THE
SOCIETY
OF SHAME

ALSO BY JANE ROPER

Double Time

Eden Lake

THE
SOCIETY
OF SHAME

Jane Roper

ANCHOR BOOKS
A DIVISION OF PENGUIN RANDOM HOUSE LLC
NEW YORK

AN ANCHOR BOOKS ORIGINAL 2023

Library of Congress Cataloging-in-Publication Data
Name: Roper, Jane, [date] author.
Title: The society of shame / by Jane Roper.
Description: First edition. | New York : Anchor Books, 2023.
Identifiers: LCCN 2022009222 (print) | LCCN 2022009223 (ebook)
Classification: LCC PS3618.O7 S63 2023 (print) |
LCC PS3618.O7 (ebook) | DDC 813/.6—dc23
LC record available at https://lccn.loc.gov/2022009222
LC ebook record available at https://lccn.loc.gov/2022009223

Anchor Books Hardcover ISBN: 978-0-593-46876-0
eBook ISBN: 978-0-593-46877-7

Book design by Nicholas Alguire

anchorbooks.com

Printed in the United States of America
10 9 8 7 6 5 4 3 2 1

For Alastair

THE
SOCIETY
OF SHAME

Day One

At seven p.m., Kathleen Held was in a taxi heading home from JFK to Greenchester, a full three hours earlier than originally scheduled.

It had worked out so perfectly, she felt almost giddy. She'd been able to switch to a nonstop flight from LA, which meant: (A) not having to change planes in Chicago—so, a 50 percent lower chance of dying in a fiery crash, or so she reasoned; and (B) that she'd get to enjoy a whole quiet evening at home, alone. After five days with her sister's family, listening to Margo drone on about the value of alternate nostril breathing and being forced by Nick to sniff and describe the various strains of genetically engineered cannabis his company grew (Pot! They all smelled like pot!), she was starving for solitude.

Her daughter, Aggie, was staying in LA for a few more days before school started—yet another forced attempt at cousin-to-cousin bonding. Margo's kids might as well have been a different species from Aggie, all long limbed, sun bronzed, and aggressively outdoorsy. But Aggie, sweet soul that she was, always went gamely along with whatever vigorous outings were planned.

Bill, meanwhile, would have just left for the large and extremely important campaign fundraiser he was attending that night at a country club in Scarsdale. Had Kathleen switched to an even earlier flight—which, in fact, she could have—he would have tried to convince her to go to said extremely important fundraiser with him. And it would inevitably have led to another one of the silent, simmering nonarguments they'd had so many of since he'd begun his US Senate campaign eight months before.

Tonight, thank god, there would be none of that. No simmering, no guilt. No having to stuff her soft middle-aged midsection into shapewear and make small talk with smug limousine liberals. Instead, just an easy, sleepy reunion when Bill came home—the kind where the light would be off and she might even be asleep but would wake up at the sound of the bedroom door opening. She wouldn't mind. She liked listening in the dark as he undressed: the *clink* of belt buckle, the *whoosh* of cloth, a muttered curse if he stubbed his toe. When he crawled into bed, she would whisper a "Hi," and he would whisper a "Hi" back. Then he would roll toward her, kiss her cheek, and slide his arm over her belly, where it would stay all night, heavy and warm and familiar.

She just wished their bedtime reunions weren't the only times things felt right between them anymore—when she didn't feel like she was being squashed into a corner by Bill's glorious career.

Maybe, she told herself, as she watched streetlights whip past along the Van Wyck Expressway, she needed to make sure that Bill knew, even if the rest of the world didn't, that she was more than just a supporting character in his story. She would start as soon as he got home tonight. Maybe she'd even wait up for him. Yes, she would. With that small gesture of engagement, she could begin the work of nudging the balance between them back into a better, healthier place.

In the meantime, though, the evening was hers.

By the time the taxi turned onto her street, she had started picturing where she'd be in a matter of minutes: sitting on the three-season porch in a fresh change of clothes (she imagined some loose, breezy linen ensemble that she didn't actually own), having a glass of white wine, catching up on her *New Yorker*s, ignoring the dog.

Instead, she came home to smoke billowing out of the garage.

"That doesn't look so good," the taxi driver said.

Kathleen bolted out of the car. The driver was close behind her.

"Is anybody in the house?" he asked.

"No—I mean yes! Nugget. Shit."

"Nugget shit?"

"Nugget, our dog," said Kathleen. "He's in there."

She started toward the house, but the driver flung his arm in front of her chest. "Don't you go in there, ma'am. You call 911. I'll go get your dog. My twin brother's a firefighter."

"What's that got to do with—"

"You want your dog to die of smoke inhalation? What does he look like?"

"He looks like a *dog*," said Kathleen. "He's the only one in there. But the house doesn't look like it's on fire. I can really just—"

"Big dog? Small dog?"

"A Yorkshire terrier. Small. With a missing eye. But—"

"Small one-eyed dog. Got it. Give me your keys."

She handed him the keys, just to get rid of him, and called 911. When she got off the phone with the dispatcher, she moved a few paces over the lawn toward the garage. The smoke was thicker than it had been seconds before, and there were now tendrils of flame creeping out from under the roof. The left-hand garage door was open, and Kathleen saw that the source of the blaze was Bill's 1969 Dodge Charger, which he'd bought on a whim the year before. It was completely engulfed in flames. In spite of herself, Kathleen felt a flare of triumph. She'd told him repeatedly it was a deathtrap. She'd been referring to its lack of three-point seat belts and airbags, but the fact that it was now on fire was not altogether surprising to her.

Still, poor Bill was going to be heartbroken. She dialed his number and was waiting for him to pick up when suddenly there he was, emerging from the garage, stumbling and coughing, a spent fire extinguisher in his hands, wearing nothing but a half-unbuttoned white dress shirt and boxer shorts.

"Bill, Jesus!" She ran toward him. "What's happening? Are you okay?"

He staggered forward a few more steps, then tossed the fire extinguisher aside, fell to his hands and knees, hacking and coughing, and vomited onto the grass. Kathleen knelt beside him and rubbed his back. After a few final mucus-drenched coughs, he looked at her. "I'm sorry, Kath," he croaked.

"Sorry for what? What happened?"

In the distance, there was the wail of sirens.

"Shit," Bill said, and commenced coughing again.

"I got him! All good!" The taxi driver was coming down the front walk, Nugget a small hairy lump in his arms. "Hey!" He pointed to Bill. "You're that guy running for president. I saw you on the news."

"Senate," Bill managed to gasp.

The driver grinned. "Sure, that's where it starts." He handed Nugget to Kathleen, nearly knocking her to the ground, then pulled his phone out of his pocket and crouched next to Bill to snap a selfie.

"Delete that!" Bill yelled, his voice suddenly strong and clear.

"Don't worry," said the driver, standing back up. "I won't show it to anyone. Just my wife."

"Please, delete," Bill said before he was wracked by another coughing fit.

An ambulance and a fire engine were pulling into the driveway now.

"All right, all right." The driver tapped at his phone in a not entirely convincing way. "I guess you being in your underwear and everything."

For the first time, it occurred to Kathleen to wonder: Why *was* Bill in his underwear? The Nantucket Reds, she saw now—an inside joke going back to when they were first dating and had gone to Nantucket for his sister's wedding, at his parents' enormous summer home. The day before the wedding, they'd gone into a shop that was entirely devoted to clothing in that simpering, stupid, milky tomato soup color. Kathleen, relatively new to the East Coast at the time, had told Bill she couldn't believe men actually wore it. He bought a pair of boxer shorts on the spot to prove that they did. She had bought him a pair every Christmas since, to the point where it wasn't quite a joke anymore.

"Bill," she said now, "why are you— Were you in the middle of getting dressed? In the car?"

He turned his head toward her, and the look in his eyes was one of utter defeat. "I'm so sorry, Kath," he rasped. "She's not . . . She just . . ."

Kathleen felt the blood drain from her limbs. *Please let him be referring to the car*, she thought. But Bill was not the kind of man who referred to cars or boats or any other mode of transportation as *she*. She wouldn't have married him if he were.

He started coughing again, and this time it sounded decidedly fake.

Kathleen stood and turned slowly around. Atop the low wall on the other side of the driveway was a woman in a disheveled blue cocktail dress, barefoot, slumped over on her side, her face partially obscured by the low-hanging branches of a rhododendron. A pair of hot-pink panties dangled from her left ankle.

"Uh-oh," said the driver.

"Who . . . is"—Kathleen could barely force the words from her throat—"that?"

Bill did not reply.

"Is she dead?" the driver eventually said.

"She drank too much," said Bill.

"I don't know," said the driver. "She looks pretty dead."

"Excuse me," Kathleen said, a scrap of breath having returned to her lungs, "could you give us some space, please?" She turned and thrust Nugget into the driver's arms. "Keep him if you want."

"Nah, I'm not really a dog person. And the missing-eye thing . . ."

"You can't keep him," said Bill. "Just *go away.*"

The driver shrugged and ambled down the lawn.

"Who is that?" Kathleen asked Bill again. She couldn't bring herself to say *she*. It would confirm the fact that there was, indeed, a *she* in their yard. A *she* in their life.

But before Bill could answer, or take his fake coughing up a notch, two EMTs appeared, one man and one woman, and clapped an oxygen mask to his face.

Kathleen turned away. Across the driveway, the *that* in the dress was also being attended to by an EMT. Kathleen recognized her now: one of a bevy of twentysomething women who worked on Bill's campaign. The one with an impossibly small waist; an incongruously bulbous, perfect ass; and huge teardrop-shaped eyes fringed with antennae-like eyelashes. She looked not unlike a cartoon ant—something Kathleen herself had pointed out to Bill. In their bed, no less. Had his laughter been strained or forced? Not that she recalled. All she remembered was that it was one of those intimate moments of connection they'd had far too few of since his campaign had begun.

And no wonder: he was fucking the ant woman. A woman half his age who was technically his employee. If he was going to do this, did he have to be such a goddamned cliché about it? Kathleen had never felt so small. So foolish. So raw and exposed—as if her very skin had been stripped away.

She felt an intense need to hold on to something. Even Nugget, maybe. But the taxi driver was down at the edge of the street now, still holding the dog, talking with the small crowd of neighbors that had assembled.

The firefighters were deluging the garage with water, and the EMT in the driveway had wrapped a blanket around the woman in the blue dress and was leading her away. She was crying hysterically. Bill, meanwhile, was arguing with his own EMTs, who were trying to convince him he should come to the hospital for monitoring.

"A man your age . . ." the woman EMT said.

"A man my *age*?" Bill practically whimpered. "I'm only forty-nine."

The EMTs exchanged a look.

"You should go to the hospital," Kathleen said. The last thing she wanted was to be alone with him in their house. Although the thought of him being in the ambulance with the ant woman wasn't much better. The thought of *anything* hurt—sent her heart smashing into a brick wall. How could this be happening?

Bill shook his head. "I'm fine. It's just a little smoke." He swallowed back a cough and then, absurdly, looked at Kathleen and mouthed *I love you*.

Kathleen felt the sudden violent urge to be as far from him as possible. "I'm going to get Nugget."

She started down the lawn to where the taxi driver was holding up Nugget's paw, making him wave at a neighbor's cellphone camera. She hadn't gotten more than a few steps when the female EMT caught up to her.

"Hey, ma'am?" the EMT said softly. She touched her palm to Kathleen's shoulder, and for a second Kathleen thought perhaps she was going to try to comfort her.

"It's okay, I'm fine," Kathleen said, though in fact, she was suddenly on the edge of tears, just from that gentle touch. (Would it be strange if she hugged the EMT? Yes, it would.)

"You just had a little, um . . . leak," the EMT said. She shrugged off her jacket and tied it around Kathleen's waist.

"A leak?"

"The fire chief will want to give the all clear before he lets you into the house, but I think you could sneak around the back door and change if you wanted. I'll cover for you."

"What do you—?"

"You're clear." She turned Kathleen toward the house and gave her a little shove. "Go!"

It wasn't until she was rounding the back corner of the house that Kathleen realized, with a growing sense of dread, what had probably happened: In her haste to get home after her flight landed, she hadn't stopped to use the bathroom at JFK. And therefore, she hadn't changed the tampon she'd been wearing since she'd left LA—

the weird, flimsy, organic hemp, made-by-women-in-Malawi tampon
she'd had to borrow from her sister when her period showed up four
days early with a vengeance, the way it so often did of late. Except, of
course, when it didn't show up at all. (What a joy it was to be forty-
seven.)

Inside the house, she flung off the EMT's jacket and raced to the
bathroom off the kitchen, where she climbed up onto the toilet and
peered over her shoulder to see herself in the mirror. And there it
was: on the very bottom of the seat of her pale green capris was a
circle of dark, ugly blood the size of a saucer.

She sat down on the toilet and sobbed.

Day Two

Kathleen woke up the next morning with her pajama top soaked in sweat, smelling like a foot. As with her periods, there was no predicting when her body would decide to release the valves on whatever hormones controlled her sweat glands, drenching her in her sleep.

Sitting up, seeing Bill's side of the bed empty, the linens flat, she was slapped with the memory of what had happened: Fire. Boxers. Floozy. Blood. Her life as she'd known it gone, never to return. Her husband was a cheater. She was a perimenopausal, middle-aged fool. Their daughter's tender heart would be shattered. Everything would change.

She closed her eyes and laid her forearm across her face to block out the light.

She couldn't believe this was happening.

But no; no, the pathetic truth was, she could. The fear that Bill might cheat—though not necessarily in this strange and dramatic a fashion—had been quietly growing, tumorlike, inside her for the past several years. Ever since he had first gotten involved in politics, first on the Greenchester board of trustees and then the state assembly, where he was currently in his third term, his energy and charisma had ratcheted steadily upward. People started telling him he was a born politician. ("Please, public servant," he'd joke.) And it was true. It amazed Kathleen, how he seemed genuinely interested in and sometimes even enraptured by everyone he spoke with, whether it was an octogenarian ranting about the Deep State controlling his insulin levels via satellite or a PTA mom in Larchmont ranting about GMO foods in the cafeteria. Even more amazing was his earnest determination to actually solve the problems people brought to him. (With the exception of the Deep State–related ones.)

But as Bill grew more comfortable in his politician's skin, the way women reacted to him changed. Kathleen saw it happening: the way they looked at him, how they angled themselves when they spoke to him—canting a hip, dipping a chin, thrusting a breast or two. And she saw the way he leaned into it, even when she was right there beside him. When he held his hand to the small of her back, as he sometimes did when they were at one event or another, she'd increasingly had the feeling that he was doing it not only to reassure her that he was still hers but to remind himself.

But, fine, dammit, if she was really, *really* honest with herself, the fact was that from the moment she and Bill had started dating, she'd harbored a quiet, low-grade worry that someday he would wake up and decide he deserved someone more attractive and exciting than her. For the first ten years of her adult life, she was the nice-enough-looking one the wingman gamely bought a drink for and chatted with while his buddy flirted with the hot one. The one that men cautiously took to lunch for their first date, instead of dinner. But then along came *this* man, seated next to her at her college roommate's wedding, a law school classmate of the groom, with a strong jaw, kind eyes, and an endearingly toothy grin. He was smart and charming and quick to laugh, and he was, for some reason, captivated by her.

At their own wedding two years later, Bill had said that he loved Kathleen's intelligence and sense of humor and the way she kept him grounded. She said she loved his idealism and boundless enthusiasm. What she didn't say was that she also loved the very fact that he thought she—ordinary Kathleen Eleanor Anderson from Ohio, whose looks were a high seven on a good day, and who had never accomplished much of anything—was enough for him.

But obviously she no longer was. If she ever had been.

Was the ant woman the only one? It didn't seem possible, given the opportunities Bill had for temptation, especially over the past eight months. He was away campaigning for days at a time, going to meetings and fundraisers and county fairs from Poughkeepsie to Buffalo. For all she knew—and, clearly, she knew next to nothing—he'd nailed a civic-minded carnie in every port. A horny liberal housewife at every whistle-stop.

And yet it wasn't as if Kathleen could have forbidden him from running for office. When Bill told her he wanted to try for the soon-to-be-vacated New York US Senate seat, she hadn't said what she really thought, which was: *If you do this, Aggie and I will have to share you with even more people. Our slice of you will grow smaller. And already it is so much smaller than it used to be.* Instead, she had put on her brave, benevolent, supportive-spouse smile and said, "I think if this is your dream, you have to do it."

After all, he'd told her the exact same thing once, back when she had a passion of her own. Before she'd accepted the fact that she wasn't nearly thick-skinned or resilient enough to hack it as a writer.

In college, she had managed to publish two short stories and a treacly sonnet in the school's literary journal. As a senior, she'd applied for fellowships that would have allowed her to research and write the novel she had in mind, a retelling of the myth of Hecate, Greek goddess of crossroads, magic, and witchcraft, who had led Demeter to the underworld to rescue her daughter Persephone, a torch in each hand. She'd had visions of herself poring over thick volumes of classical scholarship in stately academic libraries and toiling away at her manuscript in the cottages of exclusive writers' colonies. But nothing she applied for came through. (*The committee was intrigued by your interest in hexagons*, the least prestigious of the fellowships had said in its rejection note, *but we regret that we are unable to fund your research at this time.*)

Then there were the brief, devastating years of her creative writing MFA program, where she'd earned faint praise from her classmates (*There's some really nice stuff here!*) and cryptic, dismissive comments from her professors (*This is sturdy and well-constructed but ultimately slight. Several narrative junctions to admire, but the characters feel larval. Best of luck.*).

After limping her way to graduation, she didn't write anything for several years, but then she'd met Bill, who had goaded her into sharing some of her grad school stories with him and encouraged her to submit them to journals. When two out of four of her stories finally found acceptances, her confidence had been buoyed adequately enough that she'd resumed working on her Hecate novel. And when she managed to land an agent for it, she'd cried happy tears, snot running down her face. Bill bought a bottle of champagne, and they had celebratory sex on the floor of the apartment they'd just moved into together.

But there would be no further celebration. *The Hecate Chronicles* was swiftly rejected by the first ten publishers Kathleen's agent sent it to. When the agent suggested some revisions (including a more fun, Hecate-free title) and another round of submissions, Kathleen had said thanks but no thanks—every one of those rejections had felt like a pencil to the eyeball—and consigned the novel to the proverbial drawer.

Sometimes she thought of it and felt a pang of regret. Should she have persevered? Believed in herself more fiercely? She admired people who managed to push through rejection and defeat and keep on going. People like Bill. But whatever thick, fibrous stuff he and others like him were made of, she was made of something weaker.

There was a quiet knock at the bedroom door.

"Kath, you awake? Can I come in?" Bill had slept in his study, presumably. The night before, when the fire marshal told them it was safe to go back in the house, Kathleen had simply gone up to their bedroom and locked the door. When Bill had knocked, she'd told him to go away. She didn't specify where.

She told him the same thing now.

"I made you a cappuccino," he said. "At least let me give it to you."

"Dammit, Bill!" He knew there was no way she would be able to resist one of his cappuccinos. She, herself, was scared to death of the espresso machine—always had the feeling it might start hipster-splaining at her if she made an amateur move that would detract from the awesomeness of her beverage.

Bill shuffled in. He was barefoot, wearing clothes he must have scavenged from the laundry room—a pair of athletic pants and an old 5K T-shirt. Kathleen winced. Seeing him looking so soft and famil-iar, so *hers*, she felt an instinctive urge to go to him, bury her face in his neck, and let him comfort her. But you couldn't have the person who betrayed you comfort you for having betrayed you. And the sad-ness of that, twisted up with the fury she felt, was nearly unbearable.

"You smell like smoke," she said, and took the cappuccino from him.

Bill sat on the end of the bed. "Yeah." He kept his eyes on his hands, folded on his lap. The glint of his wedding band was a fist to her gut. "They're going to have to demo the garage. I'm sorry. The Honda is probably okay, but the bikes, unfortunately—"

"The garage? The *bikes*? Are you kidding? Fuck all that!"

Bill flinched. She rarely swore.

"Fuck the garage, and fuck you," she went on. What an excellent word it was—a spiky little kick to the shins. She should say it more often.

"I never meant for anything to happen, I swear to god, Kath. Tish asked if I could give her a ride to the event, because her car was in the shop, and her fiancé"—he paused carefully here for this to sink in, as if the fact that the woman was cheating, too, canceled the whole thing out—"couldn't drive her. But then I realized I'd forgotten my phone charger, so I stopped back here, and—"

God, he was a terrible liar. "No-bull Bill" he'd been dubbed with some carefully planted tweets by campaign volunteers. But she could practically hear the gears grinding in his brain. And *Tish*? That was the girl's name? What was that even short for? Tisharella? Tissue?

"When's the part where you take your pants off?" she asked.

"Well, they *fell* off actually, when I got out of the car. After it burst into flames. I guess the engine just overheated somehow and—"

"So your pants were un*done*." Undone to reveal one of the pairs of Nantucket Reds that Kathleen had so carefully rolled up, tied in jute twine, and slipped into his Christmas stocking. Did it give him even a moment's pause, knowing that these were the boxers he was wearing, that the ant woman would see? And if it had, what did it mean about Bill's feelings for her, Kathleen, that he was able to ignore that pause and keep going? Had his love for her worn that thin?

"I didn't mean for anything to happen," Bill said again. "Especially now, with the campaign going on—"

Kathleen nearly spit out her cappuccino. " 'Especially with the *campaign* going on'?"

"That came out wrong. I just meant— Please. I love you so much."

Kathleen felt the ache of tears and dug the heels of her hands into her eye sockets. Bill put a hand to her back. "Kath," he said softly.

She jerked away. "Has it happened before?"

"No," he said after a pause that was far too long. "Nothing like this."

"Oh?" She laughed, a strangled sort of sound. "Something like something else?"

He sighed and stayed silent for a long time. Kathleen closed her eyes and waited.

"There was a kiss," he finally said.

Of course there was.

"Once, about a year ago. I was drunk. It didn't mean anything. And it's not going to happen again, Kath. I swear on my life. I love you."

"Stop. Saying. That." She looked at him and tried to see the man she loved, whose life was so tightly interlaced with her own. But all she could see—all she let herself see, maybe, because it was ever so slightly less excruciating and infuriating—was an arrogant, duplicitous middle-aged man trying to save his own ass. "Go away. Please."

"Fine." Bill slowly stood and trudged toward the bathroom. "I'm just going to get my razor."

A few seconds later he emerged, electric razor in hand, looking stricken. "What happened to your pants?"

Kathleen had forgotten that she'd left her underwear and blood-stained capris soaking in the sink. Wonderful. More humiliation. "What do you *think* happened?"

"Oh." His mouth became very small, and he pinkened. He had always been weirdly, Waspily squeamish when it came to bodily functions. It was a quirk she normally found endearing. But not today. "I didn't know you still got your period that . . . badly. I mean, I know things had started getting more irregular, but I thought maybe—"

"Please stop talking."

"Okay," he said softly. "But there's just one thing. We need to be ready. In case the media finds out."

Kathleen's body flashed with panic. *Fuck.* She'd been so deeply mired in sorrow and anger for the past fourteen hours, it hadn't even occurred to her: someone—an emergency worker, a neighbor—might squawk to the media about what they'd seen. And Bill's affair wouldn't just be their own family's drama but everyone's.

His campaign had gotten higher-than-normal coverage right from the start, owing to his opponent, Kurt Kyrgowski, aka Kürt Krÿer, former front man of Toxic Lord. Krÿer, sporting a grayer and marginally less ratty version of his hairstyle from the '80s (BuzzFeed: "Is Kürt Krÿer wearing a rug? Look at these pics and vote!") had won the Republican primary in a surprise upset, and suddenly the race was one of the most watched in the country. Krÿer was an anti–gun control, anti-immigration, Blue Lives Matter, born-again Christian (he said he deeply regretted the goat-blood rituals of his '83 tour) and nobody expected him to actually win the general election in true-blue New York. But by reporting on him constantly, the media was doing its best to ensure that he might actually have a chance.

Now anything having to do with either Bill or Krÿer was national news. Most recently, it was the Wendy's incident: someone had spotted Bill coming out of a Wendy's with a vanilla Frosty, snapped a selfie with him, and posted it on Twitter, tagging Wendy's, which led to an adorable, witty tweet from Wendy's offering Bill a lifetime supply of free Frostys. This led to calls for a boycott of Wendy's by Republicans, which resulted, predictably, in endless selfies of Democrats holding Frostys. This was promptly followed by a backlash from some environmentalists, who criticized Bill and his "hypocritical, faux liberal" supporters' use of plastic straws and cup lids. At which point Wendy's started running a thirty-second online commercial touting their plan to transition to 100 percent recyclable and compostable packaging by 2040. This did not satisfy the environmentalists in the least, but by then nobody was paying attention anymore because there'd been a mass shooting at a high school in Illinois.

But if it got out that no-bull Bill Held, all-American dad, was a philanderer? The media, the internet, the *universe* would latch on and never let go. Kathleen would be the subject of other people's pity and prurient fascination for the rest of her life. She would join the staid, swollen ranks of Wronged Politicians' Wives and be forever associated with her husband's infidelity—chained to her heartbreak and shame for eternity.

It was too awful even to contemplate.

"No. They can't find out," Kathleen said. "You can't let them. You need to call the fire department and the neighbors . . . make them sign affidavits, pay them off. *Something.*"

Bill shook his head. "There's nothing we can do, Kath. We'll just have to deal with it if it happens. I'll issue a statement, tell the truth, apologize. I have enough of a margin in the polls that hopefully it won't tank the campaign completely."

Kathleen couldn't believe what she was hearing. "You're not going to drop out? Are you kidding?"

"Of course not," he said, incredulous. "You think I'm going to let that fascist Krÿer win? Jesus. No. Never. I wouldn't think you'd want that."

Of course she didn't. But now she didn't want Bill to win, either.

"We'll just need to put on a united front," he said.

"There's nothing *united* happening between us right now."

"Kath, please. You can't abandon me."

"*You're* the one who did the abandoning! Aggie and I barely ever see you anymore. When we talk, it's always about your campaign, your plans, your poll numbers and followers and groupies. We never talk about just *life* like we used to. And we definitely never talk about me or my life."

Bill's face hardened. "Because *you* never talk about you. Honestly, Kath, I don't even know what you care about anymore, besides Aggie. Whenever I ask you how work is, or how things are with the PTA, or how *you* are, it's always 'Fine, good, same as always.'"

"That's not true," she said. "Anyway, you hardly ever ask."

"And you never want to come to events with me," Bill went on. "I always have to twist your arm." She started to protest, but he held up his hand. "Yeah, yeah, I know. You don't like dressing up or making small talk. But I would think you might at least like *being* with me. And I would think you'd want to support me in doing this thing that is more important to me than anything else I've ever done."

"I don't do anything but support you! My whole *life* is nothing but you!"

"And whose fault is that?" He shot a stream of air out through his nose.

At which point Nugget skittered into the room, did a few tight circles on the floor, and skittered back out, leaving three small firm balls of poop in his wake.

———

After Bill left, Kathleen called her sister in California. She needed to talk to her about Aggie.

Oh, Aggie. Bill had done this to her, too. That was possibly the worst part of all. God, what Kathleen wouldn't have given to have Aggie here with her now, pressing her small hard forehead flat against Kathleen's shoulder like she did when she used to crawl into bed between her and Bill on weekend mornings—back before she had started the gradual tilt from childhood toward adolescence. At twelve, she was right at the fulcrum of the two, a precarious place. And a particularly terrible time for her family to fall apart.

Kathleen couldn't risk having her find out via the internet or TV what her father had done, should the media get hold of the story. She'd never been more grateful that she and Bill had held off on buying her anything more than a simple flip phone—no smartphone until her thirteenth birthday in April. As for Aggie's cousins, Flannery and Salinger, they didn't "do" TV or devices (ironic, given that Margo lived half her life on Instagram). Still, better to take every possible precaution.

Kathleen realized after she dialed that it was only seven a.m. in California, which meant that Margo most likely would be out on her morning trail run—"wilderness bathing," as she called it—her phone still locked in its device safe. But, to her surprise, Margo answered.

"I just had this *feeling* you were going to call," she said. "Is everything okay?"

"Everything's fine. We just had a little fire. In the garage."

Margo gasped. "Are you all right?"

"We're fine. Physically. But Bill . . ." Kathleen's voice caught. Which was a good thing, because it gave her time enough to realize that she couldn't tell Margo the full story. Keeping things to herself had never been one of Margo's strengths, and now she had a dangerously expansive network of followers, friends, and acquaintances, including a few celebrities, who were devotees of her Blissings! health and beauty products.

"We're just a little rattled," Kathleen said. "Listen, Mar, keep Aggie away from the news, and don't let her go online or anything, okay? In case they end up reporting on the fire for some reason. I'll call her tonight, or tomorrow, when things settle down."

"Absolutely. We've got a full day planned, and it's going to be completely analog. I'm taking the kids out to the farm where I get the lavender for this amazing new labia balm I'm making—I'll send some home with Aggie. It makes the whole mons *amazingly* supple. And then they'll go up to the lake with Nick overnight. Are you sure you're okay, though? I'm intuiting that there's something else that you're not saying. And I know you hate sharing your heart, Kath, but unspoken feelings cause all kinds of blockages."

"The only thing I'm feeling right now," Kathleen told her sister through clenched teeth, "is exhausted."

"Of course you are. And you need to honor that." Margo then suggested that Kathleen do some alternate nostril breathing and promised to send a picture of the kids at the lavender farm.

And so, several hours later, when Kathleen's phone pinged with the cuckoo ringtone she'd programmed for Margo, she assumed it would be a photo of Aggie and her cousins romping around in fields of lavender. But it wasn't.

Gwyneth just told me the news, Margo had written. *Call me.*

Kathleen was about to reply (*What news?*) when there was a sharp, violent *thunk* downstairs, like a shoe or—no, a chair being thrown at a wall, followed by Bill shouting, "FUCK, FUCK, FUCK, FUCK!"

The doorbell rang, and then rang again. Nugget yapped relentlessly. From outside, meanwhile, came an ever-loudening din of muffled voices. Car doors slamming. The beeping of a truck in reverse.

Kathleen found herself praying—she who never prayed—that it wasn't the thing she had a sinking feeling it might be. She shuffled numbly to the window and peered out through the drapes.

Outside, three news vans were parked along the curb, one from each of the metro-area network affiliates. Reporters milled on the sidewalk. A crowd of neighbors had once again assembled; and in the driveway, a woman in a fuchsia dress, holding a microphone, was taking position in front of a cameraman.

Maybe they don't know about the girl, Kathleen told herself in the most reasonable, levelheaded internal voice she could manage. *Maybe they're just reporting on the fire. Because they are idiots and will report on absolutely anything having to do with Bill.*

She retrieved her phone from the nightstand where she'd left it and tapped on the CNN app. There, she found herself faced with something worse than she could ever have imagined.

The giant headline on the home screen read: "Photo of Bill Held house fire raises questions about future of New York Democrat's Senate campaign." And beneath it was a picture: On the left side of the frame was Bill on his bare knees in their front yard, his face contorted in a spasmodic cough. On the right was Kathleen, her back to the camera, Nugget's snout poking out from over the crook of her left arm. Also clearly visible was Tish—bare feet, dangling panties, and all—on the other side of the driveway. All three of them, captured in a tidy foreshortened triangle, suffused in smoky pink-tinged light— light that also clearly illuminated the dark red blotch on the seat of Kathleen's capris.

No. No no no no no no no no.

She turned on the TV, then grabbed her laptop from her desk in the corner and opened it. Over and over and over again, there was the picture: Filling her newsfeed on Facebook and Twitter. Blaring from the home page of every news website. Sitting in a square in the upper-right corner of every cable news channel like the world's cruelest commemorative postage stamp: Bill, Tish, blotch. Bill, Tish, blotch.

Kathleen felt as if the walls of her bedroom—the house, the *universe*—had closed in around her, and now the only two things that existed were her and the picture.

She got up and locked the bedroom door, then crawled into bed and under the covers, where she curled herself into the smallest possible shape and cried until her stomach hurt.

The Mars and Topover Show

Segment: Frank Martello

REGINA MARS: Good evening. I'm Regina Mars, and we're thrilled to have with us Mr. Frank Martello.

CHARLIE TOPOVER: Thrilled doesn't even *begin* to describe it!

MARS: I'm sure you've driven people home from the airport dozens, if not thousands, of times, Mr. Martello. But last night was different. When you pulled up to Bill Held's home last night, his garage was on fire. Tell us what happened next.

FRANK MARTELLO: Well, you know, when I saw the fire, my adrenaline or whatever just kicked in, and when Mrs. Hold—

MARS: That's Kathleen Held, wife of disgraced New York Senate hopeful Bill Held.

MARTELLO: Right. When she said her dog was in the house, you know, I'm not really a dog person or anything, but it's, like, I didn't even think about it. My mind was, like, a blank, and I just said, "You wait here, stay safe, I'm going in." My twin brother's a firefighter, so it's, you know, in my blood.

TOPOVER: And what was going through your mind at that moment? I can't *even* imagine.

MARTELLO: Oh, like a million things. You know—Am I going to die, is this the end, will I see my wife and kids again? All the thoughts you have when your life is flashing in front of your eyes. But I just kept thinking, like it was a tantra or something: *Get the dog. Save that dog's life.*

MARS: And so you did. That must have been such an amazing feeling. And look, here's that selfie of you and the dog—I love this.

TOPOVER: Love. It.

MARS: Are you sure you're not a dog person?

MARTELLO: Well, it was a pretty cute dog, even with the missing eye and stuff—you sort of feel sorry for the little guy, you know?—and it didn't smell or anything. So, I don't know. Maybe someday I could be a dog person.

TOPOVER: I have a feeling there's a dog in your future!

MARS: But I think the question we're all asking is: Is there a Senate seat in Bill Held's future? You took a picture that has captured the world's attention and may have single-handedly ended what many thought was a bright political career ahead. What was going through your mind when you took that photo?

MARTELLO: I guess it was that the American people have a right to know. I see the girl over there, half-dressed, and the guy's there in that pink underwear, so I put two and two together pretty fast, you know? And his wife... Hoo, she was *pissed*. And I just was like, "I gotta get a picture of this."

MARS: Were you planning to vote for Bill Held before this scandal, Frank Martello—and will you still vote for him if his candidacy survives?

MARTELLO: I'll tell you, Regina. I don't vote much. I think politicians are all pretty much a bunch of crooks. My wife liked the guy, but now she says she thinks his wife should run instead.

TOPOVER: Now *that* would be a twist! I love it. Love. *It.*

MARS: Some people are saying *you* should run instead, Frank Martello.

MARTELLO: [*Laughs*] Nah, I'm just glad I could help.

Day Three

For approximately nine seconds after she woke up the next morning (this time, blessedly, randomly, not soaked in sweat), Kathleen was convinced that it had been a dream—a dirty trick her subconscious was playing, subjecting her to the thing she loathed most: being the target of other people's scrutiny. But a quick glance out the window—news vans and a few bedraggled-looking reporters still stationed below—confirmed that it was all very real.

She had to get out.

She knew that by rights Bill should be the one to leave, given that he was the one who had torched their marriage. But she didn't want to spend a single minute more in this smoke-smelling, lie-drenched, Bill-and-Nugget-filled house, next to the wreckage of the garage. She didn't want to look at his campaign magnets all over the fridge or his obnoxious espresso machine or that stupid fucking painting in the living room of a dog with an orange in its mouth that he had bought from the mayor's dilettante artist wife in a particularly blatant political ass-kissing move.

In fact, she didn't even really like the house itself. The ceilings were too high and the angles too sharp. It was Bill who'd convinced her that it wasn't too big (it was) and that it wasn't *really* a McMansion, given that it was built in the early '80s, before the term was even invented. But Kathleen suspected it was, in fact, invented for *this house*.

She wanted to be somewhere that was hers, not theirs.

She would go to work. When she was editing, the rest of the world fell away, and all she saw was whatever book she was working on. It was hard to imagine it would work today, but she didn't know what else to do. She got dressed, girding herself with an extra-heavy-flow tampon, packed a few days' worth of clothes and toiletries into her carry-on suitcase, and went downstairs.

In the kitchen, she was confronted by an absurdly large spray of white lilies and roses sitting on the counter. She glared at it. If this was Bill's attempt at an apology, he'd gone gravely astray. It looked like something that had been swiped from a funeral parlor.

"They're not from me."

Kathleen turned to see Bill shuffling in from his study.

"They came yesterday," he said. "From the Krÿer campaign."

She plucked the card out from among the lilies and opened it. *With deepest sympathy for the loss of your unborn child.*

"Half the country was convinced you'd had a miscarriage," Bill said. "I'm guessing you saw."

"No," Kathleen said. After the shock of seeing the picture of her period disaster plastered all over the internet, she had spent the afternoon catatonic in front of an entire season of *Will & Grace*, then eaten a packet of oyster crackers she found in her purse, dosed herself with NyQuil, and slept.

She chucked the card from the flowers to the counter. It skittered across the granite and plopped to the floor.

"Don't worry—we issued a statement late last night saying that wasn't what it was," Bill said.

"You issued a *statement*?"

"What? We didn't want people to be unduly concerned."

More like he didn't want to look like an unduly bigger asshole than he already did. *Senate Hopeful Bill Held Cheats on Pregnant Wife.*

"Wonderful. Now the whole world knows I had a bleed-through."

"Kath, come on. I know it's a little embarrassing, but it's not like it's the end of the world."

A *little* embarrassing? Did he really not comprehend the lengths girls and women went to avoid exactly what had happened to her? Had he not noticed the tampon and pad advertisements full of women frolicking in white pants and skimpy bathing suits and understood that feminine hygiene companies were appealing to every menstruating woman's greatest wish: to be free from the fear of inadvertently revealing to the world that they were, in fact, menstruating? Kathleen was still haunted by the handful of times it had happened to her before, the worst of all being a trip to France in college, when she'd left a small dark stamp of blood on her seat on the Paris Métro. (Surely this never happened to French women . . .)

"It is very much the end of the world," she said.

"You have far less to be embarrassed about than I do," said Bill. He seemed to notice her suitcase for the first time. "Where are you going?"

"To work. And then, I don't know, a hotel probably. Or an Airbnb. Someplace I can stay for a while, until we make more permanent arrangements." By the time she reached the end of the sentence, her voice was trembling. Speaking the word *permanent*, she felt, in a visceral way, the enormity of what was happening. How completely everything had changed.

"'Permanent'?" said Bill. "You're not even willing to *try* to work things out? Kath." His voice grew soft, pleading. "Come on, baby."

Kathleen's throat throbbed. Was she willing? She wanted to be willing. She wanted to be one of those wronged spouses who could find it in them to forgive. But she was filled with so much pain, so much rage, and now shame on top of it all—the thought of trying to repair and rebuild their relationship was impossible. Repellent.

She shook her head.

"What about Aggie?" Bill asked softly.

"She'll stay with me for now. You're barely ever home anyway. You can see her on weekends. Or something. I don't know. We'll figure it out later." It was too much to even try to process right now.

"You're going to take Aggie away from her house," said Bill. "Her room. Her dog. And you really think that's what's best for her?"

The contempt in his voice—it was infuriating. How dare *he* judge *her* for anything right now?

"I think what's best for her," Kathleen said, trying to keep her voice from wavering, "would have been you keeping your pants on."

"I can't believe you're doing this," he said.

"Believe it," she said, and left.

On the way to the train station, Kathleen stopped at a drugstore, where she bought the largest sunglasses they carried. They were hideous and resembled the goggle-like tinted sun shields her grandmother used to wear over her glasses when she drove. But they accomplished Kathleen's goal of concealing half her face.

Fortunately most people on the train platform had their eyes glued to their phones (probably reading about her) or their heads stuck inside their newspapers. (The headline of the *New York Post*: "BILL HELD CAMPAIGN IS HISTORY. PERIOD.")

On the train, Kathleen hunched against the window and attempted to read the book she'd been slogging through for nearly a month, a literary novel in translation by a Polish author from the 1980s whose work had been recently rediscovered. The entire thing took place inside a giant snail. Kathleen was not impressed but had persisted because her coworkers kept talking about how Important the book was. *Luminous and heartrending! A tour de force!* a blurb on the cover declared. But today she couldn't make it through more than a few overwrought sentences about snail anatomy and socialism before the pull of her phone in her purse grew too strong.

She had to see what people were saying.

She took a deep breath and opened up Twitter. Thankfully, she could watch from behind her cipher of a handle—@NotME, with a picture of George Eliot as an avatar. Maybe by now, she told herself hopefully, something more newsworthy than Bill's infidelity and her stained pants had drowned the story out.

But no. Worse: #Periodgate was now trending. Kathleen held her breath, clicked on the hashtag, and began to skim. Most tweets had to do with Bill and his campaign. But, to her horror, there were hundreds focusing on her and the stain on her capris.

The Mayo Clinic noted that heavy periods are a common symptom of perimenopause in "women of a certain age." A fortysomething former *Saved by the Bell* cast member confessed that she, too, had started having extra-heavy periods and wished she could give Kathleen a big "sister-solidarity" hug. A theater company in San Francisco had created a promotional graphic for their upcoming production of *Macbeth* using the now-famous picture, with the words *Out, damned spot!* printed over it.

It went on, and on, and on.

This couldn't be happening. It couldn't.

Kathleen tried searching for her name, and it turned up a whole other crop of tweets about her. Most were sympathetic (OMG, the poor thing!) or supportive (Twitterverse, can we please stop sharing this photo and give Bill Held's wife some dignity? Like she doesn't have enough to worry about right now. SMH). Some were childish (Uggghhh . . . Is it just me or is this the nastiest political scandal ever?), and others were just vulgar and mean (Plug your twat, libtard bitch LOL. Maybe he cheated on u cuz your butt-ass ugly).

But the worst were the ones that dismissed her plight completely, while making it seem as if somehow she was looking for pity or attention. As if she had any control over what was happening whatsoever!

Sorry, but I have exactly zero sympathy for the wife of a neoliberal con man who gives lip service to racial justice but nothing more. She's 100% complicit in his fake progressivism.

Rich white lady bleeds through her organic cotton pants on the lawn of her Gold Coast mansion. Cry me a river, Karen.

While the internet is falling over itself to feel sorry for privileged Kathleen Held, more than half of the 37 million Americans living in poverty are women. #Priorities #EqualPayNow #LivingWage #EndPoverty #MedicareForAll

The more Kathleen read, the more she felt as if the hand holding her phone were detached from the rest of her, floating in some separate, horrible reality.

She stuffed it into her bag and promised herself she wouldn't look at it again for the rest of the day. Or at least not until after lunch.

Being inside her cubicle at work was, as she'd hoped it would be, something of a relief. In the seven years she'd been a production editor at Gannet McMartin, she'd turned her work area into a cozy refuge—a space that was hers and hers alone: a miniature faux Tiffany lamp and postcards of her favorite authors and historical personages on the divider walls, along with a couple of Aggie's drawings from when she was younger, plus a framed picture of their family from a few years before. Seeing the photo today made her breath hitch. She quickly stashed it inside a drawer and got to work on the book she was currently assigned, a wry biography of William Howard Taft called *President Fat* that had already been optioned by Netflix.

For most of the day, she managed to avoid her coworkers, who kept giving her the kind of pained smiles people give one another at funerals. A few colleagues tried to engage her in casual conversation, sounding rather like aliens trying to imitate casual human conversation. A young editorial assistant pumped her fist and said, "Team Kathleen!" as she passed Kathleen in the corridor. Preston Forsythe, the ancient production editor who always wore a bow tie and refused to get hearing aids in spite of being almost completely deaf, cornered Kathleen in the kitchenette and gave her arm a pat. "WHEN MY WIFE WAS GOING THROUGH THE CHANGE, SHE DRANK A SPOONFUL OF BLACKSTRAP MOLASSES EVERY DAY," he said, then scooped up a handful of sugar packets and shuffled out.

The only person Kathleen talked to at length was her boss, Cody, who summoned her into his office via instant message. He had started just six months earlier, and Kathleen was still getting used to him. Pointy chinned and ginger haired, with ears placed slightly too high on his head, Cody was fifteen years younger than her, judging by the college graduation year on his LinkedIn profile. Having a gynecologist in her early thirties was one thing, but having a boss young enough to think of Pearl Jam as an oldies band was borderline humiliating.

Cody had been recruited from an online self-publishing platform as part of the leadership's recent drive to "implement new and innovative approaches to publishing, aligned with the way people consume content today." Mostly this seemed to mean hiring nineteen-year-old interns to keep up the company's social media feeds. Cody was one of a handful of more senior-level people (if you could be senior level at thirty-two) who'd been brought on board, but thus far he didn't seem to be doing anything differently besides referring to their weekly status meetings as "huddles."

"How are you doing?" he asked Kathleen meaningfully. He had a desk that could be adjusted to standing or sitting positions. Right now, it was somewhere in between, and he was bent over with his elbows on it, elfin chin in his hands.

"Fine, great," she said. She was really not in the mood for Cody. Or anyone, really. But especially Cody.

His eyes widened momentarily—a tic that Kathleen and her coworkers had dubbed his "anti-blink"—which had the effect of making it seem like he thought what you were saying was unbelievable in some way. "Well, you've always been really steady keeled," he said. "That's what we love about you."

"Even-keeled. Right."

He grinned. "Back to editing. Excellent." He pressed a button and the desk whirred upward. "So, I've got great news. There's this incredible new initiative I want you to be a part of: printuap publishing. It's something we're going to be piloting next year, and we want to make sure we get some experienced people"—here he poked a finger in her direction with an extra-large anti-blink—"on board."

"I'm sorry, what is it?"

"It's super exciting. We—*you*, that is—and your team will be chunking up some of our new releases and bestsellers for a new content app."

She realized now that he'd said "print-to-app." ("Printuap" had actually sounded more interesting. Possibly French.)

"Users get one free book to start," Cody was saying, "and every day they get an alert from the app and can choose a five-, ten-, twenty-, or thirty-minute read. The more they read each day, the more reward points they earn, for up to fifty percent off their next book. There are all kinds of add-ons and incentives, and if you upgrade to a premium subscription, you get the book without ads."

"Ads? Doesn't that kind of . . . disrupt the flow of the book?"

Anti-blink. "No! That's the best part—and that's where you come in. Product placement."

Kathleen felt the tug of a pernicious menstrual cramp deep within her pelvis. "Excuse me?"

Cody pushed the button on the side of his desk and it whirred downward again—so far down that now he was in a squatting position. "Here, have a seat." He rolled a stool-like object covered in what looked like yeti fur toward Kathleen.

"You work the brand names in seamlessly, and nobody even notices," he explained. "Seriously, I've read these things; it's incredible. They just, like, *seep* in. What's something you've read recently?"

"Um, I read a book about Eleanor Roosevelt's years as First Lady not too long ago." She had been reading up on politician's wives—the more empowered and interesting-seeming ones, specifically. She'd found it therapeutic, if intimidating. Now it just seemed embarrassing, identifying with Abigail or Eleanor or Michelle when, in reality, she was a poor man's Hillary.

"Okay." Cody thought for a minute. "So for something like that, we'd try to pitch some older, more classic brands that have been around since the nineteen-fifties. Coca-Cola, Tiffany, Cadillac—they had Cadillacs then, right?"

"It would be the thirties and forties. But yes." (How had this person gotten a job in publishing?)

"Great. So you'd find unobtrusive ways to work the brand names into the text once or twice. *Eleanor Roosevelt loved expensive jewelry and probably liked things from places like Tiffany's.* Something like that. But better."

Cody must have seen the seasick look on Kathleen's face, because he quickly added, "But most of the books we're piloting for this will be genre fiction and celebrity memoirs. Stuff you probably won't mind messing with."

Kathleen did her best to smile, but inside she felt like one giant wince. "And the authors are okay with this?"

"Totally. They get an extra little chunk of change for allowing us to create special print-to-app editions of their books, and they still get royalties when their books sell. It's a whole new pair of dimes."

It took Kathleen a second. "Paradigm."

"Right." This time he didn't smile at the correction. "And you'd still work on your regular titles, of course. But I have a feeling you're going to be insanely good at this." Anti-blink. "It's a chance to flex those creative muscles. You used to do a little writing, didn't you?"

A little writing. That just about summed it up, didn't it? "Not really," she said.

"Still," he said, "I know you'll rock this."

"Cool," said Kathleen.

When she returned to her desk, she clicked the link to a tutorial for the print-to-app platform that Cody had sent. *Get ready to be a*

Wallace rock star! the introduction exhorted. *Wallace is the first and only platform exclusively dedicated to the gamification of published content for today's fast-paced bibliophile.*

"Any idea why it's called Wallace?" she asked her cubicle neighbor, a sweet, young, moonfaced production editor named Simone who always looked like she was on the verge of tears.

"The guys who started it were super into David Foster Wallace," she said.

"Of course they were," Kathleen said.

Ready to give Wallace a try? the next screen read. *Choose up to three of the brand names in the box on the left to incorporate into the content below. Remember: A great Wallace experience is one where the reader doesn't even notice the sponsored content. You got this!*

Kathleen began reading the "content," which appeared to be an excerpt from a poorly written chick-lit novel.

I couldn't believe it! Mr. Perfect was going to be pulling up in his car in fifteen minutes and I was still standing there in my robe, my long auburn hair wet and glistening from the shower, staring desperately at my overstuffed closet. I was totally undecided about what to wear. Mr. Perfect had said dinner, but did that mean burgers and fries or filet mignon? Champagne or beer? Cute top, skinny jeans, and boots? Or cocktail dress and heels? Slouchy tote or beaded clutch?

Kathleen looked at the list of brand names next to the text—Kohl's, Moët & Chandon, Coors, BCBG, Mazda, Lululemon, BMW, Pepsi, Hulu, Levi's, and Tamara Mellon—and then back to the text again. She was no marketing genius, but who exactly was the audience here? Would someone who shopped at Kohl's or drank Coors really be in the market for Moët and Lululemon? What did Hulu have to do with anything? And who was Tamara Mellon?

She sank her head into her hands. Did she have to debase herself in this way, today of all days? She shut her browser and returned to *President Fat*. But she didn't manage to concentrate on that for long, either. It had been a full five hours since she'd gone on Twitter.

She decided to reward herself for her willpower by taking a quick look.

To her dismay, #Periodgate was still going strong. She switched over to Instagram, craving the normalcy of her friends' pictures of everyday life: baked goods, kids, pets, plants. (She didn't post anything herself. As was the case on Twitter and Facebook, she preferred to see but not be seen.) But the first image that greeted her was a photo of Margo in a straw-colored loose-knit poncho, delicately torn jeans, and carefully tousled hair, standing in her all-native-plant dry garden. She held a tiny brown bottle in two hands, elbows pointed outward like a choirboy with a candle. Her head, as always, listed to one side, and she wore a serene smile.

The caption read:

> If, like my wonderful older sister, Kathleen, and many other women in their forties, you are experiencing perimenopausal symptoms like night sweats, irritability, and very heavy or irregular periods, sage seed oils and lotions can work wonders to gentle the effects of your body's changing hormone and energy flow! In honor of my sister, I'm offering free shipping on all sage seed products for the next 72 hours. Blissings! #Aging #NaturalRemedies #Namaste

Her own sister. Perfect.

Kathleen stuffed her phone back into her bag and returned to *President Fat*. She'd just gotten to the part where the extra-large bathtub was being installed in the White House, which she found oddly comforting to read—Taft, too, must have known what it felt like to be humiliated—when Simone's face rose up over the partition between them. "Did you see?" she asked.

"See what?"

"The *New York Times* just published an op-ed by Lauren Trissler online. About you."

Oh god, no, thought Kathleen. *Please, no.* The *Times* was one of the few news sources she had avoided looking at so far. Once the Gray Lady deigned to cover Kathleen's sordid personal tragedy in their pages, she decided, that was it. Her dignity would be completely gone, her life over. As for Lauren Trissler, she was *the* feminist writer of the moment. Her most recent book, *Your Body Is a Battlefield*, was an international bestseller. Lauren had half a million followers on Twitter and disposed of trolls like they were lint from her pocket.

Though Kathleen considered herself a feminist, and agreed with much of what Lauren Trissler propounded, she also thought she was overrated, and at times insufferable. One thing was sure, though: if Lauren Trissler had written about Kathleen's period debacle, it was sure to spark a whole new round of controversy and debate, because everything Lauren Trissler wrote did. Which meant that the world would be talking about Kathleen's uterine emissions for at least another week. *Fuck.*

Simone's head descended from view, and she began reading aloud—very loud—from her computer: "'Reaction to the now-famous photo of Kathleen Held is an unfortunate testament to Americans' ignorance and hypocrisy when it comes to women's health needs. What does it say about us as a society that we're more fixated on one woman's mishap, the kind nearly every menstruating person has experienced at one time or another, than her husband's act of betrayal? Held inadvertently brought on a reckoning that is long overdue. It's time for women and all others who menstruate to own and celebrate their bodily functions, refuse to feel ashamed, and reject the misogynistic notion that we are unclean, irrational, or otherwise inferior when we menstruate, or that we are somehow less-than after menopause. Moreover, it's time to make free menstrual supplies mandatory in all public restrooms and tax-free nationwide. If we can't manage that, then there's no way we'll ever achieve true gender parity.'"

Simone's head appeared above the divider again, eyes solemn and rheumy once more. "Kathleen," she said, her voice hushed and awestruck. "You're a hero."

"Kathleen Held?"

Kathleen turned around to see an intern with the mail cart, offering her a box from Amazon. When the intern had moved on, she opened it to find a large package of adult diapers. She read the note on the packing slip: *LOL. KRYER 4 SENATE!! XOXO JUSTICE JONNY*

With a trembling hand, Kathleen switched off her lamp, shut down her computer, and left the office, dumping the contents of the box in the kitchenette trash on her way out.

Back in Greenchester, Kathleen sat in her CR-V in the train station parking lot and called Aggie. She hoped to god Margo had kept her promise and kept Aggie and her cousins away from the news.

"Hey, sweetie! How's the lake?" Kathleen said when Aggie picked up. She tried to convey normality but ended up sounding like a flight attendant on coke.

Bill had always been better than her when it came to discussing serious subjects with Aggie—things like death (in both generalities and specifics, e.g., her grandfather, her turtle) and the depravity of humankind. It was one of the divisions of labor between them that they'd never discussed but had fallen into place automatically, effortlessly. Bill's age-appropriate explanation of 9/11 on a trip to the city when Aggie was nine was masterful. The Holocaust, the Civil Rights Movement, Bill's father's terminal cancer diagnosis—all gently but never condescendingly presented to Aggie in a way that filled Kathleen with deep affection and appreciation.

Then again, the bastard always did know exactly what to say. *Effortlessly eloquent*, some stupid, fawning female columnist had called him once. Maybe he'd banged her, too.

"The lake is really nice!" Aggie said. "Really peaceful. We went on a rowboat and went fishing. Well, Salinger and Flannery did. But I wasn't really comfortable with it. Hooking the worms, and then bothering the fish. So, I just kind of hung out in the boat and used the binoculars."

"That sounds great. So, listen, Ag, did Aunt Margo or Uncle Nick tell you anything about what's been going on? At our house, I mean?"

"No. What is it?"

"Well," Kathleen said. She paused, still not sure how much to say. "There was a fire in the garage." She heard a sharp intake of breath from Aggie and quickly added, "But everything's fine! The house is fine! And nobody got hurt!" (*And your seat cushion is also a flotation device!!*)

"That's good," said Aggie. "Nugget's okay, too? He must have been going crazy."

Aggie, like Bill, adored Nugget, although his lunatic barking when cars and visitors approached distressed her in what seemed to be a deeply felt way. Then, Aggie felt everything deeply. She cried at commercials and, when she was younger, insisted on giving proper burials, complete with prayers, to dead squirrels and birds she spotted on the road. The far edge of the backyard was sprinkled with tiny rock piles, marking roadkill graves.

God, this was going to be hard.

"Does it look weird with the garage burned down?" Aggie asked.

"It didn't burn down quite all the way. But they'll still probably need to knock it down and rebuild it from scratch."

"It'll be cool," Aggie said, after a pause. Kathleen could picture her, tugging on her single, long braid that way she did when she was thinking hard or resolving herself to something. "Getting to see it get built, I mean. We can stay in the house while they're doing it, right? We won't have to move out?"

"Of course not!" The words spilled from Kathleen's mouth before she could stop them. She couldn't do this over the phone—tell Aggie that her life as she'd known it for the past twelve and a half years was about to change irrevocably. "Things might just be a little ... weird for a while. That's all. Dad and I had a bit of a fight over it. But everything will be fine."

"Okay . . ." said Aggie. "Can I talk to Dad?"

"He's traveling for a couple of days. But you'll see him when you get back. Everything's okay, really. I promise."

Then, in the decidedly more tweenish tone that had begun periodically popping into her voice of late, Aggie said, "Okay . . ."

"What?"

"You sound weird."

"I guess I just miss you," said Kathleen. It was the only thing she could bring herself to say.

"That goddamned narcissistic bastard," Bobbie said, and pulled Kathleen into a warm, bosomy embrace.

Kathleen had never quite understood her best friend's breasts. They seemed to converge into one great mound in the middle of her chest. But their (its?) presence made for particular snug and comforting hugs—and Kathleen wasn't generally a hugger. Tonight, she could have stood there on Bobbie's doorstep, engulfed in her arms and uni-breast forever.

"You're better off without him," Bobbie said when she finally broke the embrace. "I have the guest room all set up for you. But first, rosé."

They'd been friends since Bobbie's youngest, Andrew, and Aggie were in preschool and then elementary school together. The two children had been inseparable until second grade, bonded by their shared love of drawing, birds, pretending to be birds, and drawing pictures of themselves pretending to be birds. Kathleen wasn't working then, and she and Bobbie spent many a morning or afternoon together, taking the kids to playgrounds and children's museums, library story times and puppet shows (so many god-awful puppet shows . . .). The children grew apart when Andrew became obsessed with hockey, the Yankees, and *Minecraft*, and Aggie drifted toward books, insects, and playing the flute. But Bobbie and Kathleen's friendship endured, despite the fact that they, themselves, had little in common.

Bobbie was a joiner (League of Women Voters, Greenchester Garden Tour, Greenchester Gourd Festival Committee) and a doer. She decorated for every holiday and season and was genuinely happy to be the beneficiary of regifted scented candles. She loved hosting parties and would have traded her creaky 1920s colonial for Kathleen's house in a heartbeat. "It has such great flow," Bobbie said with a sigh every time she came over.

She was, in a way, Kathleen's conduit to the rest of Greenchester: a warmhearted, outgoing shrubbery that Kathleen could peek out from behind. She probably would have made a much better wife for Bill in his current, politician iteration except for the fact that they'd never seemed to like each other very much. And Bill would never have been able to get past the uni-boob.

Bobbie set a brimming glass of rosé in front of Kathleen and topped off her own. "Are you eating?" she asked. "You have to remember to eat. David's going to pick up a rotisserie chicken or three on the way home from work, but you're probably starving." She whirled toward the refrigerator and pulled out a dish of hairy, multicolored baby carrots and what appeared to be a half-gallon container of hummus. She shopped for food exclusively at Sorrel and Saffron, the gourmet market in the center of town, and Costco.

"No, I'm fine," said Kathleen. She'd consumed nothing that day except a subpar cappuccino in Grand Central and an old granola bar she'd found in her desk drawer. Still, she didn't feel the least bit hungry. She wondered if Bill had felt as perpetually seasick as she had for the past forty-eight hours. Hale and hardy as he was in general, he'd always had a weak stomach—needed to dose himself with Dramamine anytime he got on a boat or a plane. She hoped he'd spent the day puking his lungs out.

Bobbie gave her forehead a smack. "What am I thinking? Of course you don't want *carrots*." She whirled around again to retrieve a vat of Asian rice cracker snack mix and a tin of imported stroop-wafels. "Please. Eat *something*. You look terrible, no offense."

"Fine." Kathleen took a stroopwafel and nipped at the edge.

Bobbie stabbed at the hummus with a purple carrot. "You deserve *so* much better than him." She gave her head a fierce little shake. "I'm sorry, Kath, I don't like to say it, but watching him recently . . . I had a bad feeling. Remember the Fourth?"

Kathleen certainly did: the Fourth of July bash that Bobbie had hosted that summer. (Theme: "Independence Day in the Jazz Age.") Kathleen had been chatting with Bobbie when the two of them spotted Bill over by the pool house in a conversation with Stacy Gardner that was just a little too familiar, too arm touchy and giggly, for two people married to other people. Bill had had a few too many beers, and Stacy was that way with a lot of men, so Kathleen had persuaded herself not to make too much of it. But it hadn't been easy. Was Stacy the kiss Bill had mentioned? Or *another* kiss he hadn't confessed? Had they snuck away at some point during the party? Everything was in question: every trip he'd taken, every late night he'd worked, every word he'd ever said to her, ever.

"I worried, too," she told Bobbie. "But . . ."

"But what?"

"It's probably partly my fault he cheated."

"Oh hell no, it wasn't!" said Bobbie.

Kathleen gave a feeble smile. She loved it when Bobbie lovingly admonished her this way. But this time she was wrong. "No, it's true," she said. "I've gotten more distant. Ever since his career took off, and now with this fucking campaign . . . I know I've pulled away. He wants me to be one hundred percent enthusiastic and supportive and excited for him. Which is entirely reasonable. But I *can't*. I don't know what it is, but it's like I just can't get there. Not like he wants me to."

"Oh, honey," said Bobbie softly. "What about what *you* want for once?"

Kathleen had been determined not to cry. But the "honey" did her in. Bobbie slid a fall-themed box of tissues toward her. Kathleen started to wipe her nose but, realizing the tissue was pumpkin spice scented, balled it in her fist and tucked it discreetly into her pocket instead.

"Honestly, though, I don't even know what's worse." Kathleen gave a bitter, snot-strung laugh. "Having him cheat, having the entire *world* know he cheated, or having the entire world see my period."

Bobbie didn't reply. She just topped off Kathleen's still half-full glass.

Bobbie's oldest, Charles, slumped into the room then, along with a girl with a strangely small head. She wore turquoise leggings that revealed every crevice and curve of her lower body, paired with an oversize Greenchester High sweatshirt that did the exact opposite on top.

"Hi, Mrs. Held," said Charles, plunging a fist into the snack mix vat.

The girl looked up from her phone, and her eyes twitched to Kathleen's face. "Wait, are you—"

"Off with you," Bobbie said, shooing them away.

Charles left, but the girl remained. "It's just that I'm the assistant editor for the *Greenchester High Post*?" she said, poking at her phone. "And we're trying to do more current events? Could I ask you just a couple of super-quick questions? On the record?" She extended her phone toward Kathleen's face.

"Remind me what your name is again, sweetie?" Bobbie said.

"Addison Cole."

"Right. Bye, Addison Cole!"

"Bye, Addison Cole," Kathleen said, smothering a giggle. She was starting to feel decidedly buzzed.

Addison raised her small head imperiously, plucked a few wasabi peas from the snack mix, and stalked off toward the den.

"Charles's latest girlfriend," said Bobbie. "I'm not a fan."

"Maybe Bill would like her. She's about the right age."

Bobbie snorted.

"Honestly, though," said Kathleen, "why are so many young, gorgeous women into balding, middle-aged men?"

"Oh, but his little bald spot is so *charming*," said Bobbie, rolling her eyes. The thing Bill had hated ever since its shiny face had started peeking through his hair on his thirty-fifth birthday had turned out to be the perfect campaign asset, somehow winning him crushworthy dad status. ("BilldSpot," it had been nicknamed by the internet. People were idiots.)

"That Tish person could have anyone," Kathleen said. "She *has* someone. She's engaged."

"Doesn't matter. She's attracted to the power, the fame, the aura." Bobbie whirled a finger around her head.

"Or maybe," said Kathleen, "her fiancé can't get it up."

Bobbie snorted again. "You're terrible when you drink. I love it."

"I'm sorry, I shouldn't say that. I'm sure he's a perfectly lovely boy, who's just as pissed off as I am." It was a wonder the press hadn't dug him up yet; they'd already managed to ID Tish.

"You apologize too much," said Bobbie. "Anyway, you need to keep calm and carry on." A plaque above her sink said almost the same thing, *coffee* replacing *carry*.

"No. I want to take Aggie and leave Greenchester." The thought had been creeping darkly into the edges of Kathleen's mind all day. Saying it aloud, it didn't feel quite right, but then, nothing else did, either.

"What? No!" said Bobbie. "Please don't leave. I would miss you. And think of Aggie. She'd miss all her friends at school."

All her friends was a bit of a stretch. By the end of sixth grade, Aggie was down to just two—a loudmouth named Melissa, who treated Aggie more like a pet than a friend, and an awkward, bespectacled girl named Lucy whom Kathleen hadn't once heard speak. The rest of the girls she'd been friends with in elementary school had splintered off—one to a private school for the linguistically gifted; one to Singapore; and one of them, Anna, absorbed into the popular girl clique comprised of Ava, Ella, Bella, and other girls whose names ended in *A*. (Anna's name, of course, helped her cause, but Kathleen suspected it was her parents' massive house with indoor pool that clinched the deal.) And, as befitted popular girls, they'd commenced taunting and snickering about the kids they deemed uncool, which Aggie, not surprisingly, was. Just as Kathleen had been at her age, written off as brainy, a goody-goody, a prude.

It tore at Kathleen that now, on top of all that, Aggie would have to endure the implosion of her parents' life. And at the beginning of seventh grade of all times, while she was already grappling with the cruel hierarchies of middle school and the bewildering onslaught of puberty. Aggie hadn't gotten her period yet, but last winter her armpits had begun to assume a decidedly adult piquancy, requiring the purchase of her first deodorant. And in the spring she had confessed to Kathleen, with great, reverent solemnity, that she had three hairs on her vulva. (She was very much about using anatomically correct terms, unlike Kathleen, who'd been raised on *lady parts* and *privates*.)

In Greenchester, where Aggie's peers had already consigned her to the "different and therefore bad" category, this scandal would be disastrous. No, the best thing Kathleen could do was take Aggie and move someplace where nobody would know them or about what had happened. Iceland, perhaps. Or Paraguay.

"I just can't stand the idea of us living here anymore," Kathleen told Bobbie. "I mean, can you imagine what the Bitch Brigade is probably saying?"

The Bitch Brigade was a trio of women who ran the PTA like it was a Hollywood event-planning company. Two of them had daughters whose names ended in *A*; and the third had a son who, Kathleen had reason to believe, had once thrown Aggie's flute into a tree.

"Oh, who cares what the bitches or anyone else thinks," said Bobbie. "This whole thing is going to blow over. People have short memories."

"No. That picture is going to be up there with the sailor kissing the nurse in Times Square on V-J Day. And I saw something on Twitter about that stupid taxi driver getting his own reality TV show."

"Twitter?" said Bobbie, aghast. "Why on earth are you going on Twitter? That place is terrible!"

"I know I shouldn't, I just . . ." Kathleen couldn't explain it. She felt compelled to know what people were saying. Seeing them bash Bill was gratifying in some dark, twisted way, like looking at a car crash. Seeing people come to her defense was satisfying but kept her craving more. Seeing people mock or dismiss her, on the other hand, plunged her into fury and despair. And yet, she kept looking. Licked her lips and waited for the *good* people to jump in and rip those people new ones. And when they did, she felt a brief hit of pleasure and relief again.

What didn't feel good was reading emails and messages from friends and acquaintances, asking how she was doing and if there was anything they could do. One she'd received two hours before from an old college friend, that said simply, *Oh, Kath, I am just so sorry that this is happening to you,* had had her ugly crying in the swaying, stinking bathroom on the train, her face aching from silent sobs. The numb, out-of-body fugue of scrolling through Twitter or skimming think pieces was easy by comparison.

"No more social media," Bobbie said, giving the counter a quick pound with her fist. "No media, period. I forbid you. Come on. I'll kick the kids out of the den and we'll watch home-makeover shows until David gets home."

Kathleen wearily assented, but first she excused herself to the bathroom. She saw to her menstrual supply needs (the period seen 'round the world was still going strong), then splashed water on her face, trying to avoid eye contact with her red-nosed, middle-aged, husband-repelling reflection in the mirror. It was hard enough to look at herself on an average day, being faced with the mounting evidence of gravity's pull on her face—the way her cheeks, once pert and round, now threatened to drop into jowls, and how her mouth, which Bill had once described as "adorable," was starting to droop at the corners. Even her nose seemed to be sagging. (Who knew that was a thing? *Was* it a thing?) And then there was her hair. One of the articles she'd read had described her as "still attractive in spite of her graying, nondescript hair." Which didn't even make sense! You can't *describe* hair and then call it nondescript.

She returned to Bobbie, feeling defeated, ready to lose herself in the vapid pleasure of expensive home makeovers by men in low-slung tool belts. But Bobbie, instead of having retreated to the den, was standing in a huddle with Charles and his girlfriend, peering over her son's elbow as he slid a finger rhythmically up the screen of his phone. "Oh man, some of this stuff is nasty," Charles said.

"Charlie!" Bobbie scolded and gave him a little swat on the arm.

Seeing Kathleen, Bobbie snatched the phone from Charles's hand. "I know I just told you to stop looking at Twitter," she said, "but you should see this." She offered the phone to Kathleen.

"Is it the Trissler editorial? I already—"

"No, it's one of these hashtag thingies," said Bobbie. "And it has to do with . . . you know. You and your . . ."

"Hashtag YesWeBleed," said Addison.

"Yes we *bleed*?" said Kathleen. "Are you serious?"

"Women are testifying," said Addison. "It's actually really cool."

"Please make it stop?" Kathleen said to Bobbie.

"It's turning into, like, a thing," said Addison.

"Great," said Kathleen. "Wonderful." She took the phone and started scrolling.

She was astonished by what she saw: an endless feed of women were telling the stories of when and where they'd gotten their first periods, along with various period disasters they'd had—stained pants, bloody sheets, bathing suit embarrassments. Others were tweeting about the erratic periods and other symptoms they were having or had had during perimenopause. These were slightly comforting to read—at least she wasn't alone. But many of the things people were posting were melodramatic and borderline absurd:

@MorriganFire2 I never feel closer to the goddesses than when I'm on my moon cycle. #YesWeBleed #TeamKathleen

@NoPeriodShaming If you cough while you're peeling off your pad or dropping it into the waste bin in a public bathroom so your stall neighbors won't hear, you're part of the problem. #YesWeBleed #StopPeriodShaming

@SacredCrone When my twin sister and I had both achieved menopause, we constructed an applewood pyre and burned our leftover period supplies under a starry sky, jubilating in our new cronehood! #YesWeBleed #YesWeStopBleeding #Crones

@ShenaZ4521 I'm 19 and I'm totally regretting all the times I scrubbed my blood out of my underwear like it was a stain instead of a gift. **#YesWeBleed #TeamKathleen**

But that wasn't all. To her horror, someone had taken her face from the photo of their family on Bill's campaign website, posterized it, and transposed it onto the face of the kerchiefed Rosie the Riveter in the iconic WE CAN DO IT poster. The words had been changed to YES WE BLEED. Some people had already adopted it as their avatar.

Kathleen thrust the phone at Bobbie. "Take it away. I can't look at this anymore." She was aware for the first time that her words were coming out slightly slurred. *Canlookathish.*

"But don't you think it's kind of, like, cool, Mrs. Held?" said Addison. "I mean, we do bleed, right?"

Charles groaned.

"Yes, obviously we bleed," said Kathleen. And obviously she wished people didn't find it so newsworthy that she, in particular, bled. Heavily. "But this is just *ridiculous*. Don't these people have anything better to do?" (And weren't there more important causes to be fighting for? Racial injustice? Climate change? Distracted driving?)

"Well, personally, I think it's important," said Addison.

"Well, I think it's a bunch of silly, over-the-top, pseudofeminist crap," said Kathleen. "And they're using my picture, and my name . . .

I don't want any of this. I just want some *privacy* for once! I want . . ."
A thin metallic taste flooded the back corners of her mouth, and she
was swept with a sudden violent wave of nausea. She barely made it
to the kitchen sink, where she retched up her wine and imported
stroopwafels, then slumped over the edge, betrayed by her body once
again.

On the other side of the kitchen, Charles snorted. "Yes we puke,"
he said.

Bill Held Press Conference

BILL HELD: Good evening. Thanks for [*inaudible*].

REPORTER: We can't hear you!

HELD: Better? I'm off to a great start here, aren't I.

[*Laughter*]

HELD: Thank you for coming. I'll be brief.

REPORTER: You mean boxers?

[*Laughter*]

HELD: I deserved that . . . Those of you who have followed my
   campaign, and those of you who have been kind enough to
   support my candidacy over the past eight months, know that
   honesty and integrity are incredibly important to me. So, in
   that spirit, I'll give it to you straight: I screwed up. I breached
   the trust of my amazing wife of sixteen years, who's been my

rock throughout this campaign and throughout our lives together. Kathleen, I love you. And I'm sorry.

I also let down my friends and family and my campaign staff and volunteers, who have worked so hard and put so much faith in me. And . . . I let down the people of the great state of New York. I also showed myself to be an absolute disaster when it comes to handling a fire extinguisher.

[Laughter]

On that note, I want to take a moment to acknowledge the police and fire departments, especially the first responders, of the town of Greenchester, and personally thank them for their swift response and their professionalism. Thanks also to Frank Martello, who's getting some well-deserved attention for making sure our dog was out of harm's way.

Many people have asked me, and certainly I've asked myself, whether I plan to withdraw from the Senate race in light of what happened . . . what I did, that is. After consulting with my campaign advisors and mentors and my family, and after a lot of soul-searching, I've made the decision to remain in the race and let the voters decide whether or not they can forgive me for my actions. The stakes are simply too high, and the consequences would be too devastating, especially for working families, if I withdrew my candidacy and effectively conceded the race to my opponent. I'm not in this race for myself. I'm in it for the people of New York and the people of the United States of America.

[Applause]

Please. Thank you. Look, I'm not perfect. Not even close. But I sure as hell am sorry. And my hope is that that will be enough. Whether my wife will think so remains to be seen.

[Laughter, applause]

Thank you.

[Crosstalk, shouting]

DESMOND BAKER: No questions, please. We'll be *[inaudible]*.

REPORTER: Are you and your wife planning to get divorced?

REPORTER: Why isn't your wife here?

HELD: Can you blame her?

[Laughter]

REPORTER: Is your wife still menstruating at this time?

HELD: That's a very, uh, private matter, and it would be inappropriate for me—

BAKER: Thank you, everyone. No more questions please.

REPORTER: Do you have a message for menstruating voters?

REPORTER: What do you think of the Yes We Bleed movement?

[Crosstalk, shouting]

BAKER: Thank you, everyone, good night.

Day Four

The town of Greenchester was made up of three sections: Greenchester Village; Hampstead Village, where Kathleen lived; and Rock Hill. Rock Hill, at the edge of the next town over, was distinctly less affluent, with humbler houses and more apartment buildings. The Greenchester Junior League had recently launched a campaign to start calling the area Rock Hill Village, as part of their new focus on equity and inclusion, hanging ROCK HILL VILLAGE—PART OF IT ALL! banners from the lampposts. But the moniker never caught on, least of all in Rock Hill itself.

Today Kathleen was there, standing outside a pink, stucco apartment building with a huge brown water stain down the front, waiting for a real estate agent—a friend of a friend of Bobbie's—who was going to show her an apartment available for short-term rental. Bobbie was right: it would be too much, and too unfair to Aggie, to leave Greenchester. In Rock Hill, at least, she would be less likely to run into anyone she knew. Still, just to be safe, she wore her goggle sunglasses and hid her hair (her *graying, nondescript* hair) beneath an itchy Little League cap that Bobbie had swiped from her son Andrew's room. She looked like a complete idiot. But at least an unrecognizable one.

Or so she thought. But when the agent arrived—a sixtysomething woman named Nancy with the stretched, doll-eyed look of someone who'd had one too many procedures done—she immediately attempted to narrow her eyes at Kathleen and said, "You're Bill Held's wife, aren't you?"

"No," said Kathleen. "I mean, yes." If this woman started telling Kathleen about her periods, Kathleen was going to run away screaming.

But Nancy took a step toward Kathleen and, now standing uncomfortably close, jabbed her finger at her. "I knew he was a cheater. *Knew* it. And he was so smug last night in that press conference, wasn't he?" She gave an indignant little humph.

Kathleen suddenly liked this woman better. Bill *had* been smug. (At one point while she and Bobbie were watching the press conference together, Bobbie had, in fact, hurled an organic purple baby carrot at the TV.) Though the actual brief apology part of Bill's statement had sounded sincere, it was undercut by his little self-deprecating jokes, his politician's polish. Every second of it hurt. And whatever secret hope she'd had—because, apparently, to her surprise, she'd had some—that he might be able to let go of his own ambitions long enough to try to rebuild something between the two of them had vanished for good.

The public, for the most part, disapproved of Bill's performance, too, which was satisfying. His refusal to withdraw from the race was being denounced by writers in the *Washington Post*, Vox, and elsewhere as the epitome of white male privilege. And Twitter, of course, had savaged him—along with anyone brave enough to say that they thought his apology was adequate or that they planned to vote for him anyway, given that he was the lesser of two evils. Wow, the editor of a popular women's magazine had tweeted in response to another woman, who said it was the height of privilege not to vote in November just because Bill wasn't perfect in every way. Just . . . wow. #CancelBillHeld. (The editor's followers had, of course, obediently begun harassing the woman, one-upping each other with pithy insults and cleverly deployed GIFs.)

Meanwhile, most of America now seemed to think that Kathleen was some kind of hero for not standing at Bill's side "like a 1950s housewife" (to quote someone named @NotFairLilith). Retweet if you think Kathleen Held should be Time magazine's Person of the Year had been retweeted four thousand times. Kathleen wished she could feel proud or vindicated or *something* good about this absurdity, but she couldn't. She just wanted the world to leave her alone.

"He's always reminded me of my first husband," Nancy was saying. "Look, it's too soon for a new place of your own. You need something temporary. Something easy and comfortable. Anyway, you may decide you want your house after all, and a lease will ruin your shot at that. Trust me, I've been through this three times. Four times if you count Sergio, which I don't."

"Who's Sergio?"

"Exactly." She took her keys from her bag.

The next thing Kathleen knew, she was following Nancy's white Lincoln Navigator back to Greenchester, to the new Millstone River Residences luxury condo complex.

"I'm sorry," Kathleen said, confused, when they got there. "I'm definitely not in the market to buy anything . . ."

"Oh no, I know. There's nothing available here anyway," said Nancy. "Everything was snapped up before they'd even started building the place, when those tree huggers were still protesting. Save the ducks and whatnot." She flicked a few imaginary flying ducks away with the back of her hand.

The issue, Kathleen remembered, had been not ducks but a pair of beloved swans that nested near the marshy shallows of a river running behind the complex. The Friends of the Millstone River society, which consisted of a handful of aging, trust fund hippies and one teenage neo-hippie upstart, had named the swans Sonny and

Cher and given them their own Instagram account. When the condo complex was proposed, the society hired an environmental lawyer to oppose it and staged a sit-in at the town zoning office. Later, the teenage member of the group chained himself to a bulldozer and livestreamed his various confrontations with officials and construction workers. Ultimately, though, the complex got built anyway. Sonny and Cher didn't seem to care one way or the other.

Nancy led Kathleen into one of the town house–style condos, explaining that she was, until recently, renting it out as an Airbnb. ("Which isn't technically allowed," she said sotto voce, "but it's easy enough to persuade the neighbors to look the other way, if you know what I'm saying.") It was modern and spacious, with an open-concept first floor and two bedrooms on the second. Kathleen suspected that the decor, which was heavy on pillar candles and included a number of upbeat commands (LIVE! LAUGH! LOVE! advised a triptych of canvases over the couch), was obtained in a single epic spree at HomeGoods. Not Kathleen's style, yet there was something soothing about the mass-produced neutrality of it all—a quiet, comfortable, blank space. The two bedrooms, meanwhile, were bright and inviting, and the smaller of the two had a window seat, perfect for reading, that Kathleen knew Aggie would love.

Running the Airbnb was a nice little bit of side income, Nancy said, but then her longtime cleaning lady was deported, and she just hadn't gotten around to finding someone else yet. "The whole thing has been hugely inconvenient for me," she said. She offered the place to Kathleen at half price for up to twelve weeks.

"That's how long it takes," Nancy said, nodding sagely.

"To do what?"

"To find someone else."

Back at the house to collect her things, Kathleen headed straight for Bill's study. Nugget zipped along at her heels, barking psychotically. Kathleen planned to tell Bill that she'd found a place to stay for a while and braced herself for a confrontation about her failure to appear at the press conference. He wasn't home, to her relief. But seeing the evidence of him in the house—his sneakers in the hall, a *New York Times* loosely refolded on the kitchen table, their bed unmade, the indentation of his head still visible in his pillow (her pillow, meanwhile, was squished up into the corner against her nightstand)—came with its own lonely pain.

She dug two large suitcases out of the attic and had just started to pack when the doorbell rang. She opened the front door a crack, planning to slam it shut again if it was a reporter. But if it was a reporter, he was a reporter disguised as a chauffeur: black suit, gleaming black shoes, even a cap. He was bookishly handsome, with horn-rimmed glasses, chiseled features, and dark piercing eyes. Resting on his outstretched palms, like it was a glass slipper on a pillow, was what looked like a wedding invitation—a large creamy envelope bearing Bill's name in a looping font that resembled actual handwriting.

"For Bill Held," he said.

"He's not home," said Kathleen. "I'll make sure he gets it."

The chauffeur considered for a moment.

"Or come back some other time if you want," Kathleen said, and started to close the door.

"You're his wife?"

"Not for long."

The left-hand corner of his mouth twitched. "Kathleen Held, then, I presume."

"Yes, unfortunately."

" 'Unfortunately'?"

"Yes. Kathleen Held is not a particularly pleasant person to be at the moment." She held out her hand for the envelope, which the chauffeur now dangled at his side, one corner pinched between thumb and forefinger.

He didn't hand it to her. "Why is it so unpleasant to be Kathleen Held? You're something of a hero, from what I gather."

"Right. If that's what you call being humiliated in front of the entire world and then being used as a mascot for a movement," she said. Saying it out loud, she realized that was exactly what she felt like—a character slapped onto the T-shirts and helmets of feminist warriors that had nothing to do with who she, Kathleen, actually *was*. "Please, just give it to me. I need to go."

"All right," the chauffeur finally said, and extended the envelope to her. "No peeking."

When he was gone, Kathleen examined the envelope. The return address embossed on the back was on Park Avenue—Upper East Side, judging by the number. The plump ascenders of the font suggested a woman with an entire closet just for shoes—some expensively groomed, do-gooder housewife, probably, inviting Bill to a dinner party or fundraiser.

Kathleen left the envelope on Bill's desk for him to find and went back upstairs to finish packing. But seeing her pillow squashed into the corner of the bed like a piece of dirty laundry sent her, fuming, back downstairs to Bill's study, where she tore into the envelope and pulled out the heavy cream card inside.

Welcome, condolences, and congratulations.
Help is on the way.

You are most cordially invited to join

The Society of Shame

The honour of your presence is requested at luncheon,
Tuesday at noon
At the home of Danica Bellevue.

Discretion mandatory

Emma Hancock Wants You to Stop Period Shaming

Strumpet recently spoke with the amazing 19-year-old Emma Hancock, who's credited with starting the Yes We Bleed movement. Yes, the hashtag has been used before, and there have been calls for a long time for people to stop with the period shaming already. But now it's gone global, to become a rallying cry for women of all ages. Rumor has it a certain former FLOTUS whose initials might be M.O. is a megafan, too. Swoon! Activists everywhere are bringing menstruation out of the shadows, reclaiming the power of women's bodies, and making periods personal. (Can you tell we're fans?)

STRUMPET: We've got a pretty good idea where the inspiration for the Yes We Bleed movement came from (cough, cough, the awesome Kathleen Held) but tell us your version of the story.

EMMA: It actually came from a conversation with my mom that I had right after the picture of Kathleen Held came out. At first we were just like, "Oh my god, the poor woman," but then we stepped back and examined our reaction, and we were, like, "Wow, why should this be a source of shame, you know? We've all been there."

STRUMPET: It seems like periods are getting talked about more, and free menstrual supplies are showing up more places, but so many people, including a lot of women, still have this almost Victorian-era mindset about periods.

EMMA: Exactly. The Kathleen thing actually led to this really awesome conversation between my mom and me. I assumed my mom was going through menopause and everything, but I had *no* idea what that was like for her on a physical or emotional level. It was a real moment for me. You hear a lot of jokes about menopause—hot flashes and mood swings—but it's all pretty superficial.

STRUMPET: We searched our site and the word *menopause* came up only twice. And one of those times was in a list of our top ten favorite *McSweeney's* pieces.

EMMA: Right? And on the flip side, I'd never really talked with my mom about *my* periods. Not since I was, like, thirteen and achieved menarche.

STRUMPET: That seems to be pretty common. We did an informal poll of *Strumpet* staffers and more than half of us had never had those kinds of intergenerational conversations. It's pretty tragic.

EMMA: Right? My mom and I were, like, this really needs to be a bigger conversation. And then my mom sent me that Lauren Trissler essay in the *Times*, and I was, like, "I have to do this." I got a couple of friends on board, including my boyfriend, Damian Bax, who is awesome and supportive and a total feminist—and also a crazy talented dancer, <u>look him up on TikTok</u>—and here we are.

STRUMPET: Okay, you knew we were going to go here, but how do you respond to critics who say that Yes We Bleed ignores the fact that it's much more complicated, even risky, for women of color, Muslim women, and other women of faith to talk openly about menstruation? There's also been criticism from the LGBTQ+ community that nonbinary individuals and trans men who menstruate are being left out of the conversation.

EMMA: I absolutely get it. This has been a learning experience for me as a white, cisgender, heterosexual woman. I've got blind spots. So now I'm doing a ton of outreach to people who represent those other communities. We really want to turn Yes We Bleed into an intersectional movement.

STRUMPET: There's been some buzz about possible demonstrations and marches. Anything you want to let people in on?

EMMA: Oh, totally. We're planning a bunch of rallies, including a big one in DC, we hope, where people can tell their menstruation stories. Tons of people have already been doing it online, obviously, which is so totally amazing, but we want to give people a bigger forum and say to people, look, you can't ignore this. We bleed, and then we stop bleeding, and this is all real and normal and hard sometimes but natural, you know?

STRUMPET: YES! And we hear you're pushing for some legislation, too?

EMMA: Yes, we're working with some policy people on a menstrual rights bill, which would make it mandatory for all public bathrooms to have free menstrual supplies, no exceptions. We've got support from a couple of women in Congress who I can't name right now but am so psyched about, plus some pretty amazing celebrities.

STRUMPET: Have you tried reaching out to Kathleen Held, to see if she wants to get directly involved?

EMMA: She kind of already is involved—I mean, she's this inspiring symbol for all of us. Also, we couldn't figure out how to get in touch with her. She's not on Twitter.

STRUMPET: Okay, and because we ask all our interviewees this, we have to ask you, too. Your feminist fashion icon: Frida, Malala, Angela, or Ruth?

EMMA: Oh my god, *totally* Malala!

Big thanks, Emma! To learn more about Yes We Bleed and upcoming events, visit YesWeBleed.com.

Day Five

Aggie was coming home that night. Kathleen would have preferred to spend the day in her new bed—which was, in fact, quite comfortable once she managed to disinter it from beneath its layer of inspirational throw pillows—mentally preparing herself for talking with Aggie about what had happened. But she made herself get up and go to work, where she spent the morning alternately working on *President Fat* and clandestinely peeking at social media and reading think pieces on her phone. The #YesWeBleed tweets had proliferated, and now there was chatter over a cartoon that some conservative political website had published, in which a bunch of wild-eyed hairy women had toppled the Statue of Liberty and replaced it with a statue of her, Kathleen. The statue, depicted in profile, was clutching a box of maxi pads in one arm and raising a giant tampon aloft like a torch in the other. *The Feminist Agenda*, the caption read.

She didn't know how much longer she could take this.

And then there was the invitation. It had been gnawing at her ever since she'd opened it. Bill had betrayed her, lied to her, gone behind her back—and now, on top of it, he was being granted admittance into some sort of secret society. Once again, Kathleen was being kept on the outside—and by Danica Bellevue, of all people: a romance author published by an imprint of Kathleen's own employer.

Kathleen had never actually read any of Danica Bellevue's dozens of novels. The covers alone turned her off: they usually featured a nondescript white woman in some sort of flowing pastel ensemble, viewed from the back, often standing at the edge of an ocean, lake, or other body of water. Most became instant bestsellers, and two had been made into films, one starring Emma Stone and the other Emma Watson. In one, the leading man was played by Chris something, and in the other, the leading man was played by Chris something else. Between her royalties, speaking fees, and the proceeds from a lucrative divorce, Danica was rumored to have a net worth of nearly a hundred million.

But then there was her newest book, *Nothing Matters but This*, her first attempt at serious literary fiction—the book that had led to the *thing* that a year ago had gotten Danica canceled. Some bookstores had, with great, sanctimonious declarations, pulled it and all the rest of Danica's books from their shelves in the wake of the scandal. But there was a Barnes & Noble three blocks from the offices of Gannet McMartin. They might have it. She'd planned to leave work early to get Aggie at JFK anyway. Nobody would miss her if she ducked out a little sooner than planned.

She kept her head down and her sunglasses on as she made her way toward the fiction section at Barnes & Noble, where there was, in fact, a single copy of *Nothing Matters but This*. The cover featured no women or water, just the title, huge and all caps, on an abstractly patterned red and yellow background. On the back inside flap was a full-length picture of Danica, hands on her hips and a thoughtful, unsmiling look on her face. Her normally voluminous swirls of blond hair looked notably tamer, and her makeup was minimal. She was standing in what appeared to be an empty parking garage.

Kathleen flipped the book over and read the blurbs. Some were from authors who wrote books similar to Danica's past ones, but some were from more literary types. She'd even gotten Jonathan Franzen to praise the book, sort of: *A solid achievement from a surprisingly versatile author.*

From what Kathleen had heard, the prepublication reviews of the book in the trades were only so-so, but the publisher still had high hopes, given Danica's huge following. But then came the *Fresh Air* interview: when Terry Gross asked Danica why she'd chosen to write something that was such a departure from her usual style, Danica said she'd wanted to write something that wouldn't be read only by "fat Midwestern housewives and pensioners on cut-rate Caribbean cruises."

The response was fast and brutal. Danica's fans turned on her, her sales plummeted, her publisher backed out of the contract for her next book, and rumor had it her agent ditched her, too. People stampeded online to give her books one-star reviews and to tear her apart for her misogyny, body-shaming, and ageism. Her pretentious use of *pensioners* instead of *retirees*, given that she wasn't British, didn't help her cause, either.

Meanwhile, multiple book clubs in the Midwest reportedly held "Bellevue bonfires," where they burned copies of her books. A video of a woman—in a skimpy tank top with a baby on her hip—tossing one of Danica's novels in the air and firing at it with her Glock went viral. "Just another Midwestern housewife who's never reading your books again," the woman said into the camera. A copycat version of that video, featuring an elderly woman doing the same thing, minus the baby, also made the rounds.

Danica had issued a defensive apology, in which she said she was sorry to have offended anyone but she was obviously only joking. She was from the Midwest herself for god's sake, had been a housewife before her first book sold, and had nothing against cruises or people who took them, including her eighty-six-year-old mother. Not to mention the fact that she'd been overweight as a teenager and had struggled with her weight well into her twenties. But her apology was deemed defensive and insincere, which only made her more loathed.

And then she disappeared from view: she deleted her social media accounts, shut down her author website, and canceled all her appearances. There were rumors in the publishing community that she'd changed her phone number and address and that nobody knew how to reach her directly.

But Kathleen did.

The invitation was still in her purse. A short taxi ride and she could be at Danica's doorstep. But then what? The luncheon mentioned in the invitation wasn't until Tuesday. And she wasn't the one invited.

But she kept thinking of that one sentence on the invitation: *Help is on the way*. And if anyone needed help, it was her. By all outward appearances, Bill was doing just fine. She couldn't imagine that he felt as broken and exposed as she did. It just wasn't the way he was. Slights and setbacks only bumped him off-balance briefly. Then he was up and running again. Indefatigable. She wasn't like that. She was the one who needed help. She needed *something*, anyway, to soften the ache that had taken up permanent residence in the pit of her ribs. And if nothing else, she was curious. *The Society of Shame.* What on earth?

"Excuse me?"

Kathleen turned to see a thirtysomething woman standing a few feet away, smiling at her expectantly. She held the hand of a small girl of four or five. "I'm so sorry to bother you, but I couldn't help wondering . . . You're Kathleen Held, aren't you?" She put a hand to her chest. "I'm such a fan and—"

Kathleen pulled her goggle glasses back down over her eyes. "Thanks."

The woman shook her head frantically. "I'm so sorry! I shouldn't have bothered you. Come on, Fennel, sweetie." She started to lead the girl away.

But the little girl stood her ground and smiled, gap-toothed and joyful. "Yes we bleed!" she said, then skipped away at her mother's side.

Danica's building—which was named, not at all pretentiously, Livingston Court—was stately and gray, with what struck Kathleen as a pornographically long blue canopy protruding from the front door. She took a deep breath, preparing to explain herself to the doorman, but he simply gave her a nod and let her in. The security guard at the desk inside, a shrunken-looking man with a shock of white hair, swayed up to his feet.

"Good afternoon, ma'am," he said with a wink. "Nice to see you."

Dear god, even *he* recognized her? If he said, "Yes we bleed," she was going to kick something.

"I'm here to see Danica Bellevue," Kathleen said, pushing her sunglasses up onto her head. "Could you remind me what floor?"

"Oh. Sorry, dear, I thought you were the, ah, *special friend* of one of our residents." He winked broadly. "She wears the same sunglasses." He swayed his way back down into his chair. "I'm afraid there's no Mrs. Bellevue here."

"Are you sure? I have an invitation, and the address . . ." She took it from her purse and offered it to him, but he was busy fishing something from his jacket pocket: a handful of butterscotch hard candies, which he offered to Kathleen on a trembling palm. "Candy?"

"Don't take one. They've been in his pocket since the Nixon administration."

The voice was crisp and young, and Kathleen knew she'd heard it somewhere recently. She turned to see the chauffeur from yesterday, this time in a checked shirt, slim jeans in a slate gray–blue, and subtly distressed cordovan oxfords that whispered *Amex Black Card*.

Kathleen quickly pulled her sunglasses back down over her eyes.

"What's that you're holding?" the chauffeur asked.

"What? Nothing." She put the invitation back in her bag.

"Let me see."

"It's nothing."

"Butterscotch, sweetheart?"

"Thank you," Kathleen said to the guard, grateful for the diversion. She took one of the candies. Its cellophane wrapper seemed to have fused with the candy itself.

The chauffeur wagged a *shame on you* finger at Kathleen. "You didn't give the invitation to your husband, did you?"

"I meant to. I just . . ."

Then he gave a slight, knowing smile, eyes glinting, and suddenly, it seemed, they were in this together. "Why should he get all the fun, right?"

"No, I just wanted to know what it was. I just . . ."

"You just, you just," said the chauffeur, all business again. "You *just* everything, don't you?"

"You bus everywhere? Nah, don't take the bus." The guard reached toward the phone. "I'll call you a taxi."

"Great, thank you," said Kathleen. "I'm going to JFK."

"Hang up the phone, Norman," said the chauffeur. The guard obeyed.

"I really do need to go to the airport." Kathleen glanced at her wrist, where there was no watch. Aggie's flight didn't get in for another three hours. (Why had she come here? What was she doing?)

"Come with me." The chauffeur cocked his head toward the elevators. "You came here to see Danica, so come see Danica."

Kathleen didn't move. "I just . . ." *Dammit.*

"*Just* come with me," he said. "Say hello and leave if you want. It won't hurt a bit, I promise. And at least you can say you tried to change your life."

They didn't speak in the elevator, but as they approached Danica's door, the chauffeur said, "Look, she's not going to be happy about the fact that I didn't put the invitation directly into your husband's hands. Let me do the talking." This had already been Kathleen's plan.

The chauffeur (if he even was a chauffeur?) led her through a tiled entrance hall the size of a 7-Eleven and into a living room, where he swept his arm toward the sofa and the armchairs and told her to have a seat. The room was decorated in more shades of beige than Kathleen had ever seen in one place, with carefully orchestrated accents of turquoise and gold.

"I'll just stand," she said.

"Of course you just will," the chauffeur said, and left her there. Everything she did, it seemed, disappointed this man—except, apparently, the fact that she'd stolen the invitation in the first place.

A minute later, Kathleen began to hear snatches of hushed conversation elsewhere in the apartment: a "no" and a "Jonathan!" and a "desperate" were clear. Plus something that sounded like (but seemed unlikely to actually be) "artichoke."

Whatever they were saying, Danica clearly did not want Kathleen there—and Kathleen wasn't going to wait around to be told. At least now she could say she tried, like the chauffeur said. She started toward the entrance hall, planning to escape, but had barely made it when there was Danica Bellevue, coming toward her in a mint-green satin dressing gown like something out of a 1940s film noir, fastening a pearl earring. She was more voluptuous than Kathleen had thought, and prettier, too, though in a faded way. She looked much older than she did in her author photo—closer to sixty than the fiftyish Kathleen had thought she was. Either the lighting in that photo had been exceptional, or Danica's scandal had done a number on her. (Is this what Kathleen had to look forward to? Accelerated aging, just to kick her while she was down?)

"I'm sorry," said Kathleen. "I was just leaving."

"You see what I mean?" the chauffeur said to Danica.

Danica swatted a hand behind her in his direction, then stood looking at Kathleen, a hand on a hip. "What's that on your head?" she finally said.

"Oh, these? Sunglasses." Kathleen touched them.

"Can I see?"

She handed them to Danica, who turned them from side to side, back to front. "May I?"

Kathleen wasn't sure what exactly Danica was asking but nodded anyway.

Danica put the sunglasses on, then turned to look at herself in a gilded mirror on the wall behind her. A beat, and then she let out an insane laugh—a cross between an airhorn blast and a shriek. The chauffeur smirked in Kathleen's direction.

Danica tossed the glasses onto a credenza beneath the mirror. "Jonathan's right," she said. "You clearly need help. But you took an invitation that was meant for your husband." She gave the chauffeur a pointed look. "And you don't quite fit the membership criteria. My little group is for people who, like me, have been publicly shamed, fairly or unfairly. You didn't *do* anything, really, except marry a philanderer and pyromaniac. And, of course, you had that, you know . . ."

"Feminine hygiene malfunction," said the chauffeur.

"Thank you, Jonathan. Perfect. But . . . as far as I've seen, most of the attention you've gotten has been positive, no? Yes We Bleed and whatnot?"

"Yes, I guess so, technically," said Kathleen. She was about to apologize again for having come and make a hasty break for the door. But that word, *shamed*, tugged at her—whispered itself in her ear. "But I feel it," she said quietly.

"You feel what?" said Danica.

"Shame."

Danica lifted a carefully sculpted eyebrow. "Oh?"

"Yes. Shame for being cheated on. Shame for my stupid middle-aged hormones and for not stopping at the bathroom to change my—" Kathleen glanced at Jonathan, who scratched at his jaw and looked away. "I was humiliated in front of the entire country. And I *keep* being humiliated over and over again with this Yes We Bleed idiocy."

She thought of what Lauren Trissler had written: *What does it say about us as a society that we're more fixated on one woman's mishap, the kind nearly every menstruating person has experienced at one time or another, than her husband's act of betrayal?* If people weren't so damned shocked by the sight of menstrual blood, then they might have left *her* out of all this and focused on Bill's wrongdoing instead. The irony, of course, was that by turning that sentiment into a movement, all these Yes We Bleed zealots were keeping Kathleen in the spotlight, exactly where they were saying she *shouldn't* have to be. And where she definitely didn't *want* to be.

Danica piano-ed her fingers against her chin. "All right, so you *feel* shame," she finally said. "But it's not quite the same thing as *being* shamed. Still . . . you're slinking around, wearing terrible sunglasses. Hiding away from the world. You look like you haven't slept in a week. All the hallmarks of public shame. And you look . . ." She paused and put a finger to her lips, thinking. "You look . . . contained."

"Contained?" said Kathleen. She felt anything but contained right now. She felt, in fact, as if she'd been turned inside out, guts and emotions spilling everywhere while the entire universe looked on.

"Contained as in held back by something," said Danica. "Yourself, most likely." Her face softened. "And you came to me looking for help. Which is what I specialize in. What do you think, Jonathan?"

"I told you," said Jonathan, pinching a bit of unseen lint away from his shirt. "I think it might be a nice change of pace."

"Yes. And it could be quite inspiring to the others, if things go well." She looked Kathleen up and down, one eye narrowed. "Is that how you always dress? Ann Taylor Loft meets the Benjamin Moore Historical Collection?"

"Dani," Jonathan scolded.

"Excuse me," said Kathleen. "I didn't come here to be insulted."

Danica's eyes widened. "Ah! You've got a feisty streak after all. This is good. We can work with this."

"I don't want to be worked with. I was just looking for a little . . . I don't know what I was looking for." What *was* she looking for? Something, anything, to arrest the weightless spin she'd been in for the past four days. But now that she was here in this absurdly posh apartment with this bizarre, not terribly nice woman, she felt like a fool. "I'm sorry I bothered you. You're right—I don't belong in your group."

Danica was already sauntering off. "Tuesday at noon," she called over her shoulder. "Goggles optional."

Jonathan handed Kathleen's sunglasses back to her and ushered her to the elevator. "She's a bit much, I know," he said. For the first time, he gave her what seemed like a genuine smile.

"Just a bit," said Kathleen.

"She likes to cultivate a certain sense of . . . drama, if you will. But she means well, really. She likes to help people who've been in her shoes. It gives her something to focus her energy on now that she's persona non grata in the romance novel world. And she's right. You need help. A little camaraderie. Plus, if nothing else, it's an excellent lunch. Apple does an exquisite poached salmon."

"Apple?"

"Danica's personal chef."

"And you're Danica's . . . assistant?" Butler? Chauffeur? Lover, maybe? Although Kathleen wasn't quite sure if he was gay or straight. It was possible he was neither. Or both.

"Associate," he said. He took a business card from his pocket and handed it to her.

Jonathan Bray, Associate

"Let me know what train you take in on Tuesday," he said. "I'll send a car to Grand Central."

"I'm not coming on Tuesday," said Kathleen.

"Whatever you say," said Jonathan. He held the elevator door for her as she stepped inside.

Kathleen's heart didn't stop hammering until her taxi to the airport had left Manhattan behind. She felt like a fool for having gone to

Danica's. What exactly had she expected? That Danica would turn out to be some kind of bestselling fairy godmother who would tap her wand against Kathleen's head and make everything better? After all, this was a woman who had locked herself inside her beige Park Avenue bunker when the internet had come for her. She was one to talk about being "contained."

At JFK, Kathleen procured an escort pass so she could meet Aggie at the gate and then settled her nerves with a glass of white wine. She even tried a round of alternate nostril breathing but stopped when she noticed a man a few barstools down looking at her with a combination of lust and confusion. She paid and left, then ducked into a souvenir store to pick out some sort of welcome home gift for Aggie. But there was nothing that seemed remotely appropriate for this particular occasion. *Your father and I are separating, and your mother has been forced into feminist iconhood against her will. Here's an Empire State Building snow globe.*

When, finally, Aggie emerged from the gate, flute case in hand, Kathleen held her so hard and for so long that Aggie had to say, "Um, Mom?" before Kathleen broke away. It was so good to feel her, smell her, have her—her kind, loving, nonbleeding child.

"We have a lot to talk about," Kathleen said.

Aggie shifted her eyes to the side and tugged on her braid. "I know," she said.

"You know? What do you know?" Had Bill talked to her? Or had she caught something on the news? All those TV screens in the airport . . . She should have known there would be no way to shield Aggie from it for a whole four days.

"The fire burned up my bike, didn't it? And my croquet set."

"Oh no, Ag. Your things are fine—I think. I actually haven't checked, to be honest. But if they got damaged, we'll replace them. No, it's just that—"

Kathleen felt someone's eyes on her. She looked to her side and saw a pair of young women, heads bent together, looking at her. One held a phone and appeared to be trying to inconspicuously snap a photo. Kathleen put her arm around Aggie and hurried her away, then dipped into her purse and pulled out her sunglasses.

"Why are you wearing goggles?" Aggie asked.

"What? Oh, I went to the eye doctor today and he dilated my eyes," Kathleen lied. "They're still sensitive to the light."

"Oh. So, they're, like, special medical glasses?"

"Yes. I mean, well, yes and no. I thought I'd try a new look. You don't like them?"

"I'll get used to them," Aggie said.

"You must be starving. Let's stop someplace for dinner on the way home."

"Oh, but I really want to get home to Dad and Nugget, and my room . . ."

Kathleen took her daughter's hand—never more grateful that Aggie still sometimes allowed this—and squeezed, wishing she could fortify Aggie for this somehow. "We need to talk about some things first," she said.

The nearest decent-seeming restaurant was a place called the Merry Squire Pub and Grille, in a hotel on the outskirts of the airport. Whoever had decorated it seemed to have thought that the way to make it look like an actual English pub was to hang dartboards absolutely everywhere. Kathleen counted twelve by the time they were seated, including one that was mounted, disconcertingly, right over their booth.

At first, she kept the conversation light. But when their appetizer—a plate of limp mozzarella sticks—arrived, Kathleen clenched her hands together in her lap and began. "So, listen, Ag," she said as tenderly as she could. "Dad and I are going to take some time apart for a while."

Aggie looked puzzled. "Why? Are you mad at him because of the garage?"

Kathleen let out a sigh. How was she supposed to do this?

"No, it's because, well, Dad and I have been having some trouble for a while. We've been . . . just not as close as we used to be. And he made a mistake that really, *really* hurt me." She swallowed hard. She couldn't cry in front of Aggie.

Aggie picked up a mozzarella stick and poked it at the tartar sauce accompanying it. (Kathleen had asked for marinara, but the waitress said, apologetically, these were British-style mozzarella sticks. As if that was a thing.) Not lifting her head to meet Kathleen's eyes, Aggie said, "Did he have, you know, *intercourse* with someone?"

Kathleen's heart sank. What a terrible thing for a child to guess—to know—about her father. (What else had she guessed? Kathleen wondered. Had she sensed that the seams of her parents' marriage were straining?) Although, in fact, Kathleen didn't know what exactly Bill and Tish had done. Each time her mind wandered into that dangerous place—seeing the woman's lips against Bill's, her hand at his thigh, his hand on one of her stupid, twentysomething breasts—she yanked it away. It hurt too much. And yet, the truth was, the kiss Bill had mentioned, the intimacy of it, was even more searing to Kathleen than whatever pantsless fumbling had happened in the garage with the ant woman.

"Yes," Kathleen said. "Something like that."

Aggie continued dunking her mozzarella stick, with more force now. "Why?"

"I don't know, Ag. Sometimes even people who love each other just hurt each other. It has nothing to do with you, though. You know that, right?" God, she was messing this up horribly. Why would Aggie think this had anything to do with her? That was just something parents said on bad TV movies about divorce.

"I know." Aggie took a bite of her now saturated mozzarella stick, then let it drop to the plate. "I'm not really hungry."

"No. Me either." Kathleen went to Aggie's side of the booth, then, and put her arm around her. This part, at least—the primal, physical love she felt for Aggie—had always come easily to her. Aggie tilted her head to Kathleen's shoulder. A few seconds, and then her small body began to shudder with tears. Kathleen held her closer, kissed the crown of her head. "It's okay," she whispered. "We're going to be okay."

They barely spoke on the ride home. The way Aggie insisted on wheeling her own suitcase, helped herself to a glass of water in the kitchen of the condo, and wordlessly unpacked her things into the dresser in what would be her room—it seemed she'd aged ten years from the child who had worried about her bike and croquet set just hours before.

Kathleen tucked Aggie into bed. (DREAM DEEPLY, a decal on the wall instructed in wispy script that Kathleen couldn't help hearing in Margo's voice.) Just as she was about to close the door behind her, Kathleen heard Aggie say, "I think you should forgive him."

"I'm sorry, Ag," Kathleen said. "I don't know if I can."

Insight Hour with Jake Albright

Segment 2: Yes We Bleed

JAKE ALBRIGHT: In recent days, the Yes We Bleed movement has swept the globe, in response to a recent photo of Senate hopeful Bill Held and his wife, Kathleen. But many are asking, "So what?" Tonight, we hear perspectives on the issue from our guests Dr. Thomas Gold, chief of Obstetrics and Gynecology at Washington General Hospital and author of the recent memoir *A Life Between Legs*, and syndicated columnist Boris Kasoff. Good evening, gentlemen. Dr. Gold, you've spent your career dedicated to women's health. What's your take on the Yes We Bleed movement? Is it good for women?

DR. THOMAS GOLD: Thank you, Jake. In brief, no. My concern when it comes to this thing is that it may in fact be counterproductive, in the sense that it doesn't so much destigmatize menstruation as fetishize it. Look, let's be honest: menstruation is a perfectly natural function of the female body, no more remarkable—arguably *less* remarkable, in fact—than other bodily functions, whether you're talking about digestion, kidney function, or the intricate dance of the endocrine system. The fact that a rather mundane incident concerning Mrs. Held has ballooned into this collective hysteria over menstruation is bizarre, to say the least.

ALBRIGHT: A bit of a tampon in a teapot?

GOLD: Precisely. To put it in perspective: every year, millions of Americans die as a result of heart failure. You know how many Americans die of menstruation? Zero.

ALBRIGHT: Boris Kasoff, you wrote in a recent editorial that "Yes We Bleed, like so many female-empowerment movements, dismisses the equally valid concerns of men." What did you mean by that, specifically?

BORIS KASOFF: Thanks, Jake. Specifically, I mean that women aren't the only ones who bleed. Just talk to a man with an enlarged prostate or kidney stones.

GOLD: Oh yes, the stories my colleagues in urology could tell!

[*Laughter*]

KASOFF: And women aren't the only ones who have embarrassing things happen to them. Whether you're talking incontinence or flatulence or erectile dysfunction. But you don't see men going out and starting movements about these things.

ALBRIGHT: There have also been some who have pointed out that some transgender men menstruate. Would you say their voices are getting lost in the Yes We Bleed movement, too?

KASOFF: Yes, that's another great example. I think what it comes down to quite simply is that all blood matters.

GOLD: I concur. And honestly I think we all just need to take a step back here and think about what's actually in the best interest of women.

KASOFF: And men.

ALBRIGHT: After the break, we'll get a slightly different take on the subject from California congressman David Lee, who has come out in support of the Yes We Bleed movement. Don't go away.

Day Six

That morning, Kathleen brought Aggie over to the house so they could pack up some of her things, including the outfit she wanted to wear to school on Monday—a blue sundress printed with dragonflies that she'd bought with her allowance at a holiday craft fair the year before. Kathleen had tried to talk her out of buying it—it was strange and muumuu-like and definitely not like anything her peers wore. But Aggie had been determined. And now, she was determined to wear it to her first day of seventh grade.

Kathleen's original plan had been to call Bill and find a time to stop by the house when he wouldn't be home. But Aggie protested.

"I'm mad at him," she told Kathleen over toast and orange juice. "But I still want to see him. Is that weird?"

"No," said Kathleen. "It's not weird at all." Though Kathleen couldn't deny that there was a certain grim satisfaction in the idea of withholding Aggie from Bill out of sheer spite, she refused to be one of those terrible people who use their child as a pawn. At the same time, she was glad Aggie was angry with her father. She should be, dammit.

As they pulled into the driveway, where now there was a large dumpster in front of what was left of the garage, Aggie made a small sad sound. "It must have been so scary," she said. "It was so lucky that Dad wasn't hurt. Or Nugget."

"Mm," said Kathleen.

At the door, she started to insert her key into the lock, out of habit—at which point Nugget, inside, began barking so hysterically one would think a child had fallen down a well—but she stopped and rang the bell instead.

Bill opened the door and squinted in the sunlight. He was unshaven, in a rumpled oxford shirt, looking exhausted and old. *Good,* thought Kathleen. He'd looked so put together, so *normal,* at his press conference; she was glad to see visual evidence that he was actually suffering, at least a little.

He drew Aggie to him and hugged her, hard. "Welcome home, kid," he said.

Kathleen looked away.

"Thanks, it's good to be home," Aggie said a little stiffly, sounding much older than twelve. But seconds later, she was on the floor with Nugget, giggling, and then she was running up the stairs to her room like a kid half her age.

"You want to come in?" Bill asked Kathleen. "Have a cappuccino?"

She felt it again: the same instinct she'd had right after the fire, to interact with him as if nothing had happened—accept the cappuccino, ask him how he was, tell him how awful things had been for her. But the feeling was followed by a swift punch of grief to the diaphragm. "No," she said. "And please stop offering them to me."

"Did you just come from the optometrist?" Bill circled a hand in front of his eyes.

"No." She took off the sunglasses. "People recognize me. My face is everywhere."

"So's mine, but—"

"But you like it. You signed on for it. I didn't."

"I don't like *this*," said Bill. "The entire world thinks I'm an asshole. Half my appearances have gotten canceled. Donations have dried up. I'm getting nasty emails and death threats. Being completely ridiculed on social media, obviously. Someone named Justice Jonny sent me a pair of pants yesterday, for fuck's sake."

"Am I supposed to feel sorry for you?"

"No." He slid his palm over his head. "How much does Aggie know?"

"She knows that you cheated. She guessed on her own."

Bill nodded but said nothing. It would have been an opportune time for another apology, it seemed to Kathleen, but apparently he was done with those. Even for Aggie.

"I didn't give her any details, obviously," said Kathleen. "We don't need to tell her everything at once. But it's only a matter of time before she finds out about the picture. And the . . . other thing."

"You mean 'Yes We Bleed'?" Bill put the phrase in condescending air quotes.

"Why do you say it like that?"

Bill responded with an *are you kidding me?* look. When Kathleen didn't reply, he said, "What, you're on board with that bullshit? Bleed-ins and period confessions and blood sisters? Your face on Rosie the Riveter?"

Bullshit? Kathleen felt like she'd been slapped—though she wasn't quite sure why. The things Bill was talking about *were* stupid. And her face on the Rosie the Riveter poster haunted her dreams. But for him to dismiss it, with such condescension and derision, felt like yet another rejection of *her*. "I'm not on board with all of it," she told him. "But I think it has its merits."

"Well, its *merits* are shrinking my lead in the polls."

Had he always been this big an asshole? Was he just letting it all hang out now that their marriage had collapsed? "The election isn't for two months," Kathleen said. "I'm sure you'll come out on top, Bill. You always do." She put her sunglasses back on. "I'll be back at noon," she said, and headed for her car.

For the next hour and a half, Kathleen meandered the roads of northern Westchester County, stopping for coffee, listening to but not really hearing an episode of *This American Life* about the significance of Hostess Twinkies in the lives of three very different communities. By the time she reached Chappaqua, she desperately needed to pee. She considered stopping at a gas station, but the thought of using some nasty, ravaged-looking gas station bathroom was far too depressing. She found a little nature preserve instead and decided perhaps she'd try peeing in the woods, something she hadn't attempted since she was in grad school, when she briefly dated an outdoorsy type—a bearded, recovering alcoholic who'd recently hiked the Appalachian Trail. He'd been writing a novel about a recovering alcoholic hiking the Appalachian Trail.

She cut into a particularly dense patch of woods, found a good tree to squat against, and eased down her jeans. As she peed, she felt proud of herself—refreshed, even, for doing something she hadn't done in so long. Until she realized that the cuff of her right pants leg was completely soaked with urine. Perfect. #YesWePee.

When she returned to the house, Bill's campaign manager Desmond's bright blue Tesla was in the driveway. Desmond leaned against it, poking at his phone, his bald brown pate glinting in the sun. He smiled coolly at her as she approached and folded his arms, tight and high. Kathleen had never liked him. He'd materialized out of thin air days after Bill announced his candidacy, wearing an aggressively tailored suit and too-shiny shoes, looking more like a personal injury lawyer than the political genius he claimed to be.

"I'm a political genius," he'd said when he introduced himself to Kathleen at Bill's campaign kickoff party. "You looking forward to being a senator's wife? Maybe First Lady someday?"

Instead of saying, "God no," which would have been accurate, Kathleen had smiled, said something about it being Bill's party and that she was just here for the hors d'oeuvres, then stuffed a triangle of spanakopita in her mouth.

"Why are you here?" Kathleen asked him now. "Bill's with Aggie."

"We're meeting once she leaves. But I came early hoping to catch you." He bent through the open window of his car and retrieved a large, fat manila envelope. "Fan mail that's come in for you at the campaign office." He offered the envelope to her. "Congratulations," he said flatly.

The envelope was heavier than Kathleen expected. "There's hate mail in here, I'm sure," she said. *Skanky socialist bitch. Entitled neoliberal bitch. Get raped. Get a conscience.*

"We only printed out the friendly emails," said Desmond. "But I can't guarantee there isn't any nasty snail mail. That's usually the psycho medium of choice. If there's anything threatening, let us know. We've ramped up security for Bill, and we can do the same for you."

Kathleen nodded stiffly.

Desmond took a swig from the enormous travel coffee cup he carried with him at all times. "You know, you really fucked us over not showing at the press conference. Did it feel good?"

"Nothing feels particularly good right now."

He ignored this. "But we do appreciate the fact that you're lying low. Not doing interviews or getting involved in all this Yes We Bleed bullshit and making things worse than they already are." He chuckled to himself. "It's ironic. For once, your determination to remain invisible is actually helping Bill's cause instead of hurting it."

Invisible. So this is how Desmond, and probably the entire campaign staff, saw her. Or didn't see her, rather. Because—Desmond was right—she didn't let herself be seen.

The thought of Danica's Society of Shame luncheon gave her a pointed poke in the small of her back.

Desmond wrinkled his nose and sniffed. "Do you smell something? What is that?"

"I don't smell anything," Kathleen said. She shifted her pee-soaked ankle subtly behind the clean one.

"One of the goddamned reporters probably took a piss in the yard," he said. His phone rang then, and he honked a "Yello!" into it. Then, as if Kathleen wasn't even there, he got back into his Tesla and shut the door.

Day Eight

It was Aggie's first day of school, and Kathleen had arranged to work from home. After dropping Aggie off, Kathleen made herself a cup of coffee with Nancy's snorting, slurping Keurig machine (she could just imagine the disapproving look Bill's espresso machine would have given her if it saw) and opened up her laptop to begin work on a new book she'd been assigned, a novel based on the untold story of Henry Ford's wife called *The Woman in the Passenger Seat* that had sold for seven figures. But she hadn't gotten more than a few pages in when she had to stop. She was in no mood to spend her morning with a book about an unknown woman who spent her life quietly inspiring a famous man.

She turned to Twitter instead. The latest #YesWeBleed trend was sharing and retweeting pictures of famous women in history, real and fictional, and reminding people that they, too, menstruated. *Harriet Tubman bled. Marilyn Monroe bled. Amelia Earhart bled.* (The *Princess Leia bled* meme had spawned dozens of threads, the funnier of which were tweeted thousands of times, speculating as to whether Princess Leia or anyone else in the *Star Wars* galaxy actually menstruated, because how did we know their reproductive systems functioned the same way as ours? They were able to breathe on every planet without supplemental oxygen, so who was to say?)

But there was something else: an old picture of Bill had emerged, taken at the Greenchester Gourd Festival six years before, when Bill was running for his first term in the state assembly. In it, Bill, dressed as a scarecrow, had his arm around a woman's waist, perilously close to her hip, and was giving a thumbs-up. And there was Kathleen, a foot or two behind, a half-eaten apple in her hand, caught midchew with a bulge of fruit in her cheek. (Wonderful.) Aggie, thank goodness, had her back turned. She was reaching toward a swarm of soap bubbles.

Déjà vu! people were saying on Twitter.

"This is what a serial philanderer looks like—I should know" declared the title of an essay on Medium.

"Radical Leftist Bill Held Gropes Woman While Mocking Rural Life" read a headline on a site called LibertyFreedomEagle.com.

Kathleen wished she felt at least a tiny zing of schadenfreude, seeing Bill being picked apart like this. But all she could think about was the day that picture was taken. The weather had been crisp, the light golden. Aggie was giddy with excitement about the festival and Bill was giddy about the very fact that he was running for office. That morning, as he'd sat on the sink vanity while Kathleen drew a triangle over his nose and dabbed freckles over his cheeks with her eyeliner, they'd playfully debated whether it made sense for a scarecrow to have freckles. He said yes; Kathleen said it was ridiculous. What self-respecting farmer would bother with freckles? Bill had laughed, pulled her toward him, and kissed her ardently. She had felt his joy as if it were her own.

But Bill's hand, on that woman's hip in the picture, the way his fingers curved snugly around it—looking at it, Kathleen could hardly breathe. *Fuck him,* she thought, and gave the throw pillow on the sofa beside her a whack. *Fuck. Him.*

At two thirty, she donned her goggle glasses and Little League cap disguise and headed toward the middle school to pick up Aggie. Normally, Aggie would take the bus home, but today Kathleen planned to take her out for ice cream: a first-day-of-school tradition dating back to preschool.

But she could tell from the second Aggie got into the car—the stony look on her face and the fact that she refused to answer in anything other than monosyllables when Kathleen asked her about her day—that something was wrong.

"Is it friend stuff?" Kathleen asked.

Aggie just shrugged.

"Dad and me stuff?"

"I don't want to talk about it," she said.

It wasn't until Kathleen pulled into the parking lot of the Dairy Queen in Rock Hill (no way was she going to risk being seen in downtown Greenchester, where they usually got ice cream) that Aggie finally looked at her. Her face was so knotted with pain that Kathleen instinctively leaned over and gathered her into the closest hug she could manage over the gearshift. "I know how hard things are right now," she whispered into Aggie's hair. "I know, sweetie. I'm so sorry."

As she stroked Aggie's back, her hand bumped against something strange—some soft papery lump. "What have you got on you?" she said, and tugged at it. Whatever it was peeled right off with the hiss of an unsticking sound, and Kathleen realized before she even saw it exactly what it was: a maxi pad. The extra-large overnight kind, complete with wings.

"What . . . ?" Aggie said, twisting away from Kathleen. "What's on me?"

"Nothing! You just had a little piece of Scotch Tape on your dress for some reason. Not even noticeable." She clenched the pad in her fist, hoping she'd be able to drop it in the gap next to her seat before Aggie saw, but unlike every other object she'd ever dropped there before, it didn't fall in. It just sat there on the edge of Kathleen's seat, huge and white and geriatric looking.

Aggie stared at it for a few seconds, then covered her face with her hands and bent over until her head nearly touched her knees. "They stuck them everywhere," she said, so quietly Kathleen could only just make out the words. "All over my locker."

"Who. Who did it?"

"Some of the popular kids. Ava and Bella mostly, I think." She took in a shuddering breath. "And Anna."

"Oh my god, Aggie. I'm so sorry." Kathleen's heart ached. Suddenly, she herself was a seventh grader again, being evicted from her lunch table with chants of "Go away! Go away!" by her friends, the most confident and pretty of whom (fucking Becca Beam) had deemed Kathleen "too boring and smart" to be in their clique. For months afterward, she'd felt bruised and ashamed.

"You should have called me, sweetie," Kathleen said. "I would have come picked you up."

"It was the first day of school. I couldn't *leave*." Aggie dug in her backpack and pulled out a piece of paper folded into a tiny square. She handed it to Kathleen. "Look."

Kathleen unfolded it. It was the picture from the fire, printed in black and white, taking up almost the entire page. Someone had added speech bubbles in ballpoint pen. Bill was saying, *I just fucked!* and Tish, *I just got fucked!* Kathleen's speech bubble said, *I need to borrow one of Agie's [sic] extra-large Maxi Pads!*

"Why didn't you tell me?" asked Aggie. "About this picture . . . and the period thing? My friend Melissa said there's some whole hashtag thing and that you're famous. She showed me some picture of you as that woman from those posters—Rosie the River."

"Riveter. I was planning to, but it was so much, Ag. I didn't want to dump everything on you at once. And I'm not famous. I'm just . . ."

"You should have told me."

"Like I said, I was planning to." But Aggie was right. She should have told her sooner. She felt horrible that Aggie had found out like this.

"When? In ten years?" Aggie folded her arms and slumped in her seat. "I don't want ice cream. I have to organize my binder. And I have homework, and a flute piece to practice. Can we please just go home?"

"Ag, wait. Forget the homework. And you know what? Forget school. You don't want to go back there, with those—excuse my French—those little bitches."

This won the tiniest twitch of a smile from Aggie. "I can't skip school," she said. "I'll get in trouble."

"I'm not talking about skipping school. I'm talking about *switching* schools. You could go to a private school. You have the grades. Someplace where there are more smart, interesting kids, like you. And . . . we don't have to stay here in Greenchester, either, where everyone knows us. We could move to Connecticut, or up to Katonah or something. Remember how pretty it is up there?" Kathleen had a soothing vision of an old house on a quiet lane—a place where she and Aggie could slip away and scratch out a quiet, private new life.

But Aggie was looking at Kathleen with knitted brows. "Why would we move?"

"For a fresh start."

"But my friends are here," Aggie said. "And math league, and flute lessons. And Dad."

"But those girls, Ag. Those bitches." Kathleen tried a smile but got nothing in return this time.

"Yeah, but that's not what you're supposed to do," Aggie said, puzzled. "You're supposed to stand up to bullies. That's what Dad always says. And that's what they tell us at school."

"I know that's what everyone says you're *supposed* to do. But sometimes, when it's part of something bigger, like this, it's better to just turn your back on them and walk away. To another town. Or state."

Aggie was silent for a long time. "No," she finally said. "I don't think that's what we should do. I don't think we should be chicken."

"I think it's kind of brave, actually," Kathleen said. And wasn't it? Building something new instead of sitting around, vainly trying to reconstitute a life and two sets of pride, hers and Aggie's, that had been completely pulverized?

"No," Aggie said. "It's not. And also? I think maybe you should talk to someone. Like a therapist or something."

Kathleen had seen a therapist exactly once, at Bill's urging, in the midst of the low-grade depression she felt in the first months after she went back to work and Aggie started kindergarten. The therapist had an Eastern European accent, wore dresses that looked like figure skating costumes, and told Kathleen that she should look at this life transition as an opportunity to reconnect with herself as a sexual, adult woman as opposed to simply a mother and that as part of this, she and Bill should have some daring sexual experiences together. Kathleen had gotten the sense that the therapist meant with *her*.

She had no desire to see a therapist. But Aggie was right; Kathleen needed *something*.

The thought of Danica and the Society of Shame poked her in the spine again. Absurd as the whole concept sounded—as absurd as Danica was—it was, indeed, something: an outstretched hand. Maybe if she took a chance for once in her life and accepted it, she could clamber back onto solid ground. She could find the strength she needed to guide herself and her daughter through the storm.

"Actually," she told Aggie, "I've got an appointment to see someone in the city. Tomorrow."

Day Nine

Kathleen was determined not to be shamed by Danica again for looking excessively fast-fashion-meets-paint-chips, but her wardrobe didn't leave her many options. She ultimately settled on a scarf and a blouse she'd bought at a fashion party that Bobbie hosted. They had looked put together and sharp when Bobbie's tall, anemic-looking friend selling the clothes had tugged and tilted and knotted them just right. But wearing them now, they didn't look nearly as good. The scarf looked like it was in danger of swallowing her head, and the half-untucked thing she was supposed to do with the blouse looked postcoital, not chic. She was pretty sure the tan pants and the espadrilles she'd paired them with weren't quite right, either.

"I think it looks really nice," Aggie said when Kathleen showed her the outfit. "It's kind of like something Mrs. Coviello would wear."

"Mrs. Coviello, the secretary at your elementary school?" (Who was at least seventy?)

"Mm-hmm!" Aggie chirped.

On the train to the city later that morning, Kathleen pulled off the scarf and stuffed it into her bag. She put it back on again in the elevator up to Danica's apartment, draping it loosely around her neck and tying it in the back as she was fairly sure she'd seen done in a magazine once.

Jonathan greeted her at the door, wearing a white dinner jacket, a bow tie, and a cummerbund. Kathleen felt a bolt of panic. "I didn't know we were supposed to dress up," she said in a near whisper.

"You're fine," he said with a smile. "Nobody else is dressed up, either. Except Michael. But that's just Michael. You can take the boy out of the private school, but et cetera, et cetera." He reached inside his jacket pocket and withdrew a small laminated card, which he handed to her. In the same looping hand, on the same creamy card stock as the invitation, it read:

The Society of Shame

Phase One
Regroup. Relax. Reassess.

"Welcome to the society," said Jonathan, and gave a slight bow.

"Oh," said Kathleen, "I don't know that I want to be a member. I'm just here to—"

Danica appeared then, a martini glass in hand, instantly filling the foyer with the scents of vermouth and something flowery, charred, and expensive smelling. "Hello, hello," she said, and extended her free hand to briefly squeeze Kathleen's. "I'm afraid we're not having barbecue."

"What?"

Danica twiddled her fingers in the direction of Kathleen's scarf. "You can put your napkin on your lap."

Kathleen pressed her hand to her scarf. "Oh."

"Or maybe just turn it around so the knot's in front," said Jonathan.

"That works, I suppose," said Danica. "Come on, Kath, the gang's all here."

Kathleen followed Danica into the living room, tugging at her scarf. Four people sat on the various pieces of beige furniture. Kathleen's eye was drawn immediately, as if by some kind of unseen force, to the handsome, square-jawed man in the farthest armchair. He tilted his head against two fingers, causing his sandy-blond hair to drape lazily over one eye. His left ankle, bare above the huarache sandals he wore, rested sexily on his right knee. It never would have occurred to Kathleen before that an ankle could do something sexily, but there it was. And all at once, she realized who he was: the movie star who'd been disgraced six months earlier, when a tape from an old TV interview surfaced in which he was caught praising a makeup artist's breasts to a member of the crew, not realizing his lavaliere microphone was already on. In his soft, subtle lilt of a Southern drawl that made so many women go weak in the knees, he'd said, *"Man, those are some gorgeous tits, huh? I may just accidentally grab one next time she's over here. Bet she won't mind a bit."*

In the maelstrom of negative publicity that followed, the actor was dropped from two upcoming films, including one already in production. He was also un-nominated for a Golden Globe Award—which proved excellent late-night host pun fodder. (Ha ha, globes!) And then it came out that the makeup artist was, in fact, a breast cancer survivor; her breasts had been reconstructed after a double mastectomy. This made things infinitely worse.

The actor's fall had been particularly shocking to many people, including Kathleen. He'd been known for his advocacy of environmental causes and the bewitching way he managed to seem debonair and down-to-earth all at once, with his folksy Southern sayings. The greatest irony of all was that he'd vocally supported the Me Too movement, commenting during one red carpet interview that "It's time for us, as men, to do a lot less talking and a lot more listening."

Kathleen quickly looked away from him now, but not before he noticed her gaping and smiled with his eyes. (Those devastatingly sleepy, expressive eyes!)

"Everyone," said Danica, "meet Kathleen Held. Wife of a certain pantsless Bill Held. She swiped her husband's invite, which I sort of love, and here she is." Danica put her arm around Kathleen in an unexpectedly maternal way and gave her a little squeeze, then a shove. "Take a seat. Jonathan will bring you a drink. Martini, Pouilly-Fuissé, or lemon water?"

"Just lemon water," Kathleen said.

"Booo," said Danica, and called to Jonathan.

Kathleen took a seat on the larger of the two sofas, next to a salt-and-pepper-haired woman wearing a black linen tunic and leggings and a necklace of large red cubes. "I'm a big fan," the woman said, extending her hand for a shake. "Mona."

"Meter Mona," Danica said, draping herself onto a chair. "You may remember her starring turn in a video a few months back. She called the police on the utility worker who came to fiddle with her electric meter, because he was Black."

Kathleen sort of remembered. There were so many viral videos of white women calling the police on people of color for no good reason that it was hard to keep track.

"I called *because* he wasn't in any sort of uniform," Mona said, "and he wasn't in a utility company vehicle, and he was practically looking into my living room window. I'm a single woman living alone, and I would have done exactly the same thing if he were white." She looked to Kathleen. "I'm not a racist. One of my closest friends at my job—"

"Former job," noted Danica.

"One of my closest friends at the job I'm taking a *leave of absence from* was Black."

"She's still in denial," Danica said. "We're working on it, though it is proving quite a challenge."

"She doesn't see color," said the actor, and flashed Kathleen his famous lopsided smile. Kathleen had to look away again so she wouldn't break out into a stupid, blushing grin.

"That gentleman over there needs no introduction, of course," Danica said in the direction of the actor. "And over there, trying to blend into the draperies, is Annabelle."

Kathleen hadn't even noticed the woman at first, because she was, in fact, standing cupped inside one of the folds in the curtains, and her skin was nearly the exact same pale shade of beige as the fabric. Her arms were folded tightly against her chest. There was something familiar about her—the unusual, triangular shape of her face, perhaps—but Kathleen couldn't quite place her.

"Nice to meet you," Kathleen said.

Annabelle gave a little flap of her hand in reply, not lifting her eyes from the floor.

"You might recognize her," Danica said. "She's a GIF."

"A what?"

A sunburned, snub-nosed young man in a Florida State T-shirt, manspreading in an armchair, covered his head with his arms, stamped his feet against the carpet, and yelled, "Aaaaahhh!" like something was falling on him. Then he laughed, low and dopey. "Dude, she's the angry cereal mom!"

Annabelle gave a small sad squeak and retreated farther into the drapes.

Now Kathleen understood. Annabelle was the woman in the GIF that people regularly used on social media to indicate someone had gotten what they deserved. In it, Annabelle was scolding her son of seven or eight in the aisle of a Whole Foods, shaking an emphatic finger at him, when suddenly an entire cascade of natural and organic cereal boxes from the shelf behind her rained comically down onto her head. Kathleen had never really considered before why someone happened to be filming it, but now she realized it must have been because they judged the way she was talking to her son to be problematic. From the GIF it wasn't quite clear whether or not it was.

"I don't think I've seen it," Kathleen lied.

Annabelle looked visibly relieved and gave Kathleen a small smile.

"Dude, even my *mom's* seen it," said the manspreader.

"Brent, enough," said Danica. She glanced at Kathleen and gave a brief roll of her eyes. "The Moonabomber," she said.

"Check it," said Brent. He took his phone from his pocket and held it up so Kathleen could see the photo on the screen. In the foreground of the picture, on a deck overlooking the beach, an octogenarian couple stood together beaming, the man in a suit and tie, the woman in a peach dress with a corsage pinned to her chest. In the background, down on the sand, was a young man (Brent, it seemed) with his pants dropped, exposing his bare ass. A couple of guys standing near him, holding red Solo cups, laughed uproariously.

"Oh," said Kathleen, not quite knowing what else she *could* say.

"So, I look like the big d-bag, right?" said Brent. "Everyone thinks I was photobombing them on purpose. But, (A) I was mooning my friend Kyle, who you can't see in the picture, and I only did it for like two seconds; (B) I didn't know there was an anniversary party going on up there, or that they were taking a picture; and, three, I'd done like eight shots of Jäger."

"And?" Danica coaxed.

Brent rolled his eyes. "And the family called the cops and got me arrested for indecent exposure and disturbing the peace and underage drinking, and I got kicked out of my fraternity, and every girl on campus thought I was a total asshole, and I dropped out of school and now I'm back living with my stupid parents in Danbury and—"

"*And?*" Danica said.

Brent folded his arms and slumped in his chair, widening his manspread in the process. "Remorse and redeem. And also re*pay*, so the Greenbaums could have a whole other party and take new pictures because everyone was just *sooooo* traumatized. Not like they didn't already have, like, a million pictures *without* my butt in them."

"That's *repair*, not *repay*," Danica said. "Moving on." She smiled fondly as she extended an arm toward the man in the oversize armchair. He looked to be in his late thirties and wore a jacket and tie. The word that came immediately to Kathleen's mind to describe his looks was *pleasant*—not quite attractive or unattractive, just . . . nice.

Like someone who might work at a local bank or teach social studies. "This is Mr. Michael Mullins," said Danica with an affectionate wrinkle of her nose.

"It's nice to meet you," he said to Kathleen. "I'm sorry about everything you're going through." And then, as if Kathleen had asked, he told his story: "As for me, I got caught going on an adult webcam site, and some other sites of that nature, after-hours at work. I was a teacher at a Catholic high school, so of course they had to fire me. They tried to keep the whole thing hush-hush, because there'd been a sexual abuse scandal in the school a few years earlier with one of the priests. But some students somehow caught wind of why I left, and it went sort of viral—"

"There were some pretty awesome memes," Brent interjected.

"Yes, very clever," Michael said patiently. "And then the media picked it up, and suddenly the school was under all kinds of scrutiny again, and a few parents pulled their kids out and . . . well, here I am."

"He's very into confession, as you can see," said Danica. "Good Catholic boy."

Mona snorted. "Hardly."

"Well, we all make mistakes, don't we," said Danica, giving her a pointed look.

"Biggest mistake of my life," said Michael. "I was just . . . My marriage was not in a good place, and . . ." He held up a hand, stopping himself. "No. No excuses. Remorse, reform, and redeem."

"All these *re-* words," Kathleen said. "*Remorse, redeem, repay* . . . Are they some kind of—?"

"So, it's, like, this menu thing," Brent said. "And—"

Danica snapped up a hand to stop him. "Not yet." She turned to Kathleen. "Why don't you tell us all why you're here."

It really was incredible, Kathleen thought, the way Danica's manner could go from imperious bitch to wise, beloved talk show host within a fraction of a second.

"I think everyone knows," Kathleen said.

"I don't know," said the actor, leaning forward and tenting his fingers between his knees.

"Me either," Annabelle might have said.

At least that was one, possibly two, people in the world.

"I know what it is," Brent said with another of his dopey laughs.

"Just ignore him," said Danica.

Kathleen took a breath and let it heavily out. "My husband was cheating on me," she began. Why was it so hard to say? As if it were something *she'd* done? "And someone got a picture of it, sort of, and then posted it on Twitter."

"And also in that picture . . ." Danica said, tumbling her hand in the air.

Kathleen felt as if someone had just shoved her head into an oven. "And I was in the picture, too. And my . . . I had my . . ."

Mona made a phlegmy, exasperated sound. "You start a movement to destigmatize menstruation and you can't even *say* it?"

"I didn't start it! Other people did."

"Fine. I'll say it," said Mona. "She had her period, and she bled through her pants, which you can see in the picture. It's a gorgeous photo, actually."

"It *was* quite impressive," Danica agreed. "The composition . . ."

"And now women everywhere are talking openly about menstruation and demanding menstrual rights," Mona went on. "They're telling their period stories, their menopause stories. We're talking famous women, too—Alyssa Milano, Sarah Silverman, Ashley Judd . . . even Malala."

"I'm pretty sure Malala just said something about supporting health care for women and girls," said Michael.

"Close enough!" said Mona. "Anyway, if you ask me, it's long overdue. And there's no reason for you to feel embarrassed or ashamed, Kathleen. That's the entire fucking point—excuse my language, Michael."

Michael raised his hands in a gesture of bewilderment.

"But she's ashamed and embarrassed nevertheless," said Danica. "And her life has been wrecking balled, just like everyone else's. Which is why she came to us for help."

"I don't know about 'help,'" said Kathleen. "I guess I just want to know when it stops."

"When what stops?" said Danica.

"I don't know," said Kathleen. "The feeling like . . ."

"Like your life doesn't fully belong to you anymore?" said Michael.

Yes. That was exactly what it was like, Kathleen realized—like her life had been invaded by the public. They'd stormed her shores and planted a Yes We Bleed flag on her chest, never stopping to consider how *she* might feel about it. "Yes," she said. "I mean, how long is it going to go on?"

Mona let out a "ha!"

Annabelle made a whimpering noise.

The actor gave a low whistle. "I've felt that way for the past twenty years. Long before what happened."

"As for me," said Michael thoughtfully, "it's not so much the idea of thousands of strangers talking about me that's been the hardest. It's having everyone in my family know. And all my friends and colleagues, my students. Especially my students."

To her own surprise—because god knows she wasn't exactly in the mood for feeling charitable toward someone who had been sex camming with random women behind his wife's back—Kathleen felt a swell of something close to tenderness for Michael. There was such resignation in his voice, such regret—far more of it than she'd sensed from Bill thus far. But she chased the feeling away. He didn't deserve anyone's sympathy, least of all hers.

"Well, I *did* get national exposure," Mona broke in. "It's been, let's see, three months since I got lynched by the mob. And I still feel it."

"*Lynch mob* may not be the best choice of words," said Michael.

"The worst possible," said Danica.

"Oh, for god's sake, haven't any of you ever seen a Western? *That's* the kind of lynch mob I'm talking about." There was silence all around. It occurred to Kathleen that perhaps Mona was the reason everyone in this assemblage happened to be white. What person of color would be able to stand being in a support group—or whatever this was—with her? Kathleen felt a bit queasy about it herself.

Mona sat back and folded her arms. "You know what? Just forget it. Dani, do you think I could get another wine?"

Danica called for Jonathan, and he appeared a moment later, a white cloth slung over his arm, with a tray bearing a glass of wine. "I think I'll actually have a glass, too," Kathleen said to him. He gave her an approving nod.

For the next twenty minutes or so, the group recounted to Kathleen the stories of their first few days and weeks after they became the object of public shaming and humiliation—the sleepless nights and appetite-less days, the crying jags and feelings of panic, anger, and dejection. Annabelle, though she'd been GIF'ed three months prior, was still in what Danica called the acute stage—still reeling, the ground having not yet fully rematerialized beneath her feet. Michael, Mona, Brent, and the actor were further along and assured Kathleen that it did get better. Just not terribly quickly. They'd each had their coping mechanisms: For the actor it was Peloton and trips to an island in the Pacific he refused to name. For Mona it was hypnotherapy, acupuncture, and massage. For Michael, prayer and long solitary walks on the beach between meetings with divorce lawyers. Brent said he drank a lot of beer and watched a shit ton of ESPN.

None of it made Kathleen feel terribly hopeful about what lay ahead for her, and yet there was an undeniable comfort in knowing that she wasn't alone.

It was crazy—she knew it was crazy—but maybe she *did* want to be a member of this society. Not that these were people she would ever normally associate with. There was no excuse for what any of them had done, except in the case of poor Annabelle, perhaps. Their reputations *did* deserve to be tarnished. They *did* deserve to be called out for their actions. She wasn't like them (thank god). But there was one key thing they shared: like them, Kathleen had been exposed, thanks to the unchecked power of the internet and people's appetite for scandal. Not exposed as a racist or sexist or cheater or mooner but as a sad, clueless casualty of her charismatic husband's infidelity—a casualty with a gross, hemorrhaging body to boot.

And now, here they all were together, trying to help one another come to grips with their shame and move forward. In the midst of the maelstrom that was her life right now, being here with this group of infamous outcasts, feeling this sudden, unexpected sense of belonging, felt like a lifeline.

Lunch was served on clear glass plates that had the disconcerting effect of making Kathleen repeatedly think she'd gotten hollandaise sauce on the tablecloth. Danica gave a brief toast. "To regaining control and reclaiming ourselves," she said. The others repeated it in unison. "And to Christine. Brent, *please* don't pour one out for her onto the tablecloth again."

Michael, who'd been seated next to Kathleen, explained to her before she had to ask: "Christine as in Crafts with Christine."

"Oh," said Kathleen. "*That* Christine."

Christine Kelton was a crafting superstar who had been beloved by millions—especially born-again Christians, on account of the fact that Christine herself was one. She had shocked and appalled her fan base by adding her pronouns (*she/her*) to her social media profiles after her teenage niece came out as nonbinary. The craft supply superstore chain she was a spokesperson for dropped her like a hot potato for "politicizing crafts," and she was derided by conservatives on social media and cable news for bowing to "woke culture." Kathleen also vaguely recalled something about her being chased through an airport by a clutch of angry women brandishing knitting needles. Meanwhile, few people on the left or in the LGBTQ+ community rallied around her, given that she was vocally antichoice and a well-known donor to Republican political candidates. Some even accused her of pandering to liberals in an attempt to grow her fan base. Her craft empire crumbled, and she faded from view.

"Was she a member of this group?" Kathleen asked.

"No," said the actor. "She's a cautionary tale."

For the first time, Annabelle spoke. "She killed herself."

"Oh my god," said Kathleen. "I had no idea. How awful."

"Terribly sad," said Danica. "She had a crisis of faith, a crisis of identity. The family covered it up, but her mother contacted me after my debacle. She's a fan of my work." She paused for a faux humble lift of a shoulder. "She told me that she was sorry for what was happening to me and that she hoped I wouldn't let it destroy me the way it had destroyed her daughter—who was 'no longer with them as a result of all that ugliness.' I wrote back and said thank you, I'm sorry for your loss, et cetera. And she wrote back and said thank you, and are you going to write a sequel to *The Wisteria Sisters*? And that was the end of it." She made a dismissive gesture. "I generally ignore the sequel-prequel questions. *So* tedious, right?" She looked at Kathleen. "You're a writer, you understand."

"Oh no, I'm not a writer. I'm just a production editor."

"*Just* a production editor with an MFA in creative writing from an excellent program," said Jonathan, who'd seated himself at the end of the table opposite Danica at the beginning of the meal. He had traded his waiter's uniform for a collared shirt in a subtle, nouveau-Hawaiian print. "It was in some think piece I read," he said. "I believe it was called 'The Silence of Kathleen Held.'"

"Are you published?" Mona asked.

"Just a few short stories," said Kathleen.

"*Just*," said Jonathan.

"Drink!" said Danica.

"Impressive," said the actor.

"Not really. It was years ago."

"Perhaps you'll take it up again," said Danica. She clasped her hands girlishly to her chest. "You could write a book about this whole calamity. Launch a new career."

"Reinventing?" said the actor.

"No, reconnecting," said Mona.

"Re*tard*ing," said Brent, grinning.

Danica plucked a roll from the basket and chucked it at his head.

Kathleen was tempted to ask, again, what the *re-* words were all about but held her tongue for fear that Danica might yank it right out of her mouth if she didn't.

"Or," said Michael, "you could steer into the swerve. You know, like when you're driving in the snow." He mimed a steering wheel. "If you skid, you don't steer the opposite way, you steer—"

"Yes, yes, we get the metaphor," said Danica.

"If it's important to you," he continued, "you could help be an advocate for, uh, you know. What Mona was talking about earlier."

"*Men-stru-a-tion*," Mona said. "For god's sake, people. Am I the only one here who can say it?"

"Menstruation," Danica said. "And I think it's a fabulous idea. Mikey's right, Kathleen. Seize control of the narrative! Go on a press junket! Call up Kotex and see if they want you to be their spokeswoman!"

A feminine hygiene company had, in fact, already asked Kathleen to be their spokesperson—a start-up in Vermont that made hemp-based, compostable pads and sold CBD remedies for period and menopause symptoms. Their letter was in the packet that Desmond had given her. Over the past two days, Kathleen had worked her way through it. The large majority of notes were from individual women, sending their sympathies and sharing their own stories of spousal infidelity, their complicated emotions around menopause, and their humiliating period moments. (Or humiliating moments that had nothing to do with periods whatsoever: one woman related a detailed story about going to a family reunion in the '80s and being told by her "extremely handsome cousin" that she had a dryer sheet clinging to the back of her skirt.) These, Kathleen had to admit, were somewhat comforting to read.

Some of the sweetest notes, though, were the ones from girls and young women who told Kathleen that seeing her picture made them feel less alone. A twelve-year-old had written: *I thought I had accidents because I wasn't experienced with periods and I was doing something wrong. But you're a mom and it happened to you, too.*

It was at least a little gratifying to know that she had helped this girl, and probably others, feel less embarrassed about their own menstrual calamities. And, yes, she agreed that menstrual supplies should be more readily available. Who wouldn't? She also agreed that people should stop viewing menopause as some sort of ending—if for no other reason than that perhaps if they didn't, they wouldn't feel the need to go fuck something premenopausal behind their partner's back.

But that didn't mean she wanted to be anybody's spokesperson.

"I think I just want to wait it out," she told Danica.

"*Just*," Danica sang. She drained the last of her martini, and the actor and Mona, who seemed to have caught onto the drinking game, took slugs of their drinks, too.

"I bet Terry Gross would *love* to interview you," Mona said.

"*Please* do not mention that name in my presence again," Danica said. "But yes. I'm sure she would. You're missing out on an opportunity that none of the rest of us have, Kathleen. You're the hero in this story, not the villain. The patron saint of wronged middle-aged wives and menstruation. And you could be relishing it. Using it to your advantage."

"Or using it to help people," Michael added.

"Yes," said Danica. "You're throwing away your chance. *Just* waiting to fade back into the wallpaper."

It was true; part of the wallpaper was exactly where Kathleen had always been most comfortable and where she felt most useful. In a way, she *was* the wallpaper, she supposed: a subtle, inoffensive backdrop that pulled things together without anyone noticing, whether by attempting to tighten authors' flaccid prose, keeping the household steadily ticking, or making sure the charismatic politician was happy, fed, and adequately sexed, so he could bring his marvelousness to the masses. When she had tried to become something other than that—a writer, namely—she had failed. But what if she had persevered, or even succeeded? If she was a stronger, more fulfilled version of herself, maybe her marriage wouldn't have fallen apart. Maybe she would have had a weight and solidity to her—a gravitational pull that would have kept Bill from straying.

"You could speak at one of these events they're planning," said Mona. "It would be incredibly inspiring. There's going to be a big rally in DC, you know."

Kathleen had seen the news earlier that day. A cadre of hardcore Yes We Bleed activists had gotten permits and were amassing an impressive roster of speakers.

"I'm *really* not into public speaking," Kathleen said. She'd nearly fainted when she gave a toast at Margo's wedding. Although in that case, it may have been due in part to the lingering fumes from the sage smudge ritual a friend of Margo and Nick's had performed.

"Then just write something about being menopausal and heavy periods and all of it," said Mona. "Educate people, for god's sake."

"I'm only *peri*menopausal, actually," Kathleen said.

"Or do some interviews," said Danica. "They ask the questions, you just answer. Easy. Oprah doesn't speak to me anymore, but I know how to get in touch with her people. Or Katie Couric, or Colbert. Or all of them. The world is your oyster, Kathleen."

"But she needs some new clothes," noted Jonathan.

"And new hair," said a voice Kathleen didn't recognize. She turned to see a petite woman dressed entirely in black, including her apron, brandishing a large knife. Her hair, also black, was shot through with a bolt of electric blue. "The salmon," she stated to the group. "How is it?"

"Perfect, Apple," said Danica. She sounded a touch frightened.

"You're a peach," the actor added with a wink. Apple rolled her eyes and went back to the kitchen.

"Cat," said Annabelle.

"Where?" said Danica.

"I'm *highly* allergic," said Mona.

"No, like Kat with a *K*," said Annabelle. "Short for Kathleen? If you're going to change your hair and clothes and whatever else. And it helps, a little. Annabelle's not my real name."

"It's not?" said Mona, goggle-eyed.

She shook her head solemnly and resumed spearing tiny pieces of poached salmon on a single tine of her fork. "It's Annabeth," she whispered.

"Kat Held," said Jonathan. "It's not bad."

"No," said Danica, practically purring. "It's perfect."

"Look," Kathleen said. "I just—" Everyone moved to pick up their glasses. "I don't think it would make me feel any better. If anything, it would make things worse. And what if I say or do something wrong, and all of a sudden the entire world hates me? I don't think I'd survive it."

"You would," said Michael. "We all are."

"Christine Kelton didn't," said Annabelle.

There was a long silence.

"Well, if nothing else," said Danica, "you need to do something nice for yourself. That's what phase one is all about. Maybe freshen up your look. New hair, new clothes. Let your pig husband see just what he's missing. You're very attractive. You just need a little pizzazz. We can start as soon as tomorrow if you like."

"Maybe," said Kathleen.

"*Maybe*," said Danica, sounding suddenly bored, "is an awful lot like *just*."

"Drink!" said Brent, and chugged his entire glass of wine while everyone watched, horrified. "What?" he said after wiping his mouth with the back of his hand.

The conversation then turned to the actor, who was weighing whether it would help or harm his efforts to rehabilitate his image if he participated, unannounced, in an upcoming walk for breast cancer, in hopes that the paparazzi would snap a few pictures. The group was divided.

As Kathleen rode the train home two hours later, she found herself mouthing the name *Kat Held*, over and over, as she looked at her reflection in the train window. Could she be a Kat? Not the way she looked now, with her school-secretary wardrobe and nondescript hair, with her *justs* and her goggle sunglasses. But maybe if she looked a little better, a little bolder on the outside, it might help her at least *feel* more Kat-like.

And so, when the train emerged from the darkness of the tunnels that led away from Grand Central into the golden light of late afternoon, she fished from her purse the business card Jonathan had given her, and texted him: *Hi, Jonathan, this is Kathleen Held. Can you let Danica know that I'd like to take her up on her offer to help me with my look? I can duck out of work a little early tomorrow . . .*

He wrote back within seconds. *Absolutely, Kat.*

Aggie's friend Melissa lived at the edge of Rock Hill, in a too-tall house with crooked shutters. Kathleen had never actually exchanged more than a few quick, friendly pickup and drop-off words of greeting to Melissa's mother, Antoinette. She was small, round, and pug-nosed, with dark hair swirled atop her head, ruddy cheeks, and eyes like shiny black beads. Every time Kathleen had seen her, she was either barefoot or sporting cinder block–size clogs.

Tonight, Antoinette (barefoot) invited Kathleen in and offered her a cup of herbal tea. "I make it myself," she explained. "I'm officially menopausal, and it's excellent for managing symptoms. Black cohosh, ginseng, raspberry leaf, and a little mint for good luck. You should try it, too."

"I'm actually only perimenopausal," said Kathleen.

Antoinette didn't seem to hear her. She just gave Kathleen a large ceramic mug of steaming hot tea with tiny black leaves floating around in it and added a squirt of clear liquid. "Agave nectar," she explained.

"Thank you," said Kathleen, though she wasn't sure why. "Did the girls have fun?"

"Our young women," Antoinette said, "are channeling anger into action. Melissa told me what happened to Aggie at school the other day—which is horrible, but honestly not that big a surprise given the culture in Greenchester—and when she got here we did some brainstorming." She picked up her phone and thrust it in front of Kathleen's face. "I ordered them three hundred of these Yes We Bleed pins. You can pay me back. I'm happy to go fifty-fifty as my donation to the initiative."

"The initiative?"

"Come see," she said, and led Kathleen upstairs.

In Melissa's room, which was painted a melancholy shade of purple, Aggie, Melissa, Aggie's silent friend Lucy, and a girl with a mop of pink hair and sparkling gold Chucks who Kathleen didn't recognize were on the floor making posters.

Aggie bounced up to her feet. "We're bringing Yes We Bleed to our school," she said, all-out smiling for what Kathleen realized was the first time since she'd been home.

"We're going to *educate* those bitches' asses," said Melissa.

Kathleen waited for Antoinette to reprimand her daughter for her language, but she only snorted and elbowed Kathleen, sending tea sloshing out onto Kathleen's hand.

The girl with the pink hair giggled.

"They're going to do a speak-out at the school," Antoinette explained, "and distribute educational materials and lobby for free menstrual products in all the public school bathrooms. Other communities are doing it, and there's absolutely no reason Greenchester shouldn't, too."

"We're going to write a letter to the editor of the *Greenchester Gazette*," Aggie said. "Can you help edit it?"

"Aren't these kids amazing?" said Antoinette. "You and I should have a conversation about how we can help support them and get other parents on board. I'm thinking we could carpool down to DC next week for the rally."

"I'm going," said Melissa, raising her hand.

"Me too," said the other girl.

Lucy raised her hand as well.

"Mom?" said Aggie. "Please?"

Ever since Aggie had been home, Kathleen had been showering her with yeses. She'd had so much taken away from her, so quickly; it was the least Kathleen could do. Could she get the nicer three-ring binder even though it was more expensive? Yes! Could she stay up just a little later? Yes! Could she have another bowl of pistachio ice cream? Yes!

But getting involved with Yes We Bleed was different. Aggie had already been bullied once on the topic of menstruation. If she and her friends did this, the popular kids who had assaulted Aggie with feminine hygiene supplies might very well continue to torment her. It would have been different if they were in high school, where this kind of activism might actually be considered cool. This, however, was middle school. Boys would think it was gross, girls would think it was weird, and Aggie and her friends would almost definitely be pilloried on TikTok and Snapchat and whatever other instruments of digital torture their peers employed.

And that was only the people Aggie knew. If word got out that Bill and Kathleen Held's daughter was part of a Yes We Bleed Club— which it inevitably would—the internet would pounce, and the media along with them. Kathleen couldn't expose Aggie to that. Or to the inevitable cruelty and judgment that resulted whenever children or teenagers, especially female ones, stood up for causes. They were always accused of being pawns, exploited by adults, including their parents.

"No, Aggie," Kathleen said. "We need to discuss this. All of it."

"Yes, absolutely," said Antoinette. "Come into the kitchen and I'll get you some more tea—looks like you spilled yours—and we'll discuss."

"No. Not tonight, I mean. We need to go. Aggie, why don't you help clean up?"

"Oh, she's welcome to stay for dinner! You too!" Antoinette said, apparently determined to miss every cue Kathleen was laying down. "I just put a Swiss chard lasagna in the oven."

At which point the pink-haired girl and Melissa broke into some song about lasagna that Kathleen assumed was from some inane video currently making the twelve-year-old rounds. (*"Do you like lasagna? Bow, bow, I like cheese! Do you hate lasagna? Bow, bow, give me the cheese!"*)

"Thank you, Antoinette. But no. I've had a long day, and I've got an early morning tomorrow . . . Some other time."

"Please?" said Aggie.

"How about you let Aggie stay," Antoinette said, "and I'll drive her home later."

"For god's sake, Antoinette, I said no."

The pink-haired girl gasped, and Lucy clapped a hand to her mouth. Aggie dropped her gaze to the floor. Melissa grinned, apparently thrilled by this scandalous turn of events, and her eyes darted back and forth between Kathleen and her own mother. Antoinette, meanwhile, had stuck her fists to her hips and wore an offended expression.

As for Kathleen, she felt as if she'd just been thrust into a fire. Her whole body burned and throbbed. It wasn't a good feeling, but it wasn't exactly terrible, either. She floated inside it for a moment longer.

"I'm so sorry, Antoinette," she finally said. Her breath felt thin. "That just . . . came out. I've been under a lot of stress. I just . . ."

"No," said Aggie. "It's my fault." She climbed slowly to her feet. "Thanks for having me, Ms. Raab."

"Anytime, Aggie." Antoinette kept her eyes on Kathleen's, though she was speaking to Aggie when she said, "And remember, sweetheart, you can call me Antoinette."

———

In the car, neither of them spoke at first. It wasn't until they'd left Rock Hill and passed the WELCOME TO GREENCHESTER VIL-LAGE: IT ALL BEGINS HERE! sign that Kathleen finally said to Aggie, "I'm sorry I lost my temper."

The thing was, she *wasn't* sorry about the losing-her-temper part, only the possibility that she had embarrassed Aggie in front of her friends. It was as if her visit to Danica's had loosened something in her somehow, and where she normally would have held back and bitten her tongue, she didn't.

"It's okay," Aggie said. "Mrs. Raab—Antoinette—is . . . I understand why you did it. She's got all kinds of great ideas for our club, though."

"I'm sure she does," Kathleen said. "But about the club. The thing is—"

"We don't have to go to Washington," Aggie broke in. "I know it's really far. But maybe we could see if there's a rally in the city?"

"Ag, no. I'm sorry. You can't do this."

"What?"

"I mean," Kathleen quickly added, "I think you need to give this some more thought, not just rush into it. You're barely back to school. You're dealing with so much, with what me and your dad are going through. And those girls were so mean to you, Ag. It's only going to get worse if you start drawing more attention to yourself, right? And if anyone shares anything about your club online—and you know someone will—the whole world will end up finding out, because you're Bill and Kathleen Held's daughter. And then, for your *entire life* whenever anyone googles your name—an employer, a boyfriend, a . . . whoever—it's going to come up. The internet is forever. Remember you learned that in fifth grade?"

There had been a whole unit on internet safety, which kicked off with a somber letter home, asking parents to have a frank talk with their children—their *fifth graders*—about, among other things, dick pics. Kathleen had skipped that part.

"But this is important, Mom," Aggie said. "Do you know that the average woman spends ten million dollars on menstrual supplies in the course of her lifetime?"

"That doesn't sound quite right."

"It's true. Melissa saw it online."

"There are a lot of things online. And a lot of people who say terrible, awful things."

"I won't look at anything anyone says," said Aggie. "I don't even have social media. And anyway, you're the one who told me it didn't matter what anyone else thinks."

"I did?"

"About the popular kids who put that stuff on my locker. I don't care what they think anymore, so why should I care what a bunch of people I don't even know think?"

Kathleen sighed. "You shouldn't. Nobody should. But you do. It just happens."

"It won't happen to me. Anyway, it's not about me. It's about all people who menstruate. It's a global movement. That *you* started. I thought you would be happy."

"I didn't start anything!" Why did people keep saying she did? "And, yes, it's a good movement. It's fine. All I'm saying is slow down and give it some more thought. Maybe make a pro and con list. And I'll do the same thing, and we'll come to a decision, okay?"

"But we can't slow down," said Aggie. "Yes We Bleed is happening now. We have to strike the iron when it's on."

"While it's hot."

"What?"

"The expression is 'strike while the iron is hot.'"

"That's what I meant," said Aggie. "I'm doing this. And you can't stop me." She folded her arms with theatrical emphasis—a childish gesture that only served to reinforce to Kathleen how wrong it was for her to rush into this. Aggie upped the dramatics, then, by kicking the underside of the dashboard, causing the glove compartment to pop open. "You should support the movement, too."

"I don't *not* support it."

"That's not the same." Aggie slammed the glove compartment shut.

"It's complicated."

"You say that about everything."

Kathleen felt stung. Aggie had never been like this before—sullen and defiant. Disdainful, even. Not that Kathleen didn't expect that once she edged into adolescence their relationship might become more difficult, or that Aggie's soft shell might harden. But Kathleen didn't think she would feel quite so hurt or frustrated by it. Bill had morphed into someone she no longer knew in the span of hours, and now suddenly Aggie felt different, too. Did *everything* have to change at once?

Kathleen clamped her lips together and they drove in silence. When they got back to the condo, Aggie pounded up the stairs to her room and slammed the door.

Day Ten

The salon Danica told Kathleen to meet her at, on the Upper East Side, was called Papillon. When Kathleen stepped inside, she was immediately accosted by a towering, horse-faced but nevertheless attractive blonde who looked her up and down and said, "Can I help you?" in the way that people said it when they meant "You are not welcome here."

"I'm meeting a friend," Kathleen stammered.

"Name?"

"Danica Bellevue?"

"No," said the woman. "Your name." She clicked over the marble floor to the reception desk and jabbed at the keyboard. "Are you Kat Anderson Held?"

"Who? Oh. Yes." So then. Jonathan (Or Danica? Or both?) had taken the liberty of not only dubbing her Kat but inserting her maiden name as well. She was a touch annoyed at their presumption and yet, she had to admit, the combination had a nice ring to it. *Kat Anderson Held.*

The receptionist studied her and then lifted an expensive-looking
eyebrow. "Any relation to Bill Held?"

"Not anymore," said Kathleen.

The other eyebrow rose. "Well then, let's get you some champagne."

Seconds later, Kathleen was ensconced in a large pink chair and
presented with a glass and a split of Veuve Clicquot. Looking around
at the other patrons, it was clear that, as usual, she had dressed completely wrong. She'd tried for a casual-chic sort of look, like Bobbie
pulled off so perfectly: dark-wash jeans, flats, and a white tunic-
length top. She'd added a necklace Margo had given her a few Christ-
mases ago, a triple-strand of tiny colored stones that were supposed
to impart feelings of serenity and strength, and possibly help with
constipation. She'd *thought* she looked put together and at least marginally fashionable. But compared to the other women in the place,
with their pointy-toed heels and filmy blouses tucked just so, their
impeccably manicured nails and impossibly smooth foreheads, it was
evident that she didn't.

When Danica arrived a few minutes later, a square black tote in
one hand and an enormous Saks Fifth Avenue shopping bag in the
other, she confirmed the subpar nature of Kat's outfit. She took both
of Kathleen's hands and leaned in as if to kiss her on the cheek, then
whispered, "Good top, bad jeans, terrible shoes, passable necklace.
Next time, we'll shop." She placed her bag at Kathleen's feet. "Jonathan and I picked out a few things to get you started," she said, and
took out the items one by one: a couple of tops, a pair of designer
jeans, wide-legged linen trousers (Danica described them as "insouciant"), a sweater, a scarf, a few pieces of jewelry, a pair of towering
black heels, and some patterned canvas flats. There was also a strange
little straw porkpie hat that Kathleen couldn't imagine ever wearing,
in any scenario—or Danica recommending that she wear, for that
matter. She wondered if perhaps it had fallen into the bag by mistake.

When it was time for Kathleen's appointment, the receptionist led her and Danica to an alcove of the salon tucked away from the rest of the stylists' stations. Kathleen was directed to a chair in front of an enormous gilt-framed mirror. Danica's stylist, a thickset, unsmiling bald man named Zivko with rings on both his pinkies and an accent Kathleen couldn't place, inspected Kathleen like she was a piece of produce, tilting her head up and down, left and right. "What are you thinking?" he asked.

"I guess I'm just thinking how beautiful this place is. Definitely a step up from where I usually get my hair cut!"

"He means for your hair, love," Danica said.

Kathleen watched her face turn maroon in the mirror. "Oh." She cleared her throat, and said, like someone named Kat Anderson Held might, "I was thinking a touch shorter. Maybe with some choppy layers."

"Perfect," said Zivko.

"And a little color," said Kathleen, feeling bolder.

"Definitely a little color," said Danica.

"Some honey-colored highlights," said Zivko, flicking at her hair with a forefinger. "They'll bring out your complexion, cover the grays."

"I actually meant maybe a streak of magenta or purple or something." She'd been mulling the thought ever since the lunch at Danica's, thinking about the slash of color in Apple's hair. *This is a confident person*, it said. (A slightly scary person, in Apple's case, but confident nevertheless.)

Danica gave a sigh of a laugh. "Kat, Kat, Kat. You have to walk before you can fly. But I love the moxie." She lifted her champagne glass in salute and then drained the last of it.

Once Kathleen's hair was cut and her head was sprouting rows of foil squares, they moved to a pair of tufted, hot-pink armchairs, where they were given beverages (sparkling water for Kathleen, more champagne for Danica), offered macarons and microscopic cupcakes from a tiered silver tray, and then left alone.

"So, we just hang out here for a few minutes?" Kathleen asked.

Danica coughed out a fine mist of champagne and looked at her, aghast. "Have you never had your hair colored before?"

"Not in a salon." She'd done at-home kits a few times and had recently bought a little stick of brush-on dye meant to cover grays. But the one time she had tried it, it hadn't so much covered the gray as turn it into a vomit-like shade of tan.

Danica clapped her hands. "God, this is fun. We process for about forty-five minutes."

"Forty-five minutes?" It had already taken more than an hour to have her hair cut and the dye painted on, and then it would it need to be blow-dried. Danica had said something about an express makeover, too. At this rate she wouldn't be home until seven o'clock.

"I'm supposed to pick my daughter up from her father's house at five thirty," Kathleen said. She had grudgingly agreed to let Aggie go to Bill's for the afternoon. Aggie wanted to spend some time in her own room, with her own things, to walk Nugget and read in the hammock in the yard. She wanted *home*. And though it had pained Kathleen, she'd consented.

"So call and tell him you'll be late," said Danica. "Tough luck for him!"

"I can't. I promised to take Aggie to dinner at the Cheesecake Factory."

"The— Dear god, *why?*" said Danica.

"It's her favorite restaurant."

Kathleen was hoping that going there would put Aggie in a good enough mood that they could attempt another, more productive conversation about Aggie's involvement in Yes We Bleed. Kathleen's attempt at a calm heart-to-heart with her that morning had not gone well. She had tried, with every ounce of compassion and empathy and active listening skills she possessed, to let Aggie know that while she was proud of her for turning her hurt into action, she couldn't let her rush headlong into it. Not given the spotlight—searchlight, really—currently trained on their family. "What about an environmental club?" Kathleen had offered. "Or even a non–Yes We Bleed girl power sort of thing?"

But Aggie had just shaken her head. "You don't understand."

"I have to go," Kathleen told Danica now. She stood up and started tugging at the foils in her hair.

"What are you doing?" Danica shrieked. "Stop!"

And then, as if Danica had pressed some sort of panic button, the colorist and an assistant appeared and surrounded Kathleen, frantically refolding the foils she'd dislodged. One of them shoved her back into her chair. Another flute of champagne was thrust into her hand and a dictionary-size copy of *Vogue* dropped onto her lap. A few minutes later, a young woman appeared with a glass jar full of what looked like purple mud and glopped it onto both Kathleen's face and Danica's with a tiny wooden spatula. ("Siberian peat bog paste," Danica explained. "Incredible for the complexion.") And then they were alone again.

Kathleen called Aggie and apologized profusely. "We'll go out to dinner another night, I promise."

"It's okay," Aggie said. "We're hanging out at HQ and I think they're getting pizza later."

"Wait, Dad brought you to HQ?" Kathleen had always hated that Bill called his campaign office that. (She was almost certain it was a Desmond thing.) Hearing Aggie say it, it sounded doubly obnoxious. But what she *really* didn't like was the fact that Aggie was there at all. It felt unfair; like Bill was bringing Aggie into his team's dugout.

"He needed to do some stuff over here," Aggie explained.

"You're not bored?" But Kathleen knew she wasn't. Ever since Aggie was seven, when Bill first ran for the state assembly, she had loved being put to work for his campaign, even when the "work" was an unnecessary task thought up to give her something to do— shredding documents that could have just been recycled or drawing campaign signs to tape in the windows. (Kathleen had always suspected that the second one was Desmond's stroke of bullshit: What could be more adorable than Bill Held's daughter's earnestly cray-oned signs alongside the professionally printed ones?)

"No, it's fine. We're having fun," said Aggie. She seemed to have forgotten she was mad at Kathleen. That was good, at least.

"You wouldn't believe how ridiculous I look right now, Ag. I've got all these foils on my head and glop on my face—"

From the phone, Kathleen heard a blast of laughter in the back-ground. Music started playing. "Sorry, I gotta go, Mom," said Aggie. "Bye!"

After she hung up, Kathleen snapped a selfie of herself, putting on a mock grin and crossed eyes to look as hideous as possible. She'd show Aggie later.

"Are we done now?" Danica asked when she'd finished.

"Yes."

"Good. Never make that face again. And stop acting like you're committing some kind of sin to make yourself look beautiful."

"I don't think beautiful is exactly possible for me."

"Kat! Don't sell yourself short! You're lovely! You know, our resident movie star commented after you'd left that you were quite fetching."

Kathleen felt a swoop in the lowest part of her abdomen—a sensa-tion she couldn't remember feeling in years. "He did?"

"Mm-hmm. You know . . . a fling might be just the thing for you. A little tat for those tits in your garage."

"No," Kathleen said. "I'm not looking for a fling, and when I am, I'm going to steer clear of men who objectify women."

"Please," said Danica. "As if we don't objectify men all the time! Don't get me wrong; men can be absolute pigs. Especially the ones on power trips, as you yourself know. And people like Weinstein and Cosby obviously deserve to rot in jail. But there's a difference between sexual assault and a little locker room talk on a hot mic by otherwise lovely people. Unfortunately, the idiot mob makes no distinction."

"Well, yes, there's a difference," said Kathleen, feeling a stirring of unease. "But that doesn't mean—"

"It doesn't mean he should get off scot-free, I agree," said Danica. "But he *is* reforming, to his credit. Doing a lot of reading and learning and soul-searching and whatnot. I've been working with him on his mea culpa op-ed and it's going to be brilliant. Only four more months until he can reemerge."

"What's in four months?"

"The one-year mark," Danica said. "Remember David Reeble? The comedian who made those homophobic jokes years ago that the internet found? He stayed out of public view for almost exactly one year, spent time quietly volunteering at an organization for LGBTQ youth or some such, then wrote a glorious apology, which was published in the *Sunday Review*, and was able to resume his career, albeit in a slightly diminished fashion. So that's the model we're working off of."

"Oh," said Kathleen. The Siberian peat bog mud on her face was starting to tingle a touch too aggressively, and the unease she'd begun to feel about what Danica was saying hadn't dissipated. Or maybe it wasn't so much *what* she was saying but how: breezy and nonchalant, as if the hurtful things the actor or David Reeble had said were beside the point. "I just have to ask," she began.

"Just!"

"Sorry. I *have* to ask: Why do you do this? This society. Doing all these things for people."

"Ah!" Danica said, a smile warming her eyes. "Excellent question. I do it because it's the only thing that has kept me going through my little calamity. A way of turning lemons into limoncello, if you will. The first few weeks, before I got the idea for the society, were sheer misery. I barely slept, barely ate, barely left my apartment. Not that I had anything to leave it *for*. My speaking engagements and interviews and charity events—poof. Gone. But then I got an email. Do you remember Miss Delaware?"

"Who?"

"Miss Delaware, the Miss America contestant who botched her answer during the interview portion a few years back? They asked her which Black American historical figure she admired most, and she said it was Frederick Douglass, for finding so many uses for peanuts. Then she babbled on for a bit about what a 'tragesty' slavery was and thank goodness Martin Luther King helped end it. Not very bright. But, as it turns out, she's a fan of my work. And after I was tarred and feathered for my slip of the tongue, she wrote to say that she was praying for me, because she knew how terrible it felt to be, quote, 'castrated' by so many people. Then she told me that the thing that helped her recover was helping other people. She threw herself into volunteer work. Did all sorts of things for her church. And it gave her a sense of purpose—since, clearly, the pageant route was no longer an option. So you could say I'm taking a page from Miss Delaware's book—not that she probably owned any *actual* books, besides mine. I'm helping people in their darkest hour. But!" She lifted a finger in the air. "That doesn't mean it's the right approach for everyone. You, for example. *You* need to help yourself for once. With my help, of course." She reached over and tapped the magazine on Kathleen's lap. "Now. Let's look through the September issue and find a little inspiration for your wardrobe."

An hour and a half later, once the Siberian mud had been tenderly wiped away from Kathleen's face with a damp sea sponge that smelled of lavender and (maybe?) cabbage, her hair rinsed and blow-dried and tousled perfectly out of place, and her face painstakingly patted and penciled and powdered, she sat looking at herself in the mirror, aghast.

"I look . . ." She touched her fingertips to her cheek.

"I believe *stunning* is the word you're looking for," said Danica.

The makeup artist, Zivko, and even the horsey woman from reception clustered around her, nodding in agreement.

"Gorgeous," said Zivko.

"Ready," Danica whispered, and gave Kathleen's shoulders a squeeze.

Outside the salon, in the cool, dusky shade of the surrounding buildings, Danica (wearing sunglasses that Kathleen couldn't help noticing were rather goggle-like) dipped a hand into her tote bag and removed from it a leather folio. "This," she said, giving the cover a pat, "is phase two."

"The menu thing?"

"Yes, the menu thing, as Brent so eloquently put it. You don't have to choose your response, or responses as the case may be, right away. You have up to three weeks to wallow in phase one."

The phase one card Jonathan had given her the day before at Danica's was still in her purse: *Regroup. Relax. Reassess.*

"Up to three weeks or what?" Kathleen asked.

"Or you're out. It's not a pity party. Not primarily, anyway. It's about moving forward. And god knows there's no shortage of people I could invite into the society. But membership is restricted to eight, including me. More than that and it gets unwieldy." She wrinkled her nose. "Of course, once you're in, you're welcome to stay as long as you like. Or I like." She gave a saucy little shrug. "But three weeks, no more, to choose from the menu. It's generally about the time it takes until the ground reappears beneath your feet and you can formulate your long-term plan. In your case, however, if you decide you'd like to seize the opportunity you've been given, and all the perks inherent therein, time is of the essence. People have *incredibly* short attention spans. I'm surprised this Yes We Bleed foolishness has lasted as long as it has. What's it been, a week now?" She handed the menu to Kathleen. "To peruse on your ride home. Pay special attention to number nine. We'll discuss tomorrow on Long Island, yes?"

Danica had invited the members of the society for an overnight at her beach house in the Hamptons. When she'd mentioned it the day before at lunch, Kathleen, perhaps owing to the large volume of alcohol in her bloodstream, had said she would love to come. But now she was having second thoughts. She'd barely processed the surrealness of the society meeting the day before (Moonabombers! Movie stars! Oddly combative personal chefs!) and now, four hours of salon services that probably cost Danica more than Kathleen made in a week, and tomorrow, *another* day—two days—in the land of Danica? How had she ended up so far from her old life in such a short time?

"I don't know," she told Danica. "It sounds heavenly." (*Heavenly*? Since when did she say things like *heavenly*?) "But I'm behind on work. And I don't know what I'd do about Aggie. I could get a sitter, or have her stay at Bill's, I suppose, but I hate to—"

"Kat!" Danica snapped. Then she took Kathleen's hand and said more softly, "You need to think about what *you* want for once in your life. You look fabulous. And you *felt* fabulous, yesterday, with the society, and today, with me. Don't you? Aren't you having *fun*?" She gave Kathleen's hand a squeeze.

"Yes, but I just . . ."

"Ah, there it is," Danica said. She withdrew her hand. "So maybe you're *just* not ready after all, Kath*leen*."

Just, just, just. That was her in a nutshell, wasn't it? Never doing, always *just* doing—hedging, excusing, adding an escape clause. Over-thinking and overanalyzing to the point of paralysis. And what had it gotten her? *Just* humiliated by her husband and her hormones in front of a national audience. *Just* in a so-so job and so-so clothes. A so-so life. If she walked away from Danica now and never looked back, where would it leave her? Hiding and hurting in a condo full of decor telling her to LIVE! LAUGH! LOVE! while the only good and meaningful thing left in her life, Aggie, drifted gradually away from her and into adolescence. That's where.

Danica started to take the menu from Kathleen, but Kathleen jerked it back. "I am ready," she said. "And I'll be there tomorrow." She turned and raised her hand to hail a cab, and one seemed to materialize out of nowhere, nearly hopping the curb as it screeched to a halt. Kathleen leapt back.

Danica laughed. "See what a good haircut can do?"

———

In the taxi, Kathleen managed to wait all of four seconds to open the menu. The light was dim, but she could make out the words, embossed on cream paper in the familiar script:

The Society of Shame

Phase Two

Menu of Responses
Choose one or more

1. Repair: *Take action to directly remedy the hurt or damage you have caused. Publicize generously.*

2. Redeem: *Perform an action or actions that will earn you forgiveness in the eyes of the public.*

3. Reform: *Address your shortcomings, improve your character, and make clear that you have become a better person.*

4. Reinvent: *Make a fresh start: take on a new career, hobby, relationship, and/or lifestyle.*

5. Reconnect: *Find a sense of contentment and meaning by pouring your energy into the activities or the people most important to you.*

6. Reframe: *Change the conversation such that your action is cast in a more positive light and/or the public is cast in a more negative one. Variation (advanced): Change the topic of conversation completely.*

7. Restart: *Begin anew as someone else and/or somewhere else. (NB: May require extensive legal and surgical fees.)*

8. *Revamp: Pivot to a new look, image, attitude, and/or public persona.*

9. *Reap: Take possession of the rewards that may be available to you as a result of your incident: fame, money, opportunity, influence, philanthropy, etc.*

10. *Revenge: Self-explanatory.*

Kathleen read the menu over several times. Now she understood what everyone had been talking about—and why Danica had directed her to number nine: *Reap.* It was what she and the others had been so excited about the night before: the idea of Kathleen stepping forward and accepting the mantle of menstruation queen.

Kathleen tucked the menu into her bag and took out her phone. At this point, her index finger tapped the Twitter icon of its own volition, completely separate from anything her brain might want to do. Although it generally also wanted to go on Twitter. She told herself that what she was hoping to see was that the whole thing had blown over—there was some new cause or scandal that had everyone's attention. If there was, maybe she could let the whole thing go. Maybe Aggie and her friends would let the whole thing go, too.

And yet, as she began scrolling through her feed, she found, to her own surprise and semiconsternation, that a significant part of herself was, in fact, hoping the world *was* still talking about her menses. The top trending item now, it seemed, was a viral video of a squirrel riding a pig. (In the *Atlantic*: "The Surprisingly Long History of Our Fascination with Interspecies Friendships.") Second was the series finale of a home improvement reality show called *He Shed, She Shed* that Kathleen had never heard of, and third was a recently released UN report on climate change, predicting widespread famine within two decades.

But #YesWeBleed was still alive and well. (Along with #Wheres Kathleen, #MenBleedToo, and, regrettably, #AllBloodMatters.

Meanwhile, the family values/megachurch crowd was pushing #YesWeBreed, though not terribly successfully.)

So the iron was still hot if she, like Aggie, wanted to strike it. She just had to decide, soon, whether or not she did.

Bill's campaign headquarters occupied a large corner storefront in downtown Greenchester that was previously, for decades, a hardware store. Now its plate glass windows were plastered with BILL HELD FOR SENATE signs, and inside, where there used to be tall shelves of tools and fixtures and solvents and seeds, were desks, tables, and computers, though the smells of paint and metal and fertilizer still lingered in the air. Campaign lawn signs leaned against the walls between whiteboards and bulletin boards and easels. Life-size cardboard cutouts of Barack Obama and John F. Kennedy stood just inside the door.

Over the previous six months, Bill had spent untold hours here, sometimes sleeping overnight on a sofa he'd wedged into the room that was previously the hardware store's business office. A room that, it now occurred to Kathleen, would make the perfect place for clandestine trysts. An image of him there, tangled up with someone else, speared cruelly through her brain.

Kathleen had spent time here occasionally as well, sometimes sitting next to a volunteer or two—she liked the retiree women, who exuded a more peaceful, purposeful energy than the manic young volunteers and interns—helping with data entry. But she never failed to feel like an outsider. She didn't know the volunteers' and interns' inside jokes or share their constantly talked about battle fatigue. And for all the times she'd walked into the place, Obama and JFK at the door, looking so very lifelike, still made her flinch—sometimes with an audible gasp—and feel like an idiot as a result.

Today was no exception. (Fucking JFK. How fitting that a philanderer welcomed people to Bill Held HQ.) The volunteers scattered about the room, some young, some septuagenarian, swiveled their heads almost simultaneously to look at Kathleen as she entered, their faces dropping into slack-jawed, mildly fearful surprise. One young man, beer in hand, stopped mid-swig, lowered his bottle to the desk where he sat, and jerked his hands to his lap. It was past seven o'clock and, as such, not surprising that people had started drinking. But why this floppy-haired, baby-faced man in a Columbia sweatshirt seemed to think Kathleen would disapprove of his alcohol consumption, she had no idea. Did they all think of her as some kind of browbeating harridan? (No drinking! No having fun! No screwing campaign staffers!)

From the direction of the stockroom in the back of the store—which Desmond referred to, insufferably, as his "war room"—Kathleen heard voices and laughter. Desmond was saying something about "spinning shit into gold," and a man was making, inexplicably, a barking noise. There was a woman's laughter, too, husky and knowing.

The floppy-haired volunteer sprang from his desk and went back to the stockroom. Seconds later Bill emerged. When he saw Kathleen, his expression, the satisfied afterglow of a good laugh, morphed into what looked like mild shock. "Wow," he said. "You look great, Kath. Your hair, and your makeup . . ."

"Thanks." Hearing him compliment her didn't feel quite as satisfying as she had expected it to. Maybe it had to do with how *he* looked. Not rumpled and exhausted, like he had when Kathleen had seen him a few days earlier, but *normal*—clean-shaven and seemingly well rested, in a T-shirt and jeans, a beer in his hand. As if nothing in his life had changed at all.

"Where's Aggie?" Kathleen asked.

"She's in the office with her friend Melissa. They're working on some school project. Something about women's health or something? They were very secretive and giggly about it."

"Oh no."

"What's the problem?"

"The problem is—" Kathleen became suddenly aware of the volunteers in the room, who had returned to their tasks but in a stiff, overly intentional way, like bad movie extras, clearly eavesdropping. "Can we talk outside?"

"Yeah, sure. We can go out back. You want a beer?"

"No. I don't want a beer."

She followed Bill outside, to the small parking lot behind the store. The dumpster they stood beside stank of moldy cardboard. The smell triggered a memory she couldn't quite place of some other time she and Bill had been together—a happier time. Had they made out in the vicinity of a dumpster at some point in their courtship? It was entirely possible; there was a time, before she and Bill were married, when they couldn't keep their hands off each other. The way they were standing now—stiff and still, side by side instead of face-to-face, with a good six feet between them—it was hard to believe. It was even harder to believe that two weeks ago they'd slept together in the same bed.

She hated that there was still a piece of her that missed him.

"You really do look good, Kath," Bill said.

"Thank you." Now it was slightly more satisfying.

"But you looked good before, too. You know that, right?"

Kathleen squinted at him. "What is this? You're trying to reassure me that the reason you were cheating on me isn't because I was unattractive? Is that supposed to make me feel better?"

"No," he said testily. "I'm just telling you— Look, forget it. I don't want to fight. What's the issue with Aggie?"

"Aggie and her friends," said Kathleen, "chiefly Melissa, are trying to start a Yes We Bleed Club at their school."

"Shit," he said. "That's not good."

"No. If Aggie gets involved, you know it's going to get out. And we always said . . ." They'd always said that when it came to Bill's politicking and campaigning, they would, as much as possible, keep Aggie out of the public eye. (Which meant that Kathleen could steer clear herself. It worked out well.) No using their child as a prop to make Bill look good and thereby risk her being targeted by internet trolls, kidnappers (Bill thought Kathleen's fear of this was a bit extreme, given that he was only a state assemblyman), and mean girls—which had now happened. Case in point.

"We should talk to her," Bill said. "Together."

"Now?"

"Yeah, now."

"Okay," said Kathleen. And for a single, excruciating instant she felt almost as if they were still a pair. If there was one thing that *had* remained rock-solid in their marriage, it was the way they parented Aggie together. Other women Kathleen knew were always complaining about the arguments they got into with their spouses over differences in parenting styles or discipline, but Kathleen couldn't relate. She even used to feel a little smug about it.

As she followed Bill inside, she had to grit her teeth to hold back the sob welling in the back of her throat.

He rapped on the door of his office. "Hey, Ags. Mom's here."

He pushed the door open, releasing an overpowering wave of baby powder and floral-scented air. Aggie and Melissa sat on the floor, which was littered with opened boxes and packages of panty liners, tampons, and maxi pads.

"Welcome to Greenchester Yes We Bleed headquarters!" said Melissa. She wore a wide-necked *This is What a Feminist Looks Like* T-shirt that slipped from one shoulder, revealing a red bra strap. "Like my earrings?" She tapped at the white tubular objects dangling from her ears, which, Kathleen realized, with horror, were in fact applicatorless tampons tied by their strings to earring hooks. "We're going to give them out at school to raise menstrual awareness."

Aggie looked up at Kathleen, pink faced, blinking. "I thought you weren't coming until later," she said.

"No." Kathleen folded her arms across her chest. "I'm here now."

Aggie kept her gaze locked on Kathleen's a few seconds more, seeming to weigh her next move, then resumed stuffing handfuls of sanitary pads into ziplock bags. "We're putting together period kits to distribute to refugees," she said.

"Yeah, we just have to find some refugees," said Melissa. "And we're also going to—"

"No," said Bill. "No, no, no, no, no. No earrings, no refugees. Melissa, can you give us a minute with Aggie? There are Cokes and seltzers in the fridge out there. Help yourself."

"Is there kombucha?"

"What? No. There's no kombucha."

Melissa let out a disdainful breath, got laboriously to her feet, and left.

"Aggie," said Bill, "this needs to stop. If you want to cheer Melissa and your other friends on from the sidelines, that's fine. But you cannot—can*not*—get directly involved with this, do you understand?"

Aggie's eyes darted from Bill's to Kathleen's and back again. "I don't understand why you guys are being like this!" she said. "You always said to stand up for the things you believe in. And I believe in this."

"And that's great, Aggie," Kathleen said. "We're proud of you, really, but—"

"It's not *right* that periods have to be some big, embarrassing, scary thing."

Scary. Now Kathleen understood. How could she have been so dense not to have seen it before? This wasn't just about Aggie's convictions when it came to refugee women's menstrual needs or about standing up to the popular kids who had bullied her. It was more than that. It was personal.

Kathleen had talked with Aggie about menstruation, of course, starting when she was nine or ten. But had she ever really connected with her about it on an emotional level? She'd prided herself on handling it better than her own mother, who had merely left a book called *Growing and Changing!* on the foot of Kathleen's bed the day of her eleventh birthday with a note that said, *Let me know if you have any questions.* But maybe she'd still fallen short with Aggie.

"Is that what this is about?" she asked Aggie quietly. "Are you scared about getting your period?"

Bill cleared his throat. "I can leave you two alone if you—"

"No, it's not about that!" said Aggie. "I just hate that you feel so embarrassed and sad about the thing that happened with your period, Mom. And I hate that some people don't have all the period supplies they need. It's not right."

"Look, Ags," said Bill. He crouched down, bringing himself closer to eye level with her, and took her hand. "Your mom and I both really admire your conviction. You're an amazing kid, you know that. But if you do this and people find out, it could be really, *really* bad for my campaign."

Kathleen's jaw nearly dropped off the bottom of her face. "Your *campaign?*"

Bill twisted back toward her. "Yes, it would be bad for my campaign. It would look like our daughter is taking sides. Against me." He stood up, laughing with gentle disbelief. "I mean, Kath, come on—"

"But I'm not taking sides," Aggie said. A dent of hurt appeared between her eyebrows. "I would never do that."

"We know you're not," Kathleen said as calmly as she could manage in the midst of her mounting urge to strangle her husband. "Why don't you go find Melissa, okay? Dad and I just need a minute."

Aggie obeyed, and when she was gone, Kathleen slapped Bill's desk so hard her palm stung. "How *dare* you make this about your campaign. I was worried about the exposure Aggie might get, or the hell she'd catch from the little shits at her school. Not about how it would affect *you.*"

"Well, it's about both obviously. Of course I care how it would affect her. But how's it going to look if my own daughter becomes one of these Yes We Bleed nuts? These women *hate* me, Kath. And now there's the whole Yes We Age contingent, and they're pissed off about the fact that I was with a younger woman."

"Good," said Kathleen. She couldn't believe she'd missed that hashtag.

"You can't tell me that you *actually* don't care if I win or lose this thing, Kath."

"You won't lose," she said. "This is New York! When's the last time New York elected a Republican senator?"

"1992. Al D'Amato." This was spoken by Desmond, who had at some point sidled up and now leaned in the doorway, having apparently pushed the partially ajar door farther open. "But that doesn't mean Krÿer can't win," he continued, as if he'd been part of their conversation all along. "The old rules don't apply anymore. For the moment, female voters still hate Krÿer *slightly* more than they hate your husband. But if we want to hang on to that lead, we've got to change the conversation. More Bill and his policies. Less you and your uterus. Right, Billy boy?"

Bill seemed to shrink a few centimeters. "Right."

At which point somebody else sauntered up and draped an arm over Desmond's shoulder: an attractive blonde in her thirties, pencil skirt, blouse untucked, shoeless in her nylons. Kathleen had met her a handful of times before—Shelly or Shelby, some sort of publicist from the state Democratic Party. She always laughed too hard at Bill's jokes, tittering like an idiot.

"Oh, hi, Katrine!" she said. "I didn't recognize you at first! Your hair is so . . ." She wobbled toward Kathleen, clearly quite drunk, and began fluffing Kathleen's hair. "It's so pretty! Billy, isn't it pretty?"

"Very pretty," Bill said.

"I always thought you were *mush* prettier than Tish," the woman said. "*And* Caroline."

Desmond lunged into the room. "Okay!" he said, spearing his arm through the crook of the woman's elbow and yanking her away.

"Bye-bye, Billy and Katrine!" the woman called over her shoulder as she left.

Finally alone, Kathleen gave Bill a long, hard look. "Bye-bye, Billy," she said.

On her way out of the campaign office, after flinching at the cardboard cutouts near the door, Kathleen thrust a hand against JFK's stupid, handsome face and shoved, sending him toppling backward onto the floor.

In the car on the way to Melissa's house, Melissa, from the back seat, described in detail the other menstrual product accessories she was thinking of making, with help from her mother and the other members of the club: bracelets, necklaces, purses, and pencil cases made of tampons and pads. Tampon and pad cases made of tampons and pads. She was going to set up an Etsy store called Cycle Chic and use a percentage of the profits to put together more period packages for refugee women, once they found some.

"And obviously," Melissa added, "we'll sell the menstrual cup hats everyone's wearing."

Kathleen had seen pictures and patterns starting to circulate online: knitted and crocheted hats shaped like menstrual cups, the bottom few rows white and the rest dark red, peaking to an elongated nipple of a top. To Kathleen's eye, they made the women who wore them look more like breast-headed elves than menstrual rights warriors.

After Kathleen had dropped Melissa off, before they'd even pulled out of the driveway, Kathleen turned to Aggie. She took in a deep breath and let it out. "Listen, if this Yes We Bleed thing is really truly important to you, and you're really truly okay with the fact that some kids—some people—might not be kind about it, then you should do it."

"But if it's going to make Dad not get elected—"

"It won't make him not get elected."

"But I heard Desmond say something about his numbers being in the toilet. That's bad, right?"

Kathleen shook her head. "Desmond is full of shit."

"Mom!"

"Sorry. Full of *crap*. Dad will be fine. The more important thing, Ag, is that sometimes you need to do what makes you happy. Especially if it's something you feel strongly about."

"As long as it doesn't hurt anyone, I guess."

"Right," said Kathleen. She still felt an undeniable pinch of worry about the potential consequences of Aggie's involvement. But seeing how happy and confident working on this cause made Aggie feel in the midst of so much turmoil, and knowing how strongly she felt about it—how could Kathleen go on denying her permission?

Meanwhile, how could she deny *herself* the opportunity to make the best of her unsought fame? Life was handing her a chance to be a bolder, braver version of herself, if she was bold and brave enough to take it. She would be a part of an important cause—and, yes, fine, maybe she wasn't *passionate* about it exactly, but did it matter? Wasn't simply caring enough? And if it made Bill sweat over a few lost points in the polls—god knows he had plenty to spare—well, that was just icing on the cake.

"And you know what?" Kathleen said to Aggie. "I'm going to join the movement, too. I'm going to start speaking out, doing some interviews, getting involved. And we're going to go to Washington for the demonstration. Together."

Aggies eyes lit up. "We are?"

"Yep." Kathleen banged her fist on the center console three times. "Yes we bleed!"

Aggie laughed and did the same. "Yes we bleed!"

Kathleen rolled down her window and yelled it this time. "YES WE BLEED!"

"Yes we bleed!" Aggie shouted, laughing.

They backed out of Melissa's driveway, laughing and chanting into the dusk.

"Womenopause" Festival in Celebration of Menopause to be held in Ochre Peaks

Ochre Peaks – The Yes We Age chapter of the newly formed Yes We Bleed League of Santa Fe will host a "Womenopause" festival in Ochre Peaks, New Mexico, on October 31. The festival, themed "Women Without Pause," is geared toward self-identifying women aged forty or older, though women of all ages are welcome. Event chair Jill Schneider says, "We wanted to create a joyful, honest space for women to talk about and jubilate in the transition to postmenopausal life. The theme of the festival, 'Women Without Pause,' speaks to the fact that women's sensuality, sexuality, and vibrancy doesn't 'pause' or cease once we cease to menstruate, and that for many women, the postmenopausal decades are among the most productive, happy, and successful in their lives."

Scheduled sessions include "This Girl Is on Fire: Tapping the Secret Power of Temperature Dysregulation," "The Better to Eat You With: Reclaiming the 'Sexy Grandma' Trope," "Journey to Pleasure: Vibrators, Dildos, and Lube, Oh My!," "Moodsurfing: Learning to Ride the Wave," and "Sunrise, Sunset: Show Tunes About Aging (+ Karaoke!)" with new sessions being added daily as the schedule is finalized. Other activities will include dances (folk, disco, and expressive), sharing circles, a nightly all-you-can-drink cocktail and green tea hour, and a performance by the ProgesterTones a capella ensemble. The festival will culminate on the final evening with a primal scream at sunset.

For more information and updates, follow Womenopause on Facebook.

Day Eleven

"No writing to the paper," Kathleen told Aggie. "No signing petitions. No pictures or videos or anything like that. Okay? Pinkie swear?" They'd had this talk the night before, but she repeated the guidelines again when she dropped Aggie off at school that morning. Aggie would be spending the night at Melissa's so that Kathleen could stay overnight at Danica's Hamptons house, and who knew what the girls might have planned. Kathleen hoped they would stick to tampon-related crafts and refugee kits. She may have changed her mind about Aggie's involvement in the cause, but that didn't mean she wanted Aggie's name and face all over the internet.

"Pinkie swear," Aggie said. She hooked her pinkie finger into Kathleen's and tugged.

Moments later, as Kathleen was plugging the address of Danica's house into her Maps app, she heard a knock on the passenger side window and there was Bobbie, waving eagerly. Her expression turned to one of shocked delight. "Your hair!" she squealed as Kathleen lowered the window. "It looks amazing!"

Kathleen grinned and gave it a pat. "Like it?"

"I *love* it! Did you actually get highlights?" She leaned in, bosom spilling over the windowsill, and peered at it.

"Yep. I splurged."

"Hell yes you did! You deserve it. And is that a new top?"

"Mm-hmm!" Kathleen had worn the blue-and-white-striped blouse Danica had given her at the salon the day before, which she had described as a "little all-purpose structured thing."

The car behind Kathleen's blasted its horn.

Bobbie withdrew from the window. "Just a minute, jeez!" she yelled. "Oh, hi, Christy! Didn't realize it was you!" She laughed, then poked her breast back inside Kathleen's car. "I hate her. Let's have a drink soon, okay? What about tonight? Can I come by and see your new digs? I want to hear how you're doing. And how Aggie's holding up."

"I'd love that, Bobs, but I'm actually heading out of town for the night. Taking a couple of vacation days."

"Ooh! Good! Where are you going?"

"A work friend's place. Out on Long Island," Kathleen said. She hated that she couldn't tell Bobbie about the society. But Danica and Jonathan made very clear to Kathleen that she could tell no one— not even family. "We'll get together soon, though, okay?" she told Bobbie.

"Yes! Please!" Bobbie smooched the air in Kathleen's direction and withdrew from the car again.

On the drive to the Hamptons, Kathleen listened to the albums she'd loved in college, sneering along with Alanis Morrissette as she crossed the Throgs Neck Bridge and belting "Closer to Fine" twice in a row as she sailed down the Long Island Expressway. She felt strong and free, on the verge of something exciting. It had been years since she'd felt like this, she realized. The last time, in fact, might have been the day she finished writing *The Hecate Chronicles* and was about to send it out into the world.

When she pulled off the highway, onto the local roads approaching West Hampton, she was momentarily deflated by the glimpses of huge houses over high walls and privets, which reminded her of Nantucket and the world of Bill's blue-blooded family who, she had always sensed, found her lacking, with her middle-class, Midwestern, non-tennis-playing ways.

So she was somewhat relieved when Danica's house turned out to be not an imperious colonial or a rambling, shingled affair, like Bill's family's, but a strange, modern box of a house, all vertical planks and huge plate glass windows. It was just a few hundred yards from the Atlantic, surrounded on three sides by thickets of beach roses. The decor inside was, not surprisingly, a symphony of beige and pale earth tones, just like Danica's Manhattan apartment. There were a few nods to its beachside setting: touches of driftwood and, as if they had anything to do with Long Island, pelicans.

Jonathan, in madras shorts, a tight polo shirt, and gladiator sandals welcomed Kathleen with a Bloody Mary and led her out to one of several decks, where Danica and Michael sat. Michael rose to greet her, while Danica raised a hand that Kathleen understood, after a moment, she was supposed to take and squeeze.

"Doesn't she look fantastic?" Danica said to Michael.

"Oh. Yes," he said. "You got a haircut. It looks really nice." He smiled a little bashfully, then quickly looked to his lap. He was wearing khakis rolled to midcalf and a pale blue polo shirt and was barefoot, though his feet were tucked well beneath his chair, toes folded under, as if he felt they were unseemly. How was it possible that this was a man who had regularly sex cammed, and god knows what else, in a school classroom?

It was astonishing, and more than a little disturbing, how much people were able—and willing—to hide about themselves.

"And look at the ensemble!" Danica said, sweeping a hand up and down in front of Kathleen. "I would have paired the insouciant slacks with sandals, not flats, Kat, but you can just slip them off.

We're casual here at the beach. And speaking of sandals"—she looked at Jonathan's feet now, baldly lustful—"you wore them."

"Yes, but I'm not sure I like them."

"What do you think, Kat?" Danica said.

"I'm not sure," said Kathleen. "Shoes obviously aren't my strong suit."

"Anyone can see they're ridiculous with this outfit," Jonathan said.

"Well, yes, I'll grant you that." Danica rose from her seat. "Let's go pick out something else for you to wear with them. A bedsheet toga, maybe."

A few seconds after Danica and Jonathan had gone inside, there was laughter, a stumbling series of thumps, and then a door slamming shut.

"Are those two . . . ?" Kathleen asked Michael.

Michael gave a shy half smile. "I've always wondered."

"I wasn't quite sure if he was gay or straight or bi or . . ."

"He's pan. I asked him." This was Mona, who'd appeared inside the screen door. She slid it open and plopped herself into the chair Danica had just vacated, her necklace (a string of miniature bronze folding chairs) jangling. "I was upstairs *trying* to take a quick nap, but Brent and our thespian friend are playing the world's loudest game of Ping-Pong up on the roof deck, and the new girl was snoring like a buzz saw in the room next to mine."

"New girl?" said Kathleen. She felt a pinch of jealousy. Wasn't *she* the new girl?

"Don't get me started," said Mona.

"Sorry, what was that you said before?" asked Michael, before Kathleen could inquire further. "Pan?"

"Pansexual?" Mona said. "Hello? *Pan* means attracted to anything. All genders and sexualities. It's very important to understand these things if you want to be an ally, which I am. I put a rainbow frame on my Facebook avatar every June. That's Pride Month, FYI. And in answer to your question, Kat, yes, he and Danica sleep together sometimes. I asked about that, too. Anyway. Kat, rumor has it you're going to choose today."

"Choose?"

"From the menu."

"Oh, you are?" said Michael, turning toward Kathleen. "Already?"

Kathleen looked from Mona to Michael and back again, flustered. "Am I not supposed to do that yet? Danica said—"

"You do it whenever it's right for you," Mona said. "It's how you *re*gain control of your life. Snatch it back from everyone else! Michael, show her your card."

Michael pulled his wallet from his back pocket and took from it a laminated card, which he extended toward Kathleen. Again, the words were in a typeface version of Danica's hand.

The Society of Shame

Member
Michael Thomas Mullins
Repent. Reform. Redeem.

"Mine's *reform* and *rebuild*," said Mona. "I only wanted to do *rebuild*, because I don't need to do any reforming, since I'm not a racist, as I've mentioned. But Danica put it on there anyway and keeps bothering me about it." She made a dismissive gesture, jangling the bracelet she wore (also miniature folding chairs).

"What about you?" Michael asked Kathleen. "What are you thinking? *Reconnect*? *Reinvent*?"

"*Reap*, I think." She wished there was a slightly less grim-sounding word for it. "Join the movement, do interviews, get involved."

Mona gave a resounding clap. "What I thought you should do all along."

"Actually," said Kathleen, looking at Michael, "you were the one

who first said it, weren't you? The whole 'steer into the swerve' thing."
She mimed the gesture. He seemed distracted, or maybe confused.

"What? Oh. Right. I did. If it was something you felt strongly
about. But I got the impression you weren't really into getting
involved with the whole . . . movement. Thing."

"No, I am," said Kathleen. "I mean, I'm not some kind of menstruation militant or anything. But I support it."

"Oh, okay," Michael said. "That's great, then. Congrats."

"Say it, Michael!" said Mona. "Yes We Bleed!" She pounded her
fist against the arm of her chair with each word.

"I don't, actually," Michael said. "But sure. Yes." He gave Kathleen
a thumbs-up, then excused himself and went inside. Kathleen had
the distinct feeling she'd disappointed him somehow.

"He's happy to exploit women's bodies, but god forbid he try to
actually understand them," Mona said, shaking her head. "Typical."

Lunch, courtesy of Danica's chef, Apple, who'd come out for the
weekend, was vichyssoise, Nicoise salad, and chunks of baguette,
which they slathered with butter and local honey. Danica was thrilled
and appalled to find what she was quite sure was a bee leg in hers.

After the meal, they sat on a breezy screened porch with ginger-
and-cucumber ice pops—a low point in the day's cuisine. When
Apple handed Brent his ice pop, he immediately began fellating it,
making moaning sounds.

Apple yanked it out of his hand and dropped it back onto her tray.

The "new girl," whose name was Cindy—and who Kathleen had
instantly liked—gave a bawdy laugh and wagged a finger at Brent.
"Shame on you!" She was ruddy cheeked, redheaded, and sturdily
built. Ever since she'd arrived, she had been poking at things in the
house with an index finger like she was trying to figure out if they
were real or not: furniture, pillows, candles, pewter pelicans. Periodically, she would shake her head while smiling with bemused wonder-

ment and say, under her breath, things like "Would you look at that" and "Unbelievable." Just before lunch, she'd gone into the kitchen to ask if there was anything she could help with, and Apple had nearly stabbed her.

There was something familiar about Cindy, but Kathleen couldn't quite place her. She hadn't yet revealed why she was there, and Kathleen thought it best not to ask.

"Moving on," said Danica, giving Brent a stern look. "Let's hear how everyone is doing. Updates, progress, et cetera."

Michael shared that he'd started working as a volunteer ESL tutor and had gotten a job at Starbucks. He continued to take long, prayerful walks on the beach. And he'd started a local group called New Jersey Men Against Human Trafficking and Exploitation in the Pornography Industry.

"So specific," Jonathan commented. He was now wearing a seersucker suit and white buck wingtips.

"There's actually only one other member at the moment besides me," Michael said. "A guy from my pornography addiction recovery group. But we're hoping to grow and recruit some more people. We're going to pass out flyers at a bunch of farmers markets."

"Yes, well, those are always a good place to recruit New Jersey men who feel passionately about human trafficking and exploitation in the pornography industry," said Danica.

"You have to start somewhere," Kathleen said. "I think it's great."

Michael gave her an appreciative smile. But again, she had the feeling he wasn't quite buying what she was saying. Which was fair enough, since actually she thought that handing out flyers at farmers markets to recruit new members was on the stupid side, as ideas went. Still, she truly was happy for him that he was making progress. It was becoming increasingly clear to her that of all the members of the group, he was the one most committed to righting the wrong he'd done.

Next, the actor shared that he'd just been offered a job in a commercial in Bulgaria. "It's for a cologne called Scoundrel," he said.

"And I'd have to say something like, 'We all have a scoundrel inside us.' I turned it down. But, Jesus lordy, it would feel good to work again."

"All in good time," said Danica. She suppressed a snort of a laugh. "Scoundrel. Priceless." Then she leaned toward her phone, which lay on the glass-topped driftwood coffee table in front of her. "Annabelle?" she shouted. Annabelle hadn't been up for making the trip to the Hamptons and was listening in via speakerphone. "You still there? What gives, sweetheart?"

Eventually, Annabelle peeped that she had gone to a store.

"Wonderful!" shouted Danica. "A supermarket? Shelves full of cereal boxes and all?"

There was silence.

"Are you shaking your head, Annabelle? Nodding? We can't see you."

There was the shuddering that suggested tears, followed by a wet sniff. "No. A florist." Annabelle's voice was barely audible.

Danica patted the table as if it were Annabelle's knee. "That's still good progress. You'll get there. Baby steps."

"Which ones from the menu is she doing?" Kathleen whispered to Jonathan, who sat next to her.

"It's a custom item Danica came up with just for her," Jonathan whispered back. "Retail."

Mona then reported that she'd started applying for jobs in her field, which was fundraising for arts and culture organizations. It was not going well. On the upside, her book group had voted to allow her back in after she suggested that they read something by Ta-Nehisi Coates. She had also, as an exercise to prove to herself just how not racist she was, made a list of all the books she'd read by Black authors. "The list took up almost an entire page," she told the group. "I kid you not. Once I read that Ta-Nehisi Coates book, I'll have to flip it over and start on the back."

"There are some good books out there about understanding white privilege," Kathleen said. "Maybe one of those would be good."

"We've tried that," said Danica. "Believe me."

The next person to speak was Cindy. And as soon as she began her story, Kathleen realized who she was: Wolf Mom. Dubbed thusly because her husband had taken a picture of her standing with her twelve-year-old son, both brandishing semiautomatic rifles, with the two wolves they'd killed on their Montana ranch behind them in the bed of a pickup truck and posted it on Facebook. The photo went viral, and although hunting wolves had been recently legalized in their county due to overpopulation, the family had received death threats from both gun control advocates and animal rights activists. Now Cindy and her children were temporarily living with her aunt in Poughkeepsie for their own safety.

"A few days after it happened," Cindy told the group, "a bunch of freaks in wolf masks showed up outside the house and started howling and yipping. Ray chased them off the property, but the kids were scared to death." Her voice broke. "I don't know what to do. I feel so . . . I love animals, too. That's what's crazy. We've got three dogs, four cats, a parakeet. Horses. And the cattle, obviously." She covered her mouth and nose with her hands, squeezing her eyes shut as tears leaked from them. Jonathan fetched her a box of tissues. "I just want to go back home."

"I'm sorry this is happening to you," Michael said.

"It sounds awful," Kathleen added. The idea of children being subjected to that kind of terror filled her with fury.

"Well, personally, I don't believe in hunting of any kind," said Mona. "But I'm sorry for what you're going through."

Cindy, red-faced but no longer crying, leaned forward and put her elbows to her knees, clasping her thick fingers together. "Do you eat animals?" she asked Mona.

"Yes," Mona said. "But I don't look them in the eye and *shoot* them."

"You let someone else take care of the killing for you. Some would say hunting's more honest."

"Oh, so did you *eat* the wolves, then?" Mona shot back.

Brent stifled a laugh. "Wolfburgers."

"No, we didn't eat them," Cindy said. "But they were eating the cattle that people like *you* eat."

"Excuse me, I don't *eat* red meat," said Mona. "Only poultry, and only free range. Do you have any idea what the environmental impact—"

"Ladies, ladies!" said Danica. "Enough! We are here to help each other, not judge each other, remember? Moving on, *please*. Kathleen—Kat—your turn." She wrapped her hands around one knee and gave her shoulders a shimmy.

"Well," Kathleen said, "I got a bit of a makeover, which was fun." To her own mild disgust, she found herself shimmying, too.

"And," said Danica, "have you decided? On a menu item or two?"

Kathleen took a deep breath. "Yes. I'm going to do what you all suggested. I'm going to get involved with Yes We Bleed. Join the cause, fight for destigmatization and menstrual rights and all the rest."

"Reap the rewards!" declared Danica, shaking a fist in the air. "With a little revamping and reinventing thrown in for good measure. Not to mention a soupçon of revenge, now that I think of it, because your husband will *hate* it. Jonathan, you'll make up the card?"

He nodded and jotted a few things down in a small notebook.

"You're going to have so much fun," Danica said, beaming. "We'll set everything up for you."

"Maybe some newspaper interviews?" Kathleen said. "Or even magazines. I was thinking it might be fun to be in one of those little stories in Talk of the Town, in the *New Yorker*."

Danica let her head drop back and made a gagging sound. "Print! Looking like that and you want to waste it on *print*. You need to be *seen*, Kat."

Brent nodded vigorously. "My friend Kyle would be totally into you. He's got a cougar thing."

"Annabelle!" Danica shouted at the phone, ignoring Brent per usual. "You wouldn't believe how good she looks. I'll send you a picture."

"I don't think she's still there," Jonathan said.

"The point is, Kat," said Danica, "you should go on TV! You'll be America's sweetheart."

"And, more *important*, you'll help the movement more that way," said Mona.

"If it's what you really want to do," said Michael.

"Of course it is," said Danica. She turned to Kathleen. "You'll help the movement, like Mona said, and more to the point, you'll shed that meek little Kathleen skin you've been wearing all your life and release your inner Kat!"

Brent cupped his hands to his mouth and gave a jungle cat–like screech.

"She could use some practice for the camera, though," Jonathan noted.

"Oh, god yes," said Danica. "We'll do that tomorrow." She sat back and smiled at Kathleen, shaking her head with what looked like genuine amazement. "I'm so proud of you."

Kathleen allowed herself to be proud of herself, too. She hadn't, she realized, in quite a long time.

Midafternoon, they all went down to the beach. The sunlight had the distinctly golden tone of September, but the temperature hovered just around eighty. It was perfect. Jonathan, oiled up and wearing clinging turquoise swim trunks that looked like they were from another era, arranged beach chairs and lugged a cooler full of seltzer, beer, and wine down from the house. Apple, swatting at flies and seeming generally aggravated by the fact that the beach existed, laid out a picnic blanket and set platters of fruit and cheese on low folding tables.

Danica, in a UFO-like straw hat, immediately poured herself a tumbler of white wine. Mona sat nearby reading *The Color Purple*, periodically putting cubes of cheese into her mouth. The actor, in linen pants and an unbuttoned white shirt (looking annoyingly sexy, as always, with his chiseled physique and tousled, sun-bleached hair), snoozed in a chair, while Michael and Brent tossed a Frisbee at the water's edge.

After downing a beer, Cindy, who said she'd never actually seen the ocean before, stripped down to her green skirted one-piece and headed for the water. Kathleen joined her, wading in up to her waist. The water was cold, but she eventually managed to make it all the way in, after some goading from Cindy, who was alternately treading water and floating on her back, splashing water up onto her belly like a sea otter. While they bobbed, Cindy told Kathleen more about what had happened in the past month: How her family had to stop their mail and change their phone numbers and hire around-the-clock security. How, after the wolf-mask-people incident, they had to pay a company a huge sum to scrub any possible personal information about them and their extended family from the internet. How they were now in the process of changing the name of their ranch, which had been in the family for three generations, at the insistence of a major supermarket chain that someone, somehow, figured out carried their meat and was now subject of a boycott.

"What's your ranch called?" Kathleen asked.

"Wolf Hollow," Cindy said as she floated, wiggling her pale toes. "It's all one big fricking mess. But god bless Danica, because I haven't felt this good since the whole thing happened. Being around all of you. Staying in that fancy house and eating that amazing food. Floating in the frickin' *Atlantic Ocean*. You almost forget the rest of the world exists."

"You do," said Kathleen. And it was true, being here, miles away from Greenchester, detached from the rest of the world—she hadn't gone on her phone once since she'd arrived—she felt lighter and freer than she had in days. Maybe even longer, if she was honest with herself. The intrusive, increasingly loud and manic buzz of Bill's political career, which she'd lived with for the past five years, wasn't there. Only the sounds of gulls and sloshing water and faint voices and laughter from the beach, plus an occasional incongruously loud "Dude!" from Brent. Even the knot of pain she'd carried inside her chest ever since Bill's betrayal seemed to have loosened. The only thing that might have made it better would be if Aggie, or maybe Bobbie, were here to enjoy it with her.

Kathleen plunged into the cold water and then popped herself out like a cork. Cindy howled with laughter.

Day Twelve

The next morning, after a lavish brunch (eggs Benedict, bacon-wrapped sausages, popovers, and skewers of watermelon and some pale-yellow fruit Kathleen couldn't identify), Danica announced to the group that the next activity would be interview prep for Kathleen. She led everyone to a room separated from the rest of the house by a long breezeway. It seemed to be Danica's office—wall-to-ceiling built-in bookcases, an antique writing desk, and two armchairs. But unlike a normal office, the ceiling was hung with studio lighting, and various electrical cables snaked over the floor. In one corner stood a huge, menacing-looking camera.

"It's the set from when I was doing the weekly book club segment on *America Talks*," Danica explained. "Everyone, crowd in, find a place to stand."

Jonathan hurried around the room flipping switches and adjusting lights and reflector screens, while Danica directed Kathleen to the pair of chairs. "Wait," she said, just as Kathleen sat down. "We need you in a better outfit." She instructed Kathleen to put on a blue blouse she'd given her the day before. Kathleen went back to her room to change, and when she returned to the set, she twirled for the group's approval.

Cindy wolf whistled. Michael gave a thumbs-up. Brent started to take a video and said he was going to send it to his friend Kyle, but Danica threatened to shove his phone into his moon if he did.

"I don't know," said Mona, squinting at Kathleen's outfit. "It doesn't exactly say menstrual rights advocate to me."

"What do you think she should wear?" said Danica. "Birkenstocks and a sack dress?"

"Never mind. It's fine. I'll keep my mouth shut."

"What a concept," Jonathan murmured, and proceeded to arrange Kathleen's hair and then freshen her makeup with a cosmetics kit he produced seemingly out of thin air.

"Is there anything you don't do?" Kathleen asked him.

"Needlecrafts, martial arts, calculus, decoupage, Sub-Saharan African languages—there are too many—and fly fishing. I hate fly fishing."

Kathleen laughed. "And that's it?"

Jonathan, unsmiling, gave her eyebrows a final smooth. "Yes. That's it."

"Now," said Danica, "I'll be Anderson Cooper, and you be you. By which I mean beautiful, confident, defiant." She gave her fist a little shake.

"Anderson Cooper?" Kathleen felt suddenly queasy. For the first time, she realized just what going public in the way Danica was suggesting might lead to: Cable news networks. Morning shows. Maybe even late-night. Thousands, even millions of people watching her. Judging her. Talking about her—not just as some sort of symbol, like they were now, but as an actual *person*. "No. God, no. I can't talk to Anderson Cooper. I'm not ready for this. Sorry, everyone." She started to stand.

"Wait, Kat. Kathleen." Danica took her hand and gently pulled, then firmly yanked her back down into her chair. "Just give it a try. For fun. And for me. I haven't been on camera in ages, and I'm probably getting rusty. I'll need to be back in camera-ready shape again soon enough, so this is helpful for me, too. She's going to be great, right, everyone?"

"Right," they chorused. At some point, Apple had come in, and now she stood with the others, watching intently, clutching an immersion blender.

Kathleen was about to ask Danica what she meant about her needing to get back in camera-ready shape—did she have something planned?—but before she had a chance, Jonathan yelled, "Kat Anderson Held mock interview, take one!" and they began.

The first thing Kathleen learned, after doing it almost immediately, was to never look directly at the camera—only at the interviewer, unless the interviewer specifically directed her to do otherwise. "If they ask what you'd like to say to the American people, for example," Danica explained. (Dear god, would anyone ask her that? She hoped not . . .)

Danica began again. "Kat Anderson Held, thank you for taking the time to be with us today. Please, tell us what happened that night when you came home to your garage on fire."

"Well, so, I—"

"Cut!" said Danica. She leaned forward and pressed her fingers to Kathleen's knee, hard. "None of this *well* or *just* or *so* or any of these other *transitional* words you cling to so desperately. Just *speak*." She lowered her voice to a whisper and leaned in so close that Kathleen could smell the oily musk of her foundation, the sour tang of a mimosa on her breath. "Think of everything you felt that night and *use* it!"

"Okay." Kathleen cleared her throat. "When I came home that night and saw the fire, and realized what my husband had been doing, I was furious. I was *outraged*."

Danica frowned and blinked in an impressively Anderson Cooper–like fashion. "And then, that very intimate moment was caught on a photo that went viral, revealing you had your period at the time, and that, in fact the— Cut!"

"What?" said Kathleen. "Did I say something wrong? Did I look at the camera?"

"No, you were fine," said Danica. "The 'outraged' part—excellent. But you're turning redder than a jar of borscht. Frankly, come to think of it, Anderson probably would, too. This is an interview that should be conducted by a woman." She screwed up one eye, thinking. "Let's pretend that I'm *her*."

"Her?"

Danica's chin lifted a few millimeters and her expression transformed into an impossible, irresistible combination of imperious and utterly kind—a singular blend of warmth and strength that Kathleen recognized instantly. "Oprah?"

"Exactly."

"Excuse me," said Mona, raising her hand. "Should you really be portraying a person of color?"

"Don't you have a book to read or something?" Danica said. She swiveled back to Kathleen, crossed one knee over the other, and put her hand to her chin in a perfect Oprah gesture of genuine *hearing*. "Let's continue. Kat, what was it like, finding out that that photo of you, with evidence of your period very visible and your husband having just betrayed you, went viral?"

This is what it was going to be like, wasn't it? People pouring lemon juice in her wound and then asking her to describe how it felt. Did she really want to subject herself to this?

"Kat?" said Danica, sounding a little more annoyed than Oprah would.

Kathleen closed her eyes for a moment. She could do this. She *had* to do this. "It was awful. Completely, indescribably awful. To have everyone see a picture that captured basically the worst thing that's ever happened to me. I mean, that night I—" She had to stop.

The silence of the others in the room felt almost reverent, the sadness shared.

"You're doing great, Kat!" said Cindy.

"We're still rolling," said Jonathan.

"Sorry!" Cindy whispered.

"I know this is difficult," said Danica. She touched her fingertips to Kathleen's knee. "When you're ready."

Kathleen drew in and released a deep breath. "Like I said, it was very difficult at first. But it's been extremely edifying and inspiring, seeing women find a voice and galvanize around such an important cause. I am in full support of the measures being proposed by—"

"Cut!" said Danica.

"Now what?" said Kathleen.

"Now you sound like somebody who's running for office instead of a human being." She gave Apple a nod whose meaning she seemed to understand. Apple disappeared for a minute and returned with a large rosemary-garnished mimosa.

"Relax," Danica instructed. "Be yourself—the Kat Anderson Held version. The all-American, everywoman, confident, intelligent, glamorous feminist icon next door."

This seemed to Kathleen like an impossible combination of traits to achieve, but she took a generous sip of the mimosa and continued. And whether it was the mimosa, or the warmth of the lights or the look of admiring, Oprah-ish encouragement on Danica's face, Kathleen was able to speak with increasing firmness, clarity, and verve as the mock interview went on, using the same sort of language she'd seen in various think pieces and tweets: Body-shaming! Ageism! The hegemony of the patriarchy! Menstrual pride! And the more she said, the more she began to feel like the sort of person who actually *was* an outspoken advocate for these issues, as opposed to just someone clapping politely from the sidelines. She felt strong. Excited. Alive.

Danica started to bring the interview to a close, thanking Kathleen for coming on the show, but Kathleen said, "I'd like to say one last thing, Oprah, if I may."

"Of course," said Danica, seeming tickled that Kathleen was playing along so well.

"As much as I support the Yes We Bleed movement, I wish people hadn't gone ahead and used my face all over their posters and signs and memes without my permission or consent. It's dehumanizing. An invasion of my privacy. In fact, it's a real problem with social media culture in general, I think. The way it ignores the fact that there are living, breathing, three-dimensional *people* behind whatever the latest viral thing is."

Cindy started clapping, and Michael grinned. Brent looked bored.

But Danica's mouth had dropped open and she sat back in her chair as if she'd been pressed there by an unseen hand, looking decidedly un-Oprah-like. Jonathan stepped out from behind the camera.

"What in god's name was *that*?" said Danica.

"What?" said Kathleen. "It's what I think."

"You can't say you want privacy and at the same time be going around doing interviews."

"It's a subtle point, I know," said Kathleen, "but—"

"Kathleen!" said Danica. "Kat! There is no *subtle* in the media—and definitely not on the internet, for god's sake. It's black or white, pro or con, good or evil!"

"I know, but—"

"Stick to the menstrual rights thing and you'll be golden. Right, everyone? Let's give her a hand!"

The others all clapped, even Apple. Michael, Kathleen noticed, had left the room.

Later, after the group had dispersed from Danica's office, Kathleen went looking for him. She found him on the screened porch, alone, doing the *New York Times* crossword.

"Okay if I join you?" she asked.

Michael smiled in his brief, pleasant way. "Of course."

She sat in the wicker chair catty-corner to him. Stupidly, she hadn't brought her phone or her book or even a cup of coffee with her—nothing to keep her hands occupied. She felt suddenly awkward, being here alone with Michael, neither of them speaking. Him twiddling his pencil between his fingers. It was too—something. Too intimate.

"Bill and I always did the crossword," she blurted.

Michael looked up and nodded in a way that somehow managed to convey sympathy. He returned to the puzzle. "Jessica and I never did. She was a sudoku person." He looked up at Kathleen again, quickly adding, "That's not why I—I mean, there were plenty of things we had in common."

"I'm sure," said Kathleen. She and Bill had plenty in common, too, and that hadn't stopped him from screwing around.

"'A street for señor,'" Michael said after an uncomfortable silence. "Blank—*A*—*L*—blank—blank. I'm bad at the Spanish ones."

"*Calle*," said Kathleen. "*C-A-L-L-E*."

"Yes! Gracias."

"De nada." Kathleen leaned forward to rifle through the various sections of the newspaper spread over the coffee table. She plucked up the Arts section and scanned the headlines, seeing but not really reading them. She was trying to think of how, exactly, to ask what she'd come to ask—did Michael think she was some kind of asshole for deciding to take Danica's advice and do publicity for the movement? Is that why he had left the room early?—when suddenly he said, "I'm sorry."

"Sorry for what?" Kathleen asked.

"I know you think I'm an asshole for what I did."

This was the last thing she'd expected him to say. And the first time she'd ever heard him swear. "What? No, I—"

"It's okay," he said. "I don't blame you. You know how painful it is when someone you love betrays your trust. And then everyone finds out about it. And here you are, being reminded of those feelings all the time with me being here. So... I don't know, it doesn't quite make sense but... well, I just keep feeling like I should apologize.

To you. On behalf of all crappy husbands, maybe." He glanced up at her.

"Oh." She wasn't sure what to say. Should she thank him? She did, oddly, feel grateful. His apology—for something he didn't even do to *her*—seemed more genuine than any of the desperate sorrys that Bill had uttered for what he actually *had* done. And maybe this explained why he always seemed a little ... something ... around her. Maybe it wasn't because he disapproved of her. It was because he felt guilty, or embarrassed, or both.

"And now you think I'm an asshole *and* I'm really weird," Michael said.

"No," said Kathleen, smiling. "I don't think you're either. I'm sorry if I gave that impression. I know you're really sorry about what you did. I think my husband, on the other hand, is mostly just sorry he got caught. So, on behalf of all betrayed spouses, thanks."

Michael gave a courtly nod. "You're welcome."

"What else?" Kathleen said.

"What?"

"Clues. What else are you stuck on?"

"Oh. 'Flightless bird.' Four letters."

"*Kiwi*," she said.

"Wow, you're fast." He wrote the answer in, and in the quiet that followed, Kathleen started to actually read one of the stories in the Arts section—an interview with the director of a new musical adaptation of *Die Hard*. Michael's apology had put her at ease, and now sitting here with him felt just normal and neutral. And it didn't feel forced at all when she said, a little later, "That was pretty absurd in there, wasn't it? The lights and the cameras, and Danica pretending to be Oprah ..."

"She puts on a good show, all right." There was an unexpected edge to his voice.

"That she does," said Kathleen. "I just feel so awkward, doing that kind of thing ... I hope I don't totally blow it when I'm actually on TV."

"I don't think you will. You were great in there."

She put her hand to her sternum, relieved and, to her surprise, flattered. "I was?"

"Yes," said Michael. "Just keep telling the truth."

Before Kathleen left to go home that afternoon, Jonathan presented her with a small gift-wrapped box. "A party favor," he said. "And I'll start setting things up tonight. Interviews, appearances, meetings."

"It's all happening so fast," Kathleen said.

"It has to." Jonathan scrutinized her with one narrowed eye. "You're ready, Kat Anderson Held," he said. "You'll do fine. And we'll all be rooting for you."

"Thank you." She could have hugged Jonathan, though she suspected he would have leapt back in horror. "I really couldn't do this without you guys."

"Well, you could," Jonathan said. "But not nearly as well."

When she was in her car, just before she turned the key in the ignition, Kathleen opened the gift Jonathan had given her. Inside was a slim silver box lined with red velvet, containing a laminated card:

The Society of Shame

Member
Kat Anderson Held
Reap.

Day Thirteen

All it took were a few emails and a couple of phone calls from Jonathan, playing the part of—nay, *being*—Kathleen's publicist, and she was scheduled for an exclusive in-depth interview on CBS. When she arrived at the studio, she was whisked into a dressing room, where a makeup artist slathered her skin with foundation, painted her lips a bright coral pink, and went at her hair with a huge curling iron.

When Jonathan saw the results, a look of horror swept over his face, and he nearly dropped his clipboard. "Dear god," he said, "they made you look like Pat Nixon." He produced a packet of makeup removal wipes, a dark mauve lipstick, and a comb from his attaché case, glanced around to make sure nobody was looking, and went to work. His adjustments were a vast improvement.

The set Kathleen was led to was fashioned to look like an Ivy League lawyer's study, not unlike Bill's, although Kathleen suspected that in this case not only were the stern sets of hardcovers on the shelves unread, they most likely weren't actual books at all.

As the crew adjusted her lavaliere mic, someone put a bowl of fake fruit on the small table between the two chairs. When Kathleen joked to the host, a helmet-haired, crazy-eyed brunette in her sixties in a carnation-pink pantsuit, that a bowl of menstrual supplies might be more thematically on point, the host looked at her in much the same way Jonathan had earlier. "What do you *mean*?" she asked.

Her first question, once the cameras were rolling, was an urgent "How *are* you, Kathleen?"

"I'm doing fantastic, actually," Kathleen answered. "And you can call me Kat."

"Like the animal!" said the host. "The pet!"

"Sure," said Kathleen. A thought came to her, and she smiled. "Or a lioness if you like."

"Wonderful," the host said. She gripped the edge of the table between them as if it might walk off the set if she didn't. "*Wonderful*. But you weren't always a big cat, were you? You were a politician's wife, a mother, a"—she glanced down at the paper in her hand—"an editor, I see. Did you ever think that you'd be thrust into the lime-light in this way?"

"No, never," said Kathleen. "Definitely not. But when all this hap-pened, and I saw the way women were responding, it just—" Here she clapped her palm to her chest. "It was so moving. I never expected that this humiliating moment in my life would become a rallying cry. And I want to start giving back, helping the movement however I can. I realized that by not speaking out, I was in fact undercutting the whole point of Yes We Bleed. Women—including me—have accepted the patriarchal narrative about our periods for too long. And women in their forties, like me, and older have been hesitant to really *own* our menopause and celebrate it as a rite of passage like any other."

"I read something online about a menopause festival happening out in New Mexico somewhere," the host said, "and I thought, what a *wonderful* idea."

"Yes, it sounds like a lot of fun," Kathleen lied politely.

"What about the legislative agenda of the Yes We Bleed movement?" the host asked. "Tax-free menstrual supplies nationwide, free or affordable supplies in all public restrooms, sanctions on countries where women are isolated or ostracized during their menses. The list goes on and on." She made a show of flipping through the pages in her lap, which Kathleen wasn't convinced actually had anything written on them.

"It's vitally important," Kathleen said. "All of it. And what underlines it all is the need for more open conversations about menstruation. Making it a part of everyday life, so women don't have to suffer in silence. For example, if one of my coworkers, male or female, asks me how I am, if I have a cold or a headache, I might say, 'I'm doing fine, but I'm a little under the weather.' So why shouldn't I say, 'I'm doing fine, but I'm having some pretty bad cramps'? We've been ashamed of these normal bodily functions for far too long. It's time for it to stop."

Kathleen was amazed at how easily all the words tumbled from her lips. And, yes, maybe she exaggerated a little bit—there was no way in hell she'd tell a male coworker she was having cramps—but most of it was genuine. And everyone around her on the set, the women in particular, looked so fascinated, so pleased with her performance; and she felt so alive, so revved up, so *on*, who cared if she embellished her beliefs a little for effect? Like Danica said, there was no such thing as *subtle* in the media. And as the voice of Yes We Bleed, she couldn't hedge or equivocate or "just" the message of the movement.

But then the host threw her a crazy-eyed curveball: "Do you think there's any chance that you and your husband might reconcile?"

Jonathan had explicitly told the network that Kathleen would not answer any questions about Bill's infidelity or their marriage. This was Kathleen's decision, made chiefly for Aggie's sake: as furious as she was at Bill, she knew how upset Aggie would be if she found out Kathleen was publicly denouncing him. The host, however, apparently didn't get the memo or was ignoring it.

Without even thinking, Kathleen told her the absolute truth: "Um, yeah, no."

Kathleen Held Made Her First Public Appearance Last Night, and the Internet Loved It.

Gus Reddy Tellis

Two weeks after a photo of her with a menstrual stain on her pants went viral, Kathleen Anderson Held finally broke her silence, appearing on a prime-time interview with Deborah Morton for CBS. During the 30-minute exclusive, Held talked about period snafus, the need for Yes We Bleed and her, um, feelings about her husband, Bill Held—and the internet loved it.

The love fest began when Anderson Held opened up about periods, perimenopause and the importance of Menstrual Rights.

Barb Kassen @BarbarettaK Kat Anderson Held is running a master class in how to be an advocate for a movement: with intelligence, wit, and humility.

Paula Eoyang @TheRealPaulaE Kat Anderson Held is talking about night sweats & heavy periods on national TV, and I am so here for it. #YesWeBleed #Perimenopause

Jon Naddaff @JTNaddaff Kat Anderson Held: "If men got periods, they'd have contests to see whose lasted the longest." All men: "LET THE GAMES BEGIN."

Then Kat gave the love back to her supporters and to the #YesWeBleed activists, saying that women held her up and inspired her "in one of the worst moments of [her] life."

Krystal M. @JustKrystalOK Watching this interview I keep trying to hug my TV because OMG I want Kat Anderson Held to be my mom.

Clementine Lamont @ClemLaLa THIS is the kind of solidarity and support feminists should show each other. Infighting only benefits the patriarchy. Thank you, Kat.

But the biggest moment of the night came when host Deborah Morton asked Held if she planned to reconcile with her husband. Held's quip, "Um, yeah, no," became an instant sensation.

Faye McCoy. @FakeMcCoy "Um, yeah, no" is the perfect answer to pretty much any question my kids ask. Can I have a hamster? Can I have an iPhone? Can I have a hoverboard? #UmYeahNo #KatAndersonHeld #TeamKat

Bobby Cruz @BobMCruzShip Am I planning to vote for douchey neolib @BillHeld4Senate this November? Um, yeah, no.

At last count, #UmYeahNo had racked up 14K mentions on Twitter, edging out #VotingRightsNow and #SmoothieFails.

Day Fifteen

Kathleen sat on a sofa in the *Good Morning America* green room at ABC studios, waiting to be called onto the set for her segment, scrolling through her emails, sipping a cappuccino that a pixie-like production assistant in a headset had brought her. It was perfect: just the right temperature and the ideal amount and consistency of foam. Best of all, Bill hadn't made it. There was no ulterior motive to this cappuccino—to appease or apologize or assuage guilt. It was just something someone had given to her because it was their job. And it was delicious. As was the almond croissant and the sliced mango she'd taken from a miniature breakfast buffet set up in a corner of the room.

Kathleen couldn't believe that this world of TV studios and green rooms and people bringing her coffee was her life now. It was astonishing to the point of absurdity what a frenzy of media interest her first interview had unleashed. Within hours of the segment airing, GIFs made from the clip of her "Um, yeah, no" had galloped into every corner of the internet. (A *Washington Post* columnist called it "the quip that launched a thousand GIFs.") In the previous thirty-six hours, Kathleen had either done or scheduled interviews on CNN, ABC, MSNBC, NPR, and a handful of tristate-area local news and radio shows, plus this morning's appearance. She was scheduled for an interview for the online edition of *Vanity Fair* and a possible cameo in a hot Netflix comedy about a pair of cheeky Englishwomen who lived in a flat in Birmingham and said cheeky English things. *New York* Magazine wanted her in a year-end story on the year's thirty most influential New York women, and *People* wanted to include her in an upcoming issue. She was invited to a party at a lesser-known Kardashian's house (she declined) and Sandra Bullock sent her a fan letter. Somehow, news of the fact that she'd refused to appear on Fox News got out, because a tweet reading Fox News: "Can we interview you?" Kat Anderson Held: "Um, Yeah, No" was retweeted 22.6 thousand times.

As the media coverage had accelerated, Kathleen had started checking her phone and computer even more frequently than before. The picture of her as Rosie the Riveter was still circulating (to Kathleen's frustration; she hated that her old, drab, makeupless face was the one in it); but the Um-Yeah-No GIF was even more ubiquitous now, along with think pieces about why infidelity was so rampant among famous and powerful men, and why what Kathleen was doing—from refusing to stand by him at his press conference to changing her name and image to her now world-famous reply, encapsulated in the destined-to-be-a-classic GIF—was so rare.

At Jonathan's insistence, Kathleen had created non-anonymous Twitter and Instagram accounts for herself, along with a fan page on Facebook. She'd begun posting occasional pictures and updates about her media appearances, but mostly she stuck to retweeting and reposting other people's articles about her, and the Yes We Bleed movement. She couldn't possibly reply to all the instances of people tagging her or addressing their comments or questions or compliments directly to her. There were too many, so for the most part she just dutifully hit the little heart and thumbs-up buttons. Sometimes she managed a "Thank you" to a compliment, or an "I'm so glad" or "That's so rewarding to hear" if someone mentioned the impact she had had on their life. One such reply, to a former member of the US Women's Gymnastics team, garnered six thousand likes.

The liberal bitch/feminist bitch/unfuckable bitch/you-need-to-get-raped-bitch crowd was still at it, but they were outnumbered at least tenfold by tweets and posts in support of her, praising her courage, her intelligence, her likability (rated an 8.5 out of ten by an independent polling group). Every once in a while, though, someone would dismiss her as a "distraction" from the real substance of Yes We Bleed or make a snide comment (Anyone else feel like Kat Anderson Held is loving all this publicity just a little too much?) and she felt it like a jab to the gut. The only thing that dulled the pain was reading the replies people wrote in her defense (Who cares if she loves it? What, she's not allowed to have fun?) or the fan mail that came in through the website Jonathan had built for her (because of course he could do that, too).

She had been tempted many times to fire back retorts at the haters and the trolls. But when she felt that impulse, she would open up and skim the brand strategy deck that Jonathan and Danica had developed for her, including her key public persona attributes: *(1) Sincere, (2) Humble, (3) Thoughtful, (4) Witty*, and—of course—*(5) Deeply committed to/focused on the Yes We Bleed cause*. Replies to naysayers, critics, and Kürt Krÿer fans, not to mention posts on subjects other than Yes We Bleed and other women's health causes, were *not* on-brand. "In other words, ixnay on the climate change," Danica had said sternly after Kathleen retweeted an article about the retreat of the Greenland ice sheet. "Leave it to Al Gore and that Swedish child."

By now, Kathleen had her talking points about menstrual destigmatization and awareness down pat, but was still managing, she thought, to deliver them with genuine (or something close to it) fervor. The vast majority of social media denizens, it seemed, agreed—and loved her even more. On Instagram there was a new trend in which women posted selfies of themselves in cat ears

(#KatSelfie) when they had their periods—a sort of not-so-secret code—prompting all manner of jokes, commiseration, and sympathy from commenters.

> Me too! Day 7 and counting. WTF?

> Hang in there, girl!

> Wifely duty vacation! LOL!

A few women were even, unfortunately, wearing cat ears *on top of* their knitted menstrual cup caps, so that instead of breast-headed elves, they looked like breast-headed cats, leading to much meme-ing and ridicule by the right. (Ann Coulter: It's Official. The Left Has Lost Its Mind.)

The strangest thing to Kathleen was that it wasn't nearly as hard as she'd expected it would be to be Kat Anderson Held. It was as if this person—this very open, confident version of herself—was in her all along; she'd just never had the guts to reveal it.

But maybe it wasn't just that. Maybe she also had, without even being aware of it, purposely held herself back so that Bill could shine even brighter.

She wasn't holding back anymore. In fact, she'd even decided to take a chance that just days before would have been unthinkable to her: she had accepted the invitation to give a speech at the Yes We Bleed rally in Washington. When the organizers contacted her, her first impulse had been to feign a scheduling or childcare conflict and to offer to send some sort of video message instead. They could play it over the sound system, or Jumbotron it, if they must. Because there was no way she was going to stand up and speak in front of thousands of people. Just the thought of it made her mouth go dry. But, as she was about to tap out her reply, it was almost as if Danica was right there beside her, intoning gently in her ear: *Kathleen was afraid of public speaking. But you're Kat now, remember?*

Yes, she was, dammit. And Kat was the sort of person who would power through the fear and do it.

She wrote and told the Yes We Bleed organizers that she would be honored.

"Kat?" The production assistant leaned into the room. "They're doing the cooking segment now, and then you're up. You don't have a problem with lingering bacon fumes, do you?"

"No," she said. (Did anyone?)

"Perfect," said the assistant, and left.

Kathleen glanced down at the lid of her cappuccino. It was stamped with the wine-colored imprint of her lips. She went to the bank of lit mirrors against the wall and touched up her lipstick. It was almost embarrassing, how much better she looked now that she was wearing decent makeup and had a more stylish haircut. Why had she never done this before? Maybe because she didn't think it would actually make a difference? But it did. It most definitely did.

After extricating a clump of mascara from her lashes, Kathleen sat back down on the sofa, took her phone from her purse, and checked her email. There were at least ten new messages since she'd last checked less than an hour before, but her eye went immediately to one with the subject line "WOA!" It read:

Hi, Kat. My name is Liz Eckert, and I'm chairperson of the Women of America Conference—WOA, pronounced "whoa," for short. (Who says empowerment can't be fun?!)

As you may know, we're the world's largest gathering of female entrepreneurs, leaders, innovators, and changemakers. Each year, we present a special Women of America award to five women we believe embody the mission of our organization. Past recipients have included Toni Morrison, Madeleine Albright, and Gloria Steinem. We always save a spot for a last-minute honoree of the moment, and this year—two weeks from now, specifically—we'd be honored to present one of our Women of America awards to you.

A laugh burst from Kathleen's throat. The WOA Awards! Kathleen had seen the award ceremonies herself when Margo dragged her to the conference several years ago. Applauding for all those accomplished women up on the stage—scientists and senators, authors and television producers—it had never occurred to Kathleen for a second that she might one day be one of them. She hadn't even dared to wish.

She tapped out a text to her sister. *Mar! Guess who's getting a WOA award??*

The reply was instantaneous:

> Thank you for your message! I believe that mindful digital consumption is an important element in a heartful life. Between the hours of ten pm and eight am PST, I disable all my electronic devices and reconnect with what is truly essential: my loved ones, myself, the stars, the sunrise, and the sounds of nature. When I re-engage with my phone, you can be sure I'll reply. Blissings! Margo

Kathleen was about to write back with an offer to help Margo edit her auto-reply, to make it 25 percent shorter and 50 percent less sanctimonious, when her phone rang: Margo.

"It's five a.m. out there, isn't it?" Kathleen said.

"Yes, but oh my god, Kath," said Margo. "I am just *crazed* with work. I'm in the barn making tinctures and creams and teas all day—I'm here now, actually—and fulfilling orders and catching up on social all night. The demand for my Goddess Goodness line has gone through the roof since Yes We Bleed."

"Congratulations," said Kathleen.

"Thank you," said Margo. "I feel truly blessed."

"So, you saw my text about the WOA Conference?"

"Yes! It's wonderful news. And, Kath, I know you don't believe in cosmic resonance, but I had this *vision* the other night of a huge, beautiful new exhibition booth for Blissings! made of found wood and dried flowers and herbs. And now, you winning this award?

Clearly the universe is telling me I should exhibit at WOA this year!"

"Clearly," Kathleen said. She had hoped that for once Margo might be able to see past herself and make the conversation chiefly about her, Kathleen. Especially given that (A) this was the first time they'd actually spoken in two weeks and (B) for once Kathleen was the one to whom exciting, life-changing things were actually *happening*. But apparently that was beyond Margo's ability.

"I just hope it's not too late," Margo went on. "I'm going to email them right away and see if they still have spots left. And, Kath! You could spend a few hours the day of your award at my booth! Say hello to passersby, sign autographs, that sort of thing."

"Gin up business for you, in other words."

Margo made a phlegmy sound of annoyance, sounding, for a sliver of an instant, like the teenage non-California version of herself Kathleen knew when they were growing up together. The one who regularly got busted for smoking in the high school bathrooms and had once been suspended for streaking topless through the cafeteria with her friends, all of them drunk off their asses on wine coolers. The one Kathleen would cover for when she snuck out to see her twenty-eight-year-old boyfriend, Lance, a wedding DJ with a cocaine habit. "I'm your *sister*, Kathleen," Margo said. "I would think you'd want to help support my business."

"I already *am* supporting your business apparently," said Kathleen. "I've been supporting it, and you, for years."

Through the phone there came the shushing, ocean-like sound of intentional breathing—alternate nostril, no doubt. "Hello?" Kathleen said.

"I'm just processing," said Margo. "You don't sound like yourself."

The production assistant leaned into the room then and gestured at Kathleen. "I have to go," Kathleen said. "They need me on set." She silenced her phone and followed the assistant down the hall.

On the set—airy, brightly lit, smelling gloriously of bacon—the three smiling hosts waited, beaming, backed by the crowd outside

in Times Square, watching and cheering through the plate glass windows. Midway through the interview, one of the spectators, an apple-
cheeked tourist in a Yankees cap, held up a sign that read MARRY
ME, KAT ANDERSON HELD!

"What do you say, Kat?" George Stephanopoulos asked her, dark
eyes twinkling. "Um, yeah, no?"

"As you might imagine, I'm not feeling too keen on marriage at the
moment," she said, a touch flirtatiously. "But he *is* kind of cute." She
waved at the tourist through the window, and he clutched his heart,
feigning a swoon. Everyone laughed with unbridled delight.

When Kathleen got back to the condo that afternoon, two TV interviews and a conversation with someone from Al Jazeera later, she
nearly tripped over a mound of backpacks inside the door. The living
room, to her shock, was jammed with middle school girls and thick
with the smells of deodorant, body odor, and microwave popcorn.
On the floor, a clutch of girls in various stages of puberty—one looking all of nine years old, another with the kind of breasts women paid
money for, another who looked like she would be five feet ten, easily, standing up—were making strange thrusting motions with their
arms, laughing breathlessly. On the sofa was Melissa, who appeared
to be in a vigorous debate with the pink-haired Kia. Kathleen caught
the words "body image," "maxi pads," and "patriarchy" (the "ch" pronounced as in *cheese*). Aggie and another girl sat in the oversize armchair, scanning the pages of paperback books whose titles Kathleen
couldn't quite make out.

"Hello," said Kathleen, waving to get Aggie's attention. "What is
this?"

"Hi, Mom!" said Aggie. "Book Club!"

"Kathleen," said Melissa (who Kathleen really wished wouldn't
call her by her first name), "do you think *Are You There God? It's Me,
Margaret* is a feminist story or not? I say it totally is. Kia says no."

"It kind of reinforces society's rules about women's bodies, doesn't it?" said Kia. "The whole boob-exercises thing, and periods being, like, a contest?"

The girls sitting on the floor commenced their vigorous arm gestures and giggling, chanting, "I must! I must! I must increase my bust!"

"See?" said Kia, and stuck out her tongue at Melissa.

Melissa rolled her eyes. "It's a *commentary*. Right, Kathleen?"

"Um," said Kathleen, "well, yeah, I think it was clear some of it was supposed to be funny. Or sad. Or something. Anyway, I really liked it when I was around your age."

In fact, she'd read it when she was probably only nine or ten, the book having been passed to her by a friend who'd gotten it from her older sister. And she wouldn't exactly say she liked it. Yes, it was tantalizing and a little bit titillating, this window into a thing she'd known so little about. But it was also frightening, with its medieval-sounding descriptions of sanitary pads and sanitary belts with hooks. (There were belts? And hooks?) It wasn't until she was in fifth grade and all the girls were sent home from health class with "starter kits" from Kotex (two different sizes of pads and several coupons) that she realized, with relief, that there were no longer any belts or hooks involved.

"My mom wasn't that comfortable talking with me about things like periods," Kathleen told Melissa. "So I learned a lot from it."

"Oh my god," said Melissa. "That's so sad."

"My mom isn't, either," said another girl. To Kathleen's surprise, it was Anna—Aggie's former friend turned popular snot. She was wearing a pair of Melissa's homemade tampon earrings, this time dabbed with what looked like red Magic Marker, and a headband decked with glued-on rosettes made from pink panty liner wrappers. "I really liked the book."

"I did, too," said the girl with the huge breasts. "But y'all are crazy to want big boobs. Trust me."

"Speak for yourself," said the girl who looked nine, and took her bust-increasing flapping up a notch. The other girls laughed and joined her.

"PAT-ARCHIE," Kia said, scowling.

"Hey, Ag," said Kathleen. "Can I talk to you for a second?"

They climbed the stairs to the first landing, standing by the distressed-wood hanging painted with the words EMBRACE THE JOURNEY.

"I love that you're having fun," Kathleen said, "but I wish you'd asked me about having all these friends over."

Aggie furrowed her brow. "I did. Remember?" She brought her braid forward over her shoulder and worried the end of it.

"No. When did you ask?"

"Last night. You were sitting on the couch, looking at your computer, and I said, 'Can I have a few of my friends from the club over?' and you said, 'Okay.'"

"I did?"

"Yes." Aggie nodded resolutely. "You, like, totally did." *Like, totally did.* It sounded like something Melissa would say. Or any teenager, for that matter. "You were zoned out. You do that sometimes, you know. You *say* you're paying attention, but you're not."

"That's not true," said Kathleen. (All right, fine, maybe it was.) "And I remember now. You did ask, I just didn't realize it was going to be so many kids. This isn't our home, Aggie."

Aggie looked away. "Well maybe we should *get* our own home."

"We will," Kathleen said. "It's just—it's too soon. Dad and I are still figuring things out." Another lie; they weren't actually figuring anything out at all right now. Custody arrangements, finances, forgiveness, whatever else people did in situations like this—it was too overwhelming, too heartrending even to fathom. So she hadn't even tried. She was in survival mode. Survival by way of reaping. "We just need you to be patient. Okay?"

Aggie pursed her lips. "Fine, I guess."

"Hey, guess what," said Kathleen. "I've got exciting news. Do you remember that women's conference I went to a few years ago with Aunt Margo? Women of America?"

"Sort of."

"Well, what would you think about us going together? There'll be all kinds of awesome women there, giving talks, doing book signings. I'm sure the Yes We Bleed people will be doing something. And . . . drumroll please . . . guess who they're giving an award to? Somebody you've heard of . . ." Kathleen stretched out her arms.

Aggie's face lit up. "Michelle Obama?"

Kathleen let her arms drop. "No. Me."

"Oh. Congratulations."

"Thank you." Kathleen gave a small bow. "So, what do you say? You'll be my date?"

"Sure! It sounds cool."

Ah, her Aggie! Her sweet, enthusiastic Aggie.

"Can I go now?" Aggie gave her head a twitch, sending her braid back behind her again.

"Yes. You can go. Hey, hang on." Kathleen gave her a hug.

Aggie drew back more quickly than usual. "Your hair feels all crunchy," she said. "And smells weird."

Kathleen attempted to comb her fingers through her hair, though it wasn't quite possible. "Hair spray," she said. "They did something strange to it at CNN."

Aggie wrinkled her nose, then trotted back downstairs to her friends.

Kathleen retreated to her bedroom, relieved that the conversation had gone as well as it had. It really was amazing—though not all that surprising—how well Aggie was holding up. Letting her go forward with her Yes We Bleed Club had been the right choice. And so far, knock on wood, word hadn't gotten out that she'd become a small-scale activist for the cause. A couple of times, interviewers had asked Kathleen about Aggie: *You have a daughter. What does she think of all this?* Kathleen had kept her answers brief: *She's doing well, thanks. And she's a big fan of Yes We Bleed.* Nobody had pressed her further.

One TV host, male of course, had had the audacity to ask if Aggie had her period, but Kathleen had shut him down with a searing look (which had since been made into an Um-Yeah-No GIF).

Now Kathleen kicked off her heels, lay down on the bed, and took out her phone. Not surprisingly, there was a text from Jonathan. *The producers of* The Dog Rescuer *just called, asking if you'd be willing to be on the first episode of the show.*

The what? she replied.

He called a few seconds later. "The new reality show, with your taxi driver paparazzo friend Frank Martello," said Jonathan. "He does something involving dogs. Hang on, I'll pull up the email . . . Frank Martello, the taxi driver who et cetera, et cetera, will be starring in a new animal welfare reality show sensation, *The Dog Rescuer.* In each episode Martello will help a different American family select and adopt a dog from a local shelter . . . then he helps the dog get settled, checks the home for potential hazards—I'm paraphrasing—performs various safety drills with help from his brother the firefighter to demonstrate how the family would rescue the dog from fire, flood, or other potential catastrophes, et cetera. Your piece would just be an introductory segment of some sort. A little heart-to-heart with the taxi driver. So, yes? The dog-owning, reality-show-watching demographic is enormous, and largely female. And you'd reach an audience beyond your core audience of urban-dwelling, college-educated liberals."

"No," said Kathleen. "*Fuck* no. That fame-grubbing idiot ruined my life."

There was a pause. "Did he, though?"

Kathleen glanced around the room—this unfamiliar room with its generic, framed floral prints and faux distressed furniture. The king-size bed far too big for one person, with its infinite piles of coordinating pillows, including a small one that read, TO SLEEP, PERCHANCE TO DREAM. None of it hers, none of it *her.* On the other hand, the messages on the phone she held—in one wedding ring–less but impeccably manicured hand—contained invitation after invitation to interviews and events. She was growing, blossoming. Screwing her courage to the sticking place. (Now *there* was the pillow for her.) But there was no way in hell she was going on that man's show.

"Tell them thanks but no thanks," she said.

"Mm, you're right," said Jonathan. "I suppose it's not really on-brand anyway."

Bill Held/Kurt Kyrgowski Debate

[...]

DAVID OLIVER HARRIS: We have one final question, gentlemen, about an issue that's very much top of mind right now.
Mr. Krÿ—Kyrgowski, there has been a groundswell of support, both nationally and here in New York, for improved
access to women's health care and destigmatization of wom-
en's health concerns, including, ah, menstruation and menopause. If elected, would you support legislation that would,
among other things, expand access to feminine hygiene
products? You have three minutes.

KURT KYRGOWSKI: I gotta tell you, David. I've got a wife,
I've got two daughters, a step-daughter, a granddaughter, a
sister, and a mother. And one—no—wait, two nieces. They
get great health care. That's something that's really great
about our country. What's not great about our country right
now, and what I want to fix, is people coming here from
other countries, streaming in across the borders, and taking

advantage of our great health care. You've got liberals talking about women not getting enough tampons and maxi pads and that's great, I'm all for it. I didn't know there was some big shortage, because the bathrooms in my house are stuffed with them.

[*Laughter*]

But the real problem is people who aren't doing their fair share, taking up all the health care that should be going to women. Who, by the way, are doing great in this country. People have said I'm not a feminist, and it's true. I'm not. Feminists are annoying. But I respect women and I want to help them. I'll tell you what I *don't* want, and that's educating little girls as young as four, five, six years old—little baby girls—about quote-unquote "*consent*," which I've heard some people on the loopy left are doing.

HARRIS: Mr. Kyrgowski, your time—

KYRGOWSKI: Give me a minute here, Dave, because this is important. Strong borders, strong trade policies so we can keep those jobs making tampons here in America, and support for women. That's what we need, and what's so great about New York and all of America. You know, over in Arabia, they've got men chopping off women's heads for showing their faces in public. That's what we're up against. And we're taking about women like Bill's wife here not getting enough tampons? Sorry. I think we've got bigger problems to get angry about. And when you send me to Washington in November, I'll make sure everyone down there knows just how angry I am about those problems. Because, let me tell you, they're not good.

[*Applause*]

AUDIENCE MEMBER: Toxic Lord rules!!

[*Laughter*]

HARRIS: Please. Mr. Held, your response?

BILL HELD: Thanks, David. You know, Kurt, we may not agree on much, but I do agree that we've got good health care in America, in the sense that we have some of the best doctors and hospitals in the world. But I also believe we've gotta do a lot better, especially when it comes to women. We need more access to family planning resources—including safe and legal abortions—and more access to vital health services. And access to, you know, supplies. So, I look to the women leading the way on these critical issues and will do whatever I can to support their work when I'm in Washington.

HARRIS: When you talk about the women leading the way, does that include your wife?

[*Silence*]

HARRIS: Assemblyman Held?

HELD: Yes, like I said. I support the Yes We Bleed movement. Including the work my wife is doing.

FEMALE AUDIENCE MEMBER: You're a [*expletive*] liar! You're a cheater! [*Inaudible*]

[*Crowd noises*]

HARRIS: We'll wait while security . . . Thank you.

[*Applause*]

HARRIS: Mr. Held, you may continue.

HELD: Thanks, Dave. Look, ma'am—is she still here? Did they—? Hey, look, she's right. I made a huge mistake. I'm not proud of the way I've behaved in the past. And if I've lost your vote, ma'am, I understand. But please believe me when I say that my commitment to women's health care and reproductive rights has never wavered. Ever. And I believe that on that front, we need to be an example to the rest of the world, including countries like those Mr. Kyrgowski is referring to, where women aren't treated as equals.

HARRIS: That's time.

KYRGOWSKI: Hey, no offense, Bill, but maybe you should start treating your wife like she's equal first.

[*Applause*]

HARRIS: Please. Thank you.

AUDIENCE MEMBER: Bite the snake, Krÿer!

HARRIS: Please. Please.

Day Seventeen

It was midmorning, overcast but mild, and Kathleen sat on a bench by the edge of the river behind the condo complex, drinking from a quickly cooling mug of coffee (BUT FIRST, COFFEE, read the turquoise type on one side), watching Sonny and Cher floating catatonically among the cattails on the opposite bank.

She'd taken a break from her computer—specifically, the responses she'd been writing for an interview with a French women's magazine—to consciously detach, for just a few moments, from the rest of the world. There was too much Bill in it at the moment, and it was souring her mood. The debate he'd done with Kürt Krÿer, where they sparred over who was more committed to women, had, not surprisingly, led to an uptick in chatter about whether women should vote for him in spite of his infidelity, given that he was, politically speaking, a better ally for women than Kürt Krÿer. Conservatives countered that Krÿer *did* say menstrual products should be tax free, and wasn't that what the Yes We Bleed people wanted? To which the Yes We Bleed people and others counter-countered that Krÿer had, in fact, gone on to say that he thought *everything* should be tax free, which would inevitably result in budget cuts that would hit women, children, elderly, disabled, low-income, and BIPOC individuals hardest. This led to a raging, vitriolic subdebate among liberals over whether *BIPOC* was a reductive term, followed by the forced resignation of a high school teacher in Florida after she posed the question to her Advanced Placement US History class, in violation of the district's Don't Say Race policy.

But overall, people were less focused on the substance of the debate with Kyrgowski and more interested in discussing whether Bill came off as rueful, earnest, and steady or as a pompous, unrepentant prick. Kathleen hadn't watched the debate but told herself that it must be the latter. It was far less painful to just be *angry* at him than it was to try to reconcile the way she'd loved him—the way they'd loved each other—with what he'd done. Far easier to decide that all the things she'd admired about him were an illusion.

Her coffee was officially too cool to be enjoyable now. She was just getting up to go back to the condo when her phone buzzed in her jacket pocket. It was a text from Jonathan: *I just got off the phone with an extremely powerful and strange literary agent. She wants to know if you're interested in writing a book about all this. Can you talk to her at 10:30? Call me for details.*

Kathleen felt a head-to-toe thrill—a years-later echo of the sensation she'd felt when her old agent had called to offer her representation for *The Hecate Chronicles*. But she quickly reminded herself that this wasn't that; this was not someone wanting to represent something she'd labored lovingly on for years. This was someone pouncing on a potentially lucrative opportunity.

It had occurred to Kathleen once or twice that maybe she should write a book about this whole experience. But although the thought of writing again had momentarily stirred those old feelings of hope and excitement she'd repressed for so long, she had quickly dismissed the idea. She didn't want to write some sort of sordid tell-all about her marriage or her menstrual cycle. Sharing herself with the media and the internet was one thing. A book was far more intimate.

But as she made her way back to the condo, an idea began to formulate in her mind: she could write a book about menstruation—how women across the ages had dealt with it, how it was viewed in different cultures. Maybe she could weave in some of the testimonials and stories people had been sharing online. (The good ones; not the ones involving applewood pyres and dehydrated menstrual-blood vitamin supplements.) It could be something powerful and substantive. Meanwhile, she would, at last, have her name on the cover of a book. She could call herself a writer. And if it sold well, maybe the publisher would even consider publishing *The Hecate Chronicles*.

She refilled her coffee and called Jonathan.

The agent in question, he told her, was Chrysanthemum Lowell. Kathleen had heard of her through the publishing grapevine: a recent Bennington grad who'd sold three major celebrity and political memoirs in the previous year alone. She was distantly related to F. Scott Fitzgerald and had had a recent highly publicized fling with one of her clients, an '80s child star nearly thirty years her senior.

"I should probably at least look up my old agent," Kathleen told Jonathan. "I think I'm technically still her client."

"When did you last talk to her?" Jonathan asked.

"Around 2005, I think?"

"Kat?"

"Yes?"

"You're not still her client."

Moments later, Kathleen was in her bedroom, door closed, phone in hand, heart thumping.

The call came at precisely ten thirty. "Kat Anderson Held!" Chrysanthemum Lowell cried. "This is the thrill of a lifetime for me. You have absolutely *no* idea."

Kathleen had some idea that Chrysanthemum probably said this to every one of her celebrity clients (celebrity-ish, in Kathleen's case), but it still felt good to hear.

Chrysanthemum was warm and ingratiating. She was quick to laugh, in a throaty yet girlish way, and though she peppered the conversation with hyperbolic adjectives like *marvelous* and *astounding*, it somehow came off as not pretentious but charming—a little girl clomping around in her mother's heels.

"Kat, it's miraculous," she said. "Ever since the scandal first broke there's been buzz about the possibility of a book, but now every publisher in town is salivating over the idea of a Kat Anderson Held memoir. And I will confess, I've never been interested in representing internet, insta-celebrity types, but you have such *substance*. And it's such a worthy cause. When I first got my period ages ago—goodness, it must be more than ten years now!—I felt consumed with every possible feeling *except* jubilation. But for the next generation, it will be different, thanks to you. You've sparked jubilation. Oh! I'm writing that down: *Sparking Jubilation* by Kat Anderson Held."

"Thank you so much," Kathleen managed to wedge in. "I'm excited, too, but I'm not really sure I have enough of a story to merit a whole memoir, and—"

"If we're creative, yes, there positively is," said Chrysanthemum. "It doesn't have to be a traditional memoir! It can be a memoir-slash-guide-to-life-slash-style-guide. A cookbook? Do you cook? Wait, no, too domestic probably. We'll brainstorm. There are infinite possibilities. It's so exciting! And I'm crossing out *Sparking Jubilation* right now, because the title, I just realized, obviously, has to be *Um, Yeah, No.*"

"Um—"

Chrysanthemum giggled raspily. "You're thinking, 'Um, yeah, no'! And that's *so* perfect! I was absolutely joking. But in all seriousness, you'll be in charge. This book has to be heartfelt and real, just like you. Your own expression of this adventure you are on. And I will be your steadfast advocate—if we're a match. And I *do* so hope we're a match! And, Kat, I think it's *awfully* likely I can get high six figures for this." Her voice tightened to an ecstatic whisper. "Maybe even seven!"

"That's . . . that would be amazing," Kathleen said. "But what about something that's focused more on Yes We Bleed? I was thinking a sort of cultural history of menstruation, and menstrual rights, from ancient times right up to the present."

There was a long silence. And then Chrysanthemum said, "I think it's brilliant. I truly do. Alas, I'm not sure it's what the public is *thirsting* for when it comes to Kat Anderson Held. People want to spend time with inspiring, magnetic *you*. And then, perhaps for your *second* book, you'll do something about menstruation across the ages and what have you. Think of this first book as a thrilling means to an end!"

"Thrilling" wasn't exactly how Kathleen would put it. Did she want to be a published author if it meant achieving it by way of a celebrity memoir-slash-cookbook-slash-whatever? "I just need to think it over," she said. "It's just . . . it's a lot, you know? Just, everything that's going on all of a sudden."

Just, just. She'd gotten so much better at not using that hedging, mincing little word that now, on the rare occasions she did, it was like a game show buzzer going off in her brain. (*WRONG!*) But in this case, the word seemed *just*ified.

"How about this," said Chrysanthemum. "I'll email you some paperwork, you think and consider, and we'll discuss tomorrow. We *must* move quickly." She gasped. "The big rally in DC! It's soon, isn't it?"

"The day after tomorrow, yes." Kathleen had been working on her speech every spare moment she had—which weren't many—consulting with Danica and Jonathan along the way, and asking Aggie's opinion, too.

"Take bushels of notes," said Chrysanthemum. "Pictures, video, voice memos, even. The ghostwriter will want all of it. The more the better. Ooh! Maybe it's a journal-slash-photo-album-slash-diary thing. With an interactive component. *Very* zeitgeisty."

"Wait," said Kathleen. "Ghostwriter? I didn't think, I mean, I'm a— I can write. I'm an editor." (Close enough.) "I have an MFA. And I'm published." She told Chrysanthemum about the short stories and *The Hecate Chronicles*—how she'd had an agent before and had come close to getting the book published.

"All of which is splendid!" said Chrysanthemum. "The thing is, this book needs to happen *so* remarkably fast, Kat. Once things are finalized, a ghostwriter can deliver a first draft within a fortnight or two—I have one in mind whom you will *adore*—then you give it your editor's eagle eye, and then *New York Times* bestsellers list, here you come! Foreign rights, film, and TV. The list goes on."

In other words, her name on the cover of a book, and gobs of cash that she'd barely have to work for.

She could survive without the money. She would get a good chunk of change if she and Bill divorced, owing to the formidable sum he'd inherited when his father died—though, of course, she would have significantly less than before. She'd probably have to move out of Greenchester (which wouldn't exactly break her heart) to some humbler town and humbler home. She'd take fewer vacations, eat out less, but all that was fine. In fact, it would be *better*. More like the lifestyle she and Bill used to talk about having for themselves, simple and authentic. The lifestyle they *had*, in fact, when they were just starting out: Bill fresh from law school, toiling earnestly at the district attorney's office, Kathleen working as an editorial assistant by day and writing by night in their cramped but cozy apartment.

On the other hand, if she got the kind of advance Chrysanthemum thought she would, and if the book sold well, Kathleen could quit her job and take her time finding another one—one that, she would make 100 percent sure, would *not* require her to stick commercials into the middle of perfectly good, terrible books. Or maybe she wouldn't even *have* to take another job. If this ghostwritten memoir-slash-cookbook-slash-whatever sold well and led to speaking engagements or a movie deal or who knew what else, she might make enough to live comfortably on for quite some time. And, like

Chrysanthemum said, she might be able to write and publish a more serious book. Maybe could even resurrect *The Hecate Chronicles*—do a whole series on lesser-known goddesses, perhaps. (Was there a goddess of menstruation?) It was, in fact, a natural extension of her brand. *And* she would enjoy it. The best of both worlds.

The price, though, would be a nibble out of her integrity up front. Not to mention the humiliation of having to work with a ghostwriter.

"I need to think it over," she told Chrysanthemum again.

"Of course," said Chrysanthemum. "But don't tarry too long, or the moment will pass!"

Kathleen had never told more than a handful of people about the fact that she'd once dreamed of becoming a writer. It was too humiliating—both the fact that she'd failed and the fact that she'd never brushed herself off and tried again the way you were supposed to. One of the professors in her MFA program, an old man with leonine white hair and hands that trembled from a lifetime of heavy drinking, lectured again and again about the importance of "toughening one's hide" to withstand the barrage of rejections the students would face over the course of their careers. ("*If* you have the strength of character it takes to even try," he would add with a self-satisfied little "ho ho ho.") But by the end of the program, Kathleen's hide felt not so much toughened as mutilated. And later, after *The Hecate Chronicles* was rejected, she no longer felt like she had a hide at all.

That wasn't the sort of story anyone wanted to hear. So she only told it to herself.

But she needed to talk to someone she trusted about what Chrysanthemum was offering. Bobbie was one of the few other people who knew about Kathleen's past ambitions—to a degree, anyway. Kathleen had downplayed them as a "phase" from when she was in her twenties. But she felt fortified enough by everything that had happened lately that she was prepared to tell Bobbie and get her honest, unfiltered advice on whether she should jump at Chrysanthemum's offer. (*Don't tarry too long, or the moment will pass!* Could she handle being represented by someone who used the word *tarry*?)

Promptly at five, Bobbie rang the bell, which played some sort of dark melody Kathleen couldn't place. Bobbie gave Kathleen a fierce squeeze. "I've missed you! Here." She handed Kathleen a FedEx envelope. "This was on the doorstep." Kathleen glanced at the return address: Danica's. She set it on the table by the door for later.

"This place is gorgeous!" Bobbie gushed as Kathleen ushered her inside. "Oooh, and I love that!" She pointed at LIVE! LAUGH! LOVE! over the sofa. Bobbie, too, was a fan of mass-produced life-affirming word art.

"I know. It's beautiful, and the owner is renting it to us at half price," Kathleen said. "But I'll need to find something more permanent once the dust settles. Right, Aggie?"

"I guess," Aggie said, a little sourly, from the sleek beige reclining armchair where she sat reading *Our Bodies, Ourselves*. Kathleen had hoped she would be done sulking by now. They'd gone to the mall after school for some new bras for Aggie (her tiny bust had crossed some kind of puberty Rubicon, and suddenly it was clear she needed more than just the three-to-a-pack training bras she'd been wearing for the past year), and everything had gone just fine at first. It was nice to have a reprieve from the nonstop pace of the past few days for some quality mother-daughter time. But when Kathleen took a phone call while they were waiting in line at the register, Aggie instantly became visibly annoyed—and stayed that way. Even when Kathleen explained that it had to do with logistics for the DC rally— which she and Aggie were going to *together*.

"Hello, Miss Aggie," Bobbie said now, going to Aggie and gathering her into a hug, which Aggie enthusiastically reciprocated. "You been holding up okay, sweetie?"

"Aggie and her friends are doing some *great* work for the movement," Kathleen said.

"So I've heard," said Bobbie. "Andrew told me there are some very . . . educational posters up in the halls!"

"We had to take down some of them because the principal said they were inappropriate," Aggie said. "Like the ones with the pads we painted to look like they were used."

Bobbie looked at Kathleen with bugged eyes, and Kathleen grimaced in response.

"Yeah, Aggie, that's a bit . . ." said Kathleen.

"Antoinette says sometimes you have to make people uncomfortable to make a point," said Aggie.

"Would that be Antoinette Raab?" Bobbie asked.

Aggie lit up. "Are you friends?"

Bobbie made her mouth very small. "Nooo . . . I just know who she is. She's a very, ah, *enthusiastic* participant on the Friends of the Library Committee."

"Come sit," Kathleen said to Bobbie, waving her toward the kitchen.

"Antoinette Raab is a nutjob," Bobbie said to Kathleen in a whisper through one side of her mouth.

"I know," Kathleen side-mouthed back. "But Aggie's gotten tight with her daughter, and she's been super supportive of their Yes We Bleed Club, so what can I do? Wait until you try this rosé. I got it at this incredible wine shop in SoHo. I splurged a little. But why not, right?"

She poured herself and Bobbie glasses of wine and they sat at the polished granite counter that divided the kitchen from the living room.

"I want to hear *everything*," Bobbie said, taking a hearty sip of her wine. "I mean, you're *everywhere*! On TV, on the radio. I never, ever in a million years would have expected you to want to do all that!"

"I know, me either. But"—Kathleen wrinkled her nose, gave a little shrug—"it's actually really fun. It's ridiculous—I mean some of these media people are truly idiots, Bobs—but it's *fun!*" She was aware that she might be smiling a little too hard. "And I think I'm actually pretty good at it. Don't you think?"

Bobbie laughed. "My gosh, Kath, did you pop an upper before I got here? Yes, you're really good at it." She wrenched the plastic top off the snare drum–size container of dehydrated banana chips she'd brought. "I'm only doing natural sugars now. Try."

"Thanks, but I'm actually trying to lose a little weight." Kathleen put on a faux posh voice. "Camera adds ten pounds and all, don't you know."

"Oh, well, ex*cuse* me!"

"You won't believe this: I'm doing a photo shoot with *People* in a few days."

"*People*? Kathleen 'I only read the *New Yorker*' Held in *People*? And, my god, look at your manicure." Bobbie grabbed Kathleen's hand and gave it a yank. "Who *are* you?"

"She's *Kat*," said Aggie, snottily, from the living room.

Kathleen flinched. "Excuse me, Agatha Rose. It's very common for people to have a professional name that's different from their legal name."

Aggie took her book and silently retreated upstairs.

Kathleen shook her head and topped off her wine. "There's been a lot of that lately. Tweenness. I'm trying to be patient. I know how hard all this is for her. She misses being home. She misses her dad."

"I'm sure." Bobbie crunched thoughtfully on a banana chip. "And she probably misses you, too."

"I don't think so," Kathleen said. "I mean, yes, I've been insanely busy, but I've been here in the evenings. The one time I wasn't, Chloe came over, and Aggie *loves* her." Chloe was a bookish, soft-spoken Sarah Lawrence student who used to sit for Aggie regularly. Now that Aggie was old enough to be alone during the day, she only came for the occasional evening. "Plus, she's been super busy with this Yes We Bleed stuff, so I don't really think—"

"No, I mean she misses the old *version* of you," Bobbie said. "Before the hair and clothes and TV and magazines. Before you were Kat Anderson Held. I mean, don't get me wrong, you look amazing. I love that you're having fun, but"—she reached across the counter and gave Kathleen's hand a pat—"I miss Kathleen a little bit, too."

Kathleen felt a bolt of indignation. "I'm still me. I'm just a better version. I mean, for once I'm not just wallpaper."

"Oh, Kath, honey. You were never wallpaper! And even if you were—good wallpaper is underrated."

Bobbie was trying to be kind, Kathleen knew. But she didn't want compliments about a person she didn't even feel like anymore. That person had disappeared on the front lawn of her house in a cloud of smoke and blood two weeks ago. She could never go back. She never *wanted* to go back.

"I'm happy," Kathleen said. "I really am. I'm reaping the rewards of my situation."

Bobbie made a face. "You're what?"

"Steering into the swerve. And reaping the rewards. Regaining control."

Bobbie lifted an eyebrow, then leaned in close and said in a whisper, "Kathleen, are you in some sort of cult? This is sounding very cult-y."

Kathleen laughed. "No. It's just the approach I've chosen to take to all this madness."

"The approach," Bobbie said.

"Yes." Was that so strange? To have an approach to a major life crisis? "And like I said. I'm happy."

"Okay," said Bobbie. She didn't sound convinced. "Just as long as you're taking time to, you know, process everything." She snapped a banana chip in half with her front teeth.

Process. It was the kind of thing Margo said. "I tried the wallowing-around-in-misery route," said Kathleen. "It wasn't working."

"I wasn't saying you should *wallow*."

"No, I know. I just mean—this way is better for me. I'm processing by doing."

"Okay, then, good," said Bobbie. Her smile was uncharacteristically thin. "So, what was the big news you wanted to tell me about?"

Suddenly Kathleen didn't feel so eager to share the news about Chrysanthemum with Bobbie, let alone ask for her advice. She wanted enthusiastic, just-do-it, cheerleader Bobbie—the one who'd always urged Kathleen to take chances, have fun, try something new. Not *this* version of Bobbie, who seemed to suddenly think Kathleen was betraying who she was by doing exactly that.

"It's not that big, really," Kathleen said. "I just had some interest from a literary agent who thinks maybe she could get someone to publish some sort of book I write about my experiences and the whole Yes We Bleed thing."

Bobbie brightened. "That is absolutely a big deal! Are you going to do it?"

"I think so."

"It's perfect for you, Kath. I mean let's face it, you could win a Pulitzer Prize for just your PTA flyers. And you used to want to be an author, right?"

"Well, yeah, eons ago."

Bobbie lifted her glass. "To Kathleen—Kat, whatever—the *author*!"

Kathleen raised her glass and clinked it with Bobbie's. She drained what was left of her wine in a single, burning gulp.

Later that evening, when Bobbie was gone, Kathleen tore open the express mail package from Danica. Inside was one of Danica's signature cream-colored envelopes. Kathleen withdrew the card inside.

You are most cordially invited to a very special meeting of

The Society of Shame

Featuring a special presentation
Tomorrow at 7:00 p.m. sharp
Dinner will be served
Twenty-Four 132nd Avenue, Suite 2B, Queens, New York

Please enter discreetly.
The favour of a reply is requested.

Kathleen texted Jonathan to let him know that she'd be there.

I was also wondering, she added, *if I could pick Danica's brain about this agent thing. Writer to writer. Could you ask her to call me?*

After much longer than it usually took, Jonathan replied: *She's very busy at the moment. And it's late. Can I give her a message?*

Kathleen felt a little stung by this but proceeded. *Had a great talk w. Chrysanthemum but she's talking about having a ghostwriter do the book. Just wanted to get Danica's take on whether I should do it or not.*

There was an even longer pause before Jonathan's next reply. *Danica says make like a sneaker and JUST do it. This is your big chance, and you'd be an idiot not to take it. Does that help?*

Yes, Kathleen replied. *Hugely.*

She emailed Chrysanthemum and told her she would sign with her. *But*, she said in her note, *I want to have it written into the contract somewhere that we're not going to call the book* Um, Yeah, No. *And that it won't be some kind of tell-all about my marriage. And I want to collaborate closely with the ghostwriter, not have them write the whole book for me.*

Chrysanthemum, to Kathleen's surprise (it was nearly eleven) and delight, wrote back immediately: *Absolutely within the realm of possibility! And do send me the manuscript for that novel you mentioned when we spoke—the one about Hercules. Let's see what we can do!*

Day Eighteen

It had been a week since Kathleen had been to work, or even worked from home. Returning to the grind of picking her way through manuscripts and the debasement of having to turn books into infomercials was the last thing she felt like doing, but she was out of vacation days (which seemed like a remarkably mundane detail in the midst of everything that was happening; since when did celebrities worry about things like *vacation days?*). She could have worked from home—Cody probably would have been more than cool with her continuing to disrupt the boundaries of the traditional work environment and attending the weekly team huddle via Zoom—but given that she'd be having dinner with the society in Queens that night, she decided to go into the city.

She couldn't believe she'd never noticed before how drab the offices of Gannet McMartin were: the flickering fluorescent lighting, the dingy gray cubicle partitions, the stacks of books and manuscripts everywhere. Kathleen used to find the presence of so much printed material comforting; she loved being ensconced in this world of paper and words. But now all she saw was clutter and chaos.

She did, however, appreciate the standing ovation she was given by the women when she entered the conference room for the weekly huddle. This was followed by Cody adding how great it was to have such an amazing influencer on the team. "It totally re-hooves us to have that skill set in the mix!" he said, anti-blinking madly.

After the meeting, Kathleen settled in to work on *The Woman in the Passenger Seat* but found herself growing increasingly annoyed with the number of comma splices. She managed to make progress only by giving herself the reward of a social media break every twenty-five pages.

On Instagram, women were posting nicely staged pictures of the menstrual cup hats they'd knitted or crocheted (needles resting atop, a ball of yarn nearby, and perhaps a mason jar of wildflowers) as part of a drive to supply the hats to homeless and low-income women. On Twitter, chatter about the Yes We Bleed rally in DC and associated rallies elsewhere was building, but there was also a new conservative, anti–Yes We Bleed hashtag movement, in which people (some real, some, Kathleen suspected, clearly bots and trolls) heckled every tweet bearing the #YesWeBleed hashtag with a response basically telling them to shut the hell up already, nobody cared about their period. (Hashtag: #PlugItUp.) This led to a counter-countermovement (#LetItFlow) in which women told increasingly gory and graphic period stories. Apparently some had even started posting pictures of used sanitary products, but this was quickly shut down by the powers that be at every major social media site. Which, in turn, had led to a battery of posts and rapid-fire think pieces about the hypocrisy of social media decency standards. Lauren Trissler tweeted: Racism, antisemitism, and sexism get a pass, but not pads? #QuitTwitter. (From what Kathleen could tell, none of the people posting #QuitTwitter, including Lauren Trissler, were actually quitting it.)

By midafternoon, Kathleen was nearly one hundred pages into

The Woman in the Passenger Seat when she was interrupted by her cube neighbor Simone's moon of a head rising above the partition.

"Isn't it terrible?" Simone said.

"The hashtag PlugItUp thing? I know, it's ridiculous."

"No," said Simone, looking puzzled. "The email Cody just sent. About Wallace. They're going to start *tracking* us! That little . . . *punk* was too chicken to announce it in person at the huddle this morning." She sniffed loudly, and then her face sank below the partition again.

Kathleen went to her inbox and opened the latest email from Cody:

Team! We've been having some trouble getting buy-in from some of you guys on Wallace. Totally get it: it's not always easy to ramp up with new initiatives. Change can be rough, but we need to be nimble. So, here's the deal: to incentivize adoption, we're going to gamify the gamification! We'll send a weekly update on who's clocked the most Wallace hours. Plus, check the OG leaderboard outside my office. Top three Wallacers by the end of the quarter will get a cash bonus. Bottom three, you're fired. (JK!) Hope you're all feeling pumped and ready to TURN UP!!

Feeling murderous, Kathleen opened up Wallace. She'd been randomly assigned what appeared to be a soft-porn cowboy romance novel called *Spurred to Love*. She'd just begun trying to find a place to insert a reference to Applebee's when her phone rang: Chrysanthemum.

"Kat!" Chrysanthemum breathed. "The word is getting out, courtesy of me, that we're working together, and there's already tremendous buzz! When we go out with this, I expect that we'll have a deal within days. I'll send you the draft of the letter of intent I've been working on—I put down *Yes, I Bleed* as a working title, catchy, don't you think?—and you can weigh in, and we'll go from there. Isn't this *splendid*?"

"Yes!" said Kathleen. It was starting to feel real—*really* real. Why had she even for a moment considered *not* doing this?

When she got off the phone, she went straight to Cody's office.

He was, oddly, hopping around in the middle of the room. It took her a moment to realize that he was, in fact, attempting to bobble a hacky sack on his knees and insteps. He kneed too hard and the hacky sack flew across the room, knocking over a signed photo of Zach Braff on a shelf.

"Hey! You probably remember these," he said, retrieving the hacky sack and giving it a few jaunty tosses. "They were apparently really big when my parents were in college. Here!" He anti-blinked and threw it toward her. She considered catching it and hurling it back at his stupid millennial face, but at the last instant let it sail past her into the corridor.

"I need to talk to you about something," she said.

"I'm already on it," said Cody. He took up position at his standing desk and started tapping at his computer, speaking as he typed: " 'Hi, Monica . . . Kathleen Held has rebranded . . . Please change her email address to Kat Anderson Held . . . Muchas gracias . . . Cody' . . . And send." He smiled at Kathleen. "Good?"

"No, that's not what I wanted to talk about. It's about my position here."

He anti-blinked. "Oh, I think I know what this is." He lowered his desk, sat down on his yeti-fur stool and folded his hands on the desk. "Look, Kat—such an awesome name—I know you're all about trad. books, and I get it. They're totally authentic and cool, and they're right up your wheelhouse. But we're getting serious traction on the Wallace beta. I know you've barely had time to get started, but so far you've been spending eighty percent of your clocked hours on your trad. books and only twenty percent on Wallace. And I would never ask you to flip that ratio, but we probably do have to get it to more like sixty-forty, so I'm going to need you to double down. Cool?"

Kathleen looked him square in his anti-blinking eyes. "Um, yeah, no," she said.

She turned around, walked back to her cube, and packed up her desk.

Two hours later, she was in a taxi en route to the far reaches of Queens. On the seat next to her bag were boxes of gourmet chocolates laced with flavor accents that seemed borderline disturbing—breadfruit, turmeric, filet mignon, tequila—but that Kathleen assumed must be good, given the price. She planned to hand them out as celebratory gifts to the other Society of Shame members (the tequila one was for Brent) when she shared the good news about her imminent book deal.

She had assumed that the address on the invitation Jonathan had given her was that of a restaurant, or perhaps another home that Danica owned. But when the driver pulled up to the curb, she realized it definitely wasn't the latter. (At least, it seemed awfully unlikely that Danica would have a pied-à-terre above a walk-in dental clinic within earshot of JFK.) But it didn't look like a restaurant, either. As Kathleen discovered, after making her way up a dark, steep flight of stairs, it was a spacious empty apartment, dimly lit except for strings of retro light bulbs hanging from the ceilings and candles flickering on a long harvest table in the center of the largest room. A staff of three, all decked in white, worked in the kitchen while Danica and the rest of the group milled about with drinks in what looked like high school chemistry class beakers.

When Danica spotted Kathleen, she put her beaker down and strode toward her with outstretched arms. "Kat!" she exclaimed, taking both of Kathleen's hands in hers and squeezing alarmingly hard. "Amazing. All of it. Brava. The television appearances, the interviews, the social media. And it sounds like you're on the verge of a *very* nice book deal."

"It looks that way," Kathleen said. She couldn't have suppressed her smile if she tried. "I just wanted to say thank you, Danica. For everything. You've changed my—"

"I confess, I wasn't quite sure you'd be able to pull it off. You were so . . ." Danica put an exaggerated slump into her shoulders and made a pitiful sort of face. The imitation was a touch crueler than it needed to be, it seemed to Kathleen. "But look at you now! Come, celebrate. Isn't this place marvelous?"

"What is it, exactly?"

Danica explained: It was a pop-up restaurant ("It just pops up! A different place each time!") run by an old friend of hers, a chef named Rudolph Pepys, who became briefly famous as the judge on a short-lived reality cooking show called *Soup Skirmish*. He was fired from the show and ended up shuttering both of his restaurants when the internet discovered that one of them had catered a fundraiser for an antiabortion lobbying group.

"It was early in his career, when things hadn't taken off yet, so he couldn't afford to be picky," Danica explained. "An entirely forgivable offense, if you ask me. And wait until you taste the bouillabaisse!" Then she whisked off, over to the actor, who was chuckling at a wildly gesticulating Brent while a woman with short brown hair and bright blue hoop earrings listened with a timid smile on her face. It took Kathleen a moment to realize that the woman was, in fact, Anna-belle. She was almost completely unrecognizable.

Kathleen spotted Michael, then, over on the other side of the room, alone in the dark and looking rather adrift, holding a drink in a giant test tube, garnished with what appeared to be a small tree branch. She started toward him, but Cindy intercepted her, nearly knocking her off her feet with a hug. She'd clearly made an effort to dress up, but her pants were too tight, giving her thighs an unfortu-nate, rippled look, and the teal blouse she wore was at least three years out of style, with openings at the tops of the sleeves that revealed her round, freckled shoulders. "I am so glad to see you!" she said, a touch too loud, into Kathleen's ear. "It's been so fun watching you on TV!"

Kathleen took a step backward. "Thank you so much. It's been fun *being* on TV!"

Cindy stepped forward again. "Hey, look," she said quietly. "Danica gave me that menu thing today? And I'm kind of starting to freak out a little. I just don't know if there's anything on there for me."

"I'm sure there is," Kathleen said. "There's something on there for everyone. We'll help you figure it out, okay?"

There was the sound of a throat being emphatically cleared: Mona. She wore a black tunic over white leggings, and her drink beaker was sprouting a large brown fern. "Repair," she said. "Take action to directly remedy the hurt or damage you have caused. In other words, make a large donation to Rescue the Wolves."

"Rescue the Wolves?" said Cindy. "What the heck is Rescue the Wolves?"

"Or maybe it's Save the Wolves, I don't know."

"Wolves aren't endangered," said Cindy. "Not in Montana, anyway."

"They will be if people like you keep—"

"Okay, okay!" said Kathleen. "We're here to help each other, not judge each other, remember?"

"Fine, fine," said Mona. She took a sip from her beaker, the fern folding up against her face as she did, prompting her to squeeze one eye shut. "But can I just say one more thing? It's about something else." She turned to Kat. "I don't mean any offense by this, because as a feminist I am *very* appreciative of the way you've stepped up for the Yes We Bleed movement. But at the same time, I'm looking at you, and I'm asking myself: Why?"

"Why what?"

"Why give in to the patriarchal beauty standards? The makeup, the nails, the highlighted hair . . ." She whipped a hand up into the air, jangling that evening's chunky jewelry of choice (strings of brass snails).

"Why the heck *not?*" said Cindy. She put a protective arm around Kathleen and pulled her close. She was alarmingly strong. "I think she looks great."

"I don't think there's anything anti-feminist about wanting to look good," said Kathleen. "It's not like I'm wearing corsets or something."

True, the heels she'd been wearing of late could get uncomfortable after a while, but what was she supposed to wear? Her old, plain flats or slip-on sneakers wouldn't cut it on network television. And anyway, Mona wasn't exactly in a position to judge anyone about anything. In the hierarchy of sins, Kathleen was pretty sure indulging in a little mild vanity was about a thousand rungs below calling the cops on Black people for no reason.

"I'm just saying," Mona said.

"So am I," said Kathleen.

Dinner began with a cold, curried endive and smoked herring soup that the chef Rudolph Pepys—a tiny man with a purple buzz cut and a strange, nasal variant of a British accent—explained was meant to "shiatsu massage the palate." Kathleen hoped that the entire meal wouldn't consist of soup, but when the second course turned out to be corn chowder with pancetta and vodka-cured grapes, she resigned herself the fact that it was going to be. The soup was so good, though (who knew you could cure grapes?), that she didn't care. And, as was usually the case when she was in Danica's company, she soon felt mildly, pleasantly drunk.

After the main course, the bouillabaisse—which, as Danica had promised, was exquisite—Danica tapped her spoon against her glass until everyone hushed. "We have some exciting announcements tonight!"

Kathleen readied herself to speak. But instead Danica said, "Annabelle? You go first, dear."

Annabelle's smile looked like it pained her. "I got a haircut, as you can see. And a new color. And on Monday, I'm going to get a nose job."

Cindy gasped. "Why? Your nose is fine!"

"I concur," the actor drawled. "I don't think you should change a blessed thing."

"How often do people actually recognize you?" Michael asked.

Kathleen still hadn't had a chance to talk with him, and now he was sitting several seats away.

"It's only been a couple of times." Annabelle's eyes filled with tears. "I just don't want to look like the person in that GIF anymore. I'm *not* that person. I almost never yell at Trevor, or any of my kids. I was having a terrible day, and Trevor kept asking for things. You know how it is sometimes, right?" She looked pleadingly at Cindy, and then Kathleen.

"Of *course* we do," said Cindy.

"She's revamping and restarting," said Danica. "It's her decision, and it's our job to be supportive. Right?"

The only person whose "Right" was enthusiastic was Brent. He punctuated it with a burp.

"That was lovely, Brent," said Danica.

"Thanks," said Brent. "Can I go now? I've got news, too."

"By all means," said Danica.

"Right, so, I've been doing this reform and repay and repeat shit, right?"

"No, not repeat," said Danica. "Repeating is almost never a good idea."

"Okay, whatever, so it turns out this guy I know's cousin's dad is a producer for *Dancing with the Stars*. And there was some big thing where some lady who used to work in the White House or whatever was going to be on the show, but she canceled last minute, and my friend's cousin goes to his dad and is like, 'Dude, want me to see if the Moonabomber wants to be on the show?' And his dad was like, 'No way,' but he said something about it to some other producer, and the producer was like, 'Yes, totally, we have to get the Moonabomber on the show, because we need to get more younger people and guys to watch.' So I'm doing it. Moonabomber in the hooooouse!" He turned to Mona for a high five. She gave him a horrified look, and Brent turned to the actor instead, offering his fist for a bump. Then Brent thumped his fist to his own chest a couple of times and pointed at Kathleen. "You inspired me, man."

"I did?" The three soups in Kathleen's stomach sloshed uncomfortably.

"Totally. You're all, like, capitalizing and shit. The only thing I need to figure out, and maybe you guys can help me, is whether I should moon the camera or not. It's kind of my brand and everything, right?"

Kathleen expected Danica to immediately and haughtily dismiss this last idea, but instead Danica just laughed. "It absolutely is your disgusting, juvenile brand, and you might as well wholeheartedly embrace it. I'm embarrassed that I didn't think of it myself." She lifted her glass in a toast. "To Brent's ass."

Kathleen lifted her glass but didn't drink. The thought of Brent's exposed ass was far too unappetizing, and the soup she'd ingested still hadn't settled down. Meanwhile, the idea that her involvement in a feminist movement had inspired an idiotic man-child to plan to expose himself to the nation a second time made her feel less than celebratory.

"And, Kat," said Danica, smiling warmly at her. "I have to say, you've been an inspiration to me, too. Jonathan? Showtime." She clapped her hands twice over her head, and seconds later, from some unseen speaker, "Ride of the Valkyries" began playing.

Jonathan rose from the table and brought over an easel that had somehow been in the corner of the room the whole time. He positioned it next to Danica's chair and swept off the blue silk cloth that covered it, revealing a full-length photo of Danica in a clinging black dress and bright red heels, arms crossed in front of her chest. Above her, in bright red, airbrush-styled script, were the words *Elitist Bitch*.

Danica pressed her folded hands to her chin. "I get chills every time I see it," she said. "Thank you, Jonathan. Didn't he do a beautiful job? God, I look good."

And she did, although it wasn't exactly *her*. The fine lines on Danica's face had clearly been blurred, and either she was wearing medieval-armor-grade shapewear underneath her dress or the photo had been retouched, because she looked at least ten pounds thinner than she actually was, and about ten years younger, too.

"What is it, a book?" Cindy asked.

"It will be," said Danica. "A memoir. About me, and how I went from fat Midwestern nobody to not-fat, incredibly successful somebody. But that's just the beginning. It's a whole brand. I'm reinventing, revamping, and—this is a new one—reappropriating. Everyone already thinks I'm an elitist bitch—ironic, of course, given that I grew up in a shabby two-bedroom ranch with a single mother and went to a second-rate state school—so I'm reappropriating the insult. They think I'm a bitch now? Just wait. Next, Jonathan."

Jonathan removed the picture of Danica, revealing another poster behind it, with a bulleted list of things Danica had planned: the memoir and other books, a complete PR campaign and a social media push, guerrilla marketing and publicity stunts, a line of cosmetics and Elitist Bitch–branded tours and cruises for fans, featuring high-end hotels and VIP entrances to museums and attractions with the attendant opportunities to scoff at lowly tourists.

She hadn't finished writing the memoir yet, she explained, but would soon. Meanwhile, she was working with Jonathan and Apple ("Especially Apple," she noted) on perfecting her persona for the press junket: a thoroughly bitch-ified version of her own only slightly bitchy self. Her signature look would be all black with a pop from bold-colored accessories. Social media accounts, URLs, and a YouTube channel had all been secured.

She also planned to put out a series of novelty books (the first two titles: *The Elitist Bitch's Guide to Fashion: Because God Knows You Need the Help*; *The Elitist Bitch's Guide to Dieting: Because Nobody Actually Thinks Fat Is Beautiful*) and was outlining a quintet of novels with a thinly veiled version of herself as the protagonist. She assumed they would be optioned for film well before they were published. Jonathan, meanwhile, was working on a treatment for a makeover show that she would host.

"Brilliant, right?" She looked Kathleen square in the eye, as if they were somehow allies in this.

"Um, yes," Kathleen said after a pause. The books would sell, the movies would follow, Danica would rack up social media followers, become even wealthier than she already was. Her old books might even get a second life. "It's just . . ."

"*Just* what?" said Danica.

Just, Kathleen was thinking, that something felt wrong about the idea of Danica making a career out of being judgmental and mean—far meaner than she actually was. For all her bluster and tough love, Danica could also be kind. And certainly, she was generous, both in money (this night alone must be costing thousands) and in spirit, the way she supported and counseled people whose lives had been upended.

On the other hand, the money she'd amassed through bestsellers, speaking events, and film contracts before her career had divebombed wouldn't last forever. Being the person people loved to hate could certainly be profitable. "Nothing," Kathleen said. "It's a great idea."

"Well, like I said. You were my inspiration, my dear. And you too, Mikey. With the whole steering wheel thing." She blew him a kiss.

Michael smiled weakly. "Did you ever think about writing the kind of stuff you used to write?" he asked. "Maybe under a pen name?"

Danica snorted. "For exactly five seconds. I didn't become a writer to let a fictional persona take credit for my work. Unless, of course, that fictional persona is the Elitist Bitch. And I'll bet you dollars to doughnuts that half of my fans who claimed they hated me will end up becoming full-on Elitist Bitch devotees."

"Maybe I should write a book," Mona said, half to herself, drumming her fingers against her jaw. "*Racist Bitch*."

"No!" everyone said in unison.

After dessert—chilled raspberry-and-elderberry soup, though Kathleen noticed that everyone, like her, went straight for the biscotti accompanying it—the conversation drifted toward Cindy. Several people thought *reframing* might be a good choice for her: changing the conversation such that she and her family came off as heroes—salt-of-the-earth, all-American ranchers just trying to make a living—and the public (and wolves) as villains—out-of-touch elitists and bloodthirsty predators, respectively, who don't understand just how hard the life of a rancher was.

"You could make a movie about it," said Brent. "I can totally see it. You zoom in on the cows, right?" He made a viewfinder shape with his hands. "Show how nice and sweet they are, with their big-ass eyes, and get some shots of you and your kids feeding them, petting them, whatever. So everyone sees how much you love them."

"Until you slaughter them," Mona commented.

"And then," Brent continued, "bum, bum, bum . . . the music changes and gets all messed up and creepy, the film goes black-and-white, and fuck! Here comes this huge pack of wolves, snarling and yapping, going right for a cow and then taking it the fuck down." He sliced his hand through the air, knocking over his not quite empty water glass.

"Brent! Down!" said Danica.

"I don't know," said Cindy. "I don't think it's gonna make anything any better. I just want to stop getting death threats. And be able to move home and send my kids back to school." Her face pinkened. "And sleep through the night without being afraid some animal rights activist is going to throw a frickin' brick through the window or some militia's gonna show up on our property trying to recruit me and my husband. All these gun nuts keep bugging us, calling us heroes, asking us to help them fight government tyranny or socialists or whatever. I mean, I don't know who's crazier, them or the animal people."

"Them," Mona said under her breath.

"You could restart," Annabelle said. She fussed nervously with one of her new hoop earrings. "Move somewhere else for good, change all your names, start a new life."

"Change my babies' names?" said Cindy. "No way. And that ranch has been in our family since forever. I grew up there. My daddy grew up there. I don't . . ."

Danica gently shushed her. "Of course," she said. "Of course. Don't worry about the menu tonight, dear. It's too soon. You're still reeling. You have another whole week to decide anyway. You want another biscotti? Everyone? One can take only so much liquid."

Jonathan snapped a finger over his head and a waiter appeared.

Later, as they were all saying their goodbyes, Michael pulled Kathleen aside. She was glad they would finally have a chance to talk. They stood together by a window overlooking the darkened street.

"I just wanted to say that it was really nice meeting you," Michael said. "And I hope you'll keep in touch." He handed her a business card for the New Jersey Men Against Human Trafficking and Exploitation in the Pornography Industry, with his name and contact information.

"You're leaving the society?"

He nodded, then glanced away. "Yeah, I don't think it's really right for me anymore."

"But it's helped you, hasn't it?" Of all the members, Michael was the last one she expected to leave. It was hard to imagine the society without his calm, steady presence.

"Yes, sure," he said. "But . . . I don't know. I used to feel like we were trying to help each other change our lives for the better. And ourselves for the better. But lately it feels like we're just . . ."

"Just!" Kathleen said.

"Ha, right." He looked at his feet, which he gave a few shuffles, then looked back up at Kathleen. "You know, there are a lot worse things you could be than the kind of person who says *just* sometimes."

Kathleen felt something close up inside her. He did disapprove of her. Like she'd thought all along. "I'll keep that in mind," she said.

But as she rode home that night, she found herself wishing she hadn't said it quite so coolly. There were things about the evening—Danica's new persona and Annabelle's impending nose job in particular—that had made her feel uneasy, too. (Brent's plan to expose his ass on national TV, while odious, wasn't particularly surprising.) The jubilant mood of the (extremely lavish, if overly liquid) dinner, meanwhile, felt discordant with the seriousness of some of the members' transgressions.

But which was worse: what they were all doing to cope, or what the public had done to them? All their lives, their very selves, had been torn open, raw and exposed, to the feeding frenzy of the media, the internet, the populace at large. Even someone like Danica or the actor, who were already well known, had a new layer of themselves peeled back, revealing something weak, tender, and flawed beneath their public skin. And in the eye of the public, their sins were the sum total of who they were. So, was it any wonder they were all desperate for a process, a plan—a way to wrest back control of their lives? And so what if some of the ways they chose to do it weren't the noblest possible? These weren't exactly noble times they were living in.

As for herself, Kathleen was quite sure that *her* plan was exactly the one she should be pursuing, given the circumstances—and hardly ignoble. She was bringing visibility to an important and meaningful cause—helping to fuel the momentum of something that might have petered out by now without her involvement. And, yes, the hair and makeup and clothes admittedly were on the frivolous side, but a little frivolity never hurt anyone; more important it was *fun*. Being on TV was fun. Being treated like someone important, instead of an appendage of someone else who was important, was not only fun but immensely satisfying. Deserved. And now: a book deal, so close she could taste it. An old love—her dream of being an author (or something like it, anyway)—being rekindled. And none of it would have happened without Danica and the society.

PAMoCA | The Pennsylvania Museum of Contemporary Art

Herocyte
Tizei (American, b. 1958)
Mixed media

Herocyte is a confrontation: between the viewer and the artist, the interior and the exterior, the male and the female. On a plywood altar, rabbits' feet and pomegranates, both traditional symbols of fertility, are juxtaposed with modern everyday objects—a flip-flop, wireless earbuds, a plastic beverage cup lid—hinting at the devaluation of the sacred feminine. Blooms of red pigment on pencil sketches of celebrated European paintings, among them Goya's *The Third of May* and Caravaggio's *Judith Beheading Holofernes*, underline the absence of female blood and female artists in the Western canon. A twelve-foot glass fishbowl stuffed with cotton, gauze, rags, and plant fibers, ringed with red votive candles, is an elegy for the materials women have used for millennia to stanch the blood of abortions, miscarriages, and menstruation. Meanwhile, the title of the installation is an example of the sly, subversive wordplay for which Tizei is known: blood, whether human or animal, is composed of cells called *hemocytes*. Within *herocyte*, we find the words *her*, *hero*, and *sight* (*cyte*). Like so much of Tizei's work, *Herocyte*, which premiered at the Whitney in 2019, has proven prescient: with the advent of the Yes We Bleed movement, the work is imbued with new relevance and urgency.

Tizei dedicates the PAMoCA installation of *Herocyte* to Kat Anderson Held.

Day Nineteen

They left for Washington at five the next morning, the sky still pale and the air cool—Kathleen, Aggie, Melissa, Kia, and the ever-silent Lucy—crammed into Antoinette's dinged-up minivan, a MY OTHER CAR IS A BROOM sticker peeling from the bumper.

Kathleen had suggested to Aggie that the two of them fly instead, thinking it would be a good opportunity for them to catch up and reconnect, suspended high above the franticness of Kathleen's schedule. Flying would also mean not having to spend six hours each way in a car with Antoinette. "We could even spring for business class," Kathleen had said. (Six figures for her soon-to-be book! Maybe even seven!) But Aggie said that the ride down with her friends was one part of the trip she was most excited about, and so here they were.

Antoinette had made up *#YesWeBleedGreenchester* T-shirts for everyone, white type on crimson (which seemed like a gratuitously menstrual color choice), along with knitted menstrual cup hats. Antoinette's hat, and the one she'd made for Kathleen, had less red on them than the others. "Since we're menopausal," she explained.

"Perimenopausal," Kathleen mumbled under her breath, and folded the shirt and hat into her bag. Yes We Bleed icon or not, she would never wear one of those hats. As for the shirt, maybe she'd wear it tomorrow. For today, Danica and Jonathan had helped her put together an ensemble that they described as "activist chic": jeans, dark red boots ("For just a *touch* of menstruality," said Danica), a black T-shirt, and a distressed olive drab blazer with dark red silk lapels and cuffs.

Antoinette spoke surprisingly little on the ride down, which was something of a relief. Melissa wanted to play the soundtrack to an angsty Broadway musical she and her friends were obsessed with, and Antoinette let them. It took them through most of New Jersey. When it was over, Antoinette attempted to lead the kids in a chorus of "We Shall Overcome." Melissa sang along in an exaggerated, clearly mocking opera-singer voice, which sent Kia into hysterics. Lucy's head stayed bent over her phone. Aggie was the only one who actually sang.

Annoyed, Antoinette put on a Fleetwood Mac CD instead.

After depositing their bags at a hotel on the outskirts of the District, they rode the Metro to the Mall, where a huge crowd of menstrual-cup-hatted women had assembled, many wielding signs:

BLEED ON THE PATRIARCHY!

ASK ME ABOUT MY MENARCHE.

THEY'RE NOT HOT FLASHES. THEY'RE POWER SURGES!

FREE TIBET. #THEYBLEEDTOO

In front of the crowd was a huge stage, topped with an enormous Yes We Bleed banner. When Kathleen spotted the podium, front and center and jammed with microphones, she felt a swoop in her belly, and felt suddenly, unbearably hot. She took off her blazer and clutched it to her chest. Why in god's name had she agreed to do this? She was doing so well with the TV and print interviews, never missing a beat or flubbing a line, never looking like a fool. Why hadn't she just left it at that?

"Sydney loves you, Kat!" a woman shrieked in an Australian accent. Kathleen turned to see a dozen or so young women in matching T-shirts (*#YesWeBleed Down Under!*) all grinning and waving furiously at her. A couple of them looked like they might be high. "Can't wait for your speech!"

Kathleen smiled and waved, then glanced back up at the empty stage again. Maybe if she pretended that the entire crowd was made up of happy, stoned Australians who loved her, she would be okay?

Antoinette was shaking her head. "This crowd is shameful," she said. "This should be *just* as big as the first Women's March. And there are only what, nine, ten thousand people here? I hope the kids won't be too disappointed. Are you all right? You're sweating. Here." She pulled a rumpled cloth from her bag and started mopping Kathleen's forehead. "The hot flashes just sneak up out of nowhere."

"Thank you. It's not a hot flash; it's just nerves," Kathleen said, tilting away from Antoinette. "I'm supposed to go check in with the organizers. Do you want to find a place to stand with the kids and I'll catch up with you later?"

"No, we should absolutely stay together. This could easily devolve into a riot. I've heard rumors of a counterprotest. Men's rights people. Which is just a euphemism for fascists. Kids? Line up." She took a Sharpie from her purse and started writing on the girls' forearms: names, phone numbers, emergency contacts.

When she'd finished, they formed a human chain and threaded their way through the crowd, toward the stage. Kathleen was hoping that, with her influence, she'd be able to get them prime spots up front. As they walked, Kathleen became aware of heads turning in her direction, her name being spoken, smatterings of applause. A woman shouted her name and suddenly hoots and cheers broke out. At one point, a young woman in a *Bleed, baby, bleed* T-shirt stopped

Kathleen to ask for a selfie. Kathleen didn't want to be rude and say no, for fear that the woman or the people nearby might say something about it on social media. So she called through the crowd for Antoinette to stop, and gripped Aggie's hand behind her while she posed for the photo. It took far longer than she expected, because the woman first had to refresh her lipstick, and then insisted on taking about a dozen shots, trying different angles and pouty-faced variations until she was satisfied.

Kathleen was able to move a few more feet after that, but then more people were approaching her, stopping her, asking for pictures. An octogenarian woman in a patchwork muumuu and all-white menstrual cup hat linked her arm through Kathleen's and, tears in her eyes, told her how she'd been waiting her whole life for this movement. Kathleen nodded and smiled and waited for a moment to escape the conversation, but Aggie was straining on her hand and then suddenly Aggie's hand slipped away altogether, and all Kathleen could see was Antoinette's menstrual cup–hatted head bobbing through the crowd. Kathleen wove her way forward, trying to keep a smile on her face, waving back to the people who waved to her. Finally, Antoinette seemed to catch on that they'd lost her, and started waving her arms overhead wildly. Kathleen cupped her hands to her mouth and shouted that she had to meet her contacts backstage; she'd find them later, after the speeches. Antoinette gave her a fierce look, then shook her head and led the kids away.

When Kathleen finally made her way into the small tent behind the stage where the organizers and scheduled speakers were, she was greeted with grins and squeals and applause from a bevy of women with clipboards. One put a can of grapefruit seltzer into her hand and another, who introduced herself as Tonya, draped a lanyard around Kathleen's neck. Also there was Emma Hancock, who'd organized the event and who was credited with starting the movement—

although this was disputed by some who said the founder was a Latinx woman, also named Emma, but that the media had seized on white, blond, Shirley Temple–faced Emma, because of course it would ("How the Mainstream Media Bleached Yes We Bleed" read an essay on *The Root*).

Emma enveloped Kathleen in a hug that nearly knocked her off her feet. "It is *such* an honor," she whispered, her mop of blond curls trembling. She didn't look or sound much older than Aggie. When Emma finally broke the embrace, she introduced Kathleen to her mother, Grace, who was more or less an older version of Emma, her own blond curls gathered into a lovely updo. She hugged Kathleen as if they were old friends.

Over Emma's mother's shoulder, Kathleen spotted a well-known feminist country music star who had peaked in the '90s, a prominent female senator talking to a reporter in one corner of the tent, and an *SNL* cast member on her phone in another. And then, when Emma finally released her grip, Kathleen saw *her*, standing in front of a long table spread with platters of food, filling a napkin with strawberries and chunks of cheese: Lauren Trissler.

She was taller than Kathleen expected, and more striking, with her asymmetrical black bob, her thick, intentionally unplucked eyebrows, and her bright red lipstick. (*See?* Kathleen wished she could tell Mona. *The world's most famous feminist wears makeup, too.*)

Kathleen approached the food table, taking a paper plate and tossing a few crackers onto it in an attempt to make it look like she had an actual reason to be there. When Lauren glanced in her direction, Kathleen finally spoke.

"Hi, Lauren?"

"Yes. Hi."

"Kath—Kat Anderson Held." She extended her hand, which Lauren shook briefly.

"Yes, I know who you are." She put on a thin smile.

"I'm a huge fan. I really loved your piece about me in the *Times*."

Lauren cocked her head. "About you," she said. "I don't recall writing anything about *you*. I wrote about the need for this movement. You just happened to bleed in the right place at the right time and be married to the right person." She put a piece of cheese in her mouth, chewed it thoughtfully, and then walked away.

Kathleen felt like she might crumple to the ground.

"You ready?"

She turned to see Tonya, the girl who'd given her the lanyard, holding out a sheet of paper with the order of events. Kathleen took it, her hands trembling slightly, and found her name: she was speaking right after Lauren Trissler. Wonderful.

"Is there a bathroom somewhere?" she asked, feeling a sudden onset of intense cramps. It had only been about three weeks since she'd had her legendary period, but nothing would surprise her at this point. Why did her uterus hate her? Why did Lauren Trissler hate her?

Tonya directed Kathleen to a Porta Potty, where she discovered that, no, her period had not yet made an appearance. Nevertheless, she put on the diaper-size maxi pad she now carried with her at all times and hoped she wasn't walking in too penguin-like a fashion as she returned to the tent. (Although she supposed if there was anywhere she would be cheered for visible use of menstrual products, this was it.) She proceeded to stuff her face with cheese while she reviewed her speech.

Far too short a time later, she was sitting in a folding chair onstage, facing the ocean of demonstrators. She scanned the front of the crowd for Antoinette and Aggie and the other girls but didn't see them. She kept looking, right up until the moment that Emma introduced Lauren Trissler.

The crowd roared.

Lauren gave a brief but rousing speech involving a lot of fist pumping and indignation. She managed to work in just about every women's issue on the planet, from menstrual rights (obviously) to equal pay to female circumcision. She said something about vegan, fair-trade wigs for women with cancer that seemed to momentarily confuse the crowd, but she got them back on track and cheering again by talking about reproductive freedom.

She said nothing about Kathleen's initial humiliation and how it had started the entire movement, but at that point Kathleen didn't expect or even really want her to anyway. She was just relieved that Lauren hadn't taken a dig at her.

Lauren did not make eye contact with Kathleen when she returned to her seat.

Emma stepped back up to the podium. "Our next speaker," she said, "needs no introduction. She is the woman who went from being a victim to being an icon and inspiration. A woman whose quote-unquote '*humiliation*' by her partner and a fame-seeking man who snapped a cell phone picture sparked a revolution. A woman who, instead of staying silent, recently, boldly joined our movement and said to the status quo of period supplies being a privilege instead of a human right . . . everybody say it with me . . . 'Um, yeah, no!'"

(The crowd caught on halfway through "yeah.")

"A woman who," Emma went on, "when asked to be a spokesperson for Big Tampon, those multinational conglomerates that have extorted us for a century, that convinced us and our mothers and grandmothers that we should be humiliated by our bodies' natural functions, selling us on quote-unquote '*discreet*' packaging and scented pads, as if we should be ashamed of our life-giving blood instead of proud of it, said . . ."

"UM, YEAH, NO!" the crowd roared.

"A woman who, instead of standing by the privileged, white, centrist Democrat man who had betrayed her, like so many women have been coerced into doing in the past, said . . ."

"UM, YEAH, NO!"

Kathleen cringed. Stupidly, it hadn't even occurred to her to prepare Aggie for the fact that her father might be brought into all this. Or "Um, yeah, no." In fact, she didn't even know if Aggie *knew* about

"Um, yeah, no." When Kathleen had shown her the CBS interview the week before, she'd stopped before that part came on. "I said something sort of stupid and embarrassing here in this part coming up," she'd said, trying to sound lighthearted. "You don't need to see your mother looking like an idiot. And neither do I." Then she'd noted that it was late, and Aggie should get to bed. It was entirely possible, of course, that Aggie had seen or heard about Kathleen's bon mot through a friend who was not as sheltered from the media as Kathleen and Bill had kept Aggie, but if she had, she hadn't said anything about it. After hearing ten thousand women yell it, however, there was a good chance she would.

Kathleen scanned the crowd one last time, searching for Aggie, not sure what she would do if she *did* spot her; as if she could convey in a single, furtive glance, *I'm sorry. I didn't do this.*

"Say it again!" said Emma.

"UM, YEAH, NO!" And then suddenly they were chanting, thundering, "UM, YEAH, NO! UM, YEAH, NO!"

Emma turned to Kathleen, grinning, and Kathleen understood that she was supposed to go to the podium now.

"Don't keep your public waiting," said Lauren Trissler.

Kathleen felt there was a decent chance if she stood up she would promptly fall to the floor, but she had no choice but to smile and do it. Carefully. As she approached the podium, she searched the crowd one last time for Antoinette and the kids, or even the stoned Australians—anyone who might help relax her just the tiniest bit— but she saw only people and signs, raised cell phones, and a knot of photographers and cameramen front and center, capturing it all.

Emma gazed admiringly at Kathleen. "And as *we* watched this brave woman's story unfold," she said, "did we say, 'Oh, that poor woman!' and buy into the media narrative that somehow she should be embarrassed because she has a female body? And that her body is aging in the natural, amazing way that female bodies age? Did we sit back and do *nothing*?"

The chants of "Um, yeah, no!" started up again. Emma retreated and Kathleen took her place at the microphone. The sea of chanting women on the Mall seemed to undulate before her. (*Happy stoned Australians,* she chanted to herself. *Happy stoned Australians.*)

"Thank you," she said repeatedly, until the chanting subsided. "Thank you so much. It's an honor to be here." The words on the paper before her seemed to throb and blur. She dabbed at the inside corners of her eyes with her fingertips to try to clear her vision, which swept a reverent silence through the crowd. They thought she was moved to tears.

When she opened her eyes again the words on the page had sharpened enough that she could read them: "Just under three weeks ago, on a warm late-summer night," she began, "my life as I knew it vanished in a cloud of smoke. Literally." There was a ripple of laughter. Kathleen managed a smile. She was feeling a little braver now. "I felt broken, humiliated, hopeless. But you, all of you, you lifted me up. You inspired me with your courage and commitment, your refusal to accept what we've been told for so long: that our bodies' natural functions are something we should hide instead of celebrate." She paused for cheers, which came. "That menstruation is a 'curse' and menopause is a joke." More cheers.

"These attitudes—these outdated, patriarchal attitudes—don't just silence women, they can also be deadly. In rural western Nepal, many people still practice the tradition of chaupadi, in which women's periods are considered impure and even toxic. During their periods, women are forced to stay in isolated menstrual huts. Though the practice was criminalized in 2005, it still continues. Over the centuries, countless women and children have died of cold, animal attacks, and smoke inhalation while in these huts."

She could sense the crowd murmuring, fidgeting. Danica, after reviewing the draft of Kathleen's speech the night before, had suggested she leave out this part. "You'll sound like a college freshman after her first women's studies course," she'd said. Kathleen was realizing now that she should have listened. On the left-hand side of the crowd, a small contingent was starting up another "Um, yeah, no" chant, while farther back a "Hey, hey, ho, ho, menstrual shaming has got to go!" chant seemed to be gaining momentum. The resultant jumble of noise sounded something like "Hey, yeah, no, go!"

Kathleen skipped past the rest of the chaupadi details, and the other menstrual atrocities she'd planned on bringing up. She ad-libbed a transition: "But I don't have to tell you all this—you already know what a terrible toll menstrual shaming takes on women's bodies, minds, and souls, and has for centuries!"

A cheer more rousing than any before sounded, and Kathleen felt a tugging inside her—almost as if the crowd were physically pulling her into their midst. They were bound together, all of them, by this strange and mysterious biological process they shared, with its inconveniences and embarrassments and messes; its power to bring relief (*not pregnant!*) and heartbreak (*not pregnant*); the thresholds it marked, between child and adult, youth and middle age. Together, they were claiming its power for themselves, celebrating it, wielding it.

Now Kathleen really *was* on the verge of tears. She stood, smiling, silent, until the crowd hushed.

"And I have something to say," she said, "to anyone who thinks they can make us feel ashamed of our bodies' power. I say, Um, yeah, no! Because yes we bleed!"

The chants started up again, this time sounding something like "Um yee bleed!"

She powered through the final few paragraphs, the passion in her voice mounting with each sentence until the final, glorious command: "It is time for us to stop hiding, stop denying, stop fearing, and stop apologizing! It's time to start bleeding with pride!" She wrapped up with some vigorous thank-yous and one rousing "Yes we bleed!" at the end. The crowd erupted.

It was exhilarating.

Feeling as if she were being carried aloft on the sound of cheers, Kathleen returned to the row of chairs, where the senator, the movie star, the *SNL* actress, and the others sat beaming. Even Lauren was clapping, her mouth in an approving frown. But at that point, Kathleen gave exactly zero fucks what Lauren Trissler thought.

After the speaker portion of the rally had finished, the speakers left the stage, and women who had registered online in advance and been chosen in a random drawing (supposedly; there was scuttlebutt online that it hadn't been exactly random) were invited to come to the stage one by one to tell their five-minute menstruation stories. Kathleen actually would have liked to listen to a few of these, but backstage, where she and the other speakers resumed chatting and drank the wine and beer that had appeared, courtesy of the feminist country music star, the audio was muddy. Kathleen helped herself to a paper cup of champagne and the *SNL* actress, who had just done the same, clinked cups with her. "To our ass-kicking speeches," the actress said.

"To our ass-kicking speeches, indeed," Kathleen said.

"So, I've been dying to talk with you," the actress said. "This whole time, I've been wondering—"

Kathleen's phone pinged with a text. It was Antoinette. *Where are you? Kids are getting tired, want to check out the hotel pool. Meet us at the corner of Constitution and 12th.*

"You need to go?" said the actress.

"No!" said Kathleen.

The actress flinched. "Okay, then!"

"Sorry. Just one second." *Have to wrap up some official stuff*, she wrote to Antoinette. *Sorry! I'll meet you guys back at the hotel.* After a quick apologetic grimace at the actress (who smiled patiently but had also started glancing around the tent), she wrote another text: *Tell Aggie I'm sorry the speakers said things about her dad. It didn't even occur to me that they might.*

She didn't wait for a reply. She'd knew she'd lose the actress if she did.

———

It was almost eight when Kathleen finally got back to the hotel. The country star had taken a big group of the event speakers and organizers out to a trendy vegan brasserie called Le Coq de Courgettes, where they ate tempeh-steak frites, tofu au vin, and some barely edible thing called Escarg-no. Kathleen stuck mainly to the fries, baguette, and copious quantities of wine being poured.

Lauren Trissler, to Kathleen's relief, didn't join them. But a sixteen-year-old TikTok sensation rapper named KeyHole had shown up, along with a podcaster named Vonda Vu who everyone was extremely excited about. Kathleen had to surreptitiously google them on her phone on a trip to the ladies' room to find out who they were.

Kathleen texted Antoinette before she left the restaurant and again in the Uber on her way back to the hotel but got no reply either time. She ducked into the hotel restaurant and then peered through the fogged window of the indoor pool area, but the kids weren't there, either. She finally found them in the room she and Antoinette were sharing, perched on the beds and sitting on the floor, eating takeout pizza while a movie flashed on the TV.

"Oh, hello," said Antoinette. "You decided to come back." She was in her bathing suit, head wrapped in a towel, sitting on the bed Kathleen had planned on sleeping in. A large wet spot encircled her ass on the comforter.

"I'm so sorry," Kathleen said. "I had to wait forever for an Uber."

"You had to wait four hours?"

"No, before that I needed to stay a while longer to wrap some things up. I texted. Twice."

"We must have been at the pool," Antoinette said.

"I'm sorry," Kathleen said again. "Thanks so much for looking after the girls."

"Shh, you guys," said Melissa. "Movie."

Kathleen crouched down next to Aggie, who sat on the floor, and started to put an arm around her. "Hey, Ag—" she began, but Aggie shouldered her away, knocking her off-balance as she did.

Melissa snort-laughed as Kathleen got herself to her feet. "Are you *drunk*, Kathleen?"

"No, of course I'm not *drunk*," Kathleen said.

"That's what my mom says when she's drunk," said Lucy.

After the movie, during which Kathleen had sat awkwardly on the non-soaked bed, scrolling through Twitter and Instagram, she pulled Aggie away for a quick talk in the corridor near the elevator.

"I'm sorry it took so long for me to get back. It was harder than I expected to get away. Did you have fun though? It was an amazing crowd, wasn't it?"

"Antoinette said it wasn't as big as the Women's March," said Aggie.

"Well, no, but I don't think anyone expected it would be. It was still great, though. Your generation . . . It's so great that these attitudes are changing, and that you're so passionate. It's really great." She realized that she was babbling. "I'm really proud of you."

Aggie was tracing the diamond pattern on the carpet with her toe. "You said we were doing this together."

"We are! We came all the way down here together, didn't we?"

"I've barely seen you all day, Mom."

Kathleen gave the side of Aggie's shoulder a rub. "Aggie, come on. You know that part of the reason I'm here was to give my speech. I told you, I'm sorry it took me so long to get back. But the group invited me out to dinner, and it ended up taking much longer than I expected." She hiccupped, hard. "You would have liked this place. It was really fun and vegan and—"

"You didn't have to go," Aggie said.

"I did have to go, actually," Kathleen said. "It was part of what I agreed to." It wasn't, really. But what would Emma and the others have thought? It would have been rude of her to just take off when they were all so eager to get to know her. And if she'd come back to the hotel, Aggie probably would have been too busy with her friends to spend time with her anyway.

Aggie glared at Kathleen, jaw tight. It was around the mouth and chin that Kathleen had always thought Aggie resembled Bill, and right now, the similarity was undeniable: pissed-off Aggie looked a lot like pissed-off Bill. "I'm working really hard with my friends," Aggie said, "to spread awareness and make a difference and change things on a grass-cut level. And you're not doing anything."

"*Grassroots*, you mean."

Aggie groaned. "Can you not *correct* people all the time?"

"I'm sorry," said Kathleen. "But what do you mean I'm not doing anything? I'm doing tons!"

"No, you're not. You're just buying new clothes and going on TV and out to dinners and doing things on your phone and your computer all the time. And now you're writing some stupid book about yourself?"

"It's not going to be stupid. And doing all that stuff *is* helping Yes We Bleed. It's just different from the way you're doing it. We're complementing each other."

Aggie looked confused. "What do you mean? I'm not complimenting you."

"No, different spelling, *complement* with—never mind. What I mean is there are different ways to support a movement, and you need all of them for it to really work."

"You need fancy hair and clothes and makeup?" Aggie said. "And you have to be on Instagram and Twitter *all* the time? You won't even let me *have* social media or a smartphone."

"Well, we can talk about that. Maybe you're old enough—"

"No, I don't even *want* one! I'm just saying."

The elevator dinged, then opened, and two men in suits having an intense conversation in German strode out, trailing toaster-size rolling suitcases. One of the men gave Kathleen and Aggie a puzzled look. "Are you going to descend, or you are just standing there?"

"We are just standing here," said Kathleen.

When they were gone, Kathleen felt suddenly much more sober than she had a few minutes before. "Aggie, look," she said. "You're right, I'm not doing the kind of activism you and your friends are. I'm doing the kind where I'm helping to publicize the cause and make it personal for people, with my story. I mean, I might as well, right?"

Aggie's arms were folded, and she was eyeing Kathleen with suspicion. "What do you mean you might as well?"

"I mean what your dad did . . . and that picture going viral, and me becoming some kind of hero—I didn't want for any of it to happen. But it did. So, I'm making the best of it. The same way you made the best of it when those popular girls did what they did to you. You took your hurt and turned it into something, right? I'm doing the same thing."

Kathleen wasn't sure how much more to say. How do you tell your daughter, whom you love beyond anything, to whom you want to be a role model, that you've been hiding from yourself for the past fifteen years? Hiding from everyone? *Should* you tell her?

Yes, she decided. She should.

"This movement," Kathleen finally said, "is important. It really is. And it's also a chance for me to be the sort of person I've never had the courage to be before. To stand up for something for once. And overcome my fears, like public speaking. Put myself out there. And, Aggie, it's a chance for me to get back to a thing I loved, with this book I may be writing. I made a stupid mistake, giving up on writing all those years ago. But now, because I'm doing this work for Yes We Bleed, I'm getting a second chance."

Kathleen searched Aggie's eyes, looking for any hint of a reaction. Nothing. "You're old enough to understand all that, right, sweetie?" Kathleen asked.

"Yeah, I understand." Kathleen could have sworn that the childlike softness of her daughter's face was hardening right there and then. "You're doing it all for yourself."

Day Twenty

On the way back to Greenchester, Antoinette declared that each of the girls should share their favorite part of their first protest experience. Melissa, who had passed out business cards for her Cycle Chic Etsy store in the crowd, said that she'd already made a few sales. She estimated that after the cost of materials and shipping, she'd clear at least two dollars toward their refugee period kit fund. (Antoinette noted that she now had a few leads on where they might be able to find some refugees.) Kia said she liked giving the stink eye to the #AllBloodMatters and #MenBleedToo counterprotesters who had shown up. Lucy was psyched about all the free swag she'd gotten from the vendor booths set up at the fringes of the protest: #YesWeBleed rubber bracelets handed out by a bank, mini red #YesWeBleed flags, a tiny sample cup of the new Bloodred Velvet Macchiato™ from a coffee chain, and a water bottle from a women's athletic-wear company that read *Blood, Sweat, and H$_2$O*.

"I thought it was kind of icky, all those companies showing up," said Aggie.

"I agree completely, Aggie," said Antoinette. "The corporatization of social change is shameful." (Antoinette, Kathleen couldn't help noticing, was also sporting one of the bank's co-branded #YesWeBleed rubber bracelets.)

"I totally agree, too," said Melissa. "But the Bloodred Velvet Macchiato was really good. Lucy and I drank, like, four each." The two of them dissolved into caffeine-charged giggles.

"My favorite part," said Kathleen, twisting in her seat to face the girls, "was just the fact that you kids are all so invested in this. It's really inspiring." She smiled at Aggie, in hopes that it might thaw the chill between them, but Aggie just turned and looked out the window. She had been taciturn since their argument the night before. The words she had spoken, that Kathleen was doing this all for herself, were a jagged little pebble in Kathleen's shoe. But Aggie was wrong. Kathleen wasn't doing it *all* for herself. Just *some* of it. And anyway, what did it matter that her motivations weren't 100 percent selfless if it all benefited Yes We Bleed in the end?

It was frustrating that a kid as smart as Aggie couldn't understand that. But, Kathleen reminded herself, she was still a kid, new maturity notwithstanding. And to kids—not unlike the Twitterati—things were black and white.

Eventually she would understand.

"What about you, Ag?" Kathleen asked. "What was your favorite part?"

"My favorite part," said Aggie, "was Lauren Trissler's speech."

There was no food in the condo. Kathleen was sick of takeout, and suspected that Aggie was, too, so just before dinner, Kathleen went to Sorrel and Saffron, where Bobbie bought the majority of her non-jumbo-size groceries. Kathleen shopped there only rarely, for their prepared foods and baked goods, or on the occasions when she got halfway through a recipe before realizing it relied on some obscure ingredient not easily found at Stop & Shop. (*Smoked Kash-*

miri turmeric is essential to the flavor of this dish! Don't substitute regular turmeric!) She hadn't dared go to Sorrel and Saffron, or pretty much anywhere in downtown Greenchester, since the debacle, because it was the sort of place where she would inevitably run into someone she knew—and often someone she didn't particularly like.

"Do you want to come?" she asked Aggie. "You can help pick out something. We'll get a good dessert, too. Pistachio ice cream?"

Aggie shook her head. "It smells like sausage in there."

"Fine." Kathleen was too drained to argue anymore. If Aggie wanted to sulk, fine. Let her sulk.

Inside, Kathleen grabbed a wicker shopping basket and made her way quickly through the aisles, trying to make it clear through her body language that she didn't care to be spoken to or gawked at or asked for selfies. She'd made it almost all the way to the prepared foods counter, when suddenly there were Margaret Foster and Dawn Herbin in smirking conversation by the charcuterie case.

Margaret and Dawn were queen and lady-in-waiting, respectively, of the Bitch Brigade. One of them was Bella's mother, and the other one Ella's. Kathleen could never remember whose daughter was whose, but it didn't really matter: both girls were interchangeably blond and expensively dressed, with nondescriptly pretty resting bitch faces. The same could be said of their mothers. There was a good chance, Kathleen realized, that it was the feminine hygiene products of these very women that Ella and Bella had pilfered to terrorize Aggie.

Kathleen was about to detour into the artisanal pasta and heirloom rice aisle to lie low until Margaret and Dawn were gone, but they spotted her before she could, and their faces broke into thrilled, gape-mouthed smiles.

"Kat!" called Margaret. "It's so good to see you!"

"Come talk to us!" said Dawn.

These were two women who had never, in the eight years Kathleen had known them, expressed any interest whatsoever in talking to her, except to ask her if she'd be willing to make baked goods or stuff envelopes. Instinctively, Kathleen froze, fearing that this was some sort of trap—that whatever they said to her (some compliment that meant the exact opposite of itself, most likely), and however she reacted, they'd laugh cattily about it later when she wasn't there.

And yet, the way they were looking at her now, with what seemed like genuine, benevolent fascination, was decidedly different from the way they had looked at her before. She put on the most Kat-like smile she could muster and headed toward them.

"You were *so* incredible in that interview last week," Margaret said.

"Which one?" said Kathleen, casually adjusting an earring.

Margaret and Dawn both broke into laughter, as if Kathleen had just said something fantastically clever.

"I meant CBS, but I know, you're everywhere," said Margaret.

Dawn gently clutched Kathleen's forearm. Her hand was icy and dry. "It's just amazing," she said. "And it's so inspiring, what Aggie and her friends are doing at the school with their little club."

"Isn't it?" Margaret said. She turned to Kathleen and put on a wry, conspiratorial smile. "I mean, god, I never thought Ella had a feminist bone in her body. Until a few days ago, all she cared about was field hockey and getting likes on Instagram. And not necessarily in that order." Dawn tittered at this. "But last week she came home wearing a Yes We Bleed button someone had given her."

"Wow," was all Kathleen could think to say.

Margaret and Dawn laughed again, flipping back their meticulously highlighted hair.

"But you know," said Dawn, "it doesn't surprise me at all when it comes to Aggie. She's always been very serious about things, hasn't she? I'll never forget, on the field trip up to Mystic Seaport when the kids were in, what, third grade? Fourth? While all the other kids were fooling around, she had the smartest little questions to ask!"

"Well, sometimes she's maybe a little *too* serious," Kathleen said. "But she's very committed to the cause."

"I think it's adorable," Margaret said.

"And it's smart," added Dawn. "College admissions committees love this kind of thing."

"*All* admissions committees love this kind of thing," said Margaret, as if it were obvious. Dawn shrank slightly inside her blouse. "I told Ella she has to stay in the club at least until her applications to Miss Porter's and Choate are in."

"Oh my gosh, that's *so* smart," said Dawn.

"Hm," said Margaret.

"So," said Dawn, moving a step closer, holding Kathleen's forearm once again. "A few of us were talking the other day, and we want to do a fundraiser for Yes We Bleed at the club. Black tie, jazz quartet, silent auction . . ."

"Not black tie," Margaret said. "We decided cocktail attire, remember? A red theme. And, of course, you'd *have* to be the honorary committee chair, Kat."

"And say a few words?" said Dawn. She was practically caressing Kathleen's arm now.

They both trained their hard, pretty eyes on Kathleen, awaiting her reply. The prospect of spending an evening at the Greenchester Country Club with the Bitch Brigade and their investment-banking, golf-playing husbands, along with fifty or more people exactly like them, was unpleasant to say the least. But if she said no, god knows what they might say about her behind her back—or what kind of revenge their evil daughters might exact upon Aggie.

"Of course," Kathleen finally said, as brightly as she could.

"Oh, yay!" said Dawn, releasing Kathleen's arm to perform a silent, mini-clap of her hands.

Then, blessedly, Kathleen's phone rang. She plunged her fist into her bag to retrieve it, planning to answer regardless of who it was. In fact, it was Chrysanthemum.

"I'm so sorry," Kathleen said, "I have to take this. It's my agent."

Seeing the looks of awe on Margaret's and Dawn's faces was, she had to admit, delicious.

It was even more delicious to hear Chrysanthemum's breathless words: "We just got an eight-hundred-thousand-dollar preemptive offer on your book from Gunther House. Isn't it marvelous?"

Periods and Privilege

AN OPEN LETTER TO YES WE BLEED SUPPORTERS

Shelley Raynham

Dear Yes We Bleed Supporters,

For the past three weeks, I've watched my TikTok and Instagram feeds fill up with your stories of your periods: First periods, last periods, embarrassing period disasters. Periods like Niagara Falls and periods you barely realized you were having. Skipped periods that scared you to death or filled you with hope. I've seen selfies of you wearing menstrual cup hats and marching in Washington, demanding free menstrual products. #YesWeBleed, you tag your posts.

But who, exactly, does "we" include? More importantly, who does it exclude?

Because here's the thing: I don't bleed. I have a rare metabolic disorder that causes me to be chronically underweight—I'll save the thin-shaming I get for *that* for another time. My low weight causes amenorrhea: the absence of periods. I've never had one, and I most likely never will. It's unlikely that I'll ever be able to sustain a pregnancy. I've learned to accept my reality, but that doesn't make it easy.

Never once, in the entirety of the Yes We Bleed coverage, have I heard anyone acknowledge the way this movement excludes women like me. Not to mention women who have had hysterectomies, who I'm sure also, like me, feel marginalized by your "period pride."

I am a feminist, and I support the goals of Yes We Bleed in theory. But I wish more of you would check your privilege and stop with the microaggressive generalizations like "all women" and "As women, we . . ." I wish you'd spend less time talking about your experiences and more time listening to women who don't share them.

If you're reading this, it's a start, anyway. Now do better.

Sincerely,
Shelley

COMMENTS:

Please keep your comments civil, in accordance with our community guidelines. Posts containing hate speech or threats will be removed by the moderators.

Calla K. THANK YOU for this. As a uterine cancer survivor (full hysterectomy and oophorectomy) I've been waiting for someone to check Yes We Bleed supporters on their privilege. Despite what the MSM says, YWB is not a "women's movement." It's a SOME women's movement. Honestly, the entitlement is sickening.

B2londe1 Speaking of privilege: you neglected to acknowledge the fact that #YesWeBleed almost always leaves non-cis women out of the picture. Look in the mirror, Shelley, and ask yourself if you're not part of the problem, too. Cis-centric feminism isn't feminism at all.

Zack H. I get, it, Shelley. Every liberal feels like they missed out on the Civil Rights movement and can't wait to create one of their own. Trans rights! Black Lives Matter! Periods! A senator's wife woke up one day and decided to be Menstruation Luther King. The whole thing is obnoxious.

> **V-Spot** Wow. You're putting Trans rights and BLM in the same category as YWB?? Two of those are about human rights. I don't understand why the moderators don't remove comments like yours.

>> **Zack H.** Because of the first amendment? Ever heard of it? Oh wait, no, only liberals are allowed to cry freedom of speech. Everyone else has to shut up and suck up.

DarthLater Poor Shelley. You know who else is left out of this movement? I'll give you a hint. We don't get periods either. Welcome to the dark side! #Men #YesWeBreed

> **V-Spot** Oh, great, incel troll Darth Later is here. Don't you have anything better to do?

>> **DarthLater** I wouldn't mind doing Shelley. She's thin and she doesn't bleed. Sounds hot.

>>> **V-Spot** Don't you have a Proud Boys meeting to go to somewhere?

Gracie I get where the author is coming from, but honestly it's beside the point. The real problem with the Yes We Bleed thing is that there's only a tiny subset of people within the movement talking about the sheer quantity of disposable period products that end up in landfills every year, or cause serious problems with sewer infrastructure and wastewater management. Seriously, it's more like #YesWeWaste.

Debs THIS!!

Stacy Um, what? The hat for the movement is in the shape of a (reusable, sustainable) menstrual cup!!

Gracie Uh huh. How many women who wear that hat do you think actually USE menstrual cups?

Tia FYI, a cup costs btwn. $25-40. For someone living paycheck to paycheck or a child in a low-income family that's a lot.

Dan T. If the DNC would get out of the way and let voters put progressives in office, then you'd see wages rise enough that $25 wouldn't be a make or break for working families.

K.D. Sometimes I wonder, why is our democracy going down the drain? Then I read comment threads like this and I remember.

Day Twenty-Two

The cocktail party Gunther House threw together for an impromptu celebration and get-to-know-you session following their acquisition of Kathleen's as-yet-unwritten book was in the lounge of a boutique hotel in Hudson Yards called Adjective. Dense tangles of what looked like desiccated bird carcasses hung at random intervals from the ceiling; a huge circular sofa upholstered in faux (or not?) zebra fur ringed a column in the center of the room, while baroque gilt-framed mirrors and paintings of plump cherubs and toga-wearing women lined the walls. The bar and the tables, meanwhile, were all clear Lucite, lit from within by hot-pink neon lights. (What, exactly, was the adjective the place was going for: Nightmarish? Seizure-inducing?)

The deal with Gunther House—like everything in the past three weeks—had happened with dizzying speed. Kathleen had spent the previous morning on the phone with the team that would be working on her book to see if it was "the right fit," as Chrysanthemum put it. ("But it's *Gunther House*, for goodness' sake!" she'd gushed. "The top of the top! I just *know* you'll love them.")

Kathleen had spent most of the conversation talking with a bright-voiced, sharp-witted editorial assistant named Fiona, whom she had instantly liked. Fiona had assured Kathleen and Chrysanthemum that Kathleen would be deeply involved in the writing process if that's what she wanted. "We really do see this being more of a cowrite with you and the ghostwriter," Fiona had said. "Think of her—and we're definitely going to make sure it's a her, and that you like her, of course—as your writing assistant. Someone to help lighten your load, so you can keep doing all the things you need to do."

The editor with whom Kathleen would primarily be working if she accepted the offer—someone named Theo Balbakis whom Chrysanthemum described as a "brilliant talent"—was on the call only briefly. He had come down with a virulent stomach virus of some sort that morning, he explained with copious apologies. "But please believe me when I tell you," he'd said groggily, "that it would be a highlight of my publishing career to work with you on this book. I may be a guy, but I'm a guy who is seeing things in a whole new way, thanks to your work. Part of why I jumped at the chance to work on this book was so I could keep learning." Then he'd excused himself through a suppressed burp, saying he feared he needed to "bow to the porcelain god." "Sorry, ladies," he'd said before the line went dead.

His use of *ladies* was the only thing about the whole call that gave Kathleen pause, but she told herself she was being ridiculous. Fiona was wonderful, as was the marketing director she spoke with, who said that Kathleen's book would be the breakout title in a whole series of books about influential women that Gunther House was launching. And it was Gunther House! Years ago, when her agent tried to sell *The Hecate Chronicles*, Gunther House was the publisher Kathleen most hoped to land a deal with—the most powerful and prestigious of them all.

Immediately after the call, she had told Chrysanthemum yes: she would take their offer.

Now, less than twenty-four hours later, here she was. At Adjective. Kathleen had invited Aggie to come with her, thinking that maybe if she made her daughter more a part of some of the things she was doing, Aggie would see things differently. She would see that they were on the same team, and she would see Kathleen in her element, being the sort of strong female role model Kathleen wished she could have been to Aggie all along. She wanted Aggie to witness the way she stood straighter. Spoke less haltingly. (No *justs*!) Smiled more easily.

She offered, in turn, to help Aggie and her friends with whatever they needed for their latest Yes We Bleed efforts. Antoinette wasn't the only one who could have pins and buttons and T-shirts made. "How can I help?" Kathleen had asked Aggie. "Say it, and it's done."

"Oh," Aggie said. "Thanks. We did need some things for a thing we're doing, but Antoinette got them, I think."

"Oooh, what kind of thing?"

Aggie's expression, which seemed to have opened up the slightest bit seconds before, for the first time since their trip to DC, had shuttered itself again. "Nothing. Just some signs and things." And she'd rather not come to the city for the book party, she said; she had a big test in the morning. "Could you just have Chloe come instead?"

In the moment, Kathleen had felt deflated. But now, looking around the insanity that was Adjective, she was glad that Aggie hadn't come. It was all too strange, too adult, too . . . adjectival. Not the right place for a wholesome melding of their Yes We Bleed worlds. Aggie never would have made it past the desiccated bird carcasses.

There was a girlish cry as Kathleen approached the bar. "Kathleen! You're here, at last!" Chrysanthemum's expression was so intensely delighted that Kathleen half expected her head to explode into a mass of blossoms and butterflies. Although she had seen pictures of Chrysanthemum online, she'd had no idea how tiny she was—barely five feet if you didn't count the Gibson girl–esque pile of frothy red hair atop her head. Kathleen, wearing the four-inch Tamara Mellon heels she'd splurged on for her appearance on *Good Morning America*, felt gangly and stork-like next to her.

"Everybody!" Chrysanthemum yelled—a very large sound from

her very tiny body. She grasped Kathleen's hand and raised it aloft as though Kathleen had just won a boxing match. "Look who's here!"

A few people turned and applauded. Chrysanthemum squeezed Kathleen's hand so hard Kathleen felt something crack. "This is magnificent, isn't it?" Chrysanthemum whispered, standing on tiptoe. "And highly unusual. Why, I haven't seen this sort of lavish fete for a deal since Wolf Blitzer's children's book!"

For the next thirty minutes, Chrysanthemum guided Kathleen through the lounge, introducing her to various Gunther House executives and publicists and marketing staff. Kathleen smiled and nodded and did her best to answer their questions and be as charming and as interesting as they seemed to expect her to be, but it wasn't long before she started to feel the same combination of weariness, boredom, and low-grade anxiety she'd always had when she went to events with Bill—or any other festive event where small talk and mingling were required. She was relieved when Chrysanthemum finally led her to a table in the corner near a large wicker sphere, saying, "Your editor awaits!"

At the table sat a man of indeterminate age in a rumpled white shirt unbuttoned one button too low, with a five-o'clock shadow so dark and patchy it wasn't so much a shadow as a Rorschach blot on the lower half of his face. His eyes were bloodshot, and three rocks glasses sat on the table in front of him, two of them empty, along with an untouched plate of shrimp skewers in a puddle of amber liquid.

This couldn't possibly be the "brilliant talent" of whom Chrysanthemum had spoken. But he could most definitely be the sort of person who referred to women as "ladies."

"Theo Balbakis!" Chrysanthemum announced and gestured to the chair across from him. "I'll leave you two to get acquainted!"

Feeling slightly queasy, and suddenly aware of the fact that her pumps were cutting into her insteps, Kathleen sat, and attempted a smile.

"You all right?" said Theo when Chrysanthemum had left. "You're looking a touch *peaked*, as Chrysanthemum might say."

"No, I'm fine," said Kathleen.

"I'm sorry I was indisposed the other day when we talked on the old horn." From the way he drew out his vowels, Kathleen suspected he was well on his way to indisposed now. In fact, he looked like he might fall asleep at any second. "But fear not, Kat Anderson Held. You're working with the best. Doctorate in comparative lit from Columbia. Postdoc at Oxford. Best and brightest." He gave a little salute, then pulled a skewer out from the shrimp it speared and commenced picking his teeth with the sharp end.

"That's great," said Kathleen. Maybe if he wasn't soused, he wouldn't be so bad? "I actually have an MFA. And I have a novel manuscript that I'd love for you to—"

"And now, the pinnacle of my brilliant career," Theo went on, in a voice sloshing with sarcasm, "working on a ghostwritten social media celebrity memoir about a period hashtag. I mean, what an honor."

Kathleen felt suddenly Chrysanthemum-sized. "Why did you take on the book, then?"

"Rehab," Theo said through a suppressed burp. "Of the career variety. Every other submission I go to bat for gets turned down by the muckety-mucks with dollar signs in their eyes. I needed a hit."

This had to be a mistake. "I can write, you know. Very well," Kathleen said. "I told Fiona I want this book to be something interesting. Substantial. When I spoke with her the other day, she assured me that we could push it in that direction."

Theo laughed groggily. "Fiona's sweet that way. But that's not what's gonna happen. What's gonna happen is we're gonna hire the best and fastest ghostwriter in town, crank this puppy dog out before the public forgets who you are, and you buy yourself a nice car or a tiara or whatever the fuck, and I'll have the distinct pleasure of working in this wonderful industry for a few more years." He propped an elbow on the table, dropped his patchy-chinned face to his fist, and put on a dreamy look. "Doesn't that sound nice?"

No; this couldn't be. There was no way in hell Kathleen was going to work with this man. How could Chrysanthemum have thought that he would be a good match for her book, for her? She was about to tell Theo that perhaps there'd been some kind of misunderstanding when his drooping eyelids rose a few millimeters and he trained his gaze over Kathleen's shoulder, toward the entrance to the lounge. "Holy shit," he said. "Will you look at that."

Kathleen turned to see. There, at the hostess podium by the door, was Danica in a clinging black dress and red stilettos—her outfit from the Elitist Bitch poster she'd shown them at the most-recent society meeting. She was engaged in a heated conversation with the hostess and a man who looked like some sort of manager. When Danica caught Kathleen's eye, she lifted an arm and gave her a beckoning wave.

With a steadily growing sense of dread, Kathleen stood and made her way across the lounge.

"Hello, love," Danica said when Kathleen approached. "Will you please tell this girl that I'm your guest? Somehow, somebody neglected to put my name on the list. And I'm being treated *extremely* rudely."

"She's with me," Kathleen told the hostess weakly.

"There's absolutely no smoking," the manager said to Danica, who was now removing a brown cigarette from a crystal-encrusted case.

"Ridiculous," Danica said, and snapped the case shut. She put her arm through Kathleen's and said in a low voice as she guided her away, "I hope somebody caught all that on film. I wasn't *quite* as bitchy as I probably should have been, but I wanted to make sure I made it in the door. You look fabulous, by the way. I love the shoes."

"What are you doing here?" Kathleen whispered.

"Coming out," Danica replied. "Where's Nasturtium?"

"Who?"

"Your agent. Mine won't return my calls."

"Danica—"

"Sh, sh, sh, I know. It's your party, your night. That's why I didn't come earlier. Just play along. You're doing wonderfully."

Kathleen became suddenly aware of people staring at them, phones being held aloft, the occasional flash going off. The small of her back clenched. This was not going to look good: her being cozy with a woman who was considered by many to be the antithesis of feminism—a traitor to her sex—now looking like a combination of Cruella de Vil, Catwoman, and Alexis Carrington. Kathleen attempted to pull away from Danica, but Danica clung fiercely to her arm.

Danica spotted Chrysanthemum, chatting with another woman beneath one of the desiccated bird clumps, before Kathleen did. "That's her, isn't it?" she asked. "The one with the saloon girl hair?" She began sauntering toward Chrysanthemum, her arm still hooked through Kathleen's. Kathleen attempted to convey, through her body language, that she was not, in fact, Danica's best friend, but her hostage. But the effect, if there had been one, was blown when Danica introduced herself to Chrysanthemum as one of Kathleen's dearest friends. She then proceeded to pitch her Elitist Bitch literary franchise: the memoir, the novelty books, the novels, the product tie-ins, everything.

"I'm afraid it's not for me," Chrysanthemum said curtly when Danica had finished.

"What do you mean it's not for you?" said Danica. "Are you opposed to making money?"

Chrysanthemum lifted her little chin a few centimeters. "I'm not in this business for the money."

Danica gave a squawk of a laugh that sounded decidedly more disdainful than any Kathleen had heard issue from her throat before. "Please. Do you honestly expect me to believe that your motivations were purely artistic when you signed my dear friend here? No offense, Kat," she added in a low voice. "But let's be real here, shall we? This is all about money."

"I signed Kat because I am a passionate feminist," said Chrysanthemum, hoisting her chin even farther. "And I would never take on a client I didn't respect."

Danica gasped theatrically, and bellowed, "*What* did you just say?"

The din of voices of the room hushed noticeably, and Kathleen saw a couple of people raising their phones again. *Shit.* It was bad enough that people had been snapping photos of her and Danica before, but now Danica was clearly attempting to stir up some kind of confrontation—and Kathleen was not in the mood to be embroiled in another viral scandal.

"Danica," Kathleen said, trying to calm her. "Maybe you should just—"

But Danica, still fuming—or putting on a good show of it, at least—ignored her. Next thing Kathleen knew, Danica had ripped Chrysanthemum's champagne flute from her hands and tossed its contents onto Chrysanthemum's blouse. There were gasps and smothered laughter all around.

A pair of women rushed to Chrysanthemum's side and dabbed at her with napkins while Chrysanthemum made small squeaking sounds.

The restaurant manager and another man began ushering a laughing Danica away. "So long, losers!" she called over her shoulder.

"*That* was masterful," said Theo, who at some point had sidled up and now stood near Kathleen, listing perilously to one side. "She's going to make millions."

"Not with my help, she's not," said Chrysanthemum.

"I am so sorry," said Kathleen. She was pleasantly surprised by Chrysanthemum's conviction. "I didn't invite her, she just showed up."

"Are you actually friends with her?" Chrysanthemum asked.

"No, we're not friends. I just met her a couple of weeks ago, when everything started. She invited me—she invited me over for lunch."

Chrysanthemum dabbed daintily at her sternum. "She's a beast," she said. "And I'm gravely concerned about the effect your associating with her will have."

"I know," said Kathleen. No doubt the pictures of her and Danica were already lighting up Twitter, and god knew what people were saying. Jonathan would know how Kathleen should handle it, she thought, then immediately realized that Jonathan was, no doubt, in on Danica's stunt, too. So: in the span of three weeks she'd been betrayed by Bill, then the odious Theo Balbakis, and now Danica and Jonathan, too? What was *wrong* with her that people felt they could do this to her?

"We stand on terribly perilous ground, Kat," Chrysanthemum was saying. "We must preserve your image at all costs until this book is published."

"Eh, who cares. It's all just a bunch of bullshit anyway." This was Theo. Kathleen had forgotten he was standing there. "And all publicity is good publicity, right?" He put on a sarcastic, maniacal-looking grin.

"Theo, please," said Chrysanthemum.

"She's so cute when she's angry," Theo said with a wink at Kathleen. Then he shambled off toward the bar.

"If there's backlash, I'll just say I don't know her," Kathleen told Chrysanthemum. "And that I don't approve of her past statements. It will be easy enough."

"Good," said Chrysanthemum. "Do that."

"But we need to talk. About Theo. I just don't think he's the right editor for this book."

Chrysanthemum rolled her eyes. "Oh, I know. He can be a boor. But he's intel*lec*tual, like you. Trust me, everything will turn out exactly the way we discussed."

"But he's saying I wouldn't be involved at all with—"

"Oh, look!" said Chrysanthemum, putting a hand to her still-damp sternum. "There's our film agent, Winky! I was hoping she'd show up. Come, come." She wove her arm through Kathleen's, much in the same way Danica had, and led her across the room. Chrysanthemum practically pranced, while Kathleen stumbled in her heels to keep up.

Day Twenty-Three

The first thing Kathleen saw when she picked up her phone from her nightstand the next morning was a text from Jonathan telling her that she had an email from Danica.

Kathleen wrote Jonathan a terse reply. *I hope it's an apology. And thanks a lot to you, too.*

While she waited for his response, she opened her email, where she found the message from Danica.

Dearest Kathleen,

You're probably furious with me, but believe me, I did this for both Kat Anderson Held and the Elitist Bitch—and everything will turn out marvelously. There's already gobs of chatter on the idiot-nets, and you and #YesWeBleed are trending again for the first time in days. Fear not, you look perfectly horrified in all the pictures people are posting—a deer in the headlights of an Escalade—and they're saying it looks like I took you hostage, which was exactly my intent. The Kat fans are rallying to your side, and the detractors are flocking to the Elitist Bitch. We'll raise a glass at the next society meeting. (Details to come!)

Mwah!

D.

Postscript: In the time it took me to write this email, the Elitist Bitch gained two hundred more idiot followers on Instagram and five hundred on Twitter. It's almost too easy.

With a feeling of dread already having taken up residence in her gut, Kathleen opened Twitter. And, indeed, there were the pictures, dozens of them. In all of them, with the exception of the ones showing Danica's scuffle with the hostess and the manager at the front desk, Kathleen was right at Danica's side—exactly where Danica had so manipulatively kept her. Fortunately, Kathleen did, in fact, look stricken and bewildered in most, which was noted by the people who commented.

> OMG, poor Kat Held—she looks like she's being kidnapped.

> LOL, she's like "WTF why is this bitch here?"

> Elitist Bitch/Kat Held cage match, please!!

But not everyone gave Kathleen the benefit of the doubt—particularly when it came to the video someone had posted to TikTok of Danica yelling at Chrysanthemum, culminating in the theatrical tossing of the champagne. In this, Kathleen looked much more like she was on Danica's side. She hadn't even realized it at the time, but when she had pleaded with Danica to stop, Kathleen had put her hand on Danica's arm in the intimate way only a close friend or family member might.

> Is it just me, or do they look like they've known each other, like, a while?

> Not surprised. "Kat" Held is obv a total publicity whore, so it makes sense that she'd hang out with other ones.

> Kind of regretting the Kat Stan t-shirt I just ordered. :-(

> Kat Held gets famous, and now she's hanging around with people like Danica Bellevue. Nice feminist.

> Wow. Just wow.

Kathleen felt the familiar buzz in her limbs, the sensation that her hands had risen up from the keyboard, no longer attached to the rest of her body. For five minutes she lay in bed, paralyzed, crafting replies in her head, thinking about what she could tweet herself to make clear that Danica was, in no way, the good friend she appeared to be. Kathleen had been so disciplined up until now, avoiding impulsive or angry (or drunk) social media posting, sticking to the brand guidelines Jonathan and Danica had crafted for her. But now, all she wanted was to skewer Danica with the bitchiest tweet she could muster.

She forcibly redirected herself by calling Jonathan, who still hadn't replied to her text from before. She was surprised when he actually answered.

"I would have warned you ahead of time," he said, instead of "Hello." His voice was less clipped and more human than usual. Quieter, too; it was clear that he was trying not to be heard. "But Danica wanted to make sure you looked genuinely shocked and appalled and whatnot."

"I *was* shocked and appalled and whatnot!"

"Yes, that was the plan. Now, what you do is craft a concise, sincere, on-brand Kat Anderson Held tweet in which you make it clear that you met Danica only once, in passing—some sort of publishing-world thing—and you are not a fan. That she ambushed you and made a scene."

"Which she did."

"Exactly. You don't even have to lie. And then stay above the fray. Stay on message and on-brand. If Danica takes swipes at Yes We Bleed, don't take the bait. Let other people do the dirty work for you."

This was what Kathleen had done all along when it came to critics of Yes We Bleed, though it wasn't always easy. Especially when it came to the menstrual extremists who didn't think Yes We Bleed went nearly far enough and were vying for a new government program that would provide a lifetime supply of period products, free of charge, to all menstruating US residents. (Of course, the people who dared to comment that perhaps there were other things that more urgently needed funding were promptly attacked as fascists, misogynists, centrists, etc.)

"So, I take it the Elitist Bitch is anti–Yes We Bleed?" Kathleen asked Jonathan.

"Naturally. Look, I realize this is a bit of a wrinkle you hadn't planned on, but it's going to be all right."

"I could lose my book deal over this."

"No, you won't. If anything, you've added a few more chapters. It's just a matter of controlling the narrative."

Controlling the narrative—it sounded like something Desmond would say.

"I liked the narrative I had before! And I liked it when Danica was on my side, not just *using* me for her own selfish—"

"Look at where you are," Jonathan snapped, with a vehemence Kathleen didn't know he was capable of. "Look at everything she's done for you. Look what she does for *everyone*. I mean, good god, when she found me, I was passed out in Central Park, covered in my own frozen vomit, halfway to hypothermia. If it weren't for her—" His words screeched to a halt. "Never mind. The point is, she *is* on your side."

"Wait." Kathleen was still trying to process what Jonathan had just revealed. "Why were you covered in frozen vomit?"

Jonathan ignored her. "Just do it, Kat."

"Do what?"

"Steer into the swerve."

Later that morning, Kathleen went for a mani-pedi at a tiny nail salon in Rock Hill called Lovely Nails, wedged between a Salvadorian grocery and some sort of off-brand cell phone store. It was preparation for a photo shoot she had for a Finnish magazine that afternoon. Its name, the editor had explained, translated to *Very Ardent Woman!*

We wish to photograph you clutching sanitary napkins, the editor had written in the note Jonathan forwarded. *Therefore, your hands must look very nice, with red fingernails. Toenails as well. Please arrange this?*

Originally, Kathleen's appointment had been at Polish, a day spa in the center of Greenchester that Bobbie—snickeringly pronouncing the name with a long *O*, as in something from Poland—had dragged Kathleen to once, way back when. But she had canceled at the last minute, not wanting to risk being seen at any place that could be perceived as Elitist Bitchesque, and come here instead.

Earlier, she had taken Jonathan's advice and crafted what she thought was an artfully genuine-sounding tweet to disabuse the internet of any possible perception that she was a friend of Danica's:

> OK, cat's out of the bag: Yes, I'm in talks w. Gunther House about a book! And yes, Danica Bellevue, whom I met once years ago at an event, before she revealed her inner "Elitist Bitch," randomly crashed the party. The low point of an otherwise great night! #YesWeRead

Now she sat in a large vinyl massage chair having her back kneaded in an almost violent fashion while she scrolled through her phone to make sure that her tweet was doing its job. It seemed to be, although several people had sternly pointed out that Kathleen was essentially giving Danica free publicity by mentioning the incident at all. They had a point, and Kathleen felt frustrated and annoyed at herself for playing into Danica's hand. Stupid. At the same time, it was wearing on her, how everyone expected her to be so *perfect* all the time. Who were these high-and-mighty people always tapping out their critiques? To a person, they supported Yes We Bleed but always seemed to feel the need to add *But I just feel the need to add* to their posts. Maybe it distracted them from their own faults and hypocrisies to constantly point out hers. Why confront your own mistakes when you can attack other people's instead?

And then there was Margo, who had just posted a new photo of herself on Instagram, sitting cross-legged on a pillow-strewn window seat with her eyes closed, a slight smile on her lips, while rose-colored candles burned behind her on the windowsill.

> As you know I'm not usually a fan of the b-word. (And I'm no elitist!) But when my cycle approaches, my inner ornery tiger starts to growl. I find that lighting some of my Beach Plum Soy Candles and taking moments of quiet mindfulness throughout the day reconnects me with my best self and makes my consciousness purr. I hope you'll give this gift of serenity to yourself. I'm offering free shipping on all candles for the next 48 hours. Blissings! #YesWeBreathe #YesWeBleed #PMS #ElitistBitch

After her pedicure and manicure were finished, and shortly after she'd shuffled over in her flip-flops to the drying table, Kathleen's phone rang. The manager obligingly tucked it against Kathleen's shoulder.

"Hello!" said a spritely female voice. "It's Mrs. Minelli at the middle school! Everything is okay, don't worry, but I do need to make you aware that Aggie's actions today, admirable though they may be, will be considered an unexcused absence."

"What actions?"

The assistant principal laughed, as if Kathleen had just made a joke. "I *so* admire Aggie and her friends' activism. And yours, too, of course! I've been meaning to ask: Would you be interested in setting up a meeting to discuss how we might incorporate menstrual awareness into the curriculum?"

Ten minutes later, her nails only borderline dry, Kathleen was speeding toward the middle school. When she arrived, she couldn't believe what she saw: a huge crowd of students in front of the school, a significant portion of them, including a few boys, wearing menstrual cup hats. Some people were holding hand-lettered signs demanding free tampons and an end to period shaming. A good number appeared much too old to be in middle school—sixteen, seventeen, even older. They all looked like they were having a fantastic time—laughing, chanting, pumping fists in the air. At the edge of the crowd, some boys in Greenchester High football jerseys tossed a football, and a large clutch of girls stood talking and laughing, sucking from tall water bottles and scrolling through their phones. In front of it all, at the top of the stairs leading into the school, was Melissa, bullhorn in hand, leading chants of "Yes we bleed." On one side of her, Kia and a couple of other girls were, for some reason, emptying boxes of tampons and pads into a garbage can. On the other side of Melissa, a few steps down, a barefoot older woman in a skintight maroon bodysuit was doing what appeared to be some kind of interpretive dance. It wasn't clear whether she was officially part of the proceedings or had wandered onto the scene from elsewhere.

There were a few other adults at the edge of the crowd: a cluster of younger women who looked like they might be teachers and a handful of parents, including Margaret and Dawn, holding large Starbucks cups.

"Excuse me?" said a childish voice. Kathleen turned to see the youngest-looking of the girls who had been in her living room days before holding a cardboard box lid hung from a string around her neck. It was filled with menstrual product merchandise, which Kathleen assumed had been crafted by Melissa and her minions: crocheted menstrual cup hats, tampon jewelry, and more, as well as a small series of incongruously sleek bottles the size of hotel toiletries.

"Hi, Mrs. Held!" the girl chirped. "Can I interest you in any of our Cycle Chic products? They're ten percent off today. And if you buy something, you get a free gift!" She held up one of the mini bottles. "They're lavender labia balm samples that Aggie's aunt sent. Want to smell?"

For fuck's sake. "No, thanks."

"Kathleen!" someone called. It was Antoinette, in her menopausal menstrual cup hat, over by the bike rack, talking with a prematurely balding young man.

Kathleen tried pretending that she hadn't seen her, but Antoinette called out again and waved her over.

Antoinette put her arm around Kathleen. "This is her," she said to the man. "One of my closest friends, Kat Anderson Held. She was the inspiration for today's direct action, of course, but it was my daughter and hers who catalyzed it into this incredible event."

The young man fumbled his notebook under his arm and extended a hand to Kathleen. "Jack Urchek of the *Greenchester Gazette*. You must be very proud of your daughter and her friends."

"I am," said Kathleen. Although she wasn't sure yet whether she was proud of them for *this*.

"Look at this next part coming up," Antoinette said, nodding toward the stage. "We wanted to bring a musical element into the event."

Up on the steps of the school, a boy with a tuba, another with a snare drum, and a couple of girls with clarinets began playing "The Star-Spangled Banner" at a dirgelike tempo while Melissa's amplified voice bleated, "Until there are free period supplies in all school bathrooms everywhere, we're living in the United States of Shame!"

"I came up with that," Antoinette commented with a smile.

"Can I get a picture of you and Antoinette?" Jack Urchek asked. He hoisted the camera that hung on a strap around his neck and snapped a photo of Kathleen and Antoinette before Kathleen had a chance to protest. "That was great," he said. "I got the girl dressed as a tampon in the background."

Please let it not be Aggie, Kathleen thought. She turned to look and was relieved to see that it was some other girl she didn't recognize, in white tights and white face paint, wrapped hips to neck in toilet paper. On her head the girl wore a white beanie with a long white string attached, which she was at present chewing on absently.

Kathleen spotted Aggie then—not dressed as a feminine hygiene product, thank god, except for her menstrual cup hat—working her way along the edge of the crowd, handing out flyers. Most of the kids she offered them to didn't even give them a glance once they took them. Others refused them altogether.

"Will you excuse me, please?" Kathleen said. She hurried over to Aggie, whose face registered a strange combination of anger, shock, and relief when she saw her mother.

"What *is* all this?" Kathleen asked her.

"What are you doing here?" said Aggie, apparently deciding to go with the anger. "Don't you have a photo shoot or something to be at?"

"Not until later," Kathleen said. "You and your friends organized this whole thing?"

"Yes," said Aggie. "But it's going all wrong." Suddenly, she sounded like she was on the edge of tears. "It was supposed to be just our club and whoever wanted to support what we were doing. There were going to be speeches and a speak-out for girls to talk about their periods. But now . . . The popular kids are just here because it's a way to get out of class and make fun of us. A bunch of kids showed up from the high school who aren't supposed to be here. And nobody's even looking at my flyers."

"Can I see?"

"Why?" said Aggie, petulant again. "You don't care."

"Yes, I do."

Aggie thrust a flyer at her. *Menstruation Injustice Is a Global Problem* read the bold type at the top. Below were several thick paragraphs of information about menstruation taboos and stigmas around the world: menstruating women not being able to touch cows in India or use communal water sources in parts of Southeast Asia; girls in rural East Africa too ashamed to attend school while menstruating; even the deadly isolation huts in rural Nepal that Kathleen had mentioned at the rally in Washington. Kathleen read every word. "This is great, Ag," she said. "You should be really proud."

But Aggie was no longer there. She'd been somehow conveyed through the crowd and was being thrust up onto the steps next to Melissa, who yelled, "Everybody give it up for my best friend, Aggie Held!" The crowd broke into cheers, including manic hooting and screeching from a clutch of boys up front that sounded decidedly sarcastic. Kathleen started working her way through the crowd, propelled by equally urgent desires to rescue Aggie and to rip the boys' prepubescent larynxes from their throats.

Now Melissa was holding the bullhorn in front of Aggie's mouth, urging her to speak. Aggie shrank back from it like it was a hot dog she didn't want to eat.

Kia and Lucy, meanwhile, were dousing the trash can full of feminine hygiene supplies with what appeared to be paint thinner.

The bullhorn squealed with feedback in front of Aggie's face, causing groans in the crowd and one (obnoxiously exaggerated) moan of agony from one of the little shits up front. "Sorry," Aggie said into the bullhorn—as if it had been her fault.

The crowd began to chant her name: "Ag-EE! Ag-EE! Ag-EE!"

Aggie stood there silent, frozen. Her eyes twitched in panic. "Um . . ."

Somewhere, some girl said, snottily, "This is so sad."

Kathleen's heart felt like it was being ground by the world's largest, most calloused heel. She couldn't let this happen to Aggie; couldn't let her just stand there, terrified, being mocked by her classmates.

"Aggie," Kathleen said. She stood right at the bottom of the steps now and barely had to raise her voice. Aggie saw her, locked eyes with her. "Let's go," said Kathleen.

"Yeah, let's go, Aggie sweetie!" some boy somewhere mocked in falsetto. Kathleen whirled around to see who it was, but it wasn't clear—all the boys were smirking, holding back laughter. A few girls stood with them, too, also smirking, giving each other cruelly knowing looks—including, Kathleen was fairly sure, Bella and Ella.

"This isn't a joke!" an amplified voice said.

Kathleen turned back around. It was Aggie—sounding suddenly much older. Her face had changed; she still looked scared but at the same time resolute. She clenched the bullhorn so tightly, her knuckles strained at her skin.

" 'This isn't a joke!' " came a boy's mocking falsetto again, a little more muted now.

Aggie lifted the stack of flyers she was still holding, let out a shuddering breath, and began to read: " 'Menstrual injustice is a global problem. It's not just here in Greenchester, or in the United States!' " The crowd had quieted a little bit, and a pair of earnest-looking girls to Kathleen's left were listening, nodding.

" 'Around the world,' " Aggie went on, " 'women and girls are prosecuted when they have their periods!' " (*Persecuted,* Kathleen thought. But who cared?) " 'As feminists and feminist allies, we owe it to our sisters across the globe to fight against this injustice and make periods something to be proud of.' "

"She probably doesn't even get her period," a girl just behind Kathleen said. "She looks, like, seven."

"I know, right?" said another.

Kathleen turned and locked eyes with one of the girls—the prettiest of them all, though pretty in the way of a diamond: sharply cut and colorless. Like her mother, who Kathleen was now quite certain was Margaret Foster. "Will you shut the hell up and listen?" Kathleen said. "Or leave."

The girl's jaw dropped open.

One of her friends said, "Oh, my god."

A couple of boys snorted.

Kathleen turned back around to Aggie, regret snaking its way up her spine. What had she just done? With a few impulsive words, she'd probably just signed Aggie up for a year's worth of taunting and bullying and stink eyes. Maybe longer. *Fuck.*

"If you have questions about menstruation," Aggie was saying, "don't be afraid or ashamed to ask." She was ad-libbing now, it seemed. But she was pulling it off—beautifully. Kathleen felt a brief instinctive pang of a wish that Bill were here to see it. She had loved those times when they would sit side by side in darkened auditoriums, a current of pride running between them as they watched Aggie at flute recitals and school concerts and moving-on ceremonies.

It would never happen again, Kathleen thought bitterly. And if Bill *were* here, though he would without a doubt be proud of Aggie on some level, he would also be worrying about how her involvement in this whole circus would affect his poll numbers. Asshole.

"Learn the facts," Aggie was saying. "Share them. Do what you can to make sure that menstrual products are available to everyone. Think globally and act locally!"

A cheer went up, and Aggie smiled, reddening as she did. "Yes we bleed!" she said, and a small but enthusiastic portion of the crowd began to chant: "Yes we bleed! Yes we bleed!"

Kathleen braced herself for a sarcastic rendition of the chant from behind her, but it didn't come; the mean girls were gone, and the boys now appeared to be playing some kind of game that involved shoving each other as hard as possible and yelling, "Yeet!"

Aggie handed the bullhorn back to Melissa and then trotted down the steps to Kathleen, full-on smiling at her for the first time since their argument in Washington. "What did you think?" she said.

Kathleen recognized the exhilaration in Aggie's voice—the same she'd felt in her own after she spoke at the DC rally.

"You were fantastic," Kathleen said. "I'm just sorry that some of the kids here in front were being such jerks. All that mocking—it's just their own insecurity. You know that, right? The truth is, you're going to end up having an amazing, interesting life, and those kids are going to end up exactly like their parents. Boring and full of themselves."

Aggie shrugged. "Whatever. I don't really care that much what they think. I mean, I sort of do, I guess. But I have my own friends."

Kathleen stood taking Aggie in for a moment. She seemed so calm. So placid. So securely anchored to *something* (what was it?) that was keeping her from being thrown off-balance by the judgment of her peers. Surely on some level it must have bothered Aggie more than she was letting on. (It *had* to, didn't it?) But if that was the case, she was managing it miraculously well for a seventh grader.

An idea struck Kathleen. "Do you need to stick around for the rest of the event? Or do you want to play hooky?"

"Hooky?"

"Take the rest of the day off. We could go get lunch at the Cheesecake Factory. You could even come with me to my photo shoot this afternoon. It could be fun for you to see how that kind of thing works. Look, they made me paint my nails this crazy color." She wiggled her fingers—"Code Red!" the color was called—for Aggie to see. She actually sort of loved the way it looked.

"I'll get in trouble," Aggie said, though Kathleen could tell she was excited about the idea. "Maybe just lunch? And then I can come back in time for block six."

"What's block six?"

"Orchestra."

"Deal," said Kathleen.

Together they made their way through the crowd. Just as they reached the parking lot, there was a swell of noise and cheering behind them. Simultaneously, Kathleen and Aggie turned back to see why: Kia and Lucy had set the trash can full of feminine hygiene supplies ablaze. The band was now playing "Burn, Baby, Burn," and kids in the crowd were digging in their purses and backpacks, pulling out tampons and pads—along with sheets of crumpled-up notebook paper and various individually packaged snack foods—and tossing them toward the flaming trash cans. Kia and Lucy gathered them up and added them to the rapidly growing fire.

Kia took the bullhorn from Melissa and yelled into it, "Today we burn the pay-tarchie!" She raised a copy of *Are You There God? It's Me, Margaret* aloft, then tossed it into the fire while Melissa glared at her, then attempted to wrest the bullhorn back out of her hands.

Seconds later, the principal burst through the front doors of the school, wielding a fire extinguisher. But the flames were shooting six feet in the air now, and a toxic burned-rubber smell had started emanating from the trash can.

A couple of teachers rushed the steps, trying to usher the kids away from the flames.

Meanwhile, the older woman in the bodysuit—who, Kathleen noticed now, bore a strong resemblance to Antoinette—continued to dance furiously nearby, whirling and waving her arms overhead as if to simulate flame, while a couple of the boys from before mimicked her openly. (This time, Kathleen had to admit, she was on their side.)

Aggie stood watching, transfixed by the whole calamity, her mouth a small sad line. "They're never going to give us free stuff in the bathrooms now," she said.

"I don't know about that," said Kathleen. She watched the principal go at the trash can with the fire extinguisher while someone who appeared to be a custodian took swipes at floating embers with a wet mop. "They might."

Fire trucks and a pair of squad cars were pulling up, along with the News Team Five van, and Kathleen was struck with a queasy sense of déjà vu.

"Look," Kathleen said, "you don't have to stay involved with the

Yes We Bleed Club if it doesn't feel right anymore. I mean, things are clearly getting . . ."

"Stupid," said Aggie. "They're getting stupid."

"Yeah. They kind of are. Who's the dancer?" The woman in the bodysuit was now whirling around, hands over her head and crossed at the wrists as if manacled.

"Melissa's grandmother. Antoinette invited her. She's been kind of bossy. Antoinette, I mean. And Melissa has, too. Plus, she and Kia are always fighting all the time. Lucy and me—sorry, Lucy and *I*—were thinking maybe we could do some stuff on our own. Writing letters to Congress and stuff."

"That sounds great," said Kathleen. "And you could . . . oh, shit." Emerging from the news van was the same reporter who had stood in her driveway the morning after the fire, now in a dress a suspiciously menstrual shade of burgundy.

"Mom!" Aggie scolded.

"I mean *shoot*."

"Kat Anderson Held!" the reporter yelled. She gestured frantically to a bearded cameraman and his assistant, who had begun setting up their gear nearby. "Cammie Carlisle from News Team Five! Do you approve of youth arson as a tactic in the Yes We Bleed movement?"

"Let's go," said Aggie as the trio speed-walked toward them. "You can just tell them no."

"Kat!" the reporter said again. They were only a few yards away now, advancing fast. "What about your feud with the controversial author Danica Bellevue?"

"Mom," Aggie said. "Come on!"

Kathleen couldn't believe that the local network affiliate had picked up on the Danica story. Then again, of course she could. "This will only take a second," she told Aggie. "I just have to talk to them about something that happened." In spite of her successful denial of any ties to Danica, it couldn't hurt to reemphasize the fact that they weren't friends. And then she could change the narrative—bring it back to her support of Yes We Bleed and youth activism. (But not youth arson.) "Go wait in the car," she told Aggie, digging in her purse for her keys. She was about to hand them to Aggie, but Aggie had already turned her back and was walking away, into the crowd of spectators.

"Kat! Just a few quick questions?"

Kathleen turned to face Cammie Carlisle and put on her brightest smile. "Of course. Mind if I just touch up my lipstick?"

When she had finished the interview a mere five minutes later, the crowd was dispersing, the smoke from the flaming trash barrel was dissipating, and Aggie was nowhere in sight.

When Kathleen got home from her afternoon clutching Finnish feminine hygiene products (along with various fruits, for some reason) for *Very Ardent Woman!*, she found Aggie in her room, the classical station playing on her clock radio, reading an old copy of *Ms.* Magazine—presumably something Antoinette had given her.

"Hi," Kathleen said.

"Hi," said Aggie.

"You know, if you'd waited five minutes, we could have gone to lunch. It was pretty rude of you to just take off like that."

Aggie shrugged and turned a page of her magazine. "It was pretty rude of you to talk to those reporters."

"I know you've been frustrated by all the publicity I've been doing," said Kathleen. "And I understand. I really do. I know I haven't been around as much. That's why I invited you to come with me to the party the other night. And to my shoot with *Very Ardent Woman!*"

"Who?"

"It's a Finnish magazine. But the thing with the News Team Five people—I just needed to clear up a misperception that's been going around. It took *literally* five minutes."

Aggie lowered her magazine to her lap. "What misperception?"

"The misperception that I'm friends with a woman named Danica

Bellevue. An author. Who said some not-very-nice things about her readers. That they were fat and Midwestern."

"Why is that mean? There's nothing wrong with being fat. You're kind of body-shaming."

"No, *I'm* not. But this woman Danica meant it in a fat-shaming way. And that's why I can't have people thinking I'm friends with her."

Aggie frowned. "So she never said she was sorry?"

"She did, but not well. It's complicated."

"You say everything is complicated."

"Well, it is."

Aggie went back to her magazine.

And here they were again. That brief, lovely moment after Aggie's speech was just that: a brief moment.

It seemed there was nothing Kathleen could say to get unstuck from this—Aggie being constantly disappointed in her, not understanding how complex it was to be a public figure and a spokesperson for a cause. It was always and only Bill in that role before. Kathleen couldn't blame Aggie for having a hard time adjusting to it all. But she also didn't know how to fix it. Maybe this was one of those parenting moments where she just had to let it be for now.

"I'm going to order some pizza," Kathleen said. "Maybe we can watch something later while we eat."

"Yeah, okay," Aggie said. "I guess that would be nice."

Downstairs in the kitchen, Kathleen opened her laptop and searched for mentions of her name online.

She was relieved to see that any speculation as to whether she and Danica were friends seemed to have fizzled out, thanks in part to the fact that Danica had done exactly what Jonathan had said she would: in a video interview with an online pop culture magazine, she said that Yes We Bleed activists were a bunch of "hysterical, hormonal harpies with far too much time on their hands." She'd also tweeted:

> Menstruation is the absolute least interesting thing about being a woman, and menopause is the least pleasant of all—please, ladies, can we move on?

Meanwhile, Kathleen's tweet distancing herself from Danica was up to twelve thousand retweets, and a clip from her interview with Cammie Carlisle had gone viral—specifically the part when Cammie had asked her if she was friends with Danica and Kathleen had replied, "Dear god, no." (#DearGodNo didn't seem to be getting the same traction as #UmYeahNo, but it got a decent amount of use nevertheless.)

Kathleen felt a sense of both accomplishment and relief: she'd done it. Her image was intact, and she was back on top, in control.

When the pizza came, she and Aggie sat side by side at the kitchen island eating, and then settled in on the sofa in their pajamas. Aggie's mood seemed to have improved slightly, to the point where she had even laughed at Kathleen's imitation of Antoinette's mother's interpretative dance.

They watched a new reality competition show that Aggie chose, in which contestants vied to see who could minimize their carbon footprint the most over the course of a week. It was only mildly entertaining—there wasn't anything that exciting about turning off lights and buying spices in bulk, although the host, a puckish Brit with a nose ring, did her best to make it seem *brill*iant, by saying "*brill*iant" a lot. Kathleen suspected that the show wouldn't last more than a season. But Aggie liked it. And Kathleen was enjoying the cozy normalcy of the evening far too much to care about what, in particular, they were watching. She even felt less hostile than usual toward the canvas print on the wall over the television, which read IT'S THE SIMPLE THINGS. Because it really was, wasn't it? Plus, in the past two hours she hadn't once been tempted to pick up her phone. Not even with it lying right there on the coffee table in front of her, just a few feet away. She was proud of herself.

But then, the commercial.

"Look! It's Nugget!" Aggie exclaimed.

A sonorous male voice-over boomed from the TV. "You've heard of dogs making heroic rescues. Now get ready to see what happens when the tables are turned and it's the pooches that are in peril!"

And there on-screen was Frank Martello, the taxi driver, with Nugget in his arms. Cheerful music with perky ukulele strumming played in the background. "This is the little guy who made me realize that rescuing dogs is my calling," Frank said to the camera. Next, there was a shot of Nugget running down the stairs of Kathleen's former house to Bill, who was squatting down on his haunches and holding up a treat.

She couldn't fucking believe it. She knew that Bill was willing to do just about anything for the sake of his career. But she *never* would have thought he would sink to this.

On the TV, Nugget yapped in his singular shivery way, and then the film cut to a shot of a dog who wasn't Nugget at all, just another Yorkshire terrier that closely resembled him, except for the fact that he had two eyes, not one (as if nobody would notice) standing adorably up on his hind legs and twirling around—something Nugget had never done in his life.

The voice-over came back: "Hear the heartwarming story of how this captivating one-eyed Yorkie came into Senate candidate Bill Held's life." And there was Bill, sitting at the kitchen table. "The shelter told us he'd been overlooked for weeks, because of his eye," Bill said. "But when our daughter and I saw him, we just instantly fell in love."

Then, the music turned ominous, and the voice-over said, "See what happened the night of Nugget's dramatic rescue . . ." The film turned to black and white, and then Frank Martello burst out of a door—which wasn't actually their front door—smoke billowing behind him, the Nugget stand-in in his arms. (*Dramatic reenactment* read a caption in the lower right of the screen.) The music turned bright again: "Meet the Dog Rescuer's twin brother, Dominic, and find out how to minimize safety hazards in your home"—the announcer continued over a shot of Frank's brother, in firefighting garb, changing the battery of a smoke detector—"and hear the shocking revelations!" Now the film cut to Bill at the patio table, Frank Martello next to him. The shot was composed such that the swing set and the playhouse, which Aggie never used anymore, were visible in the background.

"Was your wife, Kathleen, close with Nugget?" Frank asked.

A slight wistful smile appeared on Bill's face as Frank said it, and Kathleen wondered if he was thinking about all the times he used to tease her about her lack of ardor for Nugget—and how she teased him back. *Your soul mate pooped on the floor again.*

But then Bill said, flat and matter-of-fact as could be: "No, they weren't close at all. Just the opposite, actually. Kathleen found Nugget annoying." The camera zoomed in on him. "The truth is, she was never really a dog person. She wanted cats." There was a record scratch sound, and then the film cut to Frank looking gobsmacked.

"*Cats?*" he said.

The final shot was of Frank holding Nugget overhead like baby Simba in *The Lion King*. "Don't miss *The Dog Rescuer*!" the voice-over boomed. "Next!"

Kathleen's entire body throbbed. She clutched the nearest throw pillow so hard her fingernails hurt.

"Can we watch it?" Aggie asked.

"You go ahead," said Kathleen, straining to sound like a calm, stable adult person. "I need to make a quick phone call."

"How could you *possibly* agree to be on that asinine show?"

Kathleen paced the lamplit roads of the condo complex, an enormous glass of wine in one hand, her phone in the other. It had taken four attempts in a row, but finally Bill had answered his phone. "And what the fuck, I wanted cats? No, I didn't!" (She had wanted *a* cat, singular.)

"I didn't exactly want to go on it, either, Kathleen," Bill said. "Or *Kat*, or whoever the hell you are. But at this point, I need to do whatever it takes to rehab my image and stay competitive in this race."

"Oh? And how exactly does this help your image?" It seemed to her that, if anything, it would remind people of the fact that he'd cheated.

"People like dogs," said Bill. "And they like people who like dogs."

"People are already well aware you have a dog."

"Well, we're reminding them," Bill intoned bitterly. "Because every day you're out there being everyone's glamorous feminist superhero, reminding them that I'm an asshole, is a day I'm losing points in the polls."

Kathleen found Nugget annoying. She was never really a dog person. She wanted cats. He'd been jabbing at her, trying to paint her (and, by extension, all Yes We Bleed supporters) as bitchy, dog-hating, crazy cat ladies, while making himself look like a wholesome, disabled-dog-loving everyman. It was beyond infuriating.

"I haven't said a single disparaging thing about you," said Kathleen. "In fact, I've bent over backward *not* to." It was true. Danica had even helped her come up with the perfect quip for when hosts or interviewers persisted in asking her about Bill's infidelity: *If you don't mind, I'd prefer to talk about something a little less personal—like my period.* Though at this very moment, she was wishing she *had* ripped Bill a new one on national TV.

She had reached the road that abutted the riverbank. She stepped onto the grass and scanned the reeds for Sonny and Cher, thinking, absurdly, that they would be on her side in this argument with Bill. But if they were there, they were well hidden.

"Three words," said Bill. "Um, yeah, no."

"It was an answer to a question," said Kathleen. "And I could have said a lot worse."

"And you probably will, sooner or later, on your infinite press junket. I mean, Jesus, are you ever even at home for Aggie? And thanks a lot, by the way, for letting her get involved in all this Yes We Bleed bullshit."

"I'm home enough. And I had to let her get involved. It was the right thing to do. She's passionate about it."

Bill emitted a dry laugh. "Well, that makes one of you, at least."

"Excuse me?" Some large prehistoric-looking insect landed on Kathleen's arm, and she jerked it away, sending her wine sloshing.

"You can't tell me you're actually as into the whole thing as you pretend to be. For as long as I've known you, you've never gotten involved with feminist causes. And now, all of a sudden, you do?"

"Yes. I do. And I've always been a feminist." Maybe she didn't go around wearing a *This Is What a Feminist Looks Like* T-shirt à la Antoinette. But she'd marched in Take Back the Night rallies in college; she'd signed petitions for equal pay. And she'd sure as hell bristled every time she was introduced as Mrs. William Held. Bill knew all that.

"Not like this. This is not your style."

"Maybe my style is changing."

Bill scoffed. "Whatever it is, you're obviously doing it to get back at me."

"No, I'm not," Kathleen said. "I'm really not." It was true. Whatever tiny soupçon of revenge (as Danica put it) there might be in all this, it was just that: tiny. Bill may have been the catalyst, but he wasn't the point.

Bill ignored her. "Honestly, Kath, I'm impressed. You're doing a bang-up job. Maybe you should run for office."

There was a guttural honk from the reeds.

"Maybe you should fuck a swan."

"What?"

"I don't know. Never mind." The wine was making her head feel heavy, and the dampness of the grass was starting to soak through her espadrilles. "You really, truly think everything is about you, don't you?"

Bill seemed about to say something but stopped himself. "Bye, Kathleen," he said. "Tell Aggie I love her."

The line went dead.

Kathleen let the last of her wine dribble onto the pavement. "Asshole," she muttered.

Wearily, she opened Twitter and searched for "The Dog Rescuer." Already, it had begun.

She clicked on her messaging app and texted a single word to Jonathan. *Help.*

Kelsee & Kiki's Endless Adventures

Voted #1 pet lifestyle blog two years in a row (Squee!)

NEW POST:

Frisco, Pink Sneaks, and *The Dog Rescuer*

If you follow Kiki and me on TikTok, you know that yesterday we were exploring the sights, sounds, and tastes of San Francisco. Can you believe it was our first visit?! The weather was just right for my favorite pink suede sneaks—comfy shoes are a MUST for long days of walking, you guys—cropped mom jeans, and a slouchy jacket. (Pics below!) Naughty Kiki, as usual, preferred to go in her birthday suit, but wore her pink collar to match my shoes, because she's sweet like that. We spent a long day walking the famous hills (Hello, glutes!), riding the trolley, snapping pics of the Golden Gate, browsing boutiques, and sampling tasty bites at not one but *three* amazing dog treat bakeries. By six we were both exhausted. A cozy night at our suite back at the Fairmont was just the thing, and I invited my college bestie Sam and my cousin Maddye over for French 75s, Thai street food from Bangkok Johnnie's, room service ice cream—Kiki likes strawberry—and the series premiere of *The Dog Rescuer*.

Oh my god, you guys. Did you watch it? Things I loved: The star of the show, Nugget, obviously (Spoiler alert: SOME-BODY might be having a playdate with that cutie in the very near future . . .). The Dog Rescuer's twin brother, the firefighter, just because. And—don't kill me—Bill Held. As you know, Kiki and I don't like to get political, but we DO pay attention to the news, and we did NOT heart Bill Held. I won't get into it, but let's just say . . . I am *not* a fan of guys who cheat, and neither is Kiki. After watching the show, though, and seeing Bill Held with that cutie-pie rescue pup he adopted even though he's visually challenged, I don't think he's so bad. (Also, is it just me or is he kind of dreamy in a cute dad sort of way?? Kiki thinks so, anyway.)

But the part of the show that made me SO angry and sad and all the other feels was finding out that Kat Anderson Held doesn't like her dog or dogs in general. Kiki was so offended she sulked for the rest of the night—100% not kidding!! I was firmly on #Team-Kat ever since a certain photo went viral a few weeks ago. I don't consider myself a feminist with a capital F, but I'm totally pro Yes We Bleed. (Exhibit A: Kiki's and my matching Angora Menstrual Cup hats from Cycle Chic on Etsy.) Like so many people, I thought Kat Anderson Held was so fab. And can we talk about that adorbs jacket she wore at the Yes We Bleed rally in DC? But I was mega disappointed after I watched *The Dog Rescuer* premiere last night. Kiki and I have no problem with people who prefer cats, but "Kats" who don't like their own dog (Aren't I clever?), especially when he has a disability, are another thing.

So that's my rant. And if you're feeling like Kiki and me do, you can do what we did and donate to the Visually Impaired Pet Rescue Organization (VIPRO). And, if you're feeling political-ish, to the Bill Held for Senate Campaign. (No shade to my Republican fans. Love you too!!)

Then, don't forget to reward yourself with a little something special from San Fran, like a treat for your pooch from <u>Cookie Cur</u>
<u>Vegan Dog Bakery and Café</u> or, for you, the limited-edition super-
soft pima cotton Fairy Dog Mother T-shirt I'm wearing in the pic
below, <u>$99 at Kārpāsa</u> in Union Square. Both available on their
websites.

Happy Adventures, you guys, and be sure to check back in a
couple of days for deets and pics from our next trip: Dubrovnik!
(Kiki is practicing her Croatian. She already knows how to say
"woof"!)

Day Twenty-Five

Kathleen dragged herself out of bed and stood in front of her closet, trying to decide what to wear. She had a packed day ahead: a call-in interview with a public radio show in Seattle; a visit to a "feminist memory-care retirement home," whatever that was (a retirement home for women who had forgotten they were feminists?); and then a visit to an animal shelter that had invited her via Twitter the day before to spend a few hours with them and "see just how loving and loyal our canine guests are."

But all she really wanted to do was sleep. She'd spent most of the previous day dealing with the fallout of the *Dog Rescuer* premiere, and she was exhausted. Predictably, there had been a large contingent, including several prominent dogs-of-Instagram influencers and the past season's winner of *The Bachelor*, who lamented Kathleen's alleged distaste for dogs. Sorry, but you can't trust people who don't like dogs, the *Bachelor* winner wrote. That's just a fact.

A screen grab of one family snapshot that had appeared on *The*

Dog Rescuer, of Aggie and Bill playing with Nugget together, was making the rounds online, with comments like Hmm . . . who's missing from the photo? It took all Kathleen's willpower not to tweet: I AM MISSING BECAUSE I WAS TAKING THE GODDAMNED PICTURE.

But mostly it was Bill she was angry at, not the idiots who were clucking their tongues at her terrible, unforgivable sin of not being a dog person. Pundits were speculating that Bill's *Dog Rescuer* appearance might represent a turning point in his candidacy, earning him enough favor in the polls to lift him up into a safe margin of victory over Kürt Krÿer.

On the other hand, there were plenty of people who saw through Bill's pandering to the dog-loving public—including some key Yes We Bleed figures. Emma Hancock tweeted:

> Wow @BillHeld4Senate. Way to throw @KatAndersonHeld under the bus. Kat, we love you whether you're a cat person, a dog person, or neither! Xoxo #YesWeBleed #TeamKat

Meanwhile, the cat community quickly rallied behind Kathleen (#Cats4Kat). Women and teenage girls posted selfies of themselves in their Yes We Bleed T-shirts and hats, adding photo filters that made them look like they had cat faces—an even more unfortunate trend than the earlier spate of cat-ear postings. (Why did these women insist on setting themselves—and by extension, the whole movement—up for mockery?) Kathleen had even gotten an inquiry from *Modern Cat* magazine, proposing that she appear on the cover, holding "the cat of her choice." They wanted to do a menstruation-related tie-in story: "10 Ways to Help When Your Cat Is in Heat (#1: Get Them Spayed!)." She considered doing it, but there were enough people in the pro-dog camp caricaturing her as a crazy cat lady, as she'd predicted, that she decided to say no.

"Prudent choice," Danica had said when Kathleen told her about it.

Kathleen's annoyance with Danica still hadn't abated completely, but it was a relief to have her reassuring, two-steps-ahead advice as Kathleen navigated this stupid situation.

"Pet magazines are very déclassé," Danica said. "More to the point, you need to tread very carefully with this whole matter. Animals . . . they always complicate things."

"Shouldn't I say or do something, though?" Kathleen had asked. "I hate the idea of people thinking I'm some kind of coldhearted, dog-hating bitch. I'm really not." (Except when it came to Nugget, sort of.)

"I know," Danica had said. "And you know I'm all about regaining control of conversations. But in this case, with an issue as charged as cats versus dogs, your best move—for the moment, at least—is to stay mum and let the dog and cat people tear each other apart."

And by the end of the day, per Danica's prediction, they were, with glee. CNN kept track of the number of pro-dog versus pro-cat tweets, updating it on an hourly basis. (Cats maintained a slight, consistent edge, though many dismissed this as being the result of Russian trolls tasked with sowing dissent.) An LA-based designer was selling limited-edition T-shirts on his website that read either *CATS* or *DOGS* in black 288-point Helvetica for $69 each, pledging to donate 10 percent of the profits to the ASPCA. *What better cats or dogs?* was, for a short time, the tenth-most-searched phrase on Google.

By the time the tweet from the animal shelter came in late afternoon, inviting Kat for a visit, the cat versus dog debate seemed to have taken on such a life of its own, well beyond the matter of Kat versus Bill, that Kathleen had wondered whether she should even bother accepting. Plus, there'd been a magnitude 8.2 earthquake in Guatemala, where, as it turned out, Brad Pitt was shooting a movie; for several hours, while the world waited with bated breath for news of his condition (#WheresBrad), the volume of cat and dog content dropped nearly to zero. So was it really necessary for Kathleen to go to a shelter and glad-hand a bunch of dogs? Wouldn't it just restart the whole stupid cats-and-dogs conversation? And what if it backfired and people started accusing *her* of pandering the same way that Bill had? Coming off as sleazy and calculating would not be good either for her or for Yes We Bleed. Already, there were plenty of skeptics, with some people questioning whether the movement would actually change attitudes long-term or lead to any substantive changes—like those free menstrual supplies everyone kept talking about—or was destined to be (as a male writer on *Salon* put it) just a "flash in the pan(ties)."

But Danica advised Kathleen to go ahead and do the animal shelter visit anyway, just to be safe. "It's image insurance, if you will," she'd explained. "Jonathan will courier over some legal papers for the shelter people to sign, stipulating under penalty of monstrous litigation that only your official photographer may take or release photographs of you."

"Who's my official photographer?"

"Jonathan, obviously!" said Danica. "He has one of those little vests with all the pockets in it—it's adorable. And he has quite the impressive camera." She pretended to clear her throat suggestively, as if she'd just made a double entendre, though if she had, Kathleen wasn't quite sure what it was. "He'll take pictures of you with both dogs *and* cats," Danica continued. "And ferrets and guinea pigs and whatever other foul creatures they keep around there. Do they have birds? Birds aren't so terrible, are they? In any case, you'll have the pictures, and if it looks like it would behoove you to release them and show everyone that you're the second coming of Doctor Dolittle, you will, and if everyone has already moved on to something else, you won't. Got it?"

"Got it," Kathleen had said, and tapped out a tweet in reply to the animal shelter invitation:

> Loving and loyal? Sounds like your canine guests could teach
> @BillHeld4Senate a thing or two. (And, yes, I'd be honored
> to visit. Tell me when and where!) #TeamCats #TeamDogs
> #YesWeBleed

This was, predictably, retweeted and liked thousands upon thousands of times by dog and cat lovers alike. Yes We Bleed diehards on social media loved it, too, to Kathleen's relief:

> Love that @KatAndersonHeld is being such a great sport about
> this dog/cat dust-up.

> Animal dignity + Menstrual Rights = Proof that #YesWeBleed
> has evolved into a truly intersectional movement.

Kathleen felt as if she'd dodged a bullet. But the whole thing still left her feeling bruised, off-balance. How many more times would she have to do this? First the Elitist Bitch, now dogs and cats, for god's sake. What next? She had learned to do the dance well, at least; that much she knew. But she was getting weary. She couldn't keep up this pace. She knew she needed to be spending more time with Aggie, too. Though the two of them had seemed to have reached some kind of détente, Kathleen knew it was a fragile one.

Everything felt fragile right now.

The Women of America Conference was in a few days. After that, Kathleen decided, she would take a step back from the limelight to recharge: a little mid-reap *re*prieve. She would have to buckle down and start working on her book anyway—she intended to collaborate closely with the ghostwriter, whoever she might turn out to be, Theo Balbakis be damned.

Until then, however, she had no choice but to keep forging ahead.

She finally decided on an outfit that she thought would work for visits to both elderly feminists and shelter animals—a jewel-green knit top with a subtle stripe and a draped neckline, along with a pair of fake-fur-cuffed Finnish designer jeans the *Very Ardent Woman!* people had let her keep after the shoot. She lay them out on the bed and was just about to head for the shower when she heard Aggie's voice outside her bedroom door.

"Mom?" Aggie said. "There's a policeman downstairs."

The officer at the door was short, stocky, and chubby cheeked, with ears that protruded dramatically from beneath his cap, giving him the look of an overgrown, avuncular mouse. "Kat Held?" he said. "You got some weirdos here who are pretty ticked off at you." He thumbed over his shoulder.

Kathleen couldn't believe what she saw: three squad cars were parked at the curb of her pod of condos, and about a dozen people were standing and milling around on the sidewalk. Several were dressed as what appeared to be swans, with huge white paper-and-feather wings and bulbous papier-mâché heads and beaks. An officer had one swan person pinned against the side of his car and was attempting to put plastic zip tie handcuffs on them while trying to avoid getting a wing in his face. Another officer was chasing a bearded middle-aged swan who was flapping his wings and making honking noises. The non-swans stood cheering on the bearded swan, hoisting the signs they held up and down. KAT HELD = SWAN KILLER and SWAN BLOOD MATTERS. In the midst of it all was, to Kathleen's astonishment, Antoinette's mother—this time in a tutu and a white feathered tiara. When she saw Kathleen, she wagged a finger at her, shouted, "Shame!" and then began to do pirouettes.

"We'll get these guys out of here," the officer said. "But you might want to take some extra precautions for the next few days. Keep the doors and windows locked while you're home. Curtains closed. Don't open the door for anyone you don't know. And call us if you see or hear anything unusual or need an escort out of here, all right?"

"What is this?" Kathleen asked. "Why are they here?"

"Tree huggers," the cop said. "Well, swan huggers. Invasive species sympathizers, I call 'em. Did you know that a hundred and fifty years ago there were no mute swans in the US? None. They were all imported here by foreigners." He shook his head in disgust.

Now Kathleen realized who these people were: the Friends of the Millstone River. The ones who had tried to stop the condo complex from being built. "How did they know I was here?"

The cop reached into the pocket of his windbreaker and handed her a folded newspaper. "Don't you read the *Gazette*?"

"Sometimes." Kathleen took the newspaper.

"'Sometimes,'" the cop said. "This is why print journalism is dying."

Behind him, the bearded swan had been wrestled to the ground and was shouting something about the Geneva conventions. A few neighbors had arrived on the scene and were snapping pictures and taking videos with their phones. A gaunt, bespectacled man with a sandwich board sign that read JESUS IS LORD. REPENT! over a scene of a fiery hellscape had also wandered in from somewhere and stood at the edge of the assemblage, looking lost.

"Chuck!" one of the other officers called. "I need backup out here."

"Ah, shit," said the officer at the door. He started to go, then stopped and gave Kathleen a crooked little smile. "That's pretty funny about your doorbell, by the way."

"My doorbell?"

"The song." He rang the bell again and pointed upward, as if the haunting melody it played were issuing from the sky. "You don't recognize it?"

And all at once, Kathleen did: the theme from *Swan Lake*.

The officer swaggered off, and Kathleen locked and dead-bolted the door behind him. Then she sat at the kitchen island and read the front-page story of the *Gazette*.

Wife of Bill Held Found to Be Living in an Illegal Airbnb at Controversial Millstone River Complex

JACK URCHEK,
STAFF REPORTER AND EDITOR IN CHIEF

Greenchester – Three years ago, the town of Greenchester was rocked by a large and epic division when the luxurious Millstone River Residences complex was developed on the tranquil banks of the Millstone River, endangering a pair of two swans that came to be known as Sunny and Share, along with many other animals and ecosystems. Being as the spacious town house–style condominiums were built anyway, they were quickly occupied with residents.

(Kathleen paused and picked up a pen. She couldn't help herself; it was so abysmally written, it physically hurt her not to make notations and corrections.)

One of those residents, our sources revealed, is Kathleen "Kat" Anderson Held, wife of US Senate candidate and long-time Greenchester resident Bill Held. For approximately three weeks, Mrs. Held and her daughter have been residing in a condo belonging to local real estate agent Nancy Doyle, which is being operated as an Airbnb, in defiance of the condo association's strict rules and regulations.

Edie Cabot, founder and president of the Friends of the Millstone River, the organization that led the protesting of the building of the condominiums, including a sit-in at the town hall, said, "I am disappointed to learn that an activist like Kathleen Held is contributing to the decimation of a river ecosystem." Ms. Cabot added that her organization also disapproves of Bill Held's past use of plastic straws and soft drink cup lids.

The *Gazette* reached out to Kathleen Anderson Held, Bill Held and Nancy Doyle for this story, but they were unavailable for commenting.

"They did not reach out to me!" Kathleen said aloud, half to herself and half to Aggie, who had come and stood at her side to read the paper.

Then she remembered: one of the dozens of emails she'd received since *The Dog Rescuer* had, in fact, been from a Jack something, but she'd had no idea who he was, and the subject had been something about animal welfare, so she'd ignored it, assuming he was yet another militant dog person.

"I don't understand," Aggie said. "Why are we living here if this condo is bad for the environment? Did you know?"

Aggie had only been eight during the controversy, and clearly she didn't remember—in spite of the fact that her teacher at the time, who was vocally anti-condo, had enlisted the entire third grade to badly fold hundreds of origami swans that she sprinkled over the steps of the town hall.

"Yes," Kathleen told Aggie, "I knew." She watched as her daughter's face, once again, clouded with disappointment. Why did this keep happening? Bill was the one who cheated, and yet she, Kathleen, was the one who seemed to be letting Aggie down over and over and over. It wasn't fair, dammit. "I needed a place for us to go," she said, "and I needed it fast. It just happened." (*Just. Just.*) "And the swans are fine. You've seen them out there."

"Just because they're *alive* doesn't mean they're fine! Or happy!"

"Aggie, look, those people out there are—" Kathleen was interrupted by a loud *smack* against the kitchen window, so sudden and violent that both she and Aggie instinctively dropped to the floor, Aggie emitting a short, sharp scream as she did.

"It's okay! We're okay," Kathleen said, putting her hand to Aggie's back.

When she rose slowly to her feet, she could see that the window was splattered with what looked like lumpy brown-green mud: swan shit.

Outside there was shouting, and then a voice through a loud-speaker: "IF YOU STRUGGLE, YOU WILL BE CHARGED WITH RESISTING ARREST."

Kathleen was about to tell Aggie to go upstairs to her room, but Aggie was already on her way, moving fast. Kathleen slid to the floor and sat there with her back to the refrigerator, knees bent, head buried in her arms, heart thumping.

She had brought this upon them—made a stupid spur-of-the moment decision to accept Nancy's offer because it was the easiest thing to do, without even considering the fact that it might come back to haunt her. Never even *dreaming* that it might lead to Aggie feeling terror and fear. She thought of Cindy from the society, her children cowering while animal rights activists invaded their ranch. Would Kathleen have to do what she had? Take her child and hide somewhere?

She lifted her head from her arms, her dismay hardening to anger. She hadn't shot or tortured or so much as illegally tossed bread crusts to the goddamned swans. It wasn't her fault that the condo complex had been built—and if she had refused on principle to live here, it wasn't as if the place would have been somehow *un*built.

She was about to go up to Aggie when the doorbell played *Swan Lake* again.

The officer from before stepped inside. He assured Kathleen that the last of the swan activists had been moved off the property and that the thrower of the swan shit had been apprehended. "Guy's got a record a mile long," the officer said. "All of it involving animal excrement."

He told Kathleen they'd have an officer stick around for a few hours, and then come through periodically after that. "But," he said, "you might want to consider hiring some private security. Or get out of here for a few days, if you can. If it were me here with my kid, I would." He paused, and something seemed to catch his eye. He took a step off the path, toward the swan poop–splattered window, and frowned at it. "Huh," he said, and took a step closer. "Son of a gun."

"What?" Kathleen, still in her robe, leaned out to see.

The officer smiled like he'd just remembered a good joke and shook his head. "It's not swan shit," he said. He called over his shoulder to one of the other cops: "Hey, Terry! You're right!"

"Told you," said Terry.

"If it's not swan shit, what is it?" asked Kathleen. It definitely looked like shit of some kind.

"It's Canada goose shit," said the officer, grinning. "You can tell from the color." He winked at Kathleen. "I owe Terry five bucks."

Kathleen found Aggie in her room, lying on her stomach on the floor, legs under her bed, torso out, reading. Kathleen was glad she was tucked safely there instead of on the window seat, which had become her usual perch.

Kathleen sat down on the floor beside her. "They're gone now. I don't think they're going to come back. Are you okay?" She brushed a strand of Aggie's hair behind her ear. "I'm sorry, sweetie. I'm so sorry. This is my fault."

Aggie didn't look up from her book.

"Can I see what you're reading?"

She tilted the cover up so Kathleen could see. *Little Women.*

"Aw, I read that to you when you were ten, remember?"

Aggie nodded.

"Things were simpler back then, weren't they?" She wasn't quite sure if she meant when Aggie was ten or the 1860s.

Aggie again nodded. Then she said, "I don't want to live here anymore." Kathleen could tell from the tightness of her voice that she was trying to hold back tears.

"No, I know," said Kathleen. "We won't. We'll find something else." *What* else, she had no idea. A shabby apartment in the water-stained apartment building in Rock Hill? Bobbie's guest room? Another Airbnb? The first installment of her advance from Gunther House would be coming soon enough, and it would be more than enough to get them settled somewhere decent—somewhere *not* in an ecological hot zone.

But what if Gunther House withdrew her deal? It was only a matter of time before news of her anti-swan residence went viral. She could practically see it in the distance—yet another wave of public scrutiny gathering itself up on the horizon, getting ready to crash on top of her and hold her under. (*Wildlife hater! Habitat destroyer! Luxury condo elitist!*) What if this time she couldn't fight her way back up to the surface again? Her WOA award would be withdrawn, her appearances canceled. She'd have to go back to slinking around in goggle glasses, living in a constant state of shame and dread and humiliation.

But she couldn't think about all that right now. She yanked her mind back to the matter at hand: she had to get herself and Aggie out of here.

"I was thinking we could go stay at a hotel for a few days," she said. "What do you think? A nice one. With a pool and everything. We'll check in as soon as we can, later this morning. You can skip school. You're late anyway, right? We'll swim and watch movies. It'll be fun."

"I can't skip," Aggie said. "I have a social studies test today. And a math quiz tomorrow." She slid herself out from under the bed and went to her closet.

"Okay, sure," said Kathleen, standing. "You're right. You should go." She would put a call in to the principal, make sure they were aware of the situation and would keep an eye out for any swan activists. The school, with its locked entrances and on-premises resource officer, was probably, in fact, the safest place Aggie could be. "I'll get us all set up at a hotel, and then after school—"

"No," Aggie said. She faced Kathleen. "After school, I want to go home. I don't want to live with you anymore." Her voice pinched itself closed until it was almost a whisper. "I'm sorry." She began pulling clothes from hangers, one thing after another, and tossing them to the bed.

"Oh, Aggie," Kathleen breathed.

She should have known this was coming. And though part of her wanted to say to Aggie, *This is your father's fault to begin with, don't you see?* she knew that Aggie was right. She didn't belong in a hotel right now, as shaken and afraid as she felt; she belonged in a home. Even if it was Bill's. Her room was there. Her dog was there. And, most important, she would be safe there. The place was alarmed to the hilt, and Bill was on a first-name basis with the entire Greenchester police department.

"Okay," she told Aggie.

"Okay?" Aggie seemed surprised.

"Yes. You shouldn't have to go hide in a hotel with me. You deserve to be at—" She stopped herself before saying "at home," because it implied that her former home was still hers, too. She needed to break herself of the habit. "In your own room."

"It doesn't mean I'm not still mad at him," Aggie said.

Kathleen was glad to hear this, though she knew she probably shouldn't be. "It's okay even if you're not." She managed a smile. "Your favorite dress," she said. Aggie was holding her dragonfly dress—the one she'd worn her first day of school.

Aggie pressed it to her chest. "You think it's weird, don't you."

"No," said Kathleen. "I think it looks beautiful on you. And I think you should wear whatever you want."

Kathleen dropped Aggie off at school, watching until she was safely inside, and then called Bill to let him know the situation.

When she told him about the protesters, the projectile goose shit, and how terrified Aggie was, he was furious. "We need to press charges," he said. "Harassment, destruction of private property . . . I'll call the chief right now."

"No, Bill, stop. Listen. I don't want to do that. I don't want this to turn into any more of a circus than it's already going to be. I'm fine. Aggie's fine. But she needs to stay with you for a while."

"Damn right she does!" Kathleen could imagine what Bill looked like as he said it, nostrils flared, fingertips raking his hair.

She closed her eyes. "I'm sorry," she said. "I really am. It never even occurred to me that something like this might happen."

"Yeah, well," said Bill with a sigh, "welcome to being a public figure." He sounded as exhausted as Kathleen felt.

Miraculously, by nine a.m. word of Kathleen's anti-swan residence still didn't seem to have spread. There were no swan-related inquiries on her radio interview, and the "coffee and fireside chat" (there was no fire) with the elderly feminists was uneventful, too. Several of the women fell asleep during her talk, and one soiled herself, as she announced loudly to the assembled group in the parlor, but Kathleen had been warned in advance not to take this sort of thing personally.

But when she got to the animal shelter for her I-have-no-problem-with-dogs photo op, the manager, a woman with the physique and the coiled-spring quality of a gymnast, took Kathleen into her tiny office, sat in a chair opposite her, propped her elbows on her knees, and said, "We have a problem, Kat."

"A problem?"

"It seems like there's a pattern here. Of animal disrespect."

Kathleen glanced up at Jonathan (in his multipocketed photographer's vest, as promised), who stood just inside the door. He was scrolling furiously through his phone, his features sharpening into an expression of extreme alarm. He'd been waiting for her in the lobby when she arrived, and she'd had only a moment to fill him in on the swan situation. He assured her that if the media hadn't pounced by now—it had been a full five hours—it was unlikely they would. "Swans are not well liked," he had said.

Clearly, he'd been wrong.

The manager sat back and lifted a palm. "Look, I get it. I'm not a bird person myself. That's not why I got into this business. And frankly, I'm happy for you to stay, walk around, meet some of our guests. I really am a fan of your work for *Yes We Bleed.*"

"But I'm going to have to ask that we keep this visit private. No photos." She looked at Jonathan. "No tweets, no media of any kind. We have a very strong reputation in the tristate area animal welfare community, and we can't jeopardize that with this whole swando situation." (She put air quotes around *swando*. So that's what people were calling it. Of course.) "You get it, right?"

Kathleen nodded meekly.

The manager gave the side of Kathleen's arm a vigorous whack. "Great," she said. "Let's go see some German shepherds."

When the manager ducked into a supply room for dog treats on their way toward the kennels, Kathleen whispered to Jonathan. "How bad is it?"

"It's bad," he said. "Just get this over with and then we'll strategize."

The manager emerged and pressed a few dog treats into Kathleen's hand. "Ready?"

Kathleen closed her fist around them and gave it a little shake. "Yes we feed," she said, forcing a smile.

The manager grinned and whacked Kathleen's arm again.

An hour later, her clothes coated with dog hair and dotted with drying dog drool, Kathleen stood with Jonathan in the parking lot, both of them looking at their phones.

"Not too many think pieces yet," Jonathan said. "Something in the *Atlantic*—'The Swan Maiden Trope: The Enduring Linkage of Women's Bodies and Swan Bodies, and Why Yes We Bleed Honors Both'... And then something about— Well, no, it's more about Airbnb loopholes. You and the swans only get a brief mention... Something called the Society for the Elimination of Invasive Waterfowl Species wrote an op-ed in the *Tribune* in your defense, which isn't exactly helpful. How's the Twitter situation?"

Bracing herself, Kathleen took a look.

Sorry, Kat Held. If you don't give a shit about animals, we don't give a shit about you. #CancelKat #TeamSwans #Swando

Swans are my spirit animal, and I've always felt extra connected with them while I'm on my period. So, yeah, pretty much devastated by this news. #CancelKat #TeamSwans #Swando

Retweet this picture of a dead swan to make sure people know the truth about Kat Held. #CancelKat #YesWeHonk

Fun Fact: The average price of one of those swandos Kat Held is living in is $900K. Think how many period supplies could be bought for the NYC public schools with that.

Dogs and swans are natural enemies. @KatAndersonHeld apparently has issues w. both. Anyone else find this weird? #TeamSwans #TeamDogs

"The situation isn't great," she told Jonathan.

"Any tweets from key influencers?"

"No, not yet," said Kathleen. "And I'm not seeing anything with more than a couple thousand retweets." But she knew that it was likely only a matter of time before key influencers—writers, politicians, actors, musicians, and people famous for being famous on social media—*did* start trumpeting their disapproval of Kathleen's housing choice, and it would spread with pandemic speed across the internet and the airwaves.

Should she make some sort of public apology? Obviously she should, she had to. But one wrong word, and she'd be loathed even more. And given how furious she was at the pro-swan protesters, she doubted her ability to come up with something that sounded genuinely contrite.

God, she would give anything to be with Danica and the rest of the Society of Shame right now—getting their sympathy and advice, perhaps getting a bit blitzed. She belonged in their company more than ever now. She'd crossed the line from being purely *a*shamed to being *shamed* for something she'd done. Would she be issued a new membership card? Surely there was nothing to *reap* from the circumstances she found herself in now. She would need to repent or redeem or reboot or re-something. Reset and rebalance the scales.

Whatever it took, whatever they advised, she would do it. She'd survived Danica's Elitist Bitch sabotage curveball, she'd navigated Bill's attempt to paint her (accurately) as a non-dog-person, and she would be damned if she was going to let a bunch of freaks in papier-mâché bird heads—freaks who had terrorized Aggie and her in their own kitchen—defeat her.

"This is interesting," Jonathan said, squinting at his phone.

"What?"

"Somebody put together a whole page of pictures of swans next to pictures of Cher. There actually is a bit of a resemblance. Look." He stood next to her and showed her on his phone.

"Jonathan, I need you to focus here," said Kathleen (though she could see the similarity, particularly around the beak/nose area). "I need to get back in control of the narrative. Do you think maybe—"

Jonathan held up a finger, then dipped into one of his many vest pockets and withdrew from it the familiar cream envelope. He handed it to Kathleen with a slight bow. "Society of Shame Distributed Luncheon tomorrow. Danica, I'm sure, is already hatching a strategy. No pun intended."

Kathleen took the envelope and pressed it gratefully to her chest. "Thank you."

"But until the meeting, don't do anything. Don't tweet, don't post on Instagram or Facebook, don't respond to any media queries, et cetera."

"Okay," said Kathleen. She was about to ask Jonathan what, exactly, a Distributed Luncheon was, and where it was happening, but he was already pulling on a helmet and mounting the sleek, Euro paparazzi-style motorcycle he'd apparently ridden to the animal shelter, and then he was gone.

Before she started the drive back to the Airbnb, Kathleen sat in her car and reviewed the various messages that had come in while she was inside. There were two voice mails. The first was from Nancy Doyle, owner of the Airbnb, informing Kathleen that she needed to be out of the condo first thing in the morning. *"You've ruined my life, my career, my marriage,"* Nancy's recorded voice shrieked. (That last one, about her marriage, seemed unfair; how?) *"I was doing you a favor, I tell you to keep it hush-hush that I'm renting the place to you, and you go and become a goddamned celebrity? That's the last time I ever stick my neck out for a fucking liberal. FUCK YOU!"*

The second message was from Bobbie: *"Kath! I heard about what happened!"* she said. *"Are you okay, honey? Is Aggie? I don't know what's wrong with those people. I'm assuming you're going to get out of that place, so our guest room is yours if you want it, for as long as you need. I'll set up the air bed for Aggie. And don't give me any silly 'I don't want to be a bother.' Just come, okay? Love you."*

Hearing Bobbie's voice nearly brought Kathleen to tears. How good it would feel, how *normal*, to be safe in the bosom of her best friend. But she couldn't put Bobbie and her family at risk by staying with them. And Bobbie wouldn't understand (how could anyone who wasn't a public figure?) why it was so crucial that she commit herself entirely to dealing with the swan backlash and shifting her narrative over the next few days. Bobbie would tell her to just run away from it all: to have a glass or four of rosé, binge on home-makeover shows, and ignore the rest of the world until it moved on to the next juicy bit of scandal. All of which *was* incredibly tempting. But she couldn't do it. Not when there was so much at stake.

Got your message, Bobs, she texted. *Thx so much, but I'm actually headed for a hotel. I would hate for the swan people to trace me to your place. Xoxoxo.*

Kathleen scanned her emails next, praying there would be no withdrawals of invitations or interviews or book deals or awards. But the only item in that category so far was a sternly worded note from the editors of *Very Ardent Woman!* informing Kathleen that the whooper swan was the national bird of Finland, and that they therefore could no longer publish the story about her. This, Kathleen could live with. Especially since at one point in the photo shoot they'd had her wear a decidedly unflattering reindeer-fur hat.

She just prayed she could reclaim control before the situation got worse.

As if on cue, a new text pinged its arrival:

Kathleen, it's Margaret Foster. I hope I have the right number. Bella just told me that at the protest at the middle school you told her to shut up. Is this true?

Day Twenty-Six

Kathleen woke up drenched with sweat in a bed that wasn't her own, her head pounding. For a few seconds she was disoriented. Why was the clock radio on her right instead of her left? Where was the lamp? Why was it so dark at nearly nine a.m.? Her mind had to flip forward through two different bedrooms—the one she used to share with Bill and the one at the Airbnb—before it settled into where she was now: a Best Western just outside Yonkers that she'd checked herself into the evening before and where she'd downed close to an entire bottle of chardonnay before falling asleep.

She'd chosen this place because she figured that the likelihood of running into swan enthusiasts here was about as low as it would get within the bounds of Westchester County. She had no idea how long she would be staying. Days? Weeks?

She reached for her phone, where Margaret Foster's text was still waiting for her. Kathleen hadn't had the nerve to reply the day before. If she lied and told Margaret that she hadn't told Bella to shut up at the demonstration, she would, in essence, be calling Bella a liar. If she told Margaret the truth, well, that would come with its own consequences. She'd be shunned by Margaret and the rest of the Bitch Brigade, along with their sycophants, side-eyed and snubbed by them and their ilk whenever they crossed paths in town. Both options, at the moment, made her head pound even harder. So she decided not to reply at all.

She made herself a cup of coffee from the minuscule Keurig machine on the desk and turned on the TV. Carefully avoiding morning shows or the news, she found her way to a Hallmark movie about a young widow learning to let go and love again, with help from her wise, elderly Black neighbor and a fiery, free-spirited sculptor who was everything her late husband wasn't. It was terrible in the best possible way.

But by the time it was over, Kathleen had started to feel anxious and impatient. She still hadn't done anything to rectify the swan situation—no statement, no tweet, no replies to the media inquiries filling her inbox—just as Jonathan had instructed. But was waiting this long to respond really wise? Meanwhile, she still had no idea where she was supposed to go for today's luncheon with the society. All the invitation had said was "noon" and that she should inform Jonathan of her precise location by midnight the night before, which she had. She texted him now but received no reply.

She didn't know how to get in touch with anyone else in the society, either. Danica kept a tight lid on everyone's contact information. Personal details, she'd explained, if leaked, could result in harassment, threats, pestering by the media, and other "unpleasantness."

Then Kathleen remembered something. She pawed through her purse until she found it: the business card for the New Jersey Men Against Human Trafficking and Exploitation in the Pornography Industry that Michael had given her that night at the soup dinner. If he'd been serious about leaving the society, he wouldn't be at today's meeting. But perhaps he would have some insight into what a Distributed Luncheon was. And perhaps it would be nice to hear his voice.

She dialed his number and he answered with a soft, startled "Hello?"

"Hi, it's Kat—Kathleen, from the society. I'm sorry, should I call back later?"

"Oh. Hi. No, it's okay, I was just praying."

"Oh, I'm sorry."

"No, it's fine," he said. "I'm done. I'm glad you called. How have you been?"

"Not great. For obvious reasons."

Michael didn't answer right away. "What reasons?"

"You know, first there was the dog thing—it wasn't a big deal, just annoying, really—but now the swando thing. I'm hiding in a hotel in Yonkers right now, actually, so the people with torches and pitchforks won't find me."

"Oh!" He sounded surprised and a little confused. "I'm sorry, what are the dog and swando things?"

At least there was one person in the world who didn't know yet; that was comforting, Kathleen supposed. "My husband told everyone on national TV that I don't like dogs," she explained. "Then word got out that I was living in a condo that threatened a swan habitat. And now everybody hates me. Well, not everybody. People who like cats still like me. And some people who like dogs. And people who think swans are an invasive species." It sounded completely stupid, saying it aloud. But there it was.

"Huh," said Michael. "I'm sorry. It sounds complicated. And . . . ridiculous?"

"It is definitely that," said Kathleen. She was glad she'd called him.

"You just can't catch a break, huh."

"Apparently not. I'm guessing you're not going to this Distributed Lunch thing today, are you? I have no idea where I'm supposed to go, or what I'm supposed to do . . ."

"No. I got the invitation, but I declined. I don't know what it is either. But I'm sure all will be revealed, as Danica would say."

"I'm sure," Kathleen said. "I'm sorry I bothered you."

"It's not a bother at all," he said. Then, after a pause: "You don't have to go, you know. To the meeting."

"I want to go," she said. "I need help."

"I'm sure they'll have ideas. But there's another way, too."

"You're not going to tell me to try Jesus, are you?"

"Why does everyone think I'm going to talk to them about Jesus?" said Michael. "No, what I was going to say is that maybe you should try to just ignore the media and the internet for a while. Focus on real life. You'll see that things aren't as bad as you think. I mean, it's just a condo and some swans, right? It's not like you called the cops on a Black utility worker or shot a wolf or, you know"—he cleared his throat—"were outed as a porn addict." (She could picture him, blushing furiously, sadly, as he said it.)

"I know," she said, "but—"

"And not *everybody* knows who you are, or what you did, and is sitting around judging you."

"No, but a lot of people are."

"I'm not," he said.

This was nice to hear; she couldn't deny it.

But at the same time, it was irrelevant. Opinion writers and social media influencers and animal lovers and activists surely were. And they were the ones she counted on; the ones who held in their hands her chances of maintaining her image and getting this damned book published—and then hopefully getting *other* books published. Not to mention the success of the Yes We Bleed movement in general.

"What happened to steering into the swerve?" Kathleen asked.

"You did that," he said. "But maybe it's time to get off the road. Try a different one."

Kathleen couldn't deny that there would be a certain relief in doing just that. But to let the faceless, judging, goose-poop-slinging masses have the final word—no. She couldn't do that. "I'm not sure that's what I want right now," she said. "It was really nice talking to you, though. Let's keep in touch, okay?" She meant it.

"Yes," said Michael. "I was actually wondering if maybe sometime you wanted to get—" He stopped abruptly and cleared his throat. "A walk."

"Get a walk?"

"*Take* a walk. But never mind. I know you're probably too busy."

"No, I—"

There was sharp knock on the door. Kathleen glanced at her watch: noon.

"I'm so sorry, I have to go. I think this may be them."

She opened the door a crack, keeping the security latch in place. She didn't open it fully until it was clear that the young twig-necked man who stood there was not, in fact, a swan rights activist but a hotel employee. He kept his gaze firmly affixed to the floor as he thrust a large heavy box wrapped in silver paper into Kathleen's arms and fled. "Lunch, distributed!" he shouted when he was nearly to the elevator bank.

A cream-colored envelope was affixed to the top of the box. The card inside contained nothing but a cryptic web address, jammed with letters and numbers and, below it, the words *Bon Appétit!*

Kathleen opened the box and laid its contents on the dinette table of her suite: four clear glass plates—one salad, one dinner, one dessert, one saucer—exactly like the ones at the first society luncheon at Danica's apartment; a black cloth napkin with silverware rolled inside; a smaller box, packed with silver tissue paper, containing a water goblet, a wineglass, and a clear teacup; a bottle of white wine, a large bottle of mineral water, and a thermos, which, Kathleen assumed, contained coffee; plus several small foil boxes of food, including a salad of the most delicate and intricately shaped greens Kathleen had ever seen, a grain pilaf of some sort (What sort? She had no idea), and thinly sliced meat that Kathleen couldn't identify either by sight, smell, or taste. It was drizzled with a balsamic reduction. That much she knew.

She poured herself a goblet of water and opened her laptop.

When she typed in the URL, she was taken to what seemed to be a highly customized web conferencing app. *The Society of Shame*, in Danica's curling script, was emblazoned across the top of the page, and the borders of squares in which each person's face appeared were fashioned to look like art deco picture frames. Their names appeared on the bottom of each in an excellent facsimile of an embossed metal nameplate.

"High five, neighbor!" said Brent, whose square was next to Kathleen's, thrusting a hand in her direction. Idiotically, Kathleen did the same thing.

"Hi, everyone," Kathleen said to the group.

"Welcome, welcome," said Danica. "How's your food? Too hot? Too cold?"

"It's perfect, thanks," said Kathleen. She lowered her voice to a whisper, in case Apple was lurking nearby in Danica's apartment with a sharp object in her hand. "I couldn't quite tell what the meat is?"

Danica let out a hoot of a laugh. "Goose!"

"Oh," said Kathleen, and laughed, for the first time in at least twenty-four hours.

It was good to be here.

"It would have been swan meat," Jonathan noted, "but it's illegal in New York."

"And this way," Danica continued, "we get to say, 'Your goose is cooked.' Except in the metaphorical sense, it's not. I'm quite confident we can come up with a remedy for this little hiccup of yours if we put our heads together. Virtually speaking. Isn't this snazzy?" She twirled a hand about her. "Jonathan is quite the coder. He took a horrible, dull meeting solution and gussied it up for our society. And here we are!"

"Where's Annabelle and the sex-cam guy?" asked Brent.

"Annabelle will be joining us shortly," said Danica. "Mikey, however"—she cleared her throat—"has declined the invitation to today's little gathering, as well as our brunch a few days from now. It seems he feels he no longer has need of our assistance."

"That's awesome," said Cindy, grinning. "He seemed like he was doing really good."

"He is," Kathleen said. And then, flustered for using the present tense, quickly added, "I mean, I'll bet he is."

A walk. He'd asked her to go on a walk. Did he mean as a date? Thinking about it now—the halting way he'd asked—she was pretty sure he had. She was glad she hadn't had the chance to answer. Not that she wouldn't necessarily go out with him, in theory. (Who would have thought?) But not now. Now, the admiration of men from afar was all she needed or wanted.

"Michael is doing very well," Danica said crisply. "But he doesn't intend to do phase three. Au revoir."

"That's French for 'threesome,'" said Brent.

"No, it's French for '*goodbye*,'" said Mona.

"Yes," said Danica, wistful. "I throw a wonderful goodbye party when someone decides to leave the society. And there's a lovely little ritual. Gifts, given and exchanged. Speeches made in celebration of the member's full recovery. I'm just a tad hurt, is all. He was our first sex scandal." She gave a forlorn little shrug. "But! Let's move on. To our favorite cattle rancher. Who is *re*framing the conversation and *re*connecting with what she loves and shall henceforth be known as . . . drumroll, please?"

Brent began enthusiastically banging the table in front of him.

Cindy gave a cockeyed smile. "Rancher Mama," she said. "I don't know, it sounds stupid, saying it out loud, doesn't it? Maybe we should do one of the other ones. The Green Rancher or whatever."

"No," said Jonathan. "The focus group thought it sounded like the name of a superhero."

"Rancher Mama is perfect," Danica said. "Tell the group all about it."

"All right," said Cindy. "Plan is, I'm going to start up a blog and an

Instagram account, and it's going to be all about life on our ranch—
taking care of the animals and working on my garden—"

"Her *organic* garden," Danica noted.

"Yeah," Cindy continued. "I mean, I guess it counts as organic if
we only fertilize it with manure, right?"

"Depends on what you feed the cows," said Mona.

"Details that can be ironed out soon enough," Danica said. "The
gist of the plan is that Cindy will endear herself to the vast farm-
friendly public, with a possible overlap into the New Domesticity
demographic, via a lifestyle blog that pulls the curtain back on the
world of the all-American rancher. Lots of gorgeous pictures of
animals and snow-capped mountains and things in mason jars and
what have you. Recipes, gardening, sustainable ranching practices,
et cetera."

"Snowmobiling, too, right?" said Cindy. "In the winter?"

Danica gasped. "Snowmobiling? No, no, no!"

"No snowmobiles, no ATVs, no guns," said Jonathan. "Tractors,
yes. Farm and garden implements, yes."

"And," added Danica, "Cindy will add a teensy little statement
about wolves and how she regrets shooting them, but nothing more.
We'll do a soft launch, no bells and whistles, and look to word of
mouth via other influencers in the space to spread the word. A nice,
gentle reemergence."

"Like a Carolina sunrise," the actor drawled. He appeared to be on
a patio in some tropical locale and wore a rumpled linen shirt, unbuttoned per usual.

"And speaking of reemergence," said Danica, addressing the actor,
"what's this wonderful thing you wanted to share? Something '*revo-
lutionary*,' I believe, was the word you used, no? I'm dying of sus-
pense."

"Yes, indeed," he said. "Turns out I've been offered a part. A leading role in a bona fide big-studio Tinseltown rom-com. It's, uh—" He
gave a chuckle and pinched the bridge of his nose—in almost exactly
the way that Bill sometimes did, Kathleen noticed. (Was there some

sort of guidebook of charming gestures for charismatic men with a wandering eye?) "It's about an A-list actor who's brought down by a sex scandal. A little, teeny, corn kernel–size scandal, like mine." He pinched the air in front of him. "And he's blacklisted."

"It's really unfortunate," Mona broke in, "that, in our culture, *black* is associated with negative things, isn't it?"

"Right, right," said the actor, and took a sip from a bottle of Red Stripe. "So he's blacklisted, and his life is ruined, but then he gets to know a little firecracker of a barista who's been treated badly by men. Was assaulted, in fact, by her last boyfriend. Now, the barista hates the actor at first, of course, and he's put off by her, too, and thinks she's some sort of man-hater. But they get to know each other, and he begins to understand the repercussions of his actions, and they fall in love. He makes a public apology and gets his career back on track. The end."

"My god," whispered Danica, fingertips to her lips. It wasn't quite clear whether she was horrified or awestruck. "It's a meta-apology."

The actor inclined his head in a slight bow. "Yes, ma'am. I'll donate half of my salary to a Me Too–type organization. And as part of the press junket, I'll apologize myself silly."

"Can I say something, please?" said Mona.

Eyes rolled and at least two people groaned.

"If you must," said Danica.

"As a feminist, I have a *real* problem with this." Mona gave her necklace a tug—this time it was made of what looked like small shellacked wads of crumpled notebook paper. "Me Too is not *funny*."

"No, ma'am, you're right," said the actor. "Not at all. The movie's just got funny *moments*."

"There are no funny moments when it comes to sexual assault and harassment," said Mona. "Kat, can you please back me up here? A little sisterhood?"

"Yes," said Kathleen. "I mean no, it's not funny." She couldn't possibly imagine how a movie involving a sexual assault—even in the past—could be classified as a rom-com, or how the actor would manage to rehabilitate his image with a stunt like this. The distastefulness of it was, in fact, stunning.

Just then, a text from Chrysanthemum pinged on Kathleen's phone.

Kathleen! I wish you'd confided in me about this little swan picadillo. (*Peccadillo*, Kathleen noted to herself; she'd expected better from Chrysanthemum.) *I've just come from a meeting with the publicity team and they said the situation is most likely salvageable, as swans do not test high on likability polls, but they emphasized the importance of a swift response. Ring me at your earliest convenience!*

Kathleen clenched her teeth and silenced her phone. (Would Danica move things along, already? Kathleen was the one in crisis here.)

When she returned her attention to her computer, Annabelle had appeared. Her nose was nearly completely obscured by a large bandage, and there were dark violet circles beneath her eyes.

To Kathleen's surprise, Annabelle spoke directly to her, eye contact and all, albeit via webcam, and at full volume. Her voice was unexpectedly deep and nasal, though it might have been due in part to her recent nose job. "Kat," she said, "I saw on the news that those swan activists were on your property. Your daughter must have been so scared. Is she okay?"

"What?" said Cindy. "What happened?"

Kathleen explained the situation.

"Oh, Kat," Cindy said. "That's awful. And your poor daughter."

"She's a little shaken, but she's all right. I think I'm more upset about it than she was, honestly." She must have replayed the moment of the goose shit hitting the window and Aggie's scream a hundred times in her mind over the past twenty-four hours. "But it's nowhere near as bad as what you've had to deal with, Cindy."

"Probably because you didn't actually *shoot* anything," Mona muttered.

"Dude, I'd totally shoot a swan," said Brent. "Swans are assholes."

"Maybe so," said Mona. "But they still don't deserve to be displaced."

"Neither do *children*, out of their own homes, Mona," said Cindy. "I mean, priorities, you know?"

"That's right," said Annabelle. "And they don't deserve to be called 'GIF boy' by their classmates, either."

"No, of course they don't," Cindy said sympathetically.

The actor held his phone up to the camera, then, showing everyone the picture on it: an attractive woman in sunglasses with billowing brown hair, head down, walking swiftly, a little girl of two or three in her arms. The girl was looking straight at the camera, wearing a look of utter terror on her tiny face, strands of dark hair plastered to her cheeks with tears.

"See that?" the actor said. "That picture haunts me. That's the makeup artist I made the comment about and her little girl. Getting chased by the paparazzi." He ran his thumb over his lips. "Because of me."

There was a thoughtful silence. Even Mona kept her mouth shut.

And then Brent, through a wet mouthful of goose, said, "More like because of the dude who put the clip of what you said on Twitter."

A look of mild confusion swept over the actor's chiseled features, followed by what was most decidedly relief. He raked his hair back from his forehead and sat up straighter. "That's right," he said, and pointed a finger at the screen. "What that guy did was just as bad as what I did."

"Right?" said Brent.

"Now hold on *just* a minute—" began Mona.

Danica, who'd been oddly quiet this whole time, her gaze trained somewhere other than the screen, shushed Mona sharply. "I just had a thought. Kat, what's your daughter's name again?" she said.

"My daughter? Aggie."

"Aggie?"

"It's a family name. Agatha."

"Hm," said Danica. "And you say Aggie was frightened by these swan people."

"She was frightened when they hurled feces at our window, yes. We both were. It was terrible. And . . ." Kathleen paused. She was thinking about what had happened just before they both dropped to the kitchen floor: the searching look Aggie had given her when she'd asked, *Why are we living here if this condo is bad for the environment? Did you know?*

"And," Kathleen told the group, "she was disappointed in me for letting us live there. She's very idealistic. Really committed to causes, like the environment. And Yes We Bleed, of course."

"Like mother, like daughter," Danica said.

"Right," said Kathleen. But it wasn't entirely true. In truth, Aggie was far braver, and possessed more passion and conviction than Kathleen had ever had, or probably ever would. As far as she had come in these past short weeks, learning to stand up, speak out, be seen, Aggie was still miles ahead of her.

"I think," said Mona, "you should make a large donation to whatever that swan preservation society is."

"Totally," said Brent. "And you could do it with one of those big-ass oversize checks."

"You should sue the protesters," said Annabelle, her voice still packed tight with anger. "For scaring your daughter like that."

Danica, who seemed to have been writing something down throughout all this, said, "I have an idea. Jonathan, take a look." She handed a piece of paper to her left and Jonathan took it from his right, and Kathleen realized that they were, in fact, sitting side by side. He read the notes, then stood and moved out of the frame.

"What's going on?" asked Kathleen.

"Jonathan's going to arrange for an interview," Danica explained. "One good one is all you need. Whatever you have on your schedule for tomorrow, cancel it. You're going to *re*vamp and *re*frame." She gave an exaggerated, giddy shrug. "This is so exciting."

"Okay . . . so I'm not reaping anymore?"

"You are. But to *keep* what you've *reaped* you need to change the conversation. Not completely, of course; you're still the queen of Yes We Bleed. And you may need to do a touch of *redeem*, too. Express your regret about your choice of housing. But you can also stick it to the swan people just a little bit, without serious repercussions, I think. Jonathan and I will call and explain all after the luncheon. In the meantime, see if you can dig out one of those blah mall-store blouses you used to wear. We need to declaw the Kat just a little. Show the world your maternal side." She clasped her red-nailed hands to her chest. "It's going to be wonderful. And once again, all you have to do is tell the truth."

"I'm sorry," said Kat. "I don't understand. What am I supposed to do?"

Danica gave a twitch of a smile. "All will be revealed."

The Mars and Topover Show

Segment: Kat Anderson Held

REGINA MARS: Good evening. I'm Regina Mars.

CHARLIE TOPOVER: And I'm Charlie Topover.

MARS: And with us tonight, on this very special episode of *Mars and Topover*, is the woman who sparked a revolution in menstrual awareness and quickly became an icon for the Yes We Bleed cause. Kat Anderson Held has been called the Menopausal Messiah and the Tampon Tigress and has inspired women worldwide to say, "We're not going to apologize for our menses anymore." But lately Ms. Held has come under scrutiny, in the wake of the revelation that she has been residing in an illegal Airbnb in a luxury condominium complex some activists say threatens a fragile river ecosystem—an ecosystem that's home to a pair of beloved swans. Kat Anderson Held, welcome.

KAT ANDERSON HELD: Thank you, Regina and Charlie. It's such an honor to be here. I'm a huge fan of the show.

MARS: Tell us, Kat, did you know about the controversy surrounding the Millstone River Residences when you chose to live there?

TOPOVER: Swantroversy, more like.

MARS: I believe we have a photo of the complex we can show our viewers. Yes, there it is.

TOPOVER: Gorgeous. Such clean lines.

HELD: I'm embarrassed to say, Regina, that I did know. When I found out that my husband of seventeen years—

MARS: That's Bill Held, current frontrunner in the race for the New York Senate seat.

HELD: Yes, when I found out that Bill was cheating on me, I just wanted to get away from him, and our house, and our garage—well, what was left of it—as soon as I could. And when I was offered the unit, I didn't really stop and think. It was a mistake. And I regret it.

MARS: There's been a great deal of criticism in the media and online, of course. And you had some very angry visitors on your property.

TOPOVER: Crazy people! Swan costumes!

HELD: Yes, all of that, but honestly that's not what's been the hardest.

MARS: Oh?

[*Silence*]

TOPOVER: Are you okay?

HELD: Thank you. I'm fine. No, I was just going to say that what's been hardest is knowing I let my daughter down. She's twelve and a half, and she's amazing. She's a committed environmentalist and Yes We Bleed activist.

TOPOVER: Like mother, like daughter. I love that.

HELD: Yes. I guess so. Anyway, when those protesters showed up on our property and I told Aggie why, she said, "Mom, why are we living here if it's bad for the environment?" And she asked if I'd known.

MARS: So you had to tell her that you did know.

HELD: Yeah.

MARS: That must have been very difficult.

HELD: It was.

MARS: I think we have a picture of you and your daughter. Can we put that up there, Rick?

TOPOVER: Oh my gosh. So cute. And look, you're with the little dog!

HELD: Yes, that's Nugget. Whom I actually *do* get along with just fine, in spite of what my husband might have told you.

TOPOVER: That's what I said. Isn't that what I said, Regina? *Nobody* could not like that little dog. Such a sweetheart. And I'm sorry, but I'll take a dog over a swan any day. You know, I saw a story once where a swan—

MARS: It sounds like you and your daughter are very close.

HELD: We are. It's been a difficult few weeks for our family, obviously. And Aggie's ... well, she's still a little shaken by the incident with the protesters, and the police, and having to leave the premises so fast ... There were a couple of moments that were really scary for her.

MARS: Oh? How so?

HELD: Well, the protesters were very ... passionate. Rightly so, of course, don't get me wrong. I completely understand— and support—their position and their right to demonstrate. It was just ... Well, there was poop. Thrown. At a window. Very hard.

TOPOVER: Swan poop?

HELD: Some kind of poop, yes.

TOPOVER: Oh my god. That's disgusting!

MARS: It was thrown at the window?

HELD: Yes. The kitchen window. A few feet away from where we were standing, actually. It's a miracle it didn't break.

MARS: Your daughter must have been *very* frightened. I know my children would have been ...

TOPOVER: You have children, Reg? Just kidding! I know you do.

MARS: Mrs. Held, you were saying? Your daughter . . . ?

HELD: Yes, she was extremely scared. I mean, it sounded like a gunshot when it hit. We just both instinctively dropped to the floor.

TOPOVER: Terrifying.

HELD: It was. But she's doing okay. She's a pretty amazing kid.

MARS: I'd say she has a pretty amazing mother.

TOPOVER: *So* amazing.

HELD: Well, I'm far from perfect.

TOPOVER: Who isn't?

MARS: Kat, we certainly wish you and your daughter all the best. And if any of our viewers would like to help support efforts to protect America's river ecosystems, please text *SWAN* to the number below on your screen. It's quick, it's simple, and it makes a difference. On behalf of myself, Charlie, and Kat Anderson Held—

TOPOVER: The Tampon Tigress!

MARS: Good night.

Day Twenty-Eight

She'd told the truth.

Every time Kathleen felt uneasy about the fact that she'd talked about Aggie in the interview with Mars and Topover as Danica had recommended or felt a twist of guilt over the fact that the strategy did, in fact, seem to be working (#MamaKat was now trending on Twitter), she reminded herself that she hadn't said anything untrue. She hadn't embellished or exaggerated or been maudlin about it. She'd simply told the truth: that Aggie had been disappointed with her, and that she'd been scared. She could have apologized left and right for the terrible sin of living in a swando, but it would have been far more disingenuous to do that, wouldn't it?

Maybe the fact that Aggie was part of a PR strategy wasn't the most pure or perfect thing in the world. But Kathleen and Bill had allowed her picture to be up on Bill's campaign websites for years, hadn't they? It wasn't really any different.

Plus—and most important of all—she'd asked Aggie's permission. The day of the interview, Kathleen had called her and asked if it was okay if she mentioned her when she told the story of what had happened. And Aggie said yes.

She said yes.

And now it was done, and Kathleen could move on. And today, she would spend the day with Aggie in the city, at the Women of America Conference.

She wore her olive drab jacket with the red cuffs and lapels that had so impressed the internet when she wore it at the Yes We Bleed rally in DC. But this time, under the jacket, she wore the *#YesWeBleedGreenchester* T-shirt Antoinette had given her, to match Aggie's. And instead of boots, she wore a pair of comfy flats, to add an air of "ordinary mom." Wearing them felt a little like coming home.

Her goal today—besides enjoying time with Aggie in an inspiring, pro-women's-empowerment setting and, of course, accepting her WOA award—was to make sure people who saw her knew she wasn't some sort of antienvironmental, anti-dog, pro–Elitist Bitch hypocrite. She was someone who cared about Yes We Bleed, loved her daughter, and would be willing to put a swan protester in a headlock to protect her if need be.

And after today, her image rehabilitated and status firmly intact, she would take that step back, start looking for a permanent place to live, and get to work on her book.

She rendezvoused with Bill and Aggie at a city park on the north side of Yonkers. They'd both agreed that it would be best if Kathleen didn't come to the house to get Aggie, just in case any swan extremists were still lurking about. The smattering of reporters that had shown up when the swan story broke, hoping for a statement from Bill, didn't stay for long. But one of the swan protesters, in full swan regalia, had apparently been spotted walking around the neighborhood the day before. And someone else had left a bag of flaming poop on the doorstep, though it was never verified what kind of poop it was, or if it was related to swans, dogs, Canada geese, or something else entirely.

Kathleen found Aggie and Bill on a bench near the pond that formed the northern border of the park. A few mallards bobbed near

the shore and—goddammit—a pair of swans glided near the opposite bank.

"Nice view isn't it?" said Bill when Kathleen arrived. "All the wildlife?"

She ignored him and smiled at Aggie. "Ready?"

"I guess," Aggie said. She gave her braid a tug. "My stomach kind
of hurts."

"She didn't want any breakfast," Bill said.

"Maybe that's why your stomach hurts," said Kathleen. "We'll stop
and get something on the way."

"Okay." Aggie sighed, and kicked at an acorn, which skittered
across the path and fell into the pond with a teeny *plop*.

"You don't have to go if you really don't want to, Ags," Bill said.
"I'm tied up today, but you could hang at home, or maybe with a
friend—"

"Yes, she does have to go," said Kathleen. "Everything's all planned."
She had made dinner reservations and booked them a room at the
Hilton.

"I want to go," Aggie said now. "But do you promise not to look at
your phone the whole time?"

Bill snorted.

Kathleen shot him a look. "I absolutely promise," she said.

Back at the car, after Aggie had gotten in, Bill said to Kathleen,
"She's been anxious. I think that's what's going on with her stomach. I'm a little worried about you guys. These swan people are everywhere. Did you give the heads-up to security at the event?"

"Yes," said Kathleen. "And I hired someone." Though *hired* wasn't
quite accurate; Danica had volunteered Jonathan to act as a bodyguard for Kathleen and Aggie at the conference—he had apparently,
but not at all surprisingly, been trained in hand-to-hand combat by a
former Israeli army officer.

"Good," said Bill. He looked away. "I saw your interview, by the
way."

Kathleen stiffened. "And?"

"I'm glad you didn't let the swan people off the hook for scaring Aggie." There was the suggestion of a smile in his eyes. "Mama Kat."

In the massive glass-walled lobby of the convention center, Kathleen and Aggie were handed their VIP lanyards and conference tote bags, which were emblazoned with that year's theme ("Innovate, Empower, Enjoy!"). They stood together, scanning the program booklet, Kathleen pointing out booths and events she thought Aggie might enjoy. Jonathan, disguised as a corporate middle-management sort in a bland button-down shirt and Dockers it must have pained him to wear, stood guard nearby.

Unfortunately, events that might appeal to Aggie were fewer and further between than Kathleen had hoped. Many were too career oriented for a seventh grader ("The Princess and the Paradigm Shift: Reimagining the Tale of Your Career") or too frivolous for Aggie ("Wardrobe Your Way to Joy") or just plain terrible sounding (the former education minister of Zimbabwe in conversation with the CEO of Bev-Tek Superconductor). But a few looked promising: a nineteen-year-old pop star turned actress who'd recently been named a UN Goodwill Ambassador; a mindfulness and meditation workshop; a young adult author doing signings in the "Book Nook" section of the exhibition hall; and, especially, the ChangeMaker Place, an area dedicated to nonprofits and causes.

But the first thing Aggie wanted to do was stop by and see Margo's booth.

Kathleen was not particularly excited to see Margo herself. In fact, if it weren't for Aggie, she might find an excuse to snub her altogether. When the condo news broke and the environmental shaming had begun, Margo had called her, both to check in on her well-being and to gently chide her for her choice of housing. "You know how strongly I feel about wetlands," she had said. This in spite of the fact that she lived in what was basically a desert. "But it's terrible that people aren't treating you more gently."

"Maybe you can say something to your followers," Kathleen had said. "About how it's not spiritually enlightened to call someone a condo cunt."

"Of course," said Margo. "I'll remind them of all the good that you've brought into the universe."

This had turned out to mean a picture of Margo on Instagram, in a flowing white dress and a crown of white feathers, standing ankle-deep in a pond, arms outstretched, winglike.

My menstrual cramps take flight when I add a few drops of spearmint mugwort tincture to my afternoon tea. Try it!! For the next 72 hours I'll be donating 10% of sales of all feminine health tinctures and essential oils to the World Waterfowl Protection Fund. Blissings! #YesWeBleed #PeriodPride #WomensHealth #EmbraceTheFeminine #Swando

Before they headed for Margo's booth, Kathleen pulled from her bag two knitted menstrual cup hats, one of which she handed to Aggie. "We'll be Yes We Bleed twins."

Kathleen had never actually worn one of the hats before and suspected she looked idiotic, like most people did in them. But it had the intended effect: literally within seconds, she noticed a few people glancing their way, and as they rode the escalator down to the exhibition floor, women on their way up waved to them, some snapping photos on their phones. At the bottom of the escalator, a large clutch of young women in business casual attire asked for a picture. Kathleen cheerfully agreed and grinned while the women arranged themselves around her and Aggie, and a helpful male passerby took pictures on the women's phones. "Of course, we could just take one and send it to each other!" they all joked repeatedly, while continuing to smile and say, "Cheese," as the man cycled through one phone after another. "Now a silly one, ladies!" the man directed them. "Now one where you look angry at the patriarchy! Now, everybody, jump! Again, higher!"

The scenario repeated itself several more times as Kathleen, Aggie, and Jonathan made their way through the exhibition hall. Aggie gamely smiled and gave thumbs-ups and let herself be high-fived. But the fifth time, when a pair of matronly women in pantsuits asked for a selfie ("I'm having a hot flash right now," one snickered. "It's perfect!"), Aggie demurred.

"I'll take the picture," she said. "You guys don't really want me in it anyway."

"Of course we do, honey!" one said, and pulled Aggie rather aggressively toward her. Jonathan, who had been doing his best to stay inconspicuous, straightened to attention and lifted a *you good?* brow in Kathleen's direction. Kathleen gave him a quick nod and smiled for the photo. The expression Aggie gave the camera could be best described as "tolerant."

"I don't want to be in any more pictures," Aggie said after the women had moved on.

"Why not?" Kathleen asked.

Aggie pointed to her chin. "Look," she said. "Pimple."

Kathleen squinted. "I can barely see it!" This wasn't true; in fact, she'd noticed it before. As pimples went, it wasn't too bad. Still, it was Aggie's first, as far as Kathleen knew. She remembered when the first few pimples had sprouted on her own chin, just like Aggie's, and how conspicuous they'd felt. "But you don't have to be in any more pictures if you don't want," she said. "I know it's tiring."

She used to think it was, anyway. When she went to events with Bill, the corners of her mouth would literally ache from all the smiling; by the time they got home, she would be completely sapped of energy and dive into a book or bed. Bill, on the other hand, would be hopped up and sparking, high on the attention. He'd crack open a beer, fire up his laptop or turn on the TV, and revel in the afterglow.

These days, Kathleen could have posed for pictures all day. But she wasn't about to force Aggie to do the same. And it occurred to her—she couldn't help it—that Aggie looking uncomfortable and unhappy in pictures could be counterproductive.

"Hey, notice anything?" Kathleen asked Aggie, holding up her empty palms. She'd kept her promise of not looking at her phone once all morning.

But Aggie was looking past Kathleen, her eyes wide with worry. "Who's that guy with our bodyguard? Is it the Secret Service?"

Kathleen turned to look. To her extreme annoyance she saw Brent, in aviator sunglasses and a black suit and tie, a walkie-talkie in his hand. Jonathan was talking with him, looking supremely peeved.

"What in god's name are you doing here?" Kathleen said to Brent.

"Providing backup, looking for animal rights freaks. We got this; you just do your thing. Don't draw attention to us, okay?"

"No," said Kathleen to her reflection in his enormous, mirrored sunglasses. "I wouldn't want to do that." She gave Jonathan a pleading look.

"Suspicious woman at two o'clock," Brent said into his walkie-talkie. "Dude, you have to turn yours on," he said to Jonathan.

Jonathan glanced at the walkie-talkie he held, which Brent had apparently given him, but did nothing.

Brent pointed to Aggie. "Kat's kid, your code name is the Biscuit. Kat, you're Cougar. Get it?"

"Brent," said Jonathan.

"I'm Maverick, remember?" said Brent. "I told you, Peacock." He cocked a grin at Kat. "Get it?"

"Maverick," said Jonathan, at the edge of patience. "Why don't you go . . . secure the perimeter."

"Roger that," Brent said, and strode off.

"Don't mind him," Jonathan said to Aggie. "He's a moron."

Aggie looked to Kathleen for affirmation. "It's true," Kathleen said. "But he means well." She was starting to wonder if having their own personal security detail was even necessary. The only attention they seemed to be getting was positive. Nary a swan lover in sight.

They proceeded to Margo's Blissings! booth. Unlike most of the booths in the hall, which ranged from simple tables to sleek and high-budget corporate enclaves—mini-labyrinths of panels and banners printed with splashy renderings of logos and headlines (YOU GOT THIS, WOMEN. BECAUSE WE GET YOU, proclaimed a fifteen-foot panel at a project management software booth)—Margo's booth looked like a cross between a fairy glade and beaver lodge. An elaborate arbor of leafless vines and dried flowers sheltered tables and pedestals and faux trees laden with her soaps and creams and bottles and balms. Margo stood in the center in one of her signature loose-knit ponchos, paired with perfectly faded jeans and extremely expensive-looking boots. Her earrings were dangling bits of wood. When she saw Aggie, she spread her ponchoed arms wide and gathered Aggie into them. Kathleen gave her sister only the most perfunctory of hugs.

While Aggie explored Margo's booth, peeking into the knotholes of the fake trees, where products were displayed on beds of moss, and rubbing sample lotions into her hands, Margo pulled Kathleen aside. "How are things?" she asked, canting her head to its *I'm really listening* angle.

"Better," Kathleen said. "Thanks. I'm not getting called a bitch by keyboard activists nearly as often as I was a few days ago. Thanks for your help with that, by the way."

"I meant Aggie," said Margo. "She doesn't seem quite like herself. Something's off in her aura."

Aggie had now lain down in a heap of raw silk–covered pillows toward the back of the booth. (Jonathan hovered nearby, sniffing essential oil testers arrayed in a birdbath.)

"She's just tired," Kathleen said.

"She can rest here for a while if she likes, while you circulate," Margo offered with uncharacteristic generosity. She gave Aggie a fond look. "She looks so cute in her menstrual cup hat. Maybe I'll move my feminine health products over near her. Make a little tableau."

"You want to turn Aggie into a fucking *tableau*?" said Kathleen.

Margo's head jerked back.

"I don't care that you've been using me to sell your products for the past month," Kathleen went on. "I really don't. I would expect nothing less from you. But you're not going to use Aggie, too."

"Oh, *I'm* sorry," said Margo with a laugh. "I guess only *you* get to do that."

"What are you talking about?"

Margo glanced around her booth to make sure nobody was too close, and lowered her voice. "You know what I'm talking about, Kath. And honestly, I'm not even judging you. I talk about Salinger and Flannery and post pictures of them on my feed all the time. Motherhood is part of my brand. But don't pretend you're not doing the same thing—talking about Aggie on TV, bringing her here."

"I've been planning to bring her here ever since I was invited!" Kathleen said.

"Oh?" said Margo. "And were you planning to wear matching hats and T-shirts, too? I've never seen you do anything that cutesy in your life."

"There's nothing cutesy about it. The whole reason I'm here is to accept an award for Yes We Bleed. And I'm choosing to honor Aggie's club while I do it."

A woman in a business suit had started browsing nearby, sneaking glances at Margo and Kathleen. Noticing them, Margo put on her practiced, dreamy smile and twisted her hair up into a loose bun that somehow managed to stay intact without any sort of band or clip. "When your actions and intentions aren't in harmony," she told Kathleen, "your prana stagnates." She selected a tiny round tin from a nearby bird's nest, took Kathleen's hand, and pressed the tin gently into it. "Rose hip beeswax lip balm with juniper essence. It will help."

Kathleen dropped the tin into her bag. "Time to go, Aggie," she said.

Their next stop was the Book Nook. While Aggie went to find the young adult author she wanted to meet, money in hand to buy her book, Kathleen went immediately to the Gunther House booth to see if anyone she'd met at the party at Adjective was there.

She scanned the booth, looking for someone she might recognize, or who would at least recognize her, but she saw only one familiar face: Danica's—on a huge panel, with a life-size full-length photo of her beneath bright red letters proclaiming, COMING NEXT SUMMER: *THE ELITIST BITCH'S GUIDE TO LIFE*. Beneath it, in slightly smaller letters: DON'T LIKE HER? SHE REALLY DOESN'T CARE.

"When did Danica sign with Gunther House?" Kathleen asked Jonathan, aghast.

"Didn't she tell you?"

"No."

"The editor is appalling. Theo something. But Danica likes him. Look, there you are."

On the other side of the booth was a panel featuring a checkerboard of photographs of women whose books had been or were going to be published by Gunther House. VIRAL WOMEN! it said in chubby, bright pink type. Right in the center was a photo of Kathleen at the podium at the rally in Washington. COMING SOON! The caption read *YES, I BLEED: THE SECRET SCRAPBOOK OF KAT ANDERSON HELD*.

"*The Secret Scrapbook*?" Kathleen said. "What the hell is that?" She had never agreed to that idiotic subtitle. She knew that Gunther House wanted to include photos, which was all well and good. But a *secret scrapbook*? What was she, twelve?

Jonathan shrugged. "It's all about visual storytelling these days."

Kathleen surveyed the other photographs on the panel: To the left of hers was a picture of an older woman who'd gone viral after posting a video of herself using an age-spot-covering face cream, in which she declared, "Well, this doesn't do shit!" (Book title: *Products That Don't Do Sh*t*.) To the right: a sleepy-eyed white woman with blond dreadlocks wearing an apron, a whisk in one hand and a bong in the other. Her book was called *Baked*.

Kathleen scanned the rest of the photos, hoping at least one woman in the series had done something marginally important. The one who came closest was a pro-choice activist who had confronted a Republican senator over abortion rights. Kathleen recalled the video: it had ended with the woman proclaiming, "Get your stinking laws off my twat, you damned dirty man!" (Book title: *Twat*.)

"Your book is going to be a scrapbook?" Aggie had returned, and now stood next to Kathleen looking up at the panel.

"Not really," said Kathleen. "It just sounds catchy." As soon as she had a free moment, she was going to call Chrysanthemum. There was no way in hell she was going to allow her name to be put on something with the words *Secret Scrapbook* on the cover.

"What happened with the author you wanted to see?" she asked Aggie, noticing she was empty-handed. "You didn't buy the book?"

"Canceled," said Aggie.

"Oh, that's too bad. Maybe we can catch her at another appearance somewhere."

"No," said Aggie, "I mean, she was canceled. By people. Because of her new book. It's about this girl who's deaf, and the author said she did all this research to understand firsthand what it was like to be deaf. But it turns out she just took some online sign language lessons and then walked around wearing earplugs for a few days."

"What did you say her name was?" Jonathan said. Aggie told him, and he jotted it down in a small leather-bound notebook he pulled from the back pocket of his Dockers. He said quietly to Kathleen: "We're looking for someone to fill Michael's slot."

Kathleen's spirits lifted the moment they reached the Yes We Bleed booth, where she was welcomed with cheers and applause from the volunteers. The booth was sprawling, swathed in gauzy red fabric and jammed with posters bearing slogans and statistics and pictures of various Yes We Bleed demonstrations and events. A giant time-line tracked the four-week history of the movement, starting with the infamous period-stain photo (for as many times as Kathleen had seen it, it still made her cringe), noting key milestones and events along the way.

At the front of the booth, on a large propped-up piece of foam board, was an image of the Rosie the Riveter YES WE BLEED poster, with a hole where Kathleen's face would normally be, so people could stick their heads through to pose for pictures. A young man with a platinum-blond goatee and several eyebrow rings happened to be doing it just then, to disconcerting effect.

On a huge panel above that was a list of all the Yes We Bleed chapters around the country and the world—there must have been at least two hundred—currently working to destigmatize menstruation and make free menstrual products more widely available. On another panel was the text of a "Declaration of Menstrual Rights" that had been submitted to the United Nations.

Seeing it all in one place, Kathleen was struck by how incredible (and also slightly insane) it was that a defective all-natural tampon, an unfaithful husband, and the actions of one idiot taxi driver had resulted in *this*.

When Emma Hancock spotted Kathleen, she threw her arms around her. "It's so good to see you," she said. "I'm sorry about the whole swando thing. I mean, I get why they were upset, but throwing things at someone's window when there's a child present is totally not okay."

"I'm just sorry it happened at all," said Kathleen. "I hope it hasn't reflected too badly on the movement."

"No, it hasn't," said Emma. "Not really. I mean, the Anti-Dispos are saying they're definitely going to start their own thing now, but honestly, they were kind of psycho anyway." The Anti-Dispos were the radical environmentalist wing of Yes We Bleed, who were opposed to any disposable menstruation products (unless they were 100 percent compostable). They were the target of much right-wing troll and pundit ridicule, and Kathleen wasn't surprised that they were up in arms about swando. But it probably wouldn't be a bad thing for Yes We Bleed if they seceded, for the purposes of garnering mainstream support for goals like abolishing the sales tax on menstrual products. It was a lot easier to get people to talk about legislation when they didn't think you were going to ask them to compost used tampons in their backyard.

"And you were so good on TV the other night," Emma was saying. She gave a little gasp. "Oh my gosh, is that your daughter? She's *adorable*!"

Aggie was talking with a volunteer in a red sweatshirt strewn with tampons and pads that had appeared to have been hot-glued on, who was loading up her tote bag with free swag: #YesWeBleed stickers, pens, and key chains; free samples of some kind of strange, egg-like menstrual product; and cheap cotton versions of the menstrual cup hats, with a conspicuous logo of a major car insurance company on the back.

Jonathan lingered nearby, looking mildly uncomfortable. Brent was nowhere to be found.

When Emma introduced herself to Aggie, Aggie's face lit up. She told Emma, who listened with a sweet, eager smile, all about the things her school's Yes We Bleed Club had been doing and even willingly posed for a few photos with Kathleen and Emma and some of the other menstrual cup–hatted volunteers. Kathleen suggested that they all stand by the Rosie the Riveter posters, and they thrust up their fists and flexed their biceps. Aggie popped her face through the cutout head and smiled. Passersby stopped and snapped pictures, and the conference publicity team including a videographer also materialized. They asked Kathleen if she wouldn't mind making just a quick statement about Yes We Bleed for their conference video, and she gladly obliged. "And what about the amazing Aggie Held?" one of the PR women asked when Kathleen had finished, waving goofily at Aggie. "Sweetie, can we ask you a quick question?"

"What do you think, Ag?" Kathleen said. But she could already tell from the stiff, doubtful look on Aggie's face what the answer would be.

Aggie shrugged in reply—Aggie speak for no.

"Guess not," Kathleen told the PR woman with her own little shrug. (See? She wasn't using Aggie. Not at all.)

After leaving the Yes We Bleed booth, they browsed a few other nonprofit and social justice booths and then wove their way through the much wider and more brightly lit aisles of the main area of the exhibition hall, past the booths of credit card companies and online colleges and a panoply of food companies with the words *skinny* and *smart* in their names. Along the way, Kathleen posed for selfies and signed the occasional autograph. A few women asked for hugs, which Kathleen gave, though she wasn't thrilled about it. Brent, who had reappeared at a booth where young women in extremely tight shirts and short skirts were giving out coconut water, took a step closer each time a hug was requested. "Hey, enough, lady," he said to one particularly vigorous hugger. "Don't crowd the Cougar!"

"You're not supposed to *say* her code name, idiot," Jonathan muttered, tapping at his phone.

The final aisle they walked through, en route to the conference room level for the mindfulness and meditation workshop, was lined with cosmetic company booths, where attendees sat in high folding chairs, getting makeup touch-ups and consultations from powder-faced, black-clad women.

"Everything is fifteen percent off today!" a sixtysomething woman in front of the Estée Lauder booth called over and over again, in a remarkably steady beat.

"Why are there makeup booths here?" Aggie asked. "It's not exactly feminist."

"Well, you can be a feminist and still want to look good," said Kathleen brightly. "I wear makeup, right?"

"You didn't used to."

"Yes, I did. I just didn't do it well. Maybe I'll come back and get touched up before the award show. And I bet they could put a little cover-up on that zit if you wanted."

Aggie touched her fingertip to her chin. "You said you couldn't see it! And I was in all those pictures?"

"Oh no, only barely!" Kathleen quickly said. "I'm sure it won't show up in the pictures."

"Can we just go back to the hotel and rest for a little while? My stomach still feels weird."

"The mindfulness and meditation workshop will be relaxing. And then there's the thing with the actress that you wanted to see, remember? And then it will basically be time for the award presentation."

"Ugh," Aggie groaned, and let her head fall back. "I just want to lie down and read."

"Well, you can't," Kathleen said. "Not yet. Come on." She put her arm around Aggie's shoulder and gave her a snug squeeze. "Let's go be mindful."

But forty-two minutes of mindfulness did not improve Aggie's attitude significantly, nor did a giant pretzel in the food court. She seemed to enjoy the session with the UN ambassador actress, who was charming and sincere with an impressive grasp of the issues she was involved with. But during the Q and A, all the audience members wanted to know was whether she liked having long or short hair better (presently, her hair was in an aggressively short pixie cut), what it was like to act alongside Meryl Streep, and whether it was true she had dated Timothée Chalamet. Aggie was visibly annoyed.

By the time the session was over, it was nearly time for Kathleen to go to the presenters' lounge to meet up with the award show organizers. But as she and Aggie descended the escalators back down to the exhibition floor and made their way through the aisles, Kathleen had a distinct, uneasy sense that something had changed.

There was still the occasional swivel of heads toward her, and looks of dawning, delighted recognition. She heard more than one "Hello!" and "We love you, Kat!" But she noticed that a few women, mostly those on the younger side, were giving her overtly hostile looks. She even heard someone say, "Fuck you, Kat."

"Did you hear that?" she asked Jonathan.

"Swan person, probably," he replied.

"Where's Brent?" Kathleen asked, noticing he was no longer with them. While she didn't doubt Jonathan's ability to take down any rogue animal rights people who might appear, she also thought having Brent's bulk in the mix probably wasn't a bad idea.

Jonathan nodded back toward the Planned Parenthood booth, where Brent was bent over, pants lowered a few inches, while a few tittering young women signed his ass.

"I feel so safe," said Kathleen.

They finally found the presenters' lounge, which was a huge meeting room two doors down from the stage door entrance to the auditorium. Jonathan and Brent stood guard outside while inside, Kathleen and Aggie surveyed the refreshment tables.

"Want to grab some chips?" Kathleen suggested. "If your stomach is still bothering you, the salt might help."

"Am I allowed to?" Aggie asked. "Isn't it just for people who are, like, official?"

"You are official." Kathleen gave Aggie's name tag a playful tug. "You're a VIP, remember?"

Aggie grabbed a bag of chips and a granola bar, then found a chair in a corner, where she settled in and started reading through the various brochures and flyers she'd collected in the exhibit hall. Kathleen looked around to see if she could identify someone who seemed like they might be in charge. She was surprised to see Emma Hancock at the far end of the room, along with a few of the other women who had been at the Yes We Bleed booth, including Emma's mother. Emma was in tense conversation with a woman Kathleen recognized as the person who was in charge of things at the DC rally, Tonya. The other assembled women were dragging their index fingers up their phones in steady, rhythmic strokes.

"Oh, hey, guys!" Kathleen said walking toward them. "What are you doing here?" As she said it, it occurred to her that maybe they were going to be part of the awards ceremony, too: perhaps Emma was going to be the one to present her with the award and say something to thank her for the work she'd done for the movement. Lovely!

But when they turned to look at her, she realized that something was very wrong.

Emma's eyes were fierce and small. "'Over-the-top, pseudofeminist *crap*'?" she said as Kathleen approached.

"What?" said Kathleen. The words sounded vaguely familiar. Maybe it was something she'd seen on Twitter, from some men's rights activist?

"What do you mean, 'what'?" Tonya said. "You're the one who said it."

"I don't know what you're talking about," Kathleen said. She laughed lightly. "Why would I say that?"

Tonya rolled her eyes and handed her phone to Kathleen. "See for yourself."

A YouTube video began to play, showing a woman about Kathleen's age standing on a dock at the edge of a lake, wrapped in a plaid blanket and inhaling the steam from an oversize mug of tea, a contented smile on her face. "Menopause doesn't have to be an ending," the silky female voice-over said. "It can be the start of something wonderful. Ask your doctor about—"

"Skip the ad," Tonya said. She grabbed her phone back and jabbed at it.

When she handed it to back to Kathleen, a video was playing—a jiggly shot of a hardwood floor, with a pair of foreshortened legs in turquoise leggings in the foreground—someone accidentally filming the floor it seemed. "Kat Held Sh*ts on Yes We Bleed" the title under the video read.

Kathleen was about to ask what, exactly, this was, but then she heard her own voice in the video, a little muffled, but audible. Her words were superimposed over the image in bright pink type.

KAT HELD: Is it the Trissler editorial? I already—

KAT'S FRIEND: No, it's one of these hashtag thingies. And it
    has to do with . . . you know. You and your . . .

It was Bobbie; the voice was unmistakable. What was this?

Next came a third female voice, thin and young, identified as
Reporter: "Hashtag YesWeBleed," the voice said. The legs in the foreground shifted, so that now one knee was slightly bent.

It took Kathleen a few beats, but then she realized who it was.
What this was: Addison, Bobbie's son's tiny-headed snot of a girlfriend, had recorded the conversation that night at Bobbie's house,
when Yes We Bleed had just begun—when Kathleen was still reeling
and miserable and, at that particular moment, quite drunk. Before
she'd decided to be Kat. Before she'd decided to reap. Before she'd
decided anything.

She heard her own voice on the video again, saw the caption on
the screen.

KAT HELD: Yes we *bleed*? Are you serious?

Kathleen turned from the cluster of women now intently watching her watch the video and took a few steps away from them.

"Yeah, that's right, go hide," said Tonya.

"I told you she was just a publicity whore," said someone else.

Kathleen, her hands now turned cold, her face burning, watched
the words flash over the image in the frame while her semislurred,
angry, grief-racked voice said one damning thing after another.

KAT HELD: Please make it stop?

KAT HELD: I can't look at this anymore.

KAT HELD: Yes, obviously we bleed. But this is just *ridiculous*.
    Don't these people have anything better to do?

KAT HELD: Well, I think it's a bunch of silly, over-the-top, pseudofeminist crap.

The video changed, and there was Addison in what appeared to be her bedroom. "So there you have it, guys," she said, giving her hair a toss. "The real Kat Held. The so-called feminist hero. For more of my undercover reporting and Greenchester High news exclusives, hit that subscribe button below and be sure to follow us on Insta, Tik-Tok, and Twitter. Byyyyeeeee!"

Tonya snatched the phone from Kathleen's hands.

As she did, Kathleen remembered, with a spasm of panic in her chest, that Aggie was in the room—that she might have overheard this whole thing. (What would she think? How would Kathleen explain herself?) But a glance toward the far end of the room revealed that Aggie was still absorbed in her brochure reading, a granola bar in hand.

"Look, that was ages ago," Kathleen said to Emma. She kept her voice low just to be safe. "And you have to understand, I was a mess that night. Not to mention really, *really* drunk."

"Yeah, which is when people say what they really think," said Emma.

"They certainly do," said Emma's mother, taking a sip from the plastic cup of white wine in her hand.

Kathleen stood motionless, pinned to the spot by the women's glares. She hadn't felt so exposed, or so violated, since the picture of her period stain first went viral. Thousands of people around the country and possibly beyond were listening, right now, to the sad, sloshed snark and dismay she'd expressed that night—which were not on-brand at *all* for the Kat Anderson Held they knew.

She felt like she might be sick.

But she also felt a gathering anger. What about what *they* had all done? The way they'd used *her*?

"Fine," Kathleen said. "Maybe I wasn't fully on board at first. But nobody ever asked me what *I* wanted. People just started using my picture and my name without my consent. Meanwhile my entire *life* had just been blown up. I never asked to be the martyr for your cause."

"Well, you changed your mind at some point, didn't you?" said Emma.

"Yes. I did," said Kathleen. "Because I believe in Yes We Bleed. I've been busting my butt to get the message out and bring visibility to the movement. And it's worked."

Tonya scoffed. "Yeah, worked out pretty well for you, too. How much did you get for that book you're writing again?"

"And how much was that jacket you're wearing?" said another.

Kathleen could have screamed. It was like they wanted her to be invisible—a symbol, pure and perfect, nothing more—but visible, their champion and mouthpiece, at the same time. How in god's name was she supposed to do both?

"Kat Held?" a voice said. Kathleen turned to see a brightly smiling, dark-haired woman about her age. Her head cocked left, then right, chicken-like, and she seemed to be looking directly at Kathleen's right ear. Kathleen touched her earlobes, wondering if she was missing an earring. She wasn't.

"I'm Liz Eckert," the woman said, extending a hand. "We spoke on the phone. It's such a pleasure to meet you. Ready?"

"Ready?" Kathleen said weakly.

"Yes! We need to get you to the stage. The other awardees are already there."

"She doesn't deserve an award," said Tonya.

"I'm sorry," Liz said, cocking her head at the group. "Who are you girls here with?"

"Um, with Emma Hancock?" Tonya said. "The founder and president of Yes We Bleed? As in, the person who should *actually* be getting an award? Because she actually *gives* a shit?"

"We're up to nine thousand retweets of the video," one of the other girls commented, looking at her phone. "Nine point four ... nine point five ..."

"You used the conference hashtag?" said Tonya.

"Duh," said the girl.

Oh dear god. This meant that in addition to half the internet seeing the video, everyone's retweets and reactions to it were being broadcast right now in the live feed of #WOAConference tweets scrolling down the screens erected all over the exhibition hall. How could she possibly stand out there in front of thousands of women, 90 percent of whom probably now thought she was the world's biggest hypocrite, and 10 percent of whom were probably still mad at her because they thought she was anti-waterfowl and -dog?

There was no way out, no way to fix it. None. Not even Danica or Jonathan would know how to *re*frame this humiliation.

Kathleen felt a hot flash of epic proportions coming on, along with a twist of dark, menstrual cramp–like pain in the depths of her lower abdomen. How poetic would that be? For the floodgates of her uterus to open as soon as she stepped onto the stage. It was almost exactly a month since her most-recent period, which meant that if it did start up again, it would be the first time in more than a year that her period would be on schedule. Perfect!

"Have fun out there, *Kat*," Tonya said.

"Okay, girls," Liz said brightly, clapping her hands. "We can all just agree to disagree, can't we. And I'm sorry, but unless any of you are presenting at the conference, I'm going to have to ask you all to leave. This room is for VIPs only."

Emma was slowly shaking her head, looking at Kathleen with a blend of sorrow and simmering fury. She looked like she was on the verge of tears. She looked, in fact, like Aggie had that night at the hotel in Washington, when she'd accused Kathleen of not really caring about Yes We Bleed.

Aggie.

That was the answer: she could talk about Aggie.

It had worked for swando, and it would work now. And once again, all Kathleen had to do was tell the truth: That Aggie had inspired her with her passion for Yes We Bleed, and Kathleen had come to realize just how important the movement was, especially for her own daughter and others like her. And, yes, there may have been other, less completely pure reasons for her involvement: Reaping. Revamping. But they didn't negate the rest.

As Emma and the others filed out of the room, Kathleen scanned the room for Aggie, to tell her it was time for her to go take her seat in the auditorium. Seeing Aggie there, right in the front row, would fortify her. (Should she address some of her comments directly to her? *Aggie, I just want to thank you, for your courage, your conviction, your* . . . No. No, that was a bridge too far. Aggie would be embarrassed, and people would see through it.) But the chair Aggie had been sitting in was empty. She wasn't at the snack table, nor anywhere else in the room.

"Come, come!" Liz was saying, jerking her head furiously toward the door. "We have to go!"

"My daughter," said Kathleen. "I need to text her. I just want to make sure she gets to her seat in time."

"How nice!" said Liz. "Text fast." She stood tapping her foot, making a nasal humming-cooing sort of sound.

Where are you? Kathleen texted. *I need to go to the stage. Margo's saving a seat for you in the front row. Hurry!*

Outside the meeting room, Jonathan was still standing guard, but Brent was no longer there. "Have you seen Aggie?" Kathleen asked him.

"Ladies' room. Brent's right outside."

"Can you radio him and tell him to make sure she goes straight to her seat when she's done?"

"Roger that," said Jonathan, who now seemed to be getting into the spirit of the walkie-talkie thing.

Kathleen followed Liz Eckert down the hall to the stage door, and into the darkness of the wings. There, shielded from the audience by enormous purple panels, Kathleen and the other women being honored exchanged greetings and handshakes. Two of the three honorees seemed elated when Kathleen introduced herself to them, but the third, the CEO of Prammer, a new stroller-sharing app, gave Kathleen a cool look and a dead-fish of a handshake.

Liz explained what would happen during the ceremony, including the fact that Kathleen would be the first to be presented with her award. This would have been fine with her—the sooner she could get this over with, the better—but she needed time to make revisions to her acceptance speech. Not to mention the fact that she still wasn't sure if Aggie was in the audience.

"Do you think there's any chance I could go second or third?" she asked Liz.

"Oh no, we can't make any changes," Liz said. "There's a whole multimedia component—pictures, video clips, lighting effects!" She cocked her head at her watch. "Seven minutes to showtime!"

Kathleen found a chair a few feet away from the others, where she sat and scribbled notes in the margins and between the lines of her speech. At the top of the page, she wrote down her key brand attributes, just to remind herself: sincere, humble, thoughtful, witty, deeply committed to Yes We Bleed. (She crossed out *witty*. This was no time for jokes.)

Out in the auditorium, the din of audience noise was getting louder, more restless. Kathleen checked her phone, but Aggie still hadn't replied to her text. She was about to text again when her phone rang: it was Aggie.

A nearby conference volunteer hissed, "Shh! Ringers off!"

Kathleen hastily silenced the ringer and answered. "Ag, where are you? Are you in the audience?"

There was a pause. "I'm in the bathroom." Aggie's voice was a near whisper. A toilet flushed in the background, as if on cue. "Can you come?"

"Come where? Why?"

"Nothing! I just need help!"

"Is it your zipper?" For some reason this was the first thing that came to mind: how, when Aggie was in third grade, the school had called because she was stuck inside her winter coat, the zipper having jammed. They wanted to let Kathleen know that they were going to have to cut her out of it. That night after dinner, Aggie had come to Kathleen and Bill, hands brimming with coins and tightly folded bills—the contents of her piggy bank—saying she wanted to help pay for a new coat.

"No!" said Aggie now, exasperated. "I think I got my ... you know."

"Your ... Oh!" It all made sense now: the stomach pain, the lack of appetite, the grumpiness. How could Kathleen not have realized? She was too wrapped up in herself, that's how. She felt wretched. "That's great, Ag! ... You're sure?"

Aretha Franklin's "Respect" began blaring over the sound system, and a cheer went up from the crowd.

"I don't know!" said Aggie. "There was stuff all over my underwear that was sort of brownish, and I thought maybe it was, I don't know, diarrhea or something. But when I wiped myself it came out sort of red, and I— Can you please just come?"

Thunderous applause had now engulfed the music.

"Are you there?" Aggie said.

"Yes. Ag, I'm so sorry, I can't come—I'm about to go on. You can handle this though, trust me. Okay? You have a pad in your bag, right?" She'd been carrying one with her just in case ever since she started middle school.

"Ladies! And gentlemen—if there are any!" a rich, amplified female voice said over the sound system. Laughter rippled through the audience. "It is my pleasure to be hosting this year's Women of America Awards!"

"I *had* a pad," Aggie was saying, "but I used it on one of our educational posters for the club last week."

"What about that egg thing you got at the Yes We Bleed booth?"

"I don't know how to use it. There aren't any directions. Can you *please* just come? I need to put my underwear in a plastic bag or something. They feel all wet and gross, and I'm afraid my pants are going to get stuff on them."

Kathleen felt a hand on her shoulder. "Kat," said Liz, "we need you."

Kathleen held up a finger and mouthed *One second!* "I would come if I could, I swear," she told Aggie. "But I'm the first one on. Just put some toilet paper in your underwear, and we'll deal with it after the show, okay? We'll celebrate. But right now, you need to come to the auditorium. Love you!"

Just as Kathleen was about to put her phone back into her purse, she felt it vibrate one last time. It was a text from Aggie—a single word: *Please.*

Suddenly Kathleen heard the sound of her own voice over the sound system—a clip from the first interview she'd done, on CBS: *"I realized that by not speaking out, I was in fact undercutting the whole point of Yes We Bleed. Women—including me—have accepted the patriarchal narrative about our periods for too long. And women in their forties, like me, and older have been hesitant to really own our menopause and celebrate it as a rite of passage like any other."*

Kathleen dropped her phone into her bag and went over to the very edge of the stage, to Liz, who was gesturing at her furiously.

From where she stood now, Kathleen could see that on the giant screen behind the podium, they were playing a montage of film clips from her interviews and pictures of her taken over the past several weeks, one after another: Speaking at the rally in DC. Talking to a reporter. Smiling with her arm around a young Yes We Bleed activist in a T-shirt reading *My Favorite Aunt Is Aunt Flo.*

"Eye of the Tiger" was playing over the sound system now. But there was another sound, growing steadily louder: Boos. Shouts. Hissing.

By the time Kathleen was finally called onto the stage by the host, a small but vocal contingent of people in the crowd had begun chanting, "UM, YEAH, NO! KAT HELD HAS GOT TO GO!"

The host, a large woman in a white pantsuit, attempted to silence the crowd by flapping her arms, gull-like. But this did nothing, and the chanting and booing only intensified. Kathleen felt a strange loosening sensation in the very lowest part of her back and wondered if this was the feeling that preceded losing control of one's bowels.

The host, having failed to quell the angry crowd, handed Kathleen the WOA Leadership Award—a large brass *W* on a pedestal— then leaned in close. Kathleen hoped she was going to say something encouraging and sympathetic, but all she said was "Good luck, girl."

Alone, Kathleen took her place at the podium and stared into the cavernous auditorium. She could only dimly make out people's faces. Mostly what she saw were the white-bright lights of their phones as they filmed her. She scanned the rows in front until her eyes found Margo, who sat with the fingertips of one hand against her forehead, seeming to try to shield herself from view. The seat next to hers, the one meant for Aggie, was empty.

The row behind Margo, meanwhile, was filled with the Yes We Bleed activists who had confronted Kathleen in the green room, including Emma Hancock and her mother.

A few people in the crowd finally began shushing the chanters, yelling, "Quiet!" and "Let her speak!"

"Please," Kathleen said into the microphone. "Please."

Please. The word appeared in a small white bubble in her mind. The text from Aggie: *Please.*

The crowd hushed to a quiet, disgruntled din. Quiet enough for her to speak over. "I'd like to thank the Women of America Association for this award. It's been a great honor to help support and champion the work of the Yes We Bleed movement over the past several weeks."

"You lie!" shouted someone from the back, and another murmur rose up in the crowd, a mix of support and shushing.

"As many of you may have recently discovered," Kathleen went on, "thanks to a certain video"—she forced a laugh, which she could tell sounded pathetic—"I didn't initially understand . . . I mean, I was very upset about what had just happened to me, and . . ." The notes she'd crammed between the lines of her speech squeezed and strobed and she could barely make them out. Meanwhile, the boos and jeers were starting up again, along with a few spikes of derisive laughter. "Listen," Kathleen said, with more force. "Please, just listen."

Please.

"It was my amazing twelve-year-old daughter, Aggie, who first . . ." Kathleen's voice hitched. Aggie: in one of the conference center's dozens of women's rooms—Kathleen didn't even know which one— alone in her tiny, anonymous stall, stuffing toilet paper into the crotch of her stained underwear.

Kathleen saw the word again: *Please.*

And then she saw herself at thirteen, in a changing stall in the locker room of the YMCA before swim team practice, pushing down her underwear and finding it mottled with dried blood. She remembered with piercing clarity how she'd felt: panicked, surprised, maybe a touch excited, but more than anything affronted that her body had done this thing to her—had been planning it for some time, in fact—without her knowledge or permission. And in that swampy, chlorine-fogged locker room, full as it was with her chattering teammates, exasperated mothers with their whining toddlers, and old women with their bathing caps and pendulous breasts, she'd felt utterly alone. There was still nobody she could tell or ask for help.

Please.

This was wrong. This was all wrong.

"Cancel this bitch!" someone in the audience shouted.

"Get off the stage!" said someone else.

"I will!" said Kathleen, her voice suddenly strong and sure. She knew what she had to do. She thrust the brass *W* out toward the audience. "This award doesn't belong to me; it belongs to Emma Hancock and the other activists who started the Yes We Bleed movement."

Then she stepped down from the podium, placed the award on the lip of the stage, and strode off to the sound of the audience's victorious cheers—into the wings, out of the auditorium, past Jonathan, and down the hall to the nearest ladies' room, where Aggie was waiting.

Lauren Trissler @ThatLaurenTrissler THREAD. 1/8. So, today a lot of people finally realized what some of us have known all along: That **@KatAndersonHeld** of **#YesWeBleed** fame is not the saintly victim-turned-heroine they thought she was.

Lauren Trissler @ThatLaurenTrissler 2/8. For some people, the cracks began to show with **#Swando**. But the video of Kat ridiculing and dismissing the very movement she became a willing icon for leaves no doubt as to what she is: An opportunist. A fake.

Lauren Trissler @ThatLaurenTrissler 3/8. But you know what? She's not the one who's really at fault here. If you were an ardent member of **#TeamKat**, then you're part of the problem, too.

Lauren Trissler @ThatLaurenTrissler 4/8. Over the past month, I found myself growing increasingly uncomfortable with and then all-out furious with the way the **#YesWeBleed** movement centered Kat Anderson Held, instead of the people it actually should.

Lauren Trissler @ThatLaurenTrissler 5/8. I don't mean Emma Hancock, Emma Jiménez, and the other women who have spearheaded the movement, though they deserve more credit, too. I mean the people who have the most to gain from **#YesWeBleed**.

Lauren Trissler @ThatLaurenTrissler 6/8. I mean low-income women, and especially low-income women of color. I mean women experiencing homelessness. I mean our sisters around the world whose lives and livelihoods are threatened by oppressive menstrual constructs.

Lauren Trissler @ThatLaurenTrissler 7/8. And you better believe I mean transgender people, nonbinary people, and gender-nonconforming people who menstruate, too, whose voices are too often excluded from the **#YesWeBleed** conversation.

Lauren Trissler @ThatLaurenTrissler 8/8. Kat Anderson Held was nothing more than a distraction. A mom-next-door media darling. An empty symbol for a vital movement. Don't waste your time and breath denouncing her. We've got more important work to do. **#YesWeBleed #KatAndersonWho**

Day One

"Are you sure you can't see it?"

"I'm sure," said Kathleen.

Aggie peered over her shoulder at her image in the mirror on the door of the bathroom. "It feels like a diaper."

"I know. But you get used to it. And whenever you feel ready, you can try using a tampon. It's much better. You don't even feel it."

"How do you not feel it?" Aggie asked.

"I don't know. Once it goes in far enough, you just . . . don't." Funny how, for all the time Aggie and her friends spent talking about the cause of menstrual rights and destigmatization, they'd apparently not talked much about the actual specifics of periods—neither the mechanics of menstrual products nor the inconveniences and the unpleasantness. The evening before, when Kathleen had rescued Aggie in the ladies' room at the conference center, handing her a pad underneath the stall door, Aggie had whispered, "I didn't think this whole thing would be quite so . . . gross."

Kathleen had tried not to laugh. "I know. It kind of is. Welcome to reality."

"Come on," she told Aggie now. "Let's get breakfast."

They were almost to the elevators when Aggie stopped. "My underwear," she whispered. "It's still hanging over the tub. What if the cleaners come in and see it?"

Kathleen had shown Aggie how to rinse it in the sink the night before and had given it an extra scrub herself with the hotel soap. She suspected, however, that ultimately that particular pair of underwear would be consigned to the trash.

"So what if they see?" Kathleen said. "Yes we bleed, right?"

A smile crept onto Aggie's face. "Yes we bleed," she said.

In the restaurant, they piled their plates with waffles and strawberries and sausage from the buffet. After, they strolled up to Central Park. It was a beautiful, early fall morning, and the air smelled about as fresh as it ever did in New York. Kathleen suggested the zoo, but Aggie reminded Kathleen that she didn't really like seeing animals in captivity, so they rode the carousel instead.

All the while, Kathleen did not check her phone. She kept it powered off, in fact—safe in the bottom of her purse. Twitter and Facebook and the opinion columns of every online publication were no doubt exploding with condemnations and admonishments. Her inbox was probably brimming with media inquiries and cancellations, most likely in equal measure. She would need to respond to some of them, probably. But not now. Now there were other things she needed to do. The first was this: walking through the park with her daughter on the second day of her first period, with nary a menstrual cup hat in sight.

She told Aggie what had happened: the video and the things she'd said in it, how she'd meant them at the time but didn't mean them anymore—most of them. She also confessed to Aggie that she did still think some of the memes and hashtags and selfies and GIFs were on the silly side: spectacle and posturing instead of actual activism.

"Like burning *Are You There God? It's Me, Margaret*," Aggie noted.

"Yes," said Kathleen. "And like strangers getting into comment wars on social media about who's more menstrually woke."

She told Aggie she was sorry for not being there for her more over the past few weeks.

And she told her, once again, how much she admired her.

"Can I ask you something?" Aggie said as they sat on a bench near the Heckscher Playground, watching children zoom down the slide. Two years earlier, Aggie might have been there herself. Now she sat with one leg crossed over the other, her purse on her lap.

"Of course," said Kathleen.

"Did you really tell Bella Foster to shut the hell up?"

"Yeah," she told Aggie. "I'm sorry. I did."

Aggie laughed—her usual giggle, but with a crisp edge to it. "Good."

At eleven, Kathleen dropped Aggie back at the hotel to relax on her own for a while. An hour or so, Kathleen told Aggie, and then she'd be back. They'd have lunch (with Margo, if she could spare an hour away from her beaver lodge; Kathleen hoped she would) and then take in a museum, or just explore. Whatever Aggie wanted.

A curbside attendant at the hotel hailed a cab for Kathleen, and she gave the driver Danica's address.

Jonathan answered the door, looking like a 1980s *Tiger Beat* pinup: a white blazer that Kathleen was fairly certain had shoulder pads, a small gold earring in his left ear, and his hair teased and gelled to the hilt. Danica swept into the foyer, looking similarly Reagan-era inspired, in black leather pants, a white mohair sweater that slipped from one shoulder, and large red triangle-shaped earrings.

"Oh, Kat," she said, clutching both of Kathleen's hands and kissing her fervently on each cheek—a new gesture for her. (Was the Elitist Bitch European?) "I'm so sorry about this video nonsense. But don't worry. I already have ideas."

"Thanks, I appreciate it, but—"

Danica gave Kathleen's hands an extra-hard squeeze, then whisked off into the living room, leopard-print heels clicking against the parquet.

"Did you manage to get any sleep?" Jonathan said when she'd gone.

"Some."

"I'll get you some coffee. Or would you prefer a Bellini?"

"A Bellini sounds perfect. I won't be here long, though. Aggie and I have lunch plans."

"I see," said Jonathan. He withdrew a card from an inside jacket pocket and handed it to Kathleen.

The Society of Shame

Phase One, Redux (accelerated)
Regroup. Relax. Reassess. Rebound.

Kathleen held it between her fingers, flipping it casually back and forth.

"Can I ask you something, Jonathan?"

He gave a noncommittal sort of "Hm."

"Why do you do this?"

"Do what?"

"Work for Danica, and the society," said Kathleen. "It seems you can do just about anything, so I'm curious why you do this in particular."

He cleared his throat and glanced away. "I suppose partly because I can't do what I actually want to anymore."

"What's that?"

He let out a sigh. "Do you recall the incident two years ago when a promising young art historian at Yale claimed, with great fanfare, to have found a previously unknown sketch for Frans Hals's *Gypsy Girl* and it turned out to be a fraud? And the art historian himself had already discovered this fact but covered it up rather than admit he was wrong, as was very publicly revealed at a very large conference while said art historian was onstage?"

"No, sorry," said Kathleen. "I don't remember that."

"Well," said Jonathan, "every scholar of the Dutch Golden Age does, and always will."

"I'm sorry," said Kathleen. "So when you were in the park in the cold, and Danica found you, it was because . . ."

"Because I was an absolute wreck, yes. Trying to drink myself to death but not doing it very successfully. She saved my life, in a manner of speaking."

It all made sense now. "So, this is your way of repaying her, then."

"Yes, I suppose," Jonathan said. "But it's more than that. Danica and I, we . . . That is, I actually really . . ." He tugged uncomfortably at his earring.

"You care about her," Kathleen said.

Jonathan rolled his eyes. "I'll go get you that Bellini."

"Do you mind if I use the restroom?" Kathleen asked. She needed a moment alone to collect herself before she joined the others.

"Use the one down the hall," Jonathan said, pointing. "Brent just spent twenty minutes in the other one."

As she walked down the hall toward the bathroom, Kathleen noticed that the door of a room at the far end of the corridor was partially ajar. Sunlight poured from within, and through the gap in the doorway, Kathleen caught sight of floor-to-ceiling bookshelves.

After glancing behind her to make sure nobody was nearby, Kathleen gave the door a push with her fingertips. It swung open wide, and she found herself looking into a small but well-lit room with a pair of windows backed by a fire escape. The large walnut desk, with its huge computer monitor, was littered with papers and folders and magazines. A pilled gray sweater was draped over the back of the desk's chair, and a half-full, clear blue plastic water bottle stood on the windowsill. Interspersed among the books on the built-in shelves that lined the walls were tchotchkes (an elephant figurine, a Magic 8 Ball, a ceramic bud vase with a dry, withered rose sprouting from it) and framed photos, including a black-and-white wedding portrait of a handsome couple Kathleen assumed were Danica's parents and a snapshot of a plumper, much younger Danica in a winter coat, her head tilted against that of a woman who might have been her sister. As for the books, they were an impressive hodgepodge of titles, ranging from thrillers to short story collections to Dostoevsky. On the one bookshelfless wall hung a large framed poster of Van Gogh's *Bedroom in Arles*, a chaos of oranges and green-yellows and browns against pale blue; furniture, floor, and walls disconcertingly slanted and askew.

As Kathleen stood surveying the office—this very cozy, cluttered, ordinary office—she felt as if she'd stumbled onto something she wasn't supposed to see: the real Danica. The one she hid from the world. Looking at it all, Kathleen was filled with fondness for Danica but also frustration. Why had she kept all this rich, messy *real*ness so buried beneath her personas (both nonbitch and Elitist Bitch versions)? Couldn't she be glamorous author Danica while also revealing a bit more of ordinary, human writer Danica?

Or perhaps it wasn't so much that she was being deceptive; it was that she was keeping that part of herself safe from eyes and judgment of the world. This was her bunker. Her refuge.

One more thing caught Kathleen's eye, just as she was about to leave the room. She took a step closer to see it: on the edge of the desk was a coffee mug that looked like a relic from the 1970s. It was white, with bold brown lettering faded from hundreds of washings that spelled, canted at a diagonal, a name: *Danielle.*

Kathleen retreated and was just about to close the door when she heard a throat being cleared several yards behind her. She turned to see Jonathan. He shook his head once and put a finger to his lips. Kathleen nodded once in understanding and pulled the door shut. When she turned back around, Jonathan was gone.

Danica's living room looked so different from the last time Kathleen was here that she could hardly believe it was the same room. Instead of soft beiges and tans, it was decorated entirely in an array of grays and blacks, with pops of bold color: a black leather sofa strewn with yellow and magenta pillows, a black-and-gray-striped oversize armchair draped with a bright red throw, a black Lucite coffee table topped with a large yellow bowl of enormous, possibly plastic, green apples.

Annabelle, whose nose was still bandaged, but whose eyes were a little less battered looking, stood chatting with Danica. Brent, manspreading on the sofa, and the actor beside him, were both deeply engaged with their phones. When the actor noticed Kathleen, he gave her a wink and a laconic smile. "Hey there, Mama Kat," he said.

Cindy sprang up from the black-and-gray armchair and gave Kathleen a tight, soft hug. A Bobbie-like hug, in fact, though distinctly two-breasted. (Bobbie! Kathleen couldn't wait to see her. She planned to stay at her house tonight, in fact. The text she had sent the night before had made Kathleen laugh out loud: *Kath, I swear to god, if that little miss Addison thing ever sets foot in this house again I will strangle her with her own leggings!!!*)

"I heard about that stupid video," said Cindy. "I'm so sorry." She looked different, Kathleen noticed. Her hair was flatter and shinier, her outfit more stylish and put together, with a decidedly Western flair to it: blue jeans, cowboy-style ankle boots, a white shirt with mother-of-pearl snaps, and dangling daisy-shaped earrings. Rancher Mama.

"I'm okay," said Kathleen. "I love your outfit."

"Yeah?" said Cindy. "I don't know. It's not really my style."

"Then don't wear it," Kathleen said with a friendly shrug.

Cindy laughed. "Well, yeah, I guess I don't *have* to."

Danica, seated in a molded white plastic chair by the fireplace, clapped her hands. "Everybody!" she said. "Get settled, please."

Kathleen took a seat on a red vinyl ottoman. Jonathan appeared, now wearing a pinstripe double-breasted power suit, à la Gordon

Gekko, and presented Kathleen with her Bellini in an opaque white glass with a zigzagging stem that she wasn't entirely sure how to hold.

"We have an eventful morning ahead," said Danica. "A little TLC and brainstorming for Kat, who, as you all know, had quite the debacle yesterday. But the Kat shall land on her feet!" She lifted her Bellini. "We also have a few new candidates for inclusion in the society that I'd like to discuss: a young adult author Jonathan brought to my attention, who wrote some dreadfully unresearched book called *I Can't Hear You*; a woman who berated another woman for breastfeeding in public—I believe they're calling her Bottle Barbara; a white city councillor in Connecticut who threw a Bollywood-themed party . . . the list goes on. And on, and on." She sighed. "The humanity!"

"Can I just say something?" said Mona.

"You always do," said Danica.

"I don't know if I would be able to remain civil around that city councillor. I find that kind of cultural appropriation *extremely* offensive."

Kathleen couldn't stand it anymore. "What's really offensive, Mona, is being in denial about your own racism."

"Excuse me?" said Mona. "If I'm racist, why did I buy this extremely expensive necklace from a Black-owned business that gives ten percent of its profits to the Southern Poverty Law Center?" She tugged aggressively at her necklace, which was composed of carved wooden beehives.

"You bought it because you are obsessed with proving you're not racist. Which is useless to anyone except your own guilty conscience. Maybe you could spend a little less time thinking about yourself and a little more time thinking about the man you could have gotten killed." Kathleen was angry at herself for not having the courage to say it aloud before. She drained the last of her Bellini and placed her empty glass on the coffee table, beside a coffee-table book called *Wigs!* "Look, I'm sorry. I wish you well, Mona. I really do. I wish all of you well. But I actually just came here today to say goodbye."

"Just?" drawled the actor.

"Yes, just," said Kathleen. "As in only."

"But, Kat!" said Danica. "Don't you want our help? Refusing that award was an excellent start, I'll grant you—very shrewd—but you're still in a bit of a pickle."

"Heh," said Brent. "Pickle."

"I didn't do it to be shrewd," Kathleen said. "I did it because I didn't deserve the award."

"But you did!" said Danica. "You've worked wonders for that movement. And looked absolutely fantastic doing it. Now. I actually have the perfect approach for you. I'm thinking you could start with a bit of a reframe and a revenge one-two punch. That child's hidden-camera journalism was extremely unethical, and—"

"No," said Kathleen.

"No?"

"No." She stood up and took the card Jonathan had given her out of her pocket and laid it beside her empty Bellini glass on top of *Wigs!* "I'm refusing and rejecting," she said. "I'm refusing your very kind offer of help, and I'm rejecting the whole . . . thing."

"What 'thing'?" Danica said.

"The pickle," said Brent.

"The thing where I obsess over what other people think of me. People I don't know or even particularly like. The thing we're all doing here. Controlling narratives and changing conversations and getting back on top instead of trying to actually—I don't know, grow." Kathleen took her phone from her purse and tapped at it. "I'm getting rid of them," she said. "Twitter, Facebook, Instagram." She x-ed out the icons one by one.

Jonathan gasped.

"An empty gesture," said Mona. "You can always just download them again."

"We should smash your fucking phone," said Brent. "Hey, Apple!"

he bellowed toward the kitchen. "You got one of those meat mallet things I can borrow?"

"Nobody uses my tools but me!" came Apple's piercing reply, followed by what sounded like a pot being hurled at a wall.

"She doesn't want to smash her phone, dummy," said Cindy, grinning. "I think it's awesome, Kat. You do you!" Then she took off her dangling daisy earrings, one after the other, and tossed them onto the coffee table. "I re*ject* these dumb earrings!" she said.

The actor laughed. "My, my, it's a mutiny."

"Are you sure this is really what you want, Kat?" Danica said softly. Kathleen detected a note of hurt in her voice.

"Yes," said Kathleen. "I'm pretty sure."

Danica stood, arranging her mohair sweater, which had straightened itself, so that it slipped from her shoulder once more. "I'll walk you to the door, then. Jonathan, please go make sure Apple hasn't destroyed the cabinetry again."

"Thank you for everything, Jonathan," Kathleen said.

He bowed his head in her direction and then disappeared into the kitchen.

In the hall, Danica stood looking at Kathleen with a pinched sort of expression that seemed both pitying and mildly peeved. "It pains me to think you're going to just throw it all away, after all we've done for you. All *you've* done for you."

"I appreciate what you've done for me. I really do. And, believe me, I'm not planning to throw it *all* away." (The clothes. She was definitely keeping the clothes.)

"If you say so," Danica said. She gave Kathleen's cheek a motherly pat. "Goodbye, Kathleen."

"Goodbye, Danielle," Kathleen replied.

It was just after seven when Kathleen pulled into the driveway of what used to be her house and parked in front of the brand-new garage. Nothing was on fire. The house was quiet, lit from within. It had always been too big for just the three of them, but for just Bill—and just Bill and Aggie—it bordered on grotesque. Maybe he would sell it. Probably not.

Nugget yapped psychotically when Kathleen and Aggie went inside, and then began whizzing around Kathleen's ankles with such manic speed that if she'd dared to take a single step, she might have launched him into the air.

"Nugget! No, no, no!" Bill said, in a sharper rendition of his usual, dopey, talking-to-animals voice. Nugget skittered off into the other room, ricocheting off the wall on his way out.

"Aw, he misses you, Mom," said Aggie.

"Maybe," said Kathleen.

"You guys have fun?" Bill asked.

"Yep," said Aggie. "Guess what? I got my period yesterday."

Bill's entire head turned pink (was she imagining it, or had his bald spot expanded?), and it was clear he was exerting extreme effort to sound casual when he said, "Oh. Hey, that's great. Congratulations." He glanced at Kathleen. "Big day for both of you, huh."

"Sure was," said Kathleen.

She wondered how much he knew. It was an unpleasant yet undeniably *healthy* feeling—like exercising or refusing dessert—choosing not to know what the world was or wasn't saying about her right now. She'd found herself feeling philosophical about it all day, posing questions to herself like: If someone shames you in an internet think piece but you don't read it, have you still been shamed? If there's an email from your agent in your inbox with the subject line "your book" but you haven't opened it yet, is your book deal simultaneously alive *and* dead? What is the sound of one troll tweeting?

"I just got Pierro's if you're hungry, Ags," Bill said.

"I'm going to go use the bathroom first," said Aggie. "Period stuff."

"Right," said Bill, not turning quite as pink this time. When she'd gone, he said to Kathleen, "You're welcome to stay and eat, too, if you want."

Kathleen could smell it wafting in from the kitchen: the perfect, spicy greasiness of a pepperoni pizza with extra garlic from Pierro's. It was the smell of a night together at home, as a family.

But it was a family that no longer existed. Too much had been broken, too much changed, too much damaged—starting well before Bill's car burst into flames—for them to ever go back to being that same husband, wife, and daughter eating takeout together.

Kathleen's anger at Bill wasn't quite as raw as it had been a month ago, but it was legions away from gone. Maybe it never completely would be. But maybe, someday, she would be able to forgive him.

"Thanks," she told him. "I'll pass."

Records Show Kyrgowski Funded Abortion for Exotic Dancer

ALEX BURNHAM

A Poughkeepsie woman who performs as a stripper under the name Coco Latte told the *New York Times* that she had a sexual relationship with US Senate candidate Kurt Kyrgowski (aka Kürt Krÿer) of Rochester for several months in 2019, during which she became pregnant. Latte alleges that Kyrgowski paid for her to terminate the pregnancy and provided the *Times* with medical records, receipts, and a canceled check from Mr. Kyrgowski with "you know what" written in the memo line.

Mr. Kyrgowski, who has been married to jewelry designer and stuntwoman Ginger Rialto since 2004, is a born-again Christian and outspoken critic of abortion.

"I thought about keeping the baby," said Ms. Latte, "but Kurt encouraged me to have an abortion and offered to buy me a car if I did it. So it was kind of a no-brainer. Even though the car turned out to be a piece of [expletive]." The car, a 2017 Honda Civic, was bought at Royal Honda of Poughkeepsie. A spokesperson for the dealership would neither confirm nor deny that Kyrgowski was the buyer, citing "customer-salesperson privilege."

When asked why she was coming forward Ms. Latte replied, "I was sick of hearing Kurt out there talking about how he's against abortion, and he's all born again. It's a load of crap."

Mr. Kyrgowski's former Toxic Lord bandmate Tad Zucker (aka "Arsenic") who for a brief time performed drum solos at Kyrgowski's campaign rallies before the two had a falling-out, told the *Times* that he "totally knew" about the affair with Ms. Latte, as well as the abortion. He was not, however, aware of Mr. Kyrgowski purchasing a car for Ms. Latte. "If he did, though," said Mr. Zucker, "it makes sense it would be a used Civic. Kurt's the cheapest SOB you ever met."

Mr. Kyrgowski's campaign could not be reached for comment.

Five Months Later

On a chilly but bright Saturday in February, Kathleen evicted her tabby, Eloise, from her desk chair, sat down with the almost-perfect cappuccino she'd just made (she still hadn't quite perfected the consistency of the foam), and switched on her faux Tiffany lamp.

Her home office wasn't actually an office but a corner of the living room in the apartment in Pelham she was renting. Someday, once the financial arrangements with Bill were finalized and she managed to save enough for a down payment, she hoped to buy an actual house—a bungalow or a pocket Victorian, maybe, with lots of character but no major structural issues. For the time being, though, this place, with its large windows and leafy views, far from any endangered wetlands, was fine. It had a good-size bedroom for Aggie and wasn't too far from Greenchester, where Aggie spent weekends with Bill when he wasn't in Washington. It was also an easy drive from the school where Aggie had started just after Christmas: a small private day school with a progressive bent that Bill was footing the bill for. (After-school activities included vegan cooking, varsity yoga, and yarn bombing.) Lucy's parents had transferred her there after the book-burning incident, concerned that Lucy had gotten in with a "bad crowd," and Aggie was sufficiently intrigued by Lucy's descriptions of the place that she'd asked if they could visit. When Aggie read the lists of after-school clubs and saw the facilities and met some of the students—an assortment of oddballs and artists and brainiacs and dreamers—she was instantly smitten.

Aggie had no plans to get involved in any period-related activities, though she was looking into something called the Students' Refugee Task Force. She was also still trying to persuade Kathleen to use a menstrual cup, in spite of Kathleen's protestations that she would probably need something more akin to a bucket.

Kathleen took up her red pen. The manuscript on the desk in front of her was the latest from one of Chrysanthemum's clients and was in need of a major editorial overhaul. She had done five such editorial projects in all now. Between those jobs, the child support Bill sent, and the freelance copyediting projects Gannet McMartin gave her—the latest was a dystopian novel about a future in which the United States has relegalized Colonial-era punishments for criminals, including stocks, pillories, scarlet letters, and other forms of public humiliation—she managed to make ends meet.

Her own book contract with Gunther House, of course, was long gone—but not, however, because of Addison's video. According to Chrysanthemum, Gunther House had been prepared to ride Kat's negative publicity to the bank, just as the publishers of *I Can't Hear You* were doing. What had put the nail in the coffin of *The Secret Scrapbook of Kat Anderson Held* was the second part of the video that Addison had released two days later—the part where Kathleen joked to Bobbie that maybe Tish had screwed around with Bill because her own fiancé couldn't get it up.

The fact that Kathleen had ridiculed erectile dysfunction prompted a backlash to Yes We Bleed (#PenilePride), which would have been bad enough, but then word got out that Tish's fiancé was a combat veteran who had lost his left leg below the knee in a roadside bombing in Afghanistan. This revelation had, predictably, created an uproar and accusations from conservatives that Yes We Bleed was antiveteran. A new hashtag, #VeteransBleedForYou, was spawned. And although Kathleen was, at the time, assiduously avoiding social media and media in general, she didn't escape the scandal completely. When she and Bobbie were on their way to a B&B in New Hampshire a few days after the WOA Conference for a girls' getaway, they were tailed by a squad of wounded veterans on Harleys who threw condoms in red, white, and blue wrappers at her car. But since then, she had suffered no further harassment. Jonathan had thoughtfully reached out to her, recommending a private security firm that would monitor for online threats from haters of any sort and scrub her personal information from the internet.

After Gunther House dropped her (which, at that point, was a relief), Kathleen expected she would never hear from Chrysanthemum again. But several weeks later she got a call.

"Kat!" Chrysanthemum had breathed. "I've been bursting to tell you: my assistant happened upon your manuscript for *The Hecate Chronicles* whilst helping me sort through my files. She read a bit and *insisted* that I look at it. And it's good, Kat! Astonishingly good. I'm astounded that in my schooling I never encountered Hecate. And here she is, this fascinating figure, taking care of poor Persephone in the underworld and carrying torches and consorting with ghosts and polecats and whatnot. It's truly fascinating—and you give the story such depth, such texture. Brava!"

Kathleen had sat up straighter in her chair. "Do you think someone might want to publish it?"

Chrysanthemum sighed. "Well, no, I'm afraid not. Greek mythology fiction has been de rigueur for quite some time now, as you probably know, but people are saying it's peaked. I've had terrible luck trying to sell it of late. What publishers are really hungry for at the moment is anthropomorphized animal fiction—stories told from the point of view of bears and snakes and things. You don't have anything like that, do you?"

"No."

"Alas. But I hope it heartens you to know that you truly *are* talented, Kat."

"Talented but unpublishable," Kathleen said.

"Like so many wonderful writers, yes. Unless, of course, you want to try a small press or a university press or . . ." She lowered her voice to a whisper and said, as if it were the name of a particularly shameful venereal disease: "*self-publish*. But I have a wonderful opportunity for you. How would you feel about doing some editing for a client of mine?"

Kathleen had told her she would love to.

The book before her now was the memoir of a client of Chrysanthemum's who'd had an emotional affair with her horse, Xanadu, while her husband was dying of a brain tumor, as told through her love letters to said horse. The title, *The Equine Epistles*, was problematic, Kathleen thought; too heady for the intended audience (horse-loving women aged thirty-five to seventy), though Kathleen rather liked it herself.

She made a note to call Cindy and ask what she thought. They had kept in touch since Kathleen's last appearance at the Society of Shame, which had turned out to be Cindy's last, too. The Rancher Mama was no more. Kathleen had kept in touch with Michael as well, and they'd gotten together for walks and crosswords over coffee a few times. It wasn't clear to Kathleen—and maybe not to Michael, either—whether these outings were dates. There were moments when it felt like they were; when Kathleen felt the thrum of a connection deeper than just friendship between them. But he'd never done so much as take her hand, nor she his. And though the possibility of it happening was nice, Kathleen was also glad that, for now, it was only that: a possibility.

Kathleen made a note on the title page of the manuscript: *Maybe something simpler? e.g., "Dear Xanadu"?*

For the next few hours, she worked on the book, tightening the prose, crossing out nonsensical descriptions (several times the author referred to Xanadu's "horse-deep eyes"), and suggesting structural changes. It really was a mess. And Kathleen was loving every minute of it—the chance to flex her writing muscles again after so many years.

At noon, she showered and got dressed. She was meeting Bobbie for lunch in Greenchester—Bitch Brigade and their stink eyes be damned—and then she had an appointment to get her hair cut and her highlights touched up. The nearby salon she'd started going to was no Papillon, but it did an excellent job nevertheless. Kathleen only wished they served Veuve Clicquot. Champagne and a haircut really was a brilliant concept.

She was nearly out the door when one of her two cell phones rang—the one with the private number that she gave out only to personal and professional contacts, per the advice of the private security company. The caller ID identified it as coming from Elgin, Illinois. Kathleen's heart quickened. There was only one reason anyone from Elgin, Illinois, would be calling.

"Hi . . ." the voice on the line, a woman's, began, with hesitation, "this is Kim Harrison, and I'm the editor in chief of Hamburton University Press. I hope I have the right number . . . I'm looking for a K. E. Anderson?"

A sensation of joy unlike any Kathleen had ever felt before—the one she'd been hoping for all her life—began to rise and spread inside her. She had a feeling she would, indeed, be drinking Veuve Clicquot today. She'd pick up a bottle on her way to Bobbie's.

"Yes," Kathleen said through her smile. "This is she."

The Hecate Chronicles

A novel

K. E. ANDERSON

Hamburton University Press

ELGIN, ILLINOIS

For my daughter

Acknowledgments

I'm boundlessly grateful to the many kind, talented people who helped bring this crazy book into being. Huge thanks to the fabulous Stéphanie Abou for unwavering faith, expert advice, and much-needed pandemic venting sessions; to Anna Kaufman for welcoming me aboard the Anchor Books ship, serving up some of the most thoughtful editorial insights I've ever encountered, and making the whole process a damned delight; to copy editor Martha Schwartz and production editor Kayla Overbey for not only whipping the manuscript into shape but also making sure I got the chronology and the details of Kathleen's job (mostly) right; and to everyone else on the Anchor Books team, especially interior designer Nicholas Alguire, proofreaders Hayley Jozwiak and Lyn Rosen, publicist Jordan Rodman, and marketer Sophie Normil. Finally, to Vi-An Nguyen, who designed the exquisite cover: thank you. It was love at first swan.

People say that writing is a solitary endeavor, but I don't know what they're talking about. I'm fortunate to have a wonderful network of writer friends whose feedback, support, and off-color jokes have sustained and inspired me for years. I'm especially grateful to the merry band of novelists whose ranks I joined when I first started writing this book: Trisha Blanchet, Jenna Blum, Mark Cecil, Tom Champoux, Jennifer De Leon, Chuck Garabedian, Julie Gerstenblatt, Sonya Larson, Kimberly Hensle Lowrance, Joe Moldover, Jenna Paone, and Whitney Scharer. To the men of the group: thank you for enlightening me to the fact that you—and most of your brethren—don't know jack about periods. Mark, thanks for your contributions to the comment thread in the "Open Letter" interstitial. Jenna, I owe you a pair of clogs. Fond thanks also to Erin Almond, Steve Almond, Julianna Baggott, Lisa Sullivan Ballew, Jami Brandli, Elizabeth Christopher, Jane Foley, Sara Reish Desmond, Cathy Elcik, Rebecca Morgan Frank, Ellen Litman, Jessica Murphy Moo, Heidi Pitlor, and Anna Solomon for astute reads, encouragement, commiseration, shoptalk, and, in many cases, cheese. Love to The Thread and to my alpine pals Megan, Polly, and Marah, too, just 'cuz.

I'm grateful to the wonderful literary communities I'm a part of—A Mighty Blaze, GrubStreet, and Follow Your Art Community Studios—all of which feel like home. Portions of this book were written at Wellspring House and at the Garden Suite at Possum House. Thank you, Preston Browning and Stephanie and Steven, respectively, for your hospitality. Thanks also to the Virginia Center for the Creative Arts.

My most full-hearted gratitude is for my family. To Betsy Roper, Joyce Lewinger Moock, and Peter Moock: your steady love and various kinds of support mean everything. To Dad, wherever in the cosmos you are: I know you would have hated all the period stuff, but I like to think you would have been proud nevertheless. To Kevin: What can I say of such men? To Elm and Clio, my own Aggies: You are remarkable beyond measure. Thank you for sharing your mom with her art. Most of all, to Alastair, my love: Thank you for urging me (repeatedly) to use all my tools. And for assuring me (repeatedly) that eventually I would figure out how.

About the Author

Jane Roper is the author of two previous books: a memoir, *Double Time*, and a novel, *Eden Lake*. Her short fiction, essays, and humor have appeared in publications including McSweeney's Internet Tendency, *The Millions*, *The Rumpus*, *Salon*, and *Poets & Writers* and on NPR. Jane is a graduate of the Iowa Writers' Workshop and lives in the Boston area with her husband and two children.